D0349915

ALSO BY KATHRYN DAVIS

Labrador

THE GIRL WHO TROD ON A LOAF

THE GIRL WHO TROD ON A LOAF

Kathryn Davis

ALFRED A. KNOPF   NEW YORK

1993

THIS IS A BORZOI BOOK
PUBLISHED BY ALFRED A. KNOPF, INC.

Copyright © 1993 by Kathryn Davis
All rights reserved under International and Pan-American
Copyright Conventions. Published in the United States by
Alfred A. Knopf, Inc., New York, and simultaneously in
Canada by Random House of Canada Limited, Toronto.
Distributed by Random House, Inc., New York.

The author wishes to express her appreciation to the National Endowment for the Arts for its generous support.

Grateful acknowledgment is made to Leiber & Stoller
Music Publishing for permission to reprint from "Ruby
Baby" by Jerry Leiber and Mike Stoller, copyright © 1959
by Jerry Leiber Music & Mike Stoller Music (renewed). All
rights reserved. Used by permission.

Library of Congress Cataloging-in-Publication Data

Davis, Kathryn, [date]
   The girl who trod on a loaf : a novel / Kathryn Davis. —
1st ed.
      p.   cm.
   ISBN 0-679-41425-8
   I. Title.
PS3554.A934924G57   1993
813'.54—dc20   92-54804
                                                      CIP

Manufactured in the United States of America
First Edition

FOR LOUISE GLÜCK, LOIS HARRIS, ELAINE SEGAL

—*i più dolce amiche*—

AND FOR DAPHNE

Only music can create an indestructible complicity between two persons. A passion is perishable, it decays, like everything that partakes of life, whereas music is of an essence superior to life and, of course, to death.

—E. M. CIORAN,
Anathemas and Admirations

Part One
FANTASI

I

IN THE THIRTY-FOURTH YEAR of my life, tragedy having turned my basic languor to indolence, my skepticism
to sorrow, I came to be haunted by the ghost of a woman
almost twice my age. Helle Ten Brix, composer and murder-
ess, impenitent Helle!—within a week of her death she'd
managed to peck her way through the eggshell-thin wall that
separated her world from mine. And how did she do this?
you might ask. For the moment let's just say that she planned
my haunting as carefully as she planned each of her operas:
with the same attention to detail, to elaboration of motif; with
the same blurring of distinctions between the sublime and the
vulgar. Darling sly Helle, seraph and magpie, light of my life
and infernal engine of darkness. The truth is I still miss her,
even now, long after I have finally laid her ghost to rest.

My guess is she was putting the finishing touches on her
plan during the month before she died, after she'd at last
admitted that she was too sick to take care of herself and
had checked into the hospital. *"Dammi la mano in pegno,"* I
remember her saying. Her voice was practically inaudible, a
whispered croak; but don't be fooled, there was nothing pathetic about her. The words are those of the Commendatore
at the end of *Don Giovanni*, just before he drags the Don with

him down to hell. "Marco understands, don't you, Marco?" she asked; and the man in question, a heavyset male nurse with the radiant eyes of an ingenue, answered, *"Sì, signorina."* By then he was the only member of the hospital staff Helle would tolerate, although I knew that even Marco was going to have a hard time getting her to swallow the medicine from its pleated paper cup, or to let him take her blood pressure. I could hear it rattling behind me, that wheeled apparatus which registered so matter-of-factly the faltering of a human heart.

"*La mano*, Frances," Helle repeated. While her voice seemed to be a little stronger, almost irritable, it continued to come from that place at the back of her throat where she used to claim the Danish language—her mother tongue—likewise came from. Her arm lifted stiffly, straight above the white thermal blanket, and it made me sad to see the blue plastic band strapped around her wrist instead of the usual bracelet of silver birds, linked beak to claw, their eyes made of emeralds. She said that when she was a girl in Jutland her mother used to take her by the hand and lead her into the bog. "Like this," she said, and through her glove of loose skin I could feel a tremor in the bones, as if she'd been hit at the root with a mallet. You had to be careful, she said; the light in the bog was weak. If you weren't careful you'd blunder into a peat hag and drown. How could I know what she was up to? I thought she merely wanted to reassure herself that I was there, to get me to warm her hand, which was like a lump of ice.

By now Marco no longer bothered to try to draw blood from her. The veins were too brittle, collapsing immediately; the blood wouldn't come out and instead made a dark pool under the skin. When you're as old as I am, Helle said, the body's production of everything—cells, marrow, hair, oil—slows down; so why should any old woman in her right mind give up even a single drop of blood?

"Close your eyes, Frances," she said. "Can you remember the tufts of cotton grass brushing against your legs, the cloud of midges buzzing around your face?" But I was too dull and weary to be suspicious. It never occurred to me that what she really wanted was for me to provide the girl's hand with a layer of subcutaneous fat, with ten nails bit to the quick, with a feathering of dark hair just below the knuckles. Meanwhile all I could hear was the sound of the water cooler as it choked up a bubble of air, cards being shuffled across the hall, the chiming of the intercom, an obscenity and a sigh.

Of course she knew what she was doing. Even toward the end, when she claimed the disease had clouded her mind, she knew. She was preparing me for my legacy: "To Frances Thorn, whose distrust of material wealth provides me with no alternative, I leave the conditional wealth of my final opera, regrettably unfinished at the time of my death, secure in the knowledge that she will complete it in a manner compatible with my intentions." Her lawyer explained that I'd find a package in Helle's trailer; the trailer itself, and everything else in it—as well as her financial holdings and control of her musical estate—she'd left to two ten-year-olds, Flo and Ruby, my twin daughters. Her intentions, I thought. Good luck, Francie.

IN THIS WAY I was forced to return to what the newspapers had called the scene of the crime, to that turquoise-blue trailer mounted on cinder blocks where Helle spent the last two years of her life. It was a cold, bright afternoon in early

April—April third, to be precise, Helle having chosen to die on April Fools' Day. As I walked down the Branch Road past the sloping meadow that separated my house from hers, I had to squint my eyes to keep from being blinded: a layer of snow still adhered to the hillsides, covered with an icy crust that mirrored back the sun's own brilliance; and the puddles which had formed in the road during an earlier thaw were like smaller outcroppings of the same substance, diamonds in mud. For some reason I was wearing sneakers. Was this because, despite the snow, it was spring? Was it because I felt stealthy, an interloper? Whatever the explanation, I remember how wet and chilled my feet were by the time I'd opened the trailer door and walked inside.

Helle used to keep a fire going in the wood stove, an iron box enameled dark green, with a reindeer on each side in a raised medallion. This stove was one of the few things she'd actually gone out and bought when she moved into the trailer; for the most part she'd preferred to make do with whatever austere and makeshift furnishings its former tenants—Flo and Ruby, who'd been using it as a clubhouse—had left behind. Thus the kitchen table was nothing more than a plywood panel that swung down from a hinge in the wall opposite the door, and the three chairs arranged around it were the kind you take to the beach, their frayed blue and white webbing patched with duct tape. Helle had even retained the pictures Flo and Ruby cut from seed catalogues and taped to the walls, all those zinnias and pansies and roses, their placement obviously dictated not by any aesthetic sense but by a desire to cover up holes.

You couldn't visit Helle until four o'clock, after she'd finished working for the day, when she'd give you a cup of tea—strong black tea in a glass cup, since Flo had refused to let her keep the yellow plastic tea set. In winter, the trailer was always warm; in summer, fresh air would blow through the louvered windows, at least one of which Helle kept cranked open all year long. But when I came looking for my inheritance that day in April, the air was frigid and stale, like breath from a stranger's mouth. I was doing all right, though, until I found three onions sprouting in the wire basket that hung above the countertop. Helle would never have let such a thing happen. Never. Just as she would have found it amusing that onions had made me at last break down and cry.

I was wretched, heartsick, inconsolable. I cried and cried, crying as you sometimes do for the whole sorry universe, for the inexplicable machinery that set it in motion and then kept chugging away without regard for all of the tender shoots, as forlorn as these green onion sprouts, that lived and died in it. I cried for Helle and I cried for Sam and for myself. For the twins at school, for the rapidly approaching moment when Flo would realize that Ruby's charm would win more friends than her own strange talent; when Ruby would lose Flo as an ally and, without ballast, float away from me forever. It had been a long time since I'd cried like that—what I'd forgotten was that, at least for me, such tears stop as abruptly as they begin. Sorrow spends itself, its currency evidently not governed by those economic rules that every day allow men like my father to get richer and richer. I turned the handle of the window above the doll-sized sink, then blew my nose on a dish rag so I could smell the air: melting snow and dirt warmed by the sun. A car drove by. Water was dripping from the bushes. And there on the floor at the far end of the trailer, wedged into the corner between the bed and the wall where Helle had left it for me, was the package.

It was a cardboard carton—highly waxed and faintly moist,

as if it originally had been used for shipping lettuce—with "Frances Thorn" printed on the envelope taped to its lid. Such a difficult old woman! Did I expect that the envelope would contain anything so obvious as a set of instructions? Instead, what I found inside, wrapped in a sheet of twelve-stave composition paper on which the first four staves were filled with the music and words of what appeared to be a song, was a key with a red plastic head. Helle would have expected me to recognize the key, at least by type, immediately; she might have been less certain about the song. But she'd trained me well. I knew right away that she'd stolen it from Mozart; that it was, note for note, Barbarina's cavatina—a sweetly plaintive melody in F minor—from the beginning of the fourth act of *Le nozze di Figaro*. "Oh, miserable me," Barbarina sings, "I've lost it!" She's talking about a pin, one of the many small inanimate objects, including keys, around which the plot of that opera revolves.

However, aside from its indirect reference to the subject of search and retrieval, the libretto for the song I found in the envelope bore no resemblance to Da Ponte's. "How can it end, Frances my sweet," the song asks, "if you open the lock before it's complete? Bitter your fate if first you look under the bait to find the hook."

The carton contained four smaller boxes, the top one of which, a Whitman Sampler, still smelled like chocolate when I lifted its lid, as did the photographs stored inside. These seemed to have been gathered together haphazardly and, with the peculiar exception of a complete set of dental X-rays, were unlabeled. That woman sitting on a park bench in the middle of a snow-covered town square, the photographer's shadow falling across her wide, serious face, partially obscuring the features—could she possibly be Maeve Merrow? And whoever she was, why did looking at her make me feel so inadequate, as if no matter how hard I tried, I'd never be able to figure out what she was doing sitting there in the cold with her coat unbuttoned, or whether her presence was calculated to help me or to throw me off course?

Under the chocolate box there was a quilted, pale blue glove box, crammed full of old letters and newspaper clippings, a disorderly pile dotted with empty matchbooks and scraps torn from paper napkins. Many of the letters were in Danish; the clippings, in a variety of foreign languages, including several I'd never seen before. The messages scribbled on the matchbooks and the napkins, even when they were in English, were too private and elliptical to decipher: "Snowy owl. Koo koo skoos. Oh I am sorry. Oh I am sorry." "Monday without fail." As for the remaining boxes, their contents consisted of musical scores, most of them bound, a tape recording of the 1950 Salzburg *Don Giovanni*—the only thing Helle had listened to during the last months of her life—and the five spiral notebooks in which she'd been composing her final opera, her feminist masterpiece, the capstone to a brilliant, if enigmatic, career.

I've come, eventually, to the conclusion that she left it unfinished on purpose. In fact I sometimes wonder whether her plan started to take shape as long ago as that night in June when our paths first crossed, when she claimed to see flickering around me the faint light of possibility. Never mind that I was sitting on a porch between two lamps. Never mind her persistent urge to revise history. Maybe all Helle wanted was for me to admit that she was right. Maybe, if you want to haunt a skeptic, you have to devise a task to which the skeptic's preferred tools, the scalpel and the scales, resist application. I have no other way of explaining it, really: she left the opera unfinished because she wanted to haunt me forever.

Because certainly it had nothing to do with music. The only practical use I'd found for the manual agility developed during my four unhappy years at Juilliard was shoplifting. Would it have made any difference if, as Helle once suggested, I'd studied clarinet rather than piano? The clarinet, that dark tube glistening with silver buttons and knobs, an instrument designed for the expression of love and passion, fury and parody. Just like you, Frances, she'd said. At the time she'd been busy reworking her melancholy Shoe Aria, in which a contralto voice and solo clarinet first articulate what will emerge as a central motif, the voice ascending, the clarinet descending—on the edge of a bog.

I put everything back into the carton, folded shut the flaps, and returned it to where I'd found it. My dull life, I thought, would continue; I would continue to boil macaroni, to pair socks, to scoop tips from the crumb-laden tabletops in the diner. The twins would be getting home from school, expecting a snack. I had no idea, then, where I was headed, no idea of how, in the end, I wouldn't be able to stop myself. Of course Helle was counting on that—that once I'd conjured her up, I wouldn't be able to stop myself from scraping away at her fiendish garments, weighing the residue, the minute heap of chalk dust which had been a human soul.

A T FIRST I tried to ignore those faint, devilish stirrings, the early stages of possession. An image would come to me and I'd ignore it: Helle Ten Brix in the guise of a skinny dark-haired girl, regarding me with a familiar combination of impatience and fervor, her eyes darting this way and that. Go

away, I'd say, and she would, but not before she'd left behind
a little hole, a gap which, until I acknowledged its presence—
until I finally began to figure out how to fill it in, sifting
through the papers in the carton, through remembered conversations, through the trailer's scant furnishings—deeply
disturbed my peace of mind. Little by little it became clear
that an entire landscape was taking shape. The girl wasn't
alone; she was squirming to get free from a young woman's
grip, from the grip of her mother, pretty Ida Johansdatter,
and the two of them were poised in their green rubber boots
near the lagg of what had to be the Great Bog at Horns. This
would have been in late May or early June. The first spring
flowers, crowfoot and sundew, would have been starting to
open, the first baby tortoises starting to poke from their eggs.
Understand, I did my research. I learned, for instance, that
the sundew is carnivorous, that its complex digestive system
is capable of turning the body of a fly into a spray of white,
starry blossoms. *Sialis flavilatera* into *Drosera rotundifolia*.
Something ugly into something beautiful—a sentimental metaphor, as Helle would have been the first to point out.

Eventually, though, I could actually hear it, that voice of
hers, the deep, hoarse voice of a chain smoker, stirring
through my living room like fog through a valley. A reliance
on fact or on figurative language will get you nowhere, Frances, I would hear her saying. What about the child's runny
nose, the mother's unreliable heart? It begins where it ends,
to paraphrase Machaut: when I was a child in Jutland, back
in the days when I was still as tender and innocently deceitful
as your little girls, my mother used to take me by the hand
and lead me into the bog. If you can't understand that, you
might as well give up and head straight for the bus terminal.
Go ahead, open the locker. You've got the key.

Luckily, I'd read enough fairy tales to the twins to know what happened if you gave in to such temptation, just as I'd read enough Freud to know where the suggestion came from. In fact, as Helle had anticipated, it wasn't a plant or a fly that interested me; what interested me—frightened me, really— was my own quickening sense of complicity. For at some point I'd begun to feel it myself: the bog water pooling beneath the soles of those green rubber boots and then, gradually, higher and higher up, until my ankles grew cold and my feet vanished. Was the water rising, or was I sinking? Who would have dreamed water could be so black? According to Helle, if you took even one sip of that black, frigid water you'd submit to the Bog Queen's tyranny; just one small sip and she'd turn your blood to tannin. *Squish squish squish*—it was impossible to avoid making noise when you walked on peat. Her sleek, eyeless head revolved in its neck socket. Who is walking up there? she wondered.

Who indeed but a child and her mother, the mother so involved in her own thoughts that if it weren't for the child's unnatural attentiveness, they probably would never have made it past the first peat hag. The Danish bogs were riddled with the things—big seeping holes left by the men who cut peat, dangerous pools where the storks waded on their long orange legs, hunting for frogs, where even in early spring you could see chunks of dirty ice clinging to the waterlily roots. You had to be careful walking through a bog. The Bog Queen's daughters—Retaliation, Grudge, and Unnameable—were waiting for you to make one false move. One false move and you were done for. At least this was what Ida had told Helle before they set out. The Bog Queen's daughters, she'd said, were the reason why we had shoemakers. Hadn't Helle noticed how shoemakers were always men? Men were always busy figuring out ways to protect themselves. The only problem was, shoes wouldn't do you any good in a bog. And if you worried about your shoes, like the girl in the famous story, then you'd sink. Down down down. You'd do something stupid, something that would catch their attention, like making a stepping stone out of the loaf of bread which was supposed to be a gift for your lonely old mother, just to protect your shoes. And then Retaliation would strike you dumb, and Grudge would turn your skin to salt, and Unnameable would wind your soul right out of you on a tiny wooden spindle.

Later Helle explained to me that what Ida had actually been talking about were the Furies, whom she'd transposed from their birthplace in the Aegean to cold, flat Denmark. As I understand it, the only comparable threesome in Denmark is an indifferent lot called the Norns; to generate anything so horrible as the Furies would have required a more fiery cauldron than the North could provide. In any event, Ida's reasons for doing this remain unclear. Was she trying to instill in her daughter that love of hyperbole essential to the operatic vision—or just trying to frighten the child? And why was it that the farther they got from their house, the closer to the bog's humped center, the more reckless Ida became, as if to deny the existence of the dangers she'd been describing only an hour earlier? Because she certainly wasn't watching where she put her own feet, plunging ahead without regard for the obvious peculiarities of the landscape, pausing only when she got sucked to the knee into one of the fissures between the hummocks, or when the hem of her coat got snagged on a leatherleaf bush. But Ida, as Helle explained it to me, had a talent for dressing up her own thwarted impulses so they would come out looking like advice; most unhappy people, Helle said, were good at dressing things up. Perhaps this was why on their first visit to the bog every spring her mother insisted on bringing a handful of cotton grass back to the house with her—seven or eight thin, perfectly straight stems, surmounted by what looked like clumps of mouse fur. Ida would take the cotton grass home and arrange it in a vase of sea-green glass, which she would then set on the closed lid of her Pleyel baby grand. But not before putting down an embroidered doily first: a fine piano's wood is unbelievably susceptible to defacement, and the lightest touch of a finger leaves a print that can never be removed.

THE STORY Ida was referring to is, of course, "The Girl Who Trod on a Loaf." Originally a folksong, "Pigen, der trådte på brødet," it chronicles the horrible fate of a vain young woman from the town of Sibbo, in Pomerania, whose punishment for loving a pair of shoes more than a loaf of bread is to be "frozen like a boulder" before she's swallowed up in a mud puddle. Toward the end of the eighteenth century the song was published as a broadside, and despite its heavyhanded morality and plodding rhymes ("O human soul keep this in mind, / Abandon pride's temptation, / And leave all other sins behind, / They were her ruination . . .") it's remembered for having inspired Hans Christian Andersen's story of the same name.

In Andersen's version, a poor young girl named Inger is sent out to service in the country, where, after successfully charming her rich mistress, she's treated like a member of the family, dressed in beautiful clothes and, eventually, urged to return home for a visit. Andersen has already told us that Inger's disposition was "bad from the beginning." With his customary fondness for perverse behavior he's detailed Inger's childhood habit of pulling the wings from flies and impaling beetles on pins; with his flair for the melodramatic he's allowed Inger's mother to predict that one day her daughter will trample on her heart. Which, Andersen goes on to tell us, she does "with a vengeance." Inger's mistress sends her off with two presents: a new pair of shoes for herself and a large loaf of bread for her parents. Naturally, when the path she's following leads through a bog, Inger decides to step on the loaf rather than risk ruining her shoes.

Up to this point Andersen has more or less conformed to the narrative line of the song. But even though both girls find themselves transformed for their wickedness into statues, the girl in the song remains above ground, where everyone can see her, while Inger sinks to the bottom of the bog, where she becomes a decorative element in the devil's courtyard. How gruesome and exotic the plight of the damned! Although Inger is ravenous, she can't move a muscle to break off so much as a tiny piece of the loaf to which she's welded; although flies—the very flies she mutilated years earlier— creep all over her face, she can't raise a finger to brush them away. Her whole body is fixed in place, with the exception of her eyes—and this proves to be a dubious advantage, since the only way her eyes will turn is backwards, revealing the ugly thoughts peeking out at her from between the folds of her brain.

Years go by. Inger discovers that she's able to hear everything people say about her, none of it good. Her mother, her mistress, the cowherd who watched her sink out of sight— the effect of their judgment is to make her hard heart harder still. She hears songs about her arrogance, stories describing her vanity. Her own mother's dying words are "What a grief you've been to me." And then, amazingly, another dying woman, a stranger, weeps at the door of heaven for Inger's soul. When her tears filter down through all those layers of peat, the girl's stony carapace dissolves and a little bird is released to fly into the upper world.

At first the bird is without voice and ashamed to be seen, so it hides in a chink in a wall. Winter comes, the ponds freeze over, food is scarce—when the bird finally emerges, it is to seek out those random morsels of bread left in the baiting places or fallen in the tracks of sledges. Motivated more by sympathy than by hunger, the bird eats only a single crumb of whatever it finds and gives away the rest, until, at last, what it has given away equals the weight of the original loaf which Inger tossed so thoughtlessly, so many years ago, into the bog. The bird's dull gray wings turn white; children watch it as it flies across the sea, its body gleaming, right into the sun.

Literary critics—"to a man," as Helle was fond of saying—tend to find Andersen's punishment excessive, given the nature of Inger's crime. Puzzled, they resort to Freudian analysis. The shoe, they suggest, stands for the uterus; Inger's pride in her shoes, for her awakening sexuality. Naturally Andersen—his fear of sex legendary, his famous passion for Jenny Lind fueled as much by the purity of her moral conduct as by the purity of her voice—would have wanted to banish the uterus to hell, where it belonged.

However, in Helle Ten Brix's operatic version, likewise entitled *The Girl Who Trod on a Loaf*, Inger is no sinner but a heroine, her apparent arrogance a measure of her strength, her sojourn underground a stage of apprenticeship to that feminist ideal represented by the Bog Queen. In the opera, Inger's shoes become, quite literally, the vehicles of her enlightenment. It makes perfect sense that Helle's Inger, bent on protecting her shoes, would decide to step on what might otherwise have come to serve as a symbol of her oppression; just as it follows that, bent on uncovering the enemy's identity, she would have shown an early interest in dissection. God is now the enemy, and the Bog Queen, together with her furious daughters, the inevitable worms in the rose of creation. Without them God's mindless replication of his own heart might have gone on forever and ever: "A crystal hive," as Inger sings, "that organ which is the world analogous to man's imagining."

HELLE TEN BRIX, impossible, beloved Helle, where are you now? If I were to return to the little bog you took me to one day, in that place where the Branch Road turns to a muddy trail before disappearing entirely in a thicket of cedar trunks, if I were to peer in among the deeply puckered, pale green leaves of the Solomon's seal would I see, instead of the expected single drop of water, one of your gray, furious eyes staring back at me? Because I know you went somewhere; I was there when you died, I saw you go. *No, no, ch'io non mi pento,* you said, grabbing my hand. I could hear Marco pausing outside the door to wind his watch, as if to generate an endless stream of minutes, hours, days; as if to imply that you still had all the time in the world. All the time in the world! What could he have been thinking of? *Tick tick tick*—only a week earlier you'd told us how the air was filling up with ticking black particles, which was why you had to wear earphones in order to listen to *Don Giovanni.* Only at night, after Marco had gone home and everyone else was asleep, were you able to continue work on your own opera. *Don Giovanni* and *The Girl Who Trod on a Loaf*—two works which have little in common beyond the fact that their protagonists sink into hell.

Of course in the former case it's the fiery pit of Christian iconography; in the latter, the cold pit of a bog.

Is that where you're stuck forever—in a cold, moist cauldron of peat, consigned to an eternity of tea parties with the Bog Queen and her bad-tempered daughters? Maybe you were wrong. Maybe there actually is a heaven, and up there your musical skills have won you so much praise from the angels that you've forgotten whatever passion it was that shaped you. I hope not. Just as I hope that if you're watching me now, either up through a hole in the peat, or down through a gap in the clouds, you'd be happy to know the extent to which I am finally yours and yours alone.

II

BUT JUST WHAT did I mean when I said I was haunted? How tempting to insist that all I meant was what intelligent and sophisticated people usually mean when they say that something haunts them. That Helle Ten Brix had got, so to speak, under my skin; that after she was dead I couldn't forget her. A haunting melody. A haunting smile. Besides, who believes in ghosts these days? The ignorant and the superstitious, the religious fanatic, the recently bereaved? It used to be that children believed in ghosts, but modern children are too smart to be taken in by such nonsense; they've watched enough television, seen enough movies, to know there's nothing more to this world than what meets the eye. The eye, that coolest of organs, opaque and calculating. Who needs a window to the soul when it's generally agreed that souls don't exist?

And what about me, Frances Thorn, a modern woman, a well-born and well-educated woman who once upon a time decided to discard conventional comforts—a woman who prided herself on being a true descendant of Diogenes (although I admit I never went so far as to live in a tub)? What happens to my credibility if I confess that one morning in June as I was standing naked on the bath mat—a mild airy morning, not two months after Helle's death—I felt the beads of sunlight with which the room was spattered condense suddenly into a vibrantly humming chord, and that when I reached for the towel I felt that chord drive straight through me, from the soles of my feet to the crown of my head, as if to provide despair with an axis? The dominant seventh, just on the verge of resolving itself in the music of pure inspiration—that immaculate sound Mozart achieved during the last year of his life: the music of *Die Zauberflöte*, which, according to George Bernard Shaw, was the only music fit for the mouth of God. I could hear birds singing outside the window, the drip-drip-drip of water from the shower head, the early-morning chatter of the twins. In other words, my ears remained tuned to the sounds of this world; it wasn't that I heard the chord but that I was inhabited by it.

An unpleasant sensation, the struggle toward resolution manifested itself as a persistent faint shiver, like a piano string lacking an overdamper. Like Helle, inhabited by the sound of Lahloo's voice that night on the Gothersgade. Typical, I thought. Even the Muse, when she came to me, came to me secondhand and in a bathroom: around my body the rough wet towel; under my feet the tonguelike loops of the bath mat; on the windowsill, behind the shampoo bottles pasted over with wet dust and hair, the clear plastic box in which I'd once hidden Sam's ring among aquamarine bubble-bath capsules and which was now filled with grayish slivers of soap. How warm the air was, coming in through the screen, but it made no difference. The shivering wouldn't stop, and I found myself remembering another time when I'd felt this way, though the sensation then had been more subtle, a piano string again, only a string fastened off-kilter to a cracked bridge.

Then, too, it had been a warm morning in early summer, Helle and I sitting on the stream bank behind the trailer, our bare feet in the water. She'd come tapping at my window just after dawn, complaining that she'd tossed and turned all night. Tiny specks of sun peppered the water, winked on and off like fireflies within the dark cedar woods and, there at my side, I could see the two unwinking specks of light which floated wetly across the dark surface of Helle's eyes. In such cases the string loses its ability to "know" how long it is. It wavers, refuses to hold a note. How alike we were, Helle was saying. Look at us! A pair of rail-thin women, smoking like chimneys—who would guess, to look at us, that the music of the spheres played in our heads?

"Well, in one of our heads," I said.

She snorted. "You can't fool me, Frances." Why else, in a house otherwise furnished with junk, would I maintain a 1907 Steinway upright? And pay Cyril Beemis a small fortune to come all the way from Utica twice a year to keep it tuned? Oh, we were the same, all right. It was only men who found this idea frightening, only a man who couldn't tolerate the idea that somewhere in this world there might be another man identical to himself. When you got right down to it, wasn't that why they kept plying the doppelgänger, that tired old theme, in their art? Whereas women weren't afraid of similarity. Till death do us part, Helle pronounced, delicately stifling a cough, shifting her position on the uncomfortably root-latticed bank so our legs touched along the thighs and our pale white feet swam up against each other in the cool brown water. Frances! Maybe not even death would be sufficient to part two such kindred spirits.

I remember noticing how her toenails were abnormally

long, how they curved down over the tips of her toes, as burnished and opaque as claws. Wasn't I tired of being my own worst enemy? Helle said, exhaling a great cloud of smoke into the breezeless air. "Better me than you," she said, leaning closer. Nor did I pull away; a creature not entirely human, I thought, had singled me out. "I will never desert you," the creature was saying, "never never never."

Is it any wonder, then, that on that June morning, when I wiped the steam from the bathroom mirror, I was relieved to see my own face staring back at me? Pinched and wet, my *own* face—although there was no denying the fact that somehow it was set on my neck differently, with an uncharacteristic lift to the chin, which in turn improved my overall posture. What had become of my slouch, my tendency to scowl from beneath a lowering brow?

Meanwhile the music persisted, as if a tower of notes were fiercely intent upon erecting itself, over and over again, deep inside of me. "Forget it," I said, but when I hunched my shoulders, testing the possibility that posture itself might be destiny, I felt a sharp pain—the sharp pain of dislocation—traveling up my spine. Was this how the girl had felt after she sank to the bottom of the bog? "Go away," I said. Only the music was so beautiful—spires and peaks of unearthly beauty rising into a deep blue sky. The towers of Copenhagen, as Helle had described them to me: green towers and golden towers, towers flying flags and pennants, square towers and tapering towers, turrets and minarets and crenellations, towers twisted and sleek as a narwhal's tusk. All that was required now was one final bright point of sound, a needle-thin, end-lessly ascending note, and the music, no matter how severe and uncompromising its source, would at last manage to pierce through the sky's membrane and into the house of heaven. Helle's music, I thought. Except Helle was dead.

I pressed my lips together to keep whatever was taking shape inside me from getting out. Maybe it was nothing more than the sound of my blood, racing toward my heart. When a person is dead, she's dead, and that's the end of it. Maybe it wasn't music; is there any real difference, after all, between superstition and a belief in metaphor? "Never," Helle had said. "Never" was the key, the only key a new ghost confronted with the netherworld's outer wall—that wall composed of an infinite number of shifting and shadowy boxes, each box containing a shifting and shadowy object—might use to unlock doors into the here-and-now. Like the notes of an opera waiting to be composed, like notes unrecognized yet disturbingly familiar, these objects resembling objects from our world would be dissimilar enough that the ghost might think it was floating among the snowflakes and pine trees of a glass paperweight, only to find itself stuck in a damp blue mitten.

Winking light and rushing water; the medicinal smell of cedar, like an antidote to mystery. Nor had the message seemed anything other than clear; reassuring, even. "I will never desert you." But when I'd said she surely wasn't talking about a real ghost, Helle was suddenly disdainful, impatient. Real? *Real?* Had I ever known Helle Ten Brix to care whether something was real or not? Operas had nothing to do with reality, I should know that. No one says "Ah, the czar, to the life!" when they watch *Boris Godunov*. No one protests that in *Un ballo in maschera* Verdi changed the name of King Gustavus III of Sweden to Riccardo. Could a woman *accidentally* throw her own baby onto a lit funeral pyre? Could

Dorabella and Fiordiligi actually mistake their boyfriends for Albanians? Could a man actually be dragged to hell by a statue? Not to mention the age-old complaint that no one can manage to simultaneously die and sing an aria. Real? Feh! When I said "real," what I meant was "boring"—wasn't it?

Unlike what I meant when I said I was haunted.

III

EVERY OPERA has in it bit parts, apparently inessential roles, servants in livery and masked revelers, plume-hatted soldiers and irritable minor deities, animal trainers and orphans, toadies and slaves, harem girls and priests. These characters hover on the fringes, their costumes less lavish, their voices less remarkable than those of the men and women around whose struggles with fate the stories revolve.

Mrs. Helen Sprague, the twins' third-grade teacher, seems to me such a character, a swart and efficient matron generally clad in pea- or lime-green, her hair firmly coiffed. Mrs. Sprague served as stage manager for the Operateers, our local company, and it was her idea that Ruby, by merit of her birdlike bone structure, would be perfect for the part of the spectral child who appears during the final moments of Puccini's one-act opera *Suor Angelica.* "I'll dress her in gauze and tinsel," said Mrs. Sprague. "There won't be a dry eye in the house." Which I know for a fact wasn't the case: Helle Ten Brix's eyes remained as cool and dry as nickels, round with reproof, her mascara intact.

I was sitting on the steps of the Canaan Opera House, smoking a cigarette and waiting for Ruby, who was backstage drinking punch with her less ethereal sister and the rest of the cast. "Nonalcoholic," Mrs. Sprague had assured me. "My own mother's recipe—strictly WCTU." Still, it hadn't escaped my notice that the Abbess had a vodka bottle hidden under her habit, the contents of which she was slyly tipping out into the sisters' paper cups. A humid night in late June: the yellow cones of light projecting from the few cars that made their way along Broadway, either east toward the lake or west toward the mountains, were lively with insects, as were the bluish tents around the street lamps, the golden nimbi surrounding the two glass globes on their acanthine pedestals, one to my left, one to my right, guarding the door.

Who, I wondered, made up these stories? A young noblewoman has a love affair, gives birth to an illegitimate child, and is compelled by her family to enter a convent. Years go by; the family ignores her. It's only when her younger sister wants to get married that the Princess, her aunt, shows up, explaining that before the wedding can occur Angelica must sign a document granting her permission, a simple enough request. All Angelica asks in return is for news of her child. "Dead," says the Princess, clearly relishing her role as the bearer of bad tidings, "your child died two years ago," whereupon the disconsolate Angelica drinks poison, then prays that she should not be allowed to die in mortal sin. A miracle follows: the Virgin appears with the child on the chapel steps. As a chorus of nuns and angels sings "Thou art saved," Angelica dies.

Of course it's possible that when I disgraced myself at the age of twenty-four, my family might likewise have preferred to ship me off to a convent. My mother could have raised the twins as her own; she could have explained them to her judgmental friends as the last flowers of her womb, change-of-life babies who, according to folklore, can't be aborted unless the mother kills herself. Instead of taping cutout snow-flakes or turkeys or pumpkins to the windows of Mrs. Sprague's classroom, Ruby and Flo might have conjugated French verbs, as I did when I was their age, hypnotized by the opaque gleam of Mademoiselle Tzara's monocle. Understand, my parents are rich, their money of the kind referred to as "old," as if greed only recently entered the picture.

While I sat there on the opera house steps, a salmon-and-white convertible approached, filled with teenaged boys, their outward appearance rangy and dull, their pale arms draped over the doors and across the seats, so that you couldn't immediately recognize them for the predators they were. Only their eyes gave them away: when they swiveled their pale necks in my direction, their eyes were blunt with desire. The driver leaned on the horn. Hey, baby! I thought I recognized him from the diner, an affable creature with the coffin-shaped body of an athlete, who frequently wore a tiny silver earring in his ear. The car slowed, veering toward the curb. And then, just as I was beginning to feel the first dim tingling of fear or arousal—that common confusion which Helle claimed accounted for the Don's great success with women—the focus of their eyes suddenly shifted to a place several inches above my head. Their eyes blinked; the desire drained out of them; they turned downward, became deferential.

A hundred years ago, when the railroad barons were just settling into their elaborate mansions on what was to become Rose Hill and the green marble of the opera house façade was still folded within a Vermont cliff—when Helle Ten Brix herself was only a fleck of sea foam on the Skagerrak, a gust of wind across the Øresund, whatever form the spirit takes before it gets stuck in a body—no doubt the town would have considered itself lucky to count such a woman among its inhabitants. Whereas when I met her she was regarded more or less as a liability: an elderly Dane of ambiguous sexual orientation, a supposedly famous composer who'd decided, for reasons unknown although widely guessed at, to move in with the Blackburns. She was, it was said, Maren's aunt, otherwise Sam would never have put up with her. Of course, only in hindsight does the flaw in that statement become obvious. The truth is, no one really paid very much attention to Helle, even after the Met's ill-starred production of *Fortune's Lap* was featured in the *New York Times* Sunday magazine. That everyone knew her by sight, including a carload of seventeen-year-old boys, was evident from their response. But as for *who* she was, that was another story—one with which I was about to become acquainted.

The woman standing behind me on the porch of the opera house was no more than five feet tall, her pose oddly suggestive of a woodland creature accustomed to going about on all fours, who now has suddenly reared up on its hind legs, rigid with attention. She was wearing an ankle-length gown of black crochet work, its high Victorian collar embroidered with jet beads, as were the cuffs of its long sleeves, the narrow belt fastened with a crescent moon–shaped, pearl-studded buckle. Was she wearing gloves? I don't think so, but my memory of my first close look at Helle Ten Brix may not be entirely reliable; too much has happened since. Her face, though, I can conjure up: white, papery skin stretched thinly over a neat, nutlike skull; close-set, shining eyes; the noble blade of the nose, its bridge straining the skin to a whiteness verging on incandescence; the ironic lift of the eyebrows; the narrow lips opening to release a plume of smoke. This was a face designed to imply a severity of intellect, with disconcerting hints here and there of a desire to charm as well as to intimidate. Why else would she have painted her lips the color of poppies, outlined her eyes with what looked like kohl, thickened her lashes with mascara? In his 1957 monograph *Helle Ten Brix: Prophet or Phryne?* Joseph Kerman focuses on this ambiguity as it's reflected in the work of her middle period, specifically *The Harrowing of Lahloo.* "Ten Brix," Kerman writes, "juxtaposes the seductive power of the ascetic against the ultimately evasive stance of the libertine. It is the genius of her art to be able to make us experience, through the music itself, the inevitability of this struggle; the opera's final image, the bleached bone of the figurehead floating up into the tidal wave's crest, reminds us of how apocalypse is not only ablutionary, but also erotic."

Or you might say that Helle Ten Brix was a complicated and difficult woman. For example, she smoked like a gangster, holding the cigarette between her thumb and index finger, inserting it shallowly at the corner of her mouth and then leaving it there, hanging down at a slight angle, while she talked. "Very close, don't you think?" she said. Her voice was husky, foreign in its cadence rather than its intonation. I didn't know what she was talking about. The outcome of the opera we'd just seen? The confrontation with the convertible? She didn't wait for a reply, but plunged on in a manner which would later seem characteristic, her interpretation of the world around her happily unencumbered by reliance on fact. "You found the music pretty but unsatisfying," she said, "the music of a little boy who is trying to please his mother. Naturally you're outraged. You came knowing that Puccini is a little boy, but still you're outraged. Boys in cars, girls in robes. Soon enough we'll all be drenched, and then we'll feel much better, no?"

By now she'd made her way to the sidewalk, where she was walking rapidly to and fro, occasionally pausing to look back toward where I sat. "Too sullen," she said finally, as if having reached a decision. "*Gnaven*. The key is wrong. C-sharp minor, but bright, bright. And then the oboes, sneaky like boys." Had she in fact been the small fidgety presence which I'd noticed earlier, several rows ahead of me, seated between Sam and Maren Blackburn? At the time I'd assumed it was their son, William, one of the twins' classmates, but William was, I recalled, a blond, and the head I'd seen had been dark. It must have been the head's constant restless movement, its frequent tendency to tilt upward as if the ceiling were more interesting than the stage, which had misled me.

"Drenched?" I asked, and Helle Ten Brix responded by pointing dramatically across Broadway to where, in Dr. Kinglake's front yard, the heavy blue panicles of the lilac hedge were stirring. The wind was picking up out of the east; you could smell a storm in it, the odor of fins breaking through the swelling and far-off surface of the sea.

People were beginning to leave the opera house, stepping around me with the exaggerated precision that is meant to make you get out of the way. "Oh no," someone said, and the first drops of rain landed on the steps. The sky, I suddenly realized, was the color of mineral oil. Haphazardly, and then with increasing persistence, the rain started to fall everywhere, large heavy drops turning the concrete black, bouncing off the wrought-iron coats of the two startled deer in the doctor's yard, weighing down the daffodils in the curbside planters, tearing loose the new leaves of the sugar maples along the street. Several couples made a run for it, hunched over, the husbands' arms protectively looped around their wives' shoulders, like Adam and Eve abandoning Paradise. "Ma?"

I heard, and when I looked back I could see Flo, a perplexed expression on her face, peering out from within the crowd of bodies in the doorway. "Aren't you getting wet?" she asked.

Sometimes it seems as if what I made, then, was a choice, although at the time I would have described myself as being without motivation, in the grip of the powerful inertia that's usually a prelude to romance or to war. Either I could prove that I had enough sense to come in out of the rain, or I could remain where I was, getting more and more soaked by the second. If the former, the goodwill of my neighbors would be secured; if the latter, I'd be written off as a misfit. Across the street, flanked by the doctor's deer, Helle Ten Brix sat on an ornamental bench, getting similarly soaked. I picture her winking, but of course even if she had, at that distance, through that curtain of water, I wouldn't have been able to see it. Maybe I never had a choice. Maybe Helle was telling the truth when she said that she'd invented a landscape to contain just the two of us, a landscape both overblown and factitious, like the setting of the opera we'd recently watched, complete with its own audience.

"We needed this rain," the Abbess said. "It'll clear the air," said Mrs. Sprague, to which Sam Blackburn replied that the rain was filled with poison from a thousand midwestern smokestacks. He was lounging at the edge of the group, a character waiting in the wings; I could feel his eyes on the nape of my neck. How delicate are the first whirrings of the carnal, that intemperate engine of multiple gears, its pulleys crisscrossing the spaces between bodies, a tiny wheel here making a tiny wheel there start to spin! Too delicate, really— you get mixed up when you try to assign the source. "Can't you do something?" Maren asked. "She's your aunt," Sam pointed out.

Lightning flashed. There was the sound of wood cracking open, a brief pause, and then an extended roar, as if the heavens themselves were being drawn through the eye of a needle. Broadway became the corridor into which winds from every point of the compass penetrated, whirling madly, yanking off the red petals of Mrs. Hightower's peonies, flattening the hydrangeas in front of the pizza parlor, scooping up toy trucks and garden tools and hurling them at windows—the silver tip of a trowel smashed through the doctor's fanlight, sending wet triangles of glass into his vestibule. The rain tore sideways, or swept suddenly upward, as if smacked by a huge paw. And meanwhile the lightning kept flashing, over and over again, flickering down the trunks of the maples, rolling in greenish-yellow balls across the doctor's lawn, eventually setting fire to the bench, which, luckily, Helle Ten Brix had vacated a moment before. I could see her wandering toward the street, the pale disk of her face still tilted in my direction. "Tante Helle!" Maren yelled, but the wind caught her voice and stuffed it back into her mouth.

Feathers and rocks, frogs and keys and lockets, saucers and pearls—the air seemed to be filled with spinning objects, one of which landed in my lap. A hand? Of course not. It was a gray-and-white-striped work glove, soggy and smeared with mud. That's just to show you how confused I was. I'll admit that I'd lost all sense of proportion. From the wide black base of an anvil-shaped storm cloud, positioned directly over her, a single white finger of lightning pointed straight down at the top of Helle Ten Brix's head. She was, when it hit, standing in the middle of Broadway; as I watched, her body appeared to shrivel for an instant into a dark, forked root, into the strict, metaphysical image of pure lust, surrounded by a sulfurous aureole, a green shoot licking from its crown.

Only afterwards did I understand that what I'd thought had happened and the actual event might not be the same thing. The storm retreated; for several minutes the rain continued to fall, the drops growing larger and larger, farther and farther apart, until you could see each individual drop. Over the gabled rooftops of the mansions on Rose Hill a little crescent moon, like Helle's belt buckle, appeared. For a while I could still hear the muffled sound of thunder off to the east beyond the asphalt pits, and then nothing. Helle Ten Brix stood at the foot of the steps, smoothing down the wet folds of her skirt, the curved surface of each of her gray eyes pricked with a single dot of light. "Yours?" she asked, and I realized she was looking at Ruby and Flo, who had left the crowd in the doorway and now were standing on either side of me.

"But I thought——" I began, and then I didn't know what to say. No one else seemed surprised to see her standing there intact.

"A waste of time," she replied. "Your little girls are yawning. They can hardly stay awake."

Later she would explain to me that the whole thing had been a ploy to get my attention. "Sex is no mystery," she said. "When poor Kraka, daughter of Sigurd Fafnirsbane, removed the tarred hat her stepfather had compelled her to wear, down fell all her silky hair, and the bakers were so astonished by her beauty that they burned their bread. It's as simple as that." Going to the opera had been Sam's idea, she explained. Even though he knew Helle couldn't stand Puccini, he'd convinced Maren to buy the tickets; it was his way of getting revenge, because he knew she wouldn't be able to refuse to go without hurting Maren's feelings. A clever plan, only it backfired. "To meet you," she said, "I'd have sat through *La fanciulla del West*."

All of which left me with no clear sense of how to proceed. On the one hand there was the cardboard carton, the tangible, if chaotically assembled, evidence of a life; on the other hand, there was Helle herself, hanging around with the persistence of stale cigarette smoke near my living room ceiling, urging me to ignore that evidence. I still have a copy of the review of *Suor Angelica* which appeared in the Canaan *Sun Herald* the day following the storm. After congratulating the Opera-teers on a job well done and praising individual performers with her usual share of errata—"Rose Thorn was especially enchanting in the role of the littlest novice"—Marjory Stroup went on to describe the scene on the steps. "Upon leaving the theater," she wrote, "opera-goers were treated to a second performance. Mother Nature opened her bag of special effects, putting on a rare meteorological show complete with lightning and thunder. Although a large maple, one of the magnificent trees planted 25 years ago by the Rotary, was struck by a stray bolt, fortunately no one was hurt, and the tree itself sustained minimal damage."

IV

ACCORDING TO the birth certificate included among the papers in the quilted glove box, Helle Ten Brix was born on August 6, 1897—a reliable enough piece of information and one Helle confirmed herself. Indeed, she liked to say that she'd been born on what she called a "bad day," by which she meant those days history chooses to be the occasion for its grimmest events—the very day on which, almost fifty years later, the Americans dropped the bomb on Hiroshima. But that's where such reliability began and ended. For what was I to make of the fact that even though the signature on the certificate was that of Anders Ten Brix, Helle's father, in his capacity as physician in charge, Helle insisted that her father had been a game warden?

"He was called Anders Skovløber, or Anders Game-keeper," she told me. "At least that's how the villagers referred to him. And he met my mother one night when he was returning home from the *kro* in Horns, stone sober, and wandered into the bog." As Helle described it, a *nisse*, or bad spirit, was responsible: there was a full moon, and the road from the *kro* to the manor was, in her words, "straight as a string." Still, around and around he stumbled, getting wetter and wetter, until eventually he found himself approaching a small hillock at the very center of the bog. This hillock was never under water even during the most violent and sudden of thaws; the only way it could be reached was along a narrow strip of firm land that wound among the quagmires and peat hags. "At first he thought he saw a fairy sitting on top of the hill," Helle explained. "But on closer investigation the fairy turned out to be a human woman—Ida Johansdatter." The woman was every bit as wet as himself, although she didn't seem bothered by her condition. The minute she saw Anders she dropped the carcass of the rabbit she'd been chewing away at and opened her arms. "*Heyomdick, heyomdack, come fallerah!*" she sang invitingly. So it happened that Helle Ten Brix was conceived on a hill in a bog, her conception supernaturally engineered.

When I asked what her mother had been doing in the bog in the first place, Helle smiled condescendingly. Naturally my own parents would never have told me tales about the *natmænd*, those dark-skinned gypsies of Romany origin who wandered the Jutland heath, sharpening knives, poaching game, and speaking their own secret language. Ida, Helle said, had been the illegitimate daughter of Big-Margrethe, a notorious gypsy chieftain, which would explain both the darkness of Helle's hair and her pronounced hostility to the Danish preference for neatness and comfort. Some of her earliest compositions—the *Drallers*, or Gypsy Dances—had been inspired by her mother's extensive repertoire of bedtime songs, as had her eventual use of the so-called gypsy scale for Nanna's popular virelay in *The Harrowing of Lahloo* and for the difficult quartet with which Act One of *The Girl Who Trod on a Loaf* concludes. "Two augmented seconds," she said, "and bang! the next thing you know the ground's dropping away right beneath your feet."

To accept Helle's version of her provenance was to accept the fact that this alliance was doomed from the start. What is less clear is that at the heart of the problem, at least as Helle understood it, were opposing attitudes not so much toward the law as toward the gratification of appetite, toward food. No matter which version of Helle's childhood I ended up accepting—and there were several of them to choose from—these elements remained consistent, figuring prominently in her reconstructions of most key events. Moths in a cupboard; poison in a safe. A poacher and a gamekeeper. Sorting through her books one day I uncovered a small volume, its cover pale blue and water-stained, a collection of stories by a nineteenth-century Danish writer with the improbable name of Steen Steensen Blicher—"the Danish Jane Austen," according to the prefatory note in the English-language translation I eventually tracked down and read. I did this because certain passages in Helle's copy had been heavily underlined and starred, and I couldn't help noticing the repetition of such words as *skovløber*, *natmænd*, and *nisse*. In one story a gamekeeper is returning from Viborg on a moonlit night when he finds himself mysteriously lured into an elder bog by a red-capped sprite. In another a crazy, spade-wielding woman sings a song about betrayal, each verse of which ends with Ida's words from the hummock. Or to quote Niels Ten Brix, Helle's half-brother and the father of Maren, "The whole thing's a pack of lies."

He turned out to be still alive, running a small dry-cleaning business in Hjørring when he finally decided to respond to my letters requesting information. Ida, he wrote, had been the only daughter of a Copenhagen coffee merchant, and she met Anders—who was, Niels went on to assure me, a doctor—at a wedding party. Anders was the groom's cousin; the bride was Ida's best friend. "My father told me," Niels wrote, "that Ida had been a pretty woman, but infirm, and spoiled rotten when he met her. A spoiled little girl who ran into the arms of the village idiot the minute things didn't go her way." He went on to extol the virtues of his own mother, then closed by reminding me that the past was the past, and only fools or archaeologists dug around in it.

I wasn't surprised by any of this. Certainly on more than one occasion Helle had shared with me her ideas about invention and discovery, expanding on a theme central to her art. Women, she would say, were the world's inventors; it was only after the fact that men came along and discovered whatever it was that women had already invented. The act of invention was basically lawless, whereas the act of discovery required the making of laws, an endless cataloguing, describing, judging, and ultimately, dismantling of the thing discovered. Looked at through this lens, wild Ida, perched on her hillock, could be seen as the inevitable result of a daughter's need to invent a mother consistent with her vision of the truth. I knew that if I was going to finish Helle's opera, I would have to honor this philosophy; I also knew that Helle had been aware of my basic resistance to it when she chose me for the job. As usual, she had something up her delicate, lace-paneled sleeve—its elegance designed to divert your attention from the willful strength of the arm hidden beneath it, that strong white arm snaking toward me through the water-flecked light of a hot summer morning. Running water, the apprehensive thumping of my heart, the smell of cedar mixed with the smell of cigarette smoke. But memory merely serves to promote homage to the dead, while what Helle wanted was nothing less than resurrection.

So: Helle Ten Brix was born on August 6, 1897, in the master bedroom of a large, drafty manor house, a graceless rectangle of yellow stones located within the parish of Torslev, Dronninglund hundred, village of Horns. That's a fact, as was the presence of the Great Bog immediately outside the bedroom window. Because it was summer the window was open, letting in the faint sound of the bog's crepitations, a soft crackling noise, like a piece of paper that had been wadded up and thrown away and then, all on its own, began to uncoil. The sound of uncoiling in those days was everywhere: the world was preparing for war. In Austria the Baroness von Suttner was writing in her diary, "Cold, cold are all hearts, cold as the draft which penetrates the rattling windows," while in Essen Krupp's factories were turning metal into gold.

But on that August night the world was still at peace; the air as it ruffled the bedclothes was tepid and dissolute with the smell of roses. Empress Josephine, Louise Odier, Baroness Rothschild, Lady Caroline Lamb—they bowed their heavy, aristocratic heads, accepting the strange fate by which they'd been resurrected as flowers in a formal garden on the northern tip of the Jutland peninsula. Such an inhospitable setting, so severe and windblown! It was here that ten thousand years earlier the glacier had deposited an infertile mixture of sand and clay, hills and hollows pocked with aquatic flotsam, narwhal tusks and baleen; with chunks of amber containing the skeletons of prehistoric insects. Glacial meltwater filled the hollows and, while its tendency was to form lakes and streams, to seep out toward the sea, in some places the water got trapped. It became brown and acidic, unfit for the bacteria which promote decay, so that whatever fell into it was granted a terrible kind of immortality. Arrowheads, reindeer bones, hazel catkins, the bodies of Iron Age men and women—all of these things settled within the slowly developing layers of peat. Thus the Danish bogs were made, those self-contained landscapes, treacherous but beautiful. If Helle was right, and landscape is destiny, then it makes perfect sense that she would have been born on the edge of a bog.

Just as it makes sense that her birth would have been difficult. From what I've been able to piece together, although Ida's water broke at noon on August 5, she didn't experience the transitional stage of labor until some time shortly before midnight, then worked hard for another three hours to push the baby out. "I was born at *ulvetimen*," Helle told me, "and I will die at *ulvetimen*." This was on her deathbed, and she didn't have the energy to elaborate. But I knew that *ulv* meant "wolf," and that she was talking about that moment in the day when, according to Danish folklore, a hole appears in time's otherwise impenetrable fabric, allowing spirits to enter the world or to leave it. The birth and the death—maybe the reason I find it possible to imagine the one is because I was there to watch the other. Why else would I be able to see so clearly that little section of scalp, that dark sliver turning to an oval, to a circle? When Helle was dying she asked me to press my hand down on the top of her head because, as she explained, her spirit kept swimming up into her cranium, resisting her efforts to exhale it through her mouth. The Hindi, she said, used to trepan their dead, to make sure no spiritual residue got left behind. And I could feel it, *her*—the pulse of that life, as perverse and combative in the end as it had been in the beginning.

Unfortunately the rest of the scene has a cloudy, dim quality, the result of conflicting information. If Anders Ten Brix was, as Helle said, a gamekeeper, he must have had his hands full trying to deliver a baby. For Helle also claimed that it had been her father who cut the umbilical cord, who wiped her body clean of all signs of her mother's body, who suctioned out her nasal passages with a pointed rubber bulb. What he was doing, she said, was making sure that the first thing she smelled would be him. Hadn't I noticed the way she reacted to the odor of unwashed male hair, or that particular scent on a man's breath compounded of red wine and garlic and tobacco? At such moments she would get quieter than usual, could feel her nostrils compressing. And she would find herself thinking about how the god Loki gave birth to Odin's horse after getting himself pregnant by eating a woman's heart.

By now it would have been almost four in the morning. Shadows, blue like whey, would have been puddling in the corners of the room. In the summer, in Jutland, the sun never goes all the way down; it makes the furniture gleam like mother-of-pearl, like something you'd want to lick, something sweet and bitter at the same time, similar to packaged almond custard. The headboard of the bed, for instance, in which were carved the bodies of four crows: several years later it would infuriate Anders when he caught Helle, awake long past her bedtime, sucking dreamily on one of their clawed feet. It would infuriate him, but it was his fault. He was the one, after all, who'd insisted that Ida was too small-breasted to produce milk, who'd bottle-fed Helle a specially prepared formula, a mixture he concocted himself, even as Ida strained to expel the afterbirth. He pursed his lips; he made small kissing sounds. On the bedside table there was a metal pan where knives swam in pinkish liquid.

Four crows signify success in childbirth; it probably should have been eight for grief. Or maybe nine, for a secret. The house was called Krageslund, which means Grove of Crows. They roosted in the lindens which bordered the property, and if startled they all took off at once, darkening the sky so you'd have to light the lamps to see what you were doing. I suppose, eventually, Helle fell asleep. As for Ida, she buried the afterbirth in the rose garden the next day. You had to do this, for luck.

V

ONLY IDA WASN'T a lucky woman. Even before succumbing to the tuberculosis which finally killed her, she often suffered from fevers and migraines, spending whole days in her darkened bedroom with a damp cloth on her forehead. When at last she got up, strands of black hair would be stuck to her temples and cheeks, giving her face a crazed look, like a porcelain plate on the verge of cracking into pieces. Although Helle suggested that this was the price her mother paid for leaving the bog, for denying her gypsy origins, it seemed to me that Ida's ill health might actually have been the way she'd found to triumph over Anders: the only doctor in the parish of Torslev, and he couldn't cure his own wife.

In such a marriage it's not uncommon for the weaker partner to turn a child into an ally, a strategy that Ida developed on three separate fronts. To begin with, she encouraged Helle to join her in the complicity of the infirm, their noses lowered nightly above a steaming pot into which had been let fall three drops of eucalyptus oil. Some children are cursed with a genuinely frail constitution; if a single germ is floating on the breeze, it will seek them out. Only this didn't happen to be the case with Helle, who was merely skinny, whose longing to uncover symptoms—that faint prickling at the back of the throat as if some tiny thing were scrabbling there for purchase, that heaviness in the head which made the neck feel like a pipe cleaner—was nothing more than a longing to please her mother. "*Macbeth*, Act One," Anders would say whenever he came upon his wife and daughter thus engaged at the kitchen table. "He thought he was so funny," Helle sneered. She said she'd never known a man who hadn't been given to laughing at his own jokes. Whereas Ida rarely laughed, not having much in the way of a sense of humor. An unlucky woman, an unhappy woman. If I didn't know how dangerous it is to make a virtue out of weakness, I'd probably feel sorry for her.

The second aspect of the alliance centered around the piano, Ida's Pleyel baby grand, a wedding present from Anders to his new bride, and her only belonging that he didn't ship off to the poorhouse in Hjørring immediately following her death. Eventually this piano came to stand in the corner of what was referred to as the morning room, even though it was on the west side of the house, facing the bog, and remained cool and dim until mid-afternoon. But Ida had preferred this room to the other, sunnier room where Anders had originally put the piano; she liked to keep an eye on the bog while she played. Ida Ten Brix, so pretty and young, so eager to try out her present that she never noticed how the train of her wedding dress kept catching on its pedals. Did she really look like a cat, or was that just the romantic fancy of the artist (Viggi Brahe, I assume) who drew the little ink portrait I found in the glove box? And would she really have chosen to play "After the Ball," as Helle claimed? Certainly this would have been an odd, even premonitory choice, with its theme of broken glassware and broken hearts. Unlike Helle, however, Ida never paid attention to the words of songs.

As for Anders, he had by his own admission a tin ear. It wasn't until Ida was dead that he started to pound away at the piano, the way a child might, exposing its capacity for gibberish. Clearly his reason for keeping it had nothing to do with its sentimental value; maybe it was just too big to dispose of. In any event, Ida began giving Helle lessons in the fall of 1901, not long after her fourth birthday. Before that the only instrument she could play was a large Swiss music box, its panels hand-painted with scenes from fairy tales, and she had to be watched constantly to make sure she wasn't turning the crank in the wrong direction. Or so Helle said. For although she composed her first opera when she was twelve years old, the same age at which Mozart composed *La finta semplice*, she wanted you to know that that was where the resemblance began and ended. Even when she was a very little girl, Mozart was Helle's idol, her guiding spirit, her delight and her inspiration. Sweet Wolfgang, she called him, willing to forgive him, as she would forgive no other man, for what she referred to as an accident of gender.

The first piece she learned was Mozart's Minuet in G. Ida prepared a simple arrangement, which Helle was to play with her right hand only. Her left hand was to rest, palm up, in her lap. It would appear that Ida was an exacting teacher: she refused to let Helle touch the keyboard until she'd proved that she could curve her fingers in the proper position around an apple; if Helle's wrist drooped, Ida would hit it with a knitting needle, reminding her to think of herself as a puppet, her arm suspended from the ceiling on wires. Later came the Czerny exercises, the Leschetizky method, Breithaupt's oddly

tiring principles of relaxation. Once or twice Ida blindfolded
Helle, urging her to feel the music with the tips of her fingers,
in her elbows, along her spine.

In fact, before she made the mistake of marrying Anders,
there had been a time when Ida dreamed of the concert stage.
She'd attended the conservatory in Copenhagen, just as Helle
was to do; in her dimity shirtwaist and long blue skirt she'd
spent hours in the same third-floor practice room where Helle,
dressed like a boy, would begin composing her second opera.
Escorted by a handsome Flemish bassoon player, Ida had sat
weeping in the balcony of the Odd Fellow Palæet as, far
below, Paderewski played Brahms's Piano Concerto in B-flat.
She was serious enough, Helle said, but she lacked nerve.
That was why her pedagogy was so rigorous: nerveless mothers couldn't abide nervelessness in their daughters. Of course
it was Ida to whom Helle brought her earliest attempts at
composition, Ida whose criticisms helped shape the *Fantasi*,
those strange, tantalizing songs which flutter, as so much of
Helle's early music does, at the very portal of the ear. These
songs are the obvious precursors of *Det omflakkende Møl*'s
unsettling second-act finale; of, ultimately, "Dancing Sister"
or "More has broken than you know." Nor was Ida herself
without talent. At the end of each lesson she would nudge
Helle aside on the bench with her bony hip, and then she would
begin playing something dauntingly complex and seamless,
endlessly romantic and dark. Like a dream, Helle said; no
matter what else you might say about her, my mother played
like a dream. In those days she favored Chopin, the late
études. Meanwhile, on the other side of the open window
extended the pale, unreadable face of the bog, intent as usual
on its own destiny.

Which brings me to the last and most troubling aspect of

the alliance: Ida's infidelity. I don't know how or when Ida first met Viggi Brahe, nor do I know whether she loved him or was merely appeasing her growing sense of loneliness. Indeed, despite the implication of Niels's letter, the tone of which was too bitter to be entirely convincing, I don't even know if Ida and Viggi Brahe ever really had an affair, or if Helle made it up. What I do know is that the song Ida's supposed to have sung whenever she was setting out for an assignation is a real song; called "The Feathered Maiden," it can be found in Svaning's Manuscript I, circa 1580, and is assumed to be the inspiration behind the ghastly character of Nightingale in Helle's 1953 opera, *Fuglespil*. And I do know that in northern Jutland, in the parish of Torslev, a threadlike tributary to the Rya called Mogens Stream is spanned by six bridges and skirts what used to be a vast stretch of peat land. Or at least such was the case as late as 1915, according to the copy of the map sent to me by the Horns Historical Society. But as to what actually happened that April afternoon when Ida returned to Krageslund chilled and coughing, I only have the most fugitive of clues, a shifting mass of evidence, to augment Helle's peculiar story. Clues and evidence. I can hear her voice, pinched with disgust: did clues and evidence bring us any closer to truth in the courtroom? It's my own complicity in these events which is at issue here, and nothing, not even the ghost of a woman who once loved me, can save me from that fact.

So it was that on a sunny April afternoon in 1905 a mother and her daughter were walking along a path bordering a stream. Ida and Helle Ten Brix—I'll insist on that, just as I'll insist that the stream they were walking beside was the Mogens, not the branch of the Hunger River that turns my road to mud every spring, nor the Wissahickon Creek in Philadelphia, where my mother used to take me to feed the ducks. The path was narrow and chalky, with grooves cut through it at intervals by runoff from Nissen's pasture on the right: water always seeks to find its way to other water. Air, on the other hand, arranges itself in layers; air is hierarchical. If you took a breath when you were standing up, the smell of clean, fresh air wouldn't prepare you for what you'd smell if you bent down, scrutinizing at closer range what looked like a cluster of new shoots, white and stringy, but turned out to be a tangle of worms in a pool of spittle. "Foxes," said Ida. "They're always wormy from eating mice."

Naturally no one wants to be told such a thing when she's wearing, as Helle was, a coat made of fox fur. In fact, she and Ida were wearing matching fox coats, because, even though the wind was from the south, this was April, an unreliable time of year: soft white coats with pink satin linings, invisibly fastened with silver hooks and eyes. Did Anders Skovløber kill the foxes himself; did he skin them and then dust the pelts with flour in order to remove all traces of blood? Of course not. Who would be dumb enough to think that the figment of a dead composer's imagination could kill a fox? And while it's true that Dr. Ten Brix possessed a very fine pair of Spanish dueling pistols—one of which I'm all too familiar with—it's unlikely that he ever loaded them, let alone fired them at anything.

" 'Then he put snares on all the trees where the bird was used to sit,' " Ida sang. " 'The small bird used her eyes so well, he couldn't capture it.' " She was dragging Helle along behind her, the way she did when they went shopping together in town. Town—a horrible place! Her mother never knew what to say to the other women when she met them on the street or in the pork butcher's. The other women revered Anders, and they couldn't understand why he'd saddled himself with such an unsuitable wife or why the butcher always saved the purest, sweetest fat for Ida: leaf lard, without which you couldn't make pie crusts lighter than air—as if Ida'd ever had any interest in baking.

The farther Ida and Helle got from Krageslund, the stranger the words to the song became: " 'He cut the flesh out of his chest, to hang on the linden tree; the bird's wings fluttered with delight, such tasty meat to see.' " Now on the left there grew a row of stunted and branchless alders, a dense gray screen through which they could catch their first glimpse of the bog. The stream banks here were steeper, and the path was lined on either side with scrub willows, an indication that the first of the six bridges would soon come into view. It was a sunny day; Ida shaded her eyes in order to make it out. " 'So wins a youth his maiden,' " she sang.

Once they'd crossed this bridge, they had to find what Helle thought of as the bog's doorway: a break in the alder screen that gave onto a narrow, almost invisible trail, which, no sooner had you found it, turned to muck. This is because access to the bog—as with all things inviting worship—was made difficult, in this case by the presence of an encircling, protective moat called a lagg, a knee-deep channel filled with sluggish black water. Willow trees and leatherleaf grew thickly in the lagg, their roots snarling under its surface, hooking around your feet or recoiling, pliant and slippery, beneath them. And everywhere from out of openings in the air and brush shot living creatures: voles like drops of mercury from a broken thermometer, wrens and sparrows like fat from a skillet.

"My mother was always in a hurry," Helle told me, "any time she was going to meet Viggi Brahe." But on this particular day Ida seemed more impatient than usual. Helle was doing her best to keep up, inching bit by bit along the mucid bark of a submerged trunk, trying to squeeze sideways through a gap between two willows, when all at once an arm reached out and grabbed the hem of her coat. Only it wasn't an arm, it was a willow branch—the same kind of branch used by Fru Hansen to find hidden springs underneath the ground, or by Fru Pedersen to make schoolchildren learn their lessons, a moist black branch with reddish striations along its length—and it wouldn't let go. "Stop," Helle called out, "please wait!" but Ida only looked back coldly, as if she were trying to figure out what it was, exactly, she was dealing with. "No one," she said, "I mean *no* one, has a right to tell another person how to live." Then she took off, moving faster than before, without another backward glance.

So it happened that when Helle Ten Brix was a high-strung and suggestible child of seven, she got lost in the Great Bog at Horns. One minute her mother's white coat was there, about ten yards ahead of her, and the next it was gone, along with all signs of the trail. Was it possible you couldn't see those signs unless your vision had been sharpened by desire for another person's body? Maybe such desire could make your body completely malleable, allowing you to ease it through the wet mesh of tree limbs, your arms and legs drawn like a magician's scarves out of increasingly smaller holes. It was always dark in the lagg, and now the sun was beginning to go down and the insects that come out at dusk, mosquitoes and stinging gnats, were swarming around Helle's face, greedy for blood. If she tried to brush them away, she'd lose her balance; if she didn't, they would fly into her eyes and nose and ears.

When Helle finally managed to make her way to the other side of the lagg, what stretched out in front of her was an empty expanse of peat, an apparently colorless landscape dotted here and there with low-lying shrubs, squat clumps of sweet gale, heath, and snowberry. Three miles away, to the east, the moon was starting to brighten above the chimneys and rooftops of Viggi Brahe's crumbling estate, Sandhed; behind her, to the west, the sky was changing color, making the fur of her coat appear red at the tips. Her mother was nowhere in sight, the only evidence of her passage a single green rubber boot, lying on its side in the peat. Helle picked it up and tipped the water out of it. How could a person disappear in such a flat landscape? Although the bog's flatness, she discovered as she started out across it, was illusory; this was in fact a dense mat of sphagnum boiling up at intervals into hummocks, the way oatmeal boils up within a saucepan. The sphagnum was moist and translucent, in some places almost clear, in others deep crimson. Springy, it rebounded beneath her boots; you could be tricked into thinking your footing was secure and then, all of a sudden, sink in up to your knees. If Helle had wanted, she could have let herself fall over backwards onto the moss without taking any of the usual precautions, so soft it was. Still, she suspected that if she were to relax her control even for a second, she might never stop falling; she might end up at the bottom of the bog, where she would find herself under the jurisdiction of a disposition more intemperate, more unforgiving than her own.

She'd probably walked less than a quarter of a mile when she came upon the peat hag, its cavity filled with what looked like the same black water that flowed through the lagg, but deeper. "Mmm-uh!" said the bog, opening its mouth. "Mmm-ahh!" In school Fru Pedersen had explained how during the Iron Age men and women had been thrown into similar pits as sacrifices to Nerthus, goddess of the earth. Some of them would be found with a hazel withy tied in a noose around their necks, signifying their journey across death's threshold and into the goddess's domain; some of them had their necks broken, or slit by a knife. And all of them were perfectly preserved by the tannic acids in the water—tanned, as Fru Pedersen said, "like shoe leather." On one occasion, when a peat cutter found the body of a girl, Constable Fog had been called in to investigate what appeared to be a recent murder. But the girl had been dead for two thousand years, even though you could still see her delicate eyelashes and her long blond braid, her mouth curving mysteriously upward in a smile!

These sacrifices always occurred in the spring, to ensure a good harvest. And what about the victims? Helle wondered. She imagined the girl being led by a hushed procession of friends and relatives through the lagg and across the bog. Had she known in advance what was going to happen to her? Had she been proud? Had she walked across this same stretch of peat right before she was to die, uncertain whether or not Nerthus would find her pleasing? In the spring, the snaky crowns of the mosses put forth little stalks and pods formed at the tips; if you were very quiet, you could hear the pods cracking open, releasing their spores into the fresh air.

At the pool, Helle stopped to think things over. She was tired, but afraid that if she sat down she might ruin her coat. She was also afraid that the reason she couldn't see her mother was because her mother was no longer standing up. According to Helle, although in those days the typical Danish child learned about sex from watching cows or pigs, at least her own instruction, if not equally explicit, had been infused with a certain mournful sense of romance. Hadn't she been watching only two weeks earlier as her mother fell into Viggi Brahe's arms? He'd been waiting for her, leaning over the railing of the second of the six bridges across Mogens Stream, tossing something into the current. Twigs? Coins? Probably sticks: Helle had recognized his ugly brown dog, racing back and forth through the cattails on the far bank, wagging its soaked, ratlike tail. Romantic Viggi Brahe, dressed as usual in a long cape and a tricorn hat, like a man from another century—dramatic Viggi, whose ancestor Tycho spent most of his time looking through a tube at the stars. At her mother's approach he'd turned and his arm had emerged from under his cape, which fell in deep folds from his shoulders, the fabric as dense and stiff as a horse blanket. First he'd pulled her close to him, letting his hand come to rest on her stomach; because her coat was hanging open, Helle had been able to see how his fingers were sliding down, little by little, causing the skirt to bunch between her mother's legs. For several seconds they just looked at each other. And then, as Helle watched, her mother had lifted her arms and taken hold of Viggi Brahe's head, drawing it slowly toward her, the way she'd remove a heavy bowl from the top shelf of the kitchen cupboard.

"I'd tried it out myself," Helle told me, "so I knew. Something happened if you touched yourself like that. Your legs got weak and you wanted to lie down. I didn't have any idea what that had to do with men and women, but I knew enough to know that my mother was playing me for a fool." Similarly, although Anders may have suspected Ida's infidelity, he never dreamed that she'd go so far as to involve her own daughter in it. By now he would have shown the last of his patients to the door, and would be wandering around aimlessly the way he always did at the end of the day, still filled with a need to alter the course of events. Only he couldn't do anything about Ida; as far as he knew, she and Helle were off on another one of their pointless jaunts.

Helle regarded the boot thoughtfully. It seems unlikely that at the age of seven she would have considered it symbolic, although later that was clearly what it became for her, no doubt influencing her account of ensuing events, as well as eventually showing up in the finale to the second act of *The Girl Who Trod on a Loaf*. Probably her decision to throw the boot into the pool was nothing more than a reflex action, a simple urge to punish; certainly she couldn't have known that it would be a factor in her mother's death. Helle looked at the boot and then she looked at the pool. You couldn't tell at what point its lip of moss would suddenly droop, spilling you down into that black water across which rowed long-legged insects, leaving the thinnest of wakes. A bird called out, over and over, its song choked and liquid, like a pump starting up. Far to the north a dog started to bark, and much closer, another dog—Viggi Brahe's?—barked back.

Taking a deep breath, Helle threw the boot as far as she could. By now it was dark enough that she was just barely able to make out the boot's trajectory, the way it gracefully arced before hitting the water with a small, reserved splash. For a moment the boot floated there, suspended and upright as if preparing to walk; then it tilted to one side, gradually filling with water until its new weight sucked it under.

At this point I'm tempted to jump directly to a description of how Anders, with the help of Ove Nissen, finally retrieved

Helle from the Great Bog, and how the three of them were still sitting in the kitchen, the men drinking akvavit and smoking their long curved pipes, Helle wrapped in a quilt on the floor near the wood stove, when Ida showed up. I could describe Ida's appearance—the strands of sphagnum clinging to her coat and her hair, her face dotted with insect bites, the wool stocking on her bootless leg stained brown by the bog. I could describe the way Anders took a mop from where it was propped against the wall among the search party's spades and lengths of rope, and began pushing it fiercely back and forth through the widening puddle at his wife's feet. "Ida," he's reported to have said, "how good of you to join us." In other words, now that I've got everyone safely into the kitchen, I could refuse to look back. But if I were to do so, I'd be leaving out what Helle claimed was the most important part of the story—the part which, I admit, I have the hardest time believing.

According to Helle, within seconds after the boot had sunk into the water, it somehow managed to arouse those intransigent creatures whom, once upon a time, her mother had described to her: while she watched, terrified, the Furies began to stir within the deep pot of the bog. Initially she thought that what she was seeing were snakes or fish or branches as, immediately below the pool's surface, a huge, churning knot seemed to be engaged in the act of pulling itself undone. The water tilted up and down, back and forth, pale knobs and crescents occasionally breaking through its black skin; they glistened briefly in the moonlight before sinking down again, out of sight.

Hands appeared, then forearms, shoulders, heads. Now, Helle said, she could see them clearly, their foul, undulant locks, their blunt muzzles and their open nostrils, their eyes laid flat on skin translucent as a baby's, beneath which the blood coursed in visible loops. This, she claimed, was how the Furies looked before history made them into human women, replacing the ruthless indifference of their regard with a more familiar expression, that grudging tenderness you see on the wife's face as she welcomes her husband into bed. There were, as Ida had predicted, three of them in all. "Little girl," the first of them called out, "we accept your offering." And then the second asked, "But shouldn't we tell her the price?" "No one ever believes it," the first replied. "And in any event," the third one added, "the boot was empty." Helle stood looking down at them. "Mother," she said as one at a time they submerged themselves, each one releasing, as she went under, a wide, viscid bubble. Little by little the water crept back into place. It was as if, Helle said, none of it had ever happened.

VI

THOMAS MORLEY, in *A Plaine and Easie Introduction to Practicall Musicke*, describes a fantasy as "when a musician taketh a point at his pleasure, and wresteth and turneth it as he list, making either much or little of it according as shall seeme best in his own conceit." Helle would object to his exclusive use of the male pronoun, but otherwise I think she'd agree with me that what Morley was describing was something very close to her own method. In "*Fantasi for Mors Støvle*," for example, Helle began with the idea of her mother's boot, a simple line of melody in A minor, and elaborated on it until she'd managed to create a foot in the boot, a leg attached to the foot, and, finally, an entire woman, her face tilting upward to receive her lover's kiss as all the while she's being dragged by her ankles into a peat hag. "Red boots or green boots or blue boots, why cavil?" the lyrics read. "You're either halfway to heaven or down with the devil."

Not so very different, I came to realize, from my own method, except that I eventually found I couldn't go on unless I shifted my focus away from a boot to a man: to a specific man, one who wouldn't have been caught dead in a cape and a funny hat—to Sam Blackburn, in fact, whose eyes were hazel, flecked with orange, whereas Viggi Brahe's eyes were like glove buttons, pearly and small, his lashes pale and sparse. Or at least that's the way Viggi Brahe looks in the miniature portrait I came upon one day while sorting through Helle's jewelry. The portrait was in a gold locket, inserted in the opening on the left side of the hinge; on the right side there was no portrait, though someone had scratched an X in its place. A delicate-featured face, aristocratic and rabbity, resembling Tycho Brahe's as it appears in the frontispiece to *Astronomiae instauratae mechanica*, but without Tycho's spread-winged white mustaches, without his expression of gravity and purpose. I would never have wanted to kiss Viggi Brahe.

Whereas I certainly had no trouble kissing Sam Blackburn, although when at last I gave in to him the ballpoint pen he habitually kept in his breast pocket jabbed me in the armpit. Sam. Sometimes I still confuse the noise of birds in the bushes with his footsteps. He used to sneak up like a storybook lover, tossing pebbles from the driveway at my window. Indelicate Sam Blackburn in his brown-and-green-plaid flannel shirt, in his cloth cap with the name of a popular hybrid strain of corn printed above its visor, the kind of hat that's given away free at grain stores. The pebbles would hit—*ping pang pong*—echoing the names of the three ministers in Puccini's last opera. Peuh, they sing in their pinched falsetto voices. Who is Turandot? A woman with a crown on her head and a fringed mantle. But take off her clothes and there's flesh, raw flesh. It's stuff that isn't even good to eat.

Or so Helle encouraged me to recognize the nature of the problem. Puccini was only the tip of the iceberg, she explained. A man like Sam was more like the Don, a man in whom appetite was just a symptom of a comprehensive vanity.

They're counting on your remorse, she went on to say. That's so they'll have an excuse to lock you away with your own personal Calaf, a nice man who'll run his hands through your hair, who'll flatter you with metaphors. In exchange you'll be expected to make three promises: your heart is his, your body's his, your soul is his. What he'll be hoping for, really, is that you'll provide him with a child. Only he'll have forgotten the most important thing. He'll have forgotten that the child of vanity is violence.

Except I didn't forget. There was a gun, three fingers and a thumb closing around its pearl handle, the fourth finger—the index finger—speculatively stroking its trigger. Point that thing away, someone yelled. The sound of the stream; the first drops of rain beginning to fall. *Was* it remorse that I felt? Would that have accounted for the unnatural heaviness of my limbs—my sense, night after night, of being unable to pull myself from the sofa and go to bed? Get up, Francie, I'd tell myself; and if anything I'd sink down deeper, driving the sofa's broken springs further and further toward the floor, letting loose a cloud of dust and feathers.

But I'm getting ahead of myself. How thin the membrane containing the imagination, how easily disposed to leakage! Let me go back instead to the week following the Operateers' production of *Suor Angelica*. When the letters came—one on a page torn from a loose-leaf notebook, one on a piece of music composition paper—I wrote out my replies, stuck them in envelopes, and handed them over, one to Flo, one to Ruby, with specific instructions about the way in which they were to be delivered. Ida might have used Helle as an accomplice to her infidelity, but I improved on her crime: I used my children as go-betweens.

The letter from Sam Blackburn was the more obviously amorous of the two, and thus required a more cautious response. After remarking on my qualities of intellect, and after expressing his dismay that a bright woman like myself should be stuck waitressing at the Airport Diner, Sam went on to tell me that his Tuesday-night class had been canceled, and that he was hoping we might be able to spend a little time together. I must have realized, he said, that he was attracted to me. Why else would he choose to stop at the Airport Diner, since it was obviously three miles in the wrong direction and the food was lousy?

To be honest, it wasn't as if he, too, hadn't caught my eye. Whenever he came into the diner, Sam always used to order the same thing, tuna on rye toast and ginger ale; then he'd take a stack of student papers out of his briefcase, set them down on the table next to the ginger ale glass, remove the pen from his shirt pocket, and stare off into space. Sometimes he'd put on a pair of glasses with pinkish translucent rims; sometimes he'd turn his cap around so that a small clump of curly brown hair would stick out through the half-moon opening above the adjustable plastic band. A withdrawn and gloomy man, I thought, despite the occasional smile. Our conversations, for the most part, were not unlike the conversations I had with the other customers. Were the roads icing up? How was the hill into town? Was Mrs. Hightower once again going to keep her Christmas decorations up until Easter? Still, whenever I reached over him to remove an empty glass or plate, or to sponge away the toast crumbs, I could feel the space between us like a wedge that wasn't supposed to be there. And even though I knew that our children were friends, we never talked about them.

As for the other letter, at the time I didn't have a clue that its author's objectives might differ from those she so overtly and formally stated:

Dear Miss Thorn:
    Having had the good fortune to meet you the other night (depressed nun, the steps, smoking) I'd like to expand on the acquaintance. Would you and your charming girls be free to come for tea? Let's say Wednesday, four o'clock. I'll count on you unless I hear otherwise.

Sincerely,
Helle Ten Brix.

A tryst Tuesday night, tea the following afternoon? I wrote back on postcards, figuring that in both cases the less I said, the better. For Sam I chose a winter scene, tiny figures photographed skating on a frozen lake—a landscape intended to appeal to tourists, and one which I hoped would reflect the tone of its accompanying message. I told him I could probably manage an hour; maybe we could go somewhere for a drink. Period. Signed. Mainly, I guess, I was curious; I never planned to do anything more than flirt with him a little. Whereas I admit that Helle's card, a reproduction of a painting by Thomas Cole—a hazy panoramic view of trees and a water-fall—was selected with a desire to impress. At the time I couldn't have known that she hated the Hudson River school, that in her opinion men didn't know how to paint nature and any man who tried ought to have "his fingers cut off." We'd be delighted to come for tea, I told her. Four o'clock would be fine.

The Blackburns lived just off Broadway on Quarry Road, in a fairly large house with cinquefoil window arches, an attached semicircular tower, and three separate porches. Our town had many such houses, the railroad barons' taste for architectural excess having been stirred by the writings of John Ruskin: seductive houses, their cornices dripping with ornate molding—unlike my house, the work of a more subtle architect, one bent on seduction through pity. The twins had to walk past the Blackburns' every day on their way home from school, and occasionally they'd end up staying there with William until dinnertime. He had an older sister—Joanne? Joan?—but she was away at college. Besides, Flo had informed me, William was in love with Ruby. Thus the delivery of the cards posed no problem: Ruby was to give her card to Helle, Flo to Sam. Into their hands, I said. But not if they were together in the same room. And not if Mrs. Blackburn was watching.

Of course, once I was actually sitting at her dining room table, watching the steam rise from her Limoges teapot, watching her organdy curtains blow into the room, their motion dreamy and faintly erratic like seaweed, there was no longer any reason for keeping Maren Blackburn in the dark, at least not about her aunt's invitation. The table was mahogany and smelled as if it had been recently polished; in its center, providing a kind of barricade between hostess and guest, someone had put a mason jar filled with daffodils, around which buzzed a solitary bee, under which spread out a whitish stain where water had spilled. We were to have *Nonnefad*, Helle informed me, Nun's Platter, in honor of our meeting. *Nonnefad* and elder tea.

The twins had joined William on the porch and I could hear the squealing of the glider, the enchanting catch in Flo's deep, hoarse voice, as she explained the rules of her favorite card game to William. This was a game she'd made up herself, a variation on slapjack, in which every card had a separate action attached to it. "Diamonds," Flo was saying, "are luck cards. Clubs are hitting cards; spades are digging-for-secrets cards; hearts are love cards. Like, if I get the four of clubs I get to hit someone four times."

You could close your eyes and the breeze would wash your face: the smell of dill and bacon, of steeping elder flowers and smoked fish, of blue cheese and brandied cherries. I felt languid, distracted; I had, I knew, no business being where I was, but the idea that at any second Sam Blackburn might walk into the room, might see me sitting there across from the woman he'd told me only the night before was the bane of his existence, excited me. In fact I suddenly realized I was ravenous, and in no time at all I'd eaten everything on my plate except for three cherry pits. A summer afternoon, warm and slow. "Jack of hearts," Ruby said, her voice like a little flute. "Uh-oh, William." Hot even. So why was it that when I looked up and saw Helle's face staring at me, what I found myself thinking of was winter, of how, sometimes, black water will shine up at you all at once out of a hole in the snow?

"Thin people don't usually eat so much," she said. I told her I had a lot of nervous energy, and anyway, the food was delicious. "Acceptable," Helle said, but I could tell that she was pleased; it wasn't until much later, after she'd moved into the trailer, that I discovered just how passionate she was about cooking. By then, of course, I knew enough about her to place this fact in context, to see it in relationship to its opposing asceticism. One minute she'd be assembling the ingredients for an espagnole, chopping up veal and beef bones with a cleaver, rinsing sand from leeks, complaining about the quality of the parsley; the next minute she'd be advocating a diet of spring water and raw vegetables. Or in her own words (from the second of the five songs in the *Stedmoder* cycle), "The two horns of the moon never met in me." That day in the Blackburns' dining room, for instance, she only picked at the food on her plate, eating at most a sprig of dill, a morsel of salmon, a crumb of cheese. Then she pushed her plate away, folded her hands in front of her on the table, and sighed.

"When I was a girl," she said, "I used to have elder tea whenever I was sick, which was not infrequently." Her mother would bring her the tea, along with a book to look at, a large book with pictures of the Holy Family surrounded by beasts and angels, gold spikes radiating out from their heads, or pictures of tiny figures walking among ruined temples and trees where you could see every leaf. This was the way your eyes worked when you had a fever. But the picture she liked best was a portrait of a girl, her head bound up in a pale blue turban, her face slowly turning, her lips parting as if she were about to tell a secret. Only one of the girl's ears was visible, and from its lobe there hung a drop-shaped pearl earring, which the artist had caused to glow by adding a thick dab of white paint. "Pretty, like you," Helle said, and though she made it sound more like an accusation than a compliment, I said thank you. I didn't know what else to say.

As it turned out, I needn't have worried; Helle now lifted her razor-sharp elbows onto the table, lit a cigarette, and began a thorough interrogation. Sometimes, it is true, she looked more like a mantis than a woman. How old was I? she asked. Where had I grown up? Gone to school? Had I ever been married? Where was the twins' father? Bit by bit she plucked pieces of information from me, and then, evidently having gotten what she wanted, she proceeded to give the information back, reshaping it to suit her own purpose, not unlike the way she composed the *Fantasi*.

I was the heroine, Helle said, of a story which began ten

years ago, just after my twenty-third birthday, five years after
I'd left my parents' home in Chestnut Hill, one year after I'd
done my last exercise in counterpoint at Juilliard. Ten years
ago a woman named Frances burned her finger when she went
to put on the front porch light. This was because the whole
electrical system in the house had shorted out. None of the
lights worked. None, so that a few minutes earlier when the
dog had gotten up from where it was sleeping in the hall
closet, burrowed in among sweepings of insulation and plaster
dust, I hadn't really been able to see it; the dog hadn't barked
but had walked slowly to the door, growling. The snowmobile
had stopped and then gone on to zoom past the window where
Helle herself was sitting, composing the Overture to *Fuglespil*.
The snowmobile had gone on, yet there he was, a man walking
toward my house. The snow squeaked under his boots. For
wasn't that how children were made sometimes, even beautiful
children like Ruby and Flo? Maybe it wasn't a man after all,
but a deity, transformed by its desire.

Eventually I would learn to accept this tendency of Helle's.
In fact, no more than a week later, I was actually flattered
when she showed me her reworking of the Hunters' Trio
from *The Girl Who Trod on a Loaf*, in which the hunters now
rode across the frozen bog on snowmobiles, the sound of the
engines providing a menacing basso ostinato. But what I
remember feeling at tea that day was confusion, anger. Hadn't
she heard a word I'd said? The light in the room grew faint,
pinkish, with great arabesques of smoke near the ceiling; the
walls seemed to be moving in, the curtains to be swelling.
And Helle's voice—how hypnotic it had been, like the waves'
gentle lapping away of sand from the edge of a beach, with
hints of a darker, more comprehensive urge, the tidal pull of
an entire ocean. Had she put something in the tea, or was it

the tea itself? Elder trees, as I know now, are said to possess magical, visionary properties: while she was sitting under an elder, Helle fell into the trance in which she first heard the sound of Lahloo's voice.

I said that ten years ago I didn't own a dog, and that it was no deity who had raped me. "You misunderstand my intentions," Helle replied. Rape was an abomination. All she'd meant to suggest was that sometimes you couldn't explain the love you felt for a child without reimagining the way in which that child had been conceived. Aside from certain lizards, which are apparently able to produce both egg and sperm, and aside from the parthenogenetic behavior of some turkeys, she found the whole idea of conception disgusting. Yet, she admitted, she adored William.

At this point I heard the front door slam, the sound of footsteps, a light tread but with weight in it, moving toward the dining room. Sam, I thought. He walked down the hall, stopped, retreated a few steps. Had he seen me? No, he seemed to be going through the mail, ripping open envelopes, bills no doubt, because I could hear him swearing softly under his breath. And then, just when I thought he wasn't going to come into the dining room, there he was after all, poised in the open archway, blinking as his eyes adjusted to the watery thinness of the light. The hand repositioning his glasses on the bridge of his nose was, I knew, spotted on the back with large pale freckles. The fingernails were almond-shaped and perfectly smooth. The ring had been his father's. Once he noticed me, Sam raised his eyebrows and one corner of his mouth lifted a little. "Sorry," he said, turning as if to leave. "I didn't realize you had company."

"Nonsense." Helle waved her arm in my direction. "This

is Frances. Frances Thorn, the twins' mother. We were just talking about you."

"Oh, Francie," Sam said. "Hi."

Helle scowled. "You two know one another?"

"Sure," Sam said. "From the diner."

It became immediately clear that whatever antagonism existed between Sam and Helle offered each of them the kind of antic pleasure some people take in seeing their own worst fears confirmed. "Sam is a Platonist," Helle announced. He actually believed, she explained, that after God had mixed the soul of the universe, he poured back into the bowl what remained of the former ingredients, a gooey mass which he divided into individual souls, as many as there were stars in the sky, and this was the first generation of men. The ones who led good lives got to keep on being men; those who led bad, wicked lives, cowardly or immoral lives, got turned into women.

"You're just sore because of what Plato said about poets." Sam leaned back against the sideboard, stuck his hands down into his pockets, and smiled at me. "What do you think, Francie? Were you immoral the first time around?"

"Leave Frances out of this," Helle said. But of course that was impossible. Almost as if she knew what I was thinking, she went on to describe Plato's theory about the creation of heterosexual love. When our earliest ancestors drank, the liquid made its way through the lungs into the kidneys and thence to the bladder, where it was expelled by air pressure. At this precise spot a hole pierced the column of marrow extending from the head to the base of the spine, the column down which the "divine seed" of the brain traveled, eager for release. A man's genitals were naturally disobedient and self-willed; they would stoop to any level in their wild lust to reproduce. While the womb, Plato said, was even more disobedient. And woe to the woman whose womb was never fertilized, for such wombs wandered aimlessly around the body, blocking the breathing passages, destroying everything in their path.

Only that wasn't how it happened. Although I continued to face Helle, it was as if my own womb had inside it a tiny compass, its needle indicating correct orientation: the pole's tug was to my left, where Sam now stood, biting into a pear he'd taken from the bowl on the sideboard. The needle swung around, fluctuating briefly as I found myself recalling the beat of the neon sign on the roadhouse roof—OASIS scrolled in lurid red across the bright green fronds of two palm trees, their trunks bright yellow. On, off, on, off. When it was off, you could see the stars, evidently equal in number to the souls of men. Did I really want a drink? We were the only car parked on that side of the building, near the exhaust fans and dumpsters; a fat boy in a white T-shirt emerged from the kitchen door with a pail of garbage, but aside from that we were alone. Maybe *this* was what I wanted? *This?*

Out of the corner of my eye I could see Sam's wrist—just a segment of it, the pale underside where the veins were. "When I was a girl," Helle was saying, "there was still such a thing as dichotomy. Real dichotomy. No wonder we're doomed."

Were his eyebrows lifting again? I could smell the pear, hear the little *pfft pfft* as he spit the seeds into the palm of his hand. What if I'd gotten out of that house then and there and never come back?

"Helle thinks that synthesis is amoral," Sam told me. "She blames everything she doesn't like on Plato, including sex."

"Mom, when are we going home?" Ruby called out, and she sounded plaintive, weary.

Though the air coming in through the windows was still cottony and mild, the temperature in the room had dropped. Was it possible that one old woman, unlocking and locking so many doors in her brain, could generate a breeze of her own? Maybe it wasn't the breeze of thought but the breeze of departure, the first hints of Helle's plan to leave us forever, to disappear around the world's edge like one of those tigers stuck to the rim of its metal wheel in a shooting gallery.

Part Two

DET OMFLAKKENDE
MØL

I

HELLE TEN BRIX began composing *Det omflakkende Møl* (*The Errant Moth*) in 1909, a year notable for many events: in 1909 Halley's Comet returned to draw its fiery red tail through the blue-black skies above the Great Bog; Anders remarried; workers went on strike all over Europe; Richard Strauss was hearing the first notes of *Der Rosenkavalier*, a work requiring that the part of Octavian, the juvenile lead, be sung by a woman dressed up to look like a man. *Hosenrolle*, or trouser parts, had been an operatic convention for many years—think of the winsome Cherubino, one of Helle's great favorites—but this time Strauss, his turned-up nose forever sensitive to any whiff in the air of cultural change, had twisted the convention, giving it a purposely indecent edge. For there can be no doubt about the fact that when Octavian passionately hurls himself down onto the Marschallin's confection of a bed, tangling there with her among lace-edged linens and a profusion of pillows, we're meant to accept the possibility that it's actually two women who are embracing.

I suppose Strauss had read his Krafft-Ebing; even Dr. Ten Brix had a copy of that notorious book hidden on a shelf in his examining room behind the jars of pickled fetuses, relics from his days in medical school whose presence was no doubt calculated not so much to instruct his patients as to remind them of the Circean origins of his art. I know this because Helle admitted to having noticed the book one day when her father had called her in to check her weight; as she stood on the scales she could see its tooled binding peeking out from behind the largest of the jars, into which was crammed the slippery gray body of what looked like a blue-eyed, shell-less snail. But hadn't she told me that Anders was a gamekeeper? Understand, you could never catch Helle in a lie; she would just stare at you blankly and shrug, the implication being that you were a fool to waste your time with such details. Whereas let a mezzo embellish too freely on a coloratura passage and she'd be jumping up and down like Rumpelstiltskin. In any event, although Anders probably assumed that his daughter would never find the book, much less page through it with the wild eyes and thumping heart of the fledgling deviant, he was wrong.

In the original staging of *Det omflakkende Møl* the juvenile lead was played, likewise, by a girl. In fact Helle had created the part of Prince Carissimo with a particular girl in mind: Inger Nissen, the eldest of Ove Nissen's ten children and the first real love of her life. Sensible Inger, whose hair was long like Helle's, although it was light and made by an attentive mother to crown her stunningly round skull in plaits; whereas Helle's hair was black like the cloth the magician places over his fist, and her brain bunched like the fist beneath it.

Their friendship had been secured during the year following Ida's death, when most of the other children at school had taken to avoiding Helle. They kept their distance, but sneaked little glances; worst of all, when they did speak it was with the excessive politeness that children generally reserve for the very old, or for priests. How were they supposed to know that the reason why she sat so stiffly at her desk was to protect them? One false move, she thought, and the leathery wings which had sprouted from her shoulder blades would unfold, ripping open the starched back of her blue dress. One false move and Death itself—the Bog Queen in her grimmest, most secret aspect—would be set loose to flap around the room, plucking up a girl here, a boy there, taking them home with her like pets.

At first, when her mother had started to cough up blood, Helle tried conceiving of the problem in more general terms: there was too much movement in the world. For even though the sixteenth-century merchant who'd built Krageslund was said to have chosen its remote and windy site in a vain attempt to satisfy his young bride's longing for the Lapp tundra, where she'd been born—and even though the villagers still tended to steer clear, just as their ancestors had, of Krageslund's queer mistress—it seemed that no sooner had word gotten out that Ida was dying than there was always some visitor, a neighbor or shopkeeper, tiptoeing stealthily as a thief up the stairs. It was as if the world generated its own current, a persistent thick arm of air whose purpose was to sweep away the souls of the weak.

But Helle also knew who it was who'd thrown her mother's boot into a peat hag; she knew on whose body the raveling thread of her mother's soul had been snagged. How cautiously she'd enter the sickroom, how fearfully she'd accept each kiss and hug! Her mother's fingertips felt hot, as did her lips. Sometimes she would ask Helle to brush her long brown hair and pin it up with tortoiseshell combs; but this was hard to do, because the hair was dry and stiff, breaking off like straw from an old broom. On the other hand, there was no need for rouge; in those days Ida's cheeks were bright pink, an improvement over her formerly pasty complexion. Indeed, the disease which was killing her had set the standard for female beauty all over Europe. Across the Continent women aspired to look waiflike and candescent, their eyes wild but trusting. The only difference was that those women didn't leave brown stains on their pillowcases, on the pleated bodices of their nightdresses, on their lips, your lips. "Don't leave, darling," Ida would say, and Helle would back out the door, the thread trailing behind her. The air in the room was sour and hard to breathe; on the bedside table was a porcelain teacup, but the tea was always cold and a few tiny dark sticks floated on its surface.

Oh, Helle was stiff all right—rigid with guilt. A plaster-of-Paris replica of a child, an object that would set your teeth on edge if you touched it, she sat there at her desk trying to read as all the while her eyes skidded this way and that like a dog on ice. Like Viggi Brahe's dog, to be precise, which she now saw almost everywhere she looked, its oversized, owlish head fastened to a skinny body, its eyes—one blue, the other brown—staring off placidly into space as it shat on the frozen schoolyard lawn. How lonely she felt! All around her was the sound of paper sliding across wood as notes were passed, of quick whispers and hiccoughs of swallowed laughter, the crisp rustle of paper wrappers, the sucking of illicit candies.

Meanwhile, the whole world turned to ice. Off the tip of Jutland, where the waves of the North Sea meet those of the Kattegat, a frozen ridge extended all the way to Oslo. If Helle had been allowed—if Fru Pedersen hadn't perversely forced her to sit, day after day, at the one desk situated so close to the schoolroom stove that even an overeager and sycophantic student would've grown drowsy—then Helle might have walked along that ridge; taking in deep breaths of clear cold air, she might have made it all the way to that hall where the king of Norway lounged among his bears, picking his teeth with a raven's wingbone. If, on the one hand, Helle desired nothing more than the admiration of her schoolmates, on the other she wanted to run away to a place where her name would be so foreign that not a single inhabitant would be able to pronounce it. Undoubtedly this accounted for the unsettling mixture, later in her life, of a need for recognition combined with an impulse to hide. Fame, of course, provides for this complicated balance. According to Helle, it was a metaphor for all things adolescent and, consequently, to be reviled.

But she didn't know that then. All she knew then was the dense boredom of the outcast, the smell of wood smoke permeating every cell of her body while, on the other side of the classroom, Inger Nissen sat near the door. "Inger," Helle told me, "was a girl of snow, while I was something you'd get sick of eating, like a ham." As she watched, Inger's white fingers were busy braiding the hair of the girl sitting in front of her—Ellen Randers's hair—and how Helle hoped Inger would find nits in it! Or maybe Fru Pedersen would become bored with beating time against the wall and would direct the strokes of her willow switch at the top of Torben Toksvig's head in an attempt to speed him along in his recitation of "Balder's Death." Inger's eyes were so bright they looked as if they'd been polished. They were the bright eyes of a girl who got up at five o'clock every morning and went out into the barn to feed her ducks. The whole school knew that Inger was raising eider ducks and saving the money she made selling their down for her trousseau.

What kind of a world was this, in which Helle was forced

to watch Torben Toksvig surreptitiously scratch his crotch as he stood declaiming lyric poetry, in which the heavenly fingers of Inger Nissen disappeared into the greasy meshes of Ellen Randers's hair? For a while now, since the summer of 1906, Helle had been taking piano lessons with a woman in the village. Gamle Clara everyone called her—Old Clara— and even though she was deaf as a post and, as Ida had described her, "musically oblivious," every Tuesday afternoon Helle went to that house smelling of boiled rutabagas and urine; she did so because Clara had a gramophone on which she would play operas, recordings as scratchy as the area around Clara's mouth which Helle was forced to kiss on her way in and out the door. But it was worth it. "The first time I heard Melba it was in Clara's parlor," Helle told me. "She was singing the Queen of the Night's aria—'Du! Du! Du!'— from Zauberflöte, and it was the most beautiful thing I'd ever heard. The voice of a star passing away into the infinite, as someone said. Or maybe I'm thinking of Tetrazzini. Of course it helped that it was a recording. Melba was as big as a whale."

If only the schoolroom ceiling would suddenly lift open like the lid of a box, letting in tides of dark, swirling sky; if only the Queen of the Night would suddenly descend, balanced in the crook of the crescent moon, her hair swarming with silver stars! The clock on the wall kept ticking, but the minute hand stuck in one place and then jumped ahead all at once, as if time itself were being held in thrall to the rhythms of Torben's recitation. In an opera it might take the heroine forever to die; but that's a matter of time pooling, not of time jamming up. In opera, as Helle liked to point out, it's the women who die. A fool like Torben would be relegated to the edge of a crowd.

But when Helle glanced back across the room she saw that

Inger was smiling at her, beaming across the sea of desks like a small, competent sun. And later, in the schoolyard, when Karen Holst sidled up to Helle and whispered, "Is it true what my mother says, that your mother was a whore?" it was Inger Nissen who jumped to her defense. Karen stood very close as she spoke, so close that Helle could see the frost beginning to turn her short white eyelashes whiter still; she could feel the frost growing on her own lashes, and it didn't make any sense that two spirits as dissimilar as hers and Karen's would be housed in bodies so similar in their workings. "Leave Helle alone," Inger said. Pink blotches were forming on her cheeks and forehead, a sign that her wrath, a condition as virulent as it was uncommon, had been aroused. "Why should I listen to you?" Karen replied. "Everyone knows your family sleeps with cows."

The other children gathered around, near enough to see what was going on, but far enough away so that if Fru Pedersen should suddenly loom up, they'd be taken for nothing more than innocent bystanders. It would have been mid-afternoon and already dark. All along the hem of the sky the winter planets were shining, more sharply focused than the lights of town, floundering off to the east within the branches of the beech trees.

According to Helle, Inger had no imagination; justice was her motivation, not romance. When Inger looked down and saw in the snow at her feet the silver tip of what Helle took for a wand, like a gift from a malevolent fairy, she recognized it for what it was: one of the metal sticks the littlest girls used in the spring, tapping their hoops across the pale green grass. The little girls would race after their hoops, and the little boys would make fun of them. Inger Nissen picked up the stick and wiped off its encrustation of old snow and blackish leaves. "We don't sleep with cows," she said softly, and as Karen was opening her mouth to correct her, Inger jabbed her in the stomach.

Later Inger and Helle walked home together down the Six Bridges Road, their arms across each other's shoulders. They'd sworn their undying friendship, sealing the pledge by pricking their thumbs on a thorn bush and tasting each other's blood. "*My* idea," Helle said. "The whole thing was my idea." She told me that Inger's blood tasted sweeter than her own, and was a brighter shade of red. Wasn't such idolatry the basis of many of the friendships that spring up between young girls, providing a useful apprenticeship for marriage?

Unimaginative, opportunistic Inger. Helle could feel her shoulders, slightly pudgy even then, moving beneath her own bony arm. The first in a series of bad choices, culminating in me, Francie Thorn, arguably the worst. "Did you see the look on her face?" Inger asked. "Did you see it?" She reminded Helle of her passion for sweet rolls, the ones shaped like boats. No doubt she was already thinking about supper, about the yeasty smell of her mother's kitchen and the budlike, chewing faces of her brothers and sisters, especially the youngest girl, her favorite, whom she'd nicknamed Bodie. "Maybe some macaroons?" she added as, on a slight rise off to the left, her house came into view. The Nissens lived in a single-story farmhouse, apricot-colored with dark green timbers, surmounted by a roof of thatch out of which, in summertime, grass and bluets would sprout, upon which the eider ducks would roost, preening their valuable feathers. But now the thatch was covered with snow, and smoke rose straight out of the chimney in a thin line, the way it did when the air was very cold.

Inger had to cross the second of the six bridges to get to

her house. While Helle stood there on the stream bank, chilled and immobile as a statue, Inger slipped out from under her arm, leaving behind on the sleeve of her black coat a single strand of golden hair. How dark it was getting! Still, like a detail in a repeating nightmare, Helle kept seeing the eyes of Viggi Brahe's dog drifting among the frozen swordlike reeds that grew at the base of the bridge, dislodging from the cigar-shaped crowns of the cattails a cloud of beige fluff. She told it to go home, but the creature apparently couldn't hear her. Meanwhile, on the other side of the stream, Inger Nissen stood tightening her knapsack across her wide, strong back. Girl of snow: white and pink and gold. Those were the colors of Inger Nissen. After an ice storm those were the colors that the sun could cause to spring up out of tree branches, as if fire could actually be coaxed from ice.

In *Det omflakkende Møl* Prince Carissimo's costume is white and pink and gold, and his main attribute is a sword which when plunged into even the coldest of hearts, causes that heart to burst into flame. Watch your step, Frances, I can hear Helle saying. Watch out! Can you find anything in Mozart's childhood to explain the idiotic plot of *La finta semplice*? But Helle's dead and I'm alive. The ball, as my father would say, is in my court. Thus, despite Helle's fiercely held belief that invention had nothing to do with cause and effect, I refuse to ignore the correlation here between life and art, just as I refuse to ignore the fact that the opera's organizing event—the metamorphosis of Princess Falena into a moth—can be traced back to an actual occurrence one Saturday morning in 1908, the spring of Helle's eleventh year.

A week earlier, the third anniversary of Ida's death had come and gone, evidently without notice. Or at least Anders hadn't invited Helle to kneel with him by the grave, nor had he left any token of his grief to wilt on the granite slab pressed flat into the dirt among Ida's rosebushes. Indeed, if anything, he'd been more boisterous and good-natured than usual, whistling as he stood drinking coffee by the open kitchen window, encouraging Helle to go outside for some fresh air. The milk pot, she noticed, had been left overnight on the table, and no one had bothered to put on the cover. If you wanted, you could strain the milk through cheesecloth, but still it would taste like dust.

Of course by now Helle understood all too well the source of her father's cheerful mood, just as she knew who was responsible for the condition of the milk. Gunhild Toksvig, her stupid classmate Torben's equally stupid eighteen-year-old sister—slatternly Gunhild, the so-called housekeeper Anders had hired a year ago to restore order to their lives, even though Gunhild didn't know how to cook and, when she did, the pots boiled over and she never bothered to wipe the stove clean. If the fire went out, Gunhild would yank open a lid and blow hard on the embers, sending forth a gray shower of ash. She thought sweeping was a bore, and long after she'd gone home you could still see the prints of her large feet everywhere. On more than one occasion Helle had followed Gunhild's footprints out of the kitchen and up the back stairs—dark, ashy smudges such as an elephant might leave—until they disappeared into the flowers of the hall runner.

"I heard the rumors," Helle said, "but I tried to ignore them." Gunhild couldn't cook and couldn't clean, yet Anders went so far as to give her a raise, and then took her out to celebrate at the best restaurant in Frederikshavn, where, he claimed, she made a favorable impression on the wine steward. Harder for Helle to ignore were the changes in her father's appearance, his former look of dishevelment giving way to a new attentiveness to grooming. At Gunhild's urging he'd grown a beard, a thrush-colored bush, and strode around the house attired in a gray serge shooting jacket and a pair of black leather jackboots, all the while brandishing a walking stick with a silver handle in the shape of a fox head. "Sarastro," she said. "He was like Sarastro. Large and confident and beaming. All that was missing was the gold robe and the devotion to his daughter."

In *Den onde Stedmoder*, or *The Wicked Stepmother*—one of the three song cycles Helle was to compose during her last year at Krageslund, the other two being *Sange til Inger* (*Songs for Inger*) and *Den mørke Spisestue* (*The Dark Dining Room*)— we receive a fairly detailed, if biased, description of the woman who was to become Anders's second wife. "Round white face and pouting lips," the first song proclaims, "Hair like corn silk specked with thrips." The song goes on to describe how although Gunhild's limbs were slender, the flesh moved loosely over her bones as if once upon a time she'd been very fat. And although she wore the costume of servility—an encompassing white apron over a dress of brown hopsack—Gunhild was clearly the kind of girl who'd never been assailed by doubts, the kind of girl who always thought she was getting exactly what she wanted because she never entertained the possibility of an alternative. "My enemy," the song concludes, "dull as a poker, blunt as a log; though a king's kiss woke her she remained a frog." Or, as a later song elaborates, you could always recognize the enemy by its resemblance to whatever weapon you used to beat it off. Interestingly, the libretti for all of Helle's compositions dating to this period were in English—her original purpose in abjuring her mother tongue having evidently been to conceal from prying eyes any hint of her deepest, most shocking thoughts.

On the Saturday in question Helle had been sitting at the piano for hours, attempting to retune it according to the rules of the mean-tone system, a method of tuning originally in use around 1500. Because, in the mean-tone system, what you end up with is a perfect third and an almost perfect fifth, the triads sound much purer than those produced according to the rules of equal temperament (that division of the octave to which our ears are accustomed). Purer and yet troublesome, for as you continue projecting such a series of mean-tone fifths, an odd discrepancy is created between the sharps and the flats, a sort of hole in the harmonic texture, which is called—just like that other, mystical hole in the hours of the Danish day—a "wolf."

It isn't easy to retune a piano, and Helle was growing irritable. Rain was approaching from the west, falling out of a single dark cloud over the village, as if someone had let down a curtain on that world of idle chatter and commerce, abandoning her at the very back of the huge, quaking amphitheater that was the bog. The village, with its squat yellow houses like those mushrooms called gristleballs which popped up out of the bog in the summertime! Did the villagers actually think it would do any good to have positioned a church between their foolish houses and the sixth bridge? *Plink plink plink*—Helle could almost hear them, the little hooves of the Bog Queen's baby demons, prancing across the wooden planks. The church tried to ward the demons off with the thick, admonitory shadow of its steeple, but they couldn't have cared less. They scampered right through the shadow, intent on creating discord.

Plink plink plink. B-flat B-flat B-flat. Mozart had whole orchestras at his disposal, and Helle was stuck with a single piano! Besides, what was the difference, after all, between B-flat and A-sharp? And why had Fru Nissen picked today to take Inger with her to Hjørring to buy a confirmation dress? It served them right, Helle thought, if they were getting rained on. In his examining room Anders was lecturing one of his patients about the merits of electricity and the dangers of the Kaiser; like pebbles, the first drops of rain struck the side of the house. As the squall advanced west from the kitchen toward the morning room, Helle could hear the sound of windows being slammed shut one by one, while Anders yelled, "Mark my words, Morocco is only the tip of the iceberg!"

I don't question that Gunhild was the kind of woman who wouldn't bother to knock before entering a room, or that the first thing she'd have asked Helle, after throwing open the morning room door, was whether she wanted to end up hunchbacked like the poor creature who gave her piano lessons. But I do find it hard to believe that a woman who lived her entire life in a village in northern Jutland, who moved her lips when she read, whose idea of luxury was a chicken dinner in Frederikshavn, could have been the imperious and sly villain Helle made her out to be. Oh, I'm well acquainted with Helle's need for villains. Whereas it seems more likely to me that what Helle saw as Gunhild's villainy was merely her persistence, the dogged way she had of deciding that something was going to happen, and then not relaxing until it had. Gunhild had grown up with five other children in one of the smallest of the village's yellow houses, and probably the only thing she wanted was to be the mistress of a household that possessed electricity and running water.

I assume it was this quality which most endeared her to Anders, who by 1908, after three years alone with Helle, was no doubt completely worn out, and tired of having to rely on signs—a curled lip, a bit nail—to understand his daughter's intentions. It was bad enough that he had to do this as a doctor. Didn't cells die, regularly, even in the healthiest of bodies? But whether those cells were normal or diseased was a more difficult question. Generally, it was the sick cell which refused to die, becoming obsessive, swallowing up everything around it. When Anders looked at his daughter, what did he see? A skinny creature with long unwashed hair and sallow skin, her fingers constantly moving, deriving music you couldn't hear from the edge of any horizontal surface? There is no question that this habit of Helle's made mealtimes unbearable. Gunhild Toksvig may have been persistent, but at least she wasn't obsessed.

At first Helle continued to monkey around with the piano, adjusting pins, tapping at the keys, plucking at the strings, humming. Then she began to play a line of melody from Schlick's "Da Pacem," figuring that it was sure to bore Gunhild, whose taste in music ran toward the maudlin or, more often, the bawdy, her favorite song being "Old Mister Cock and Little Miss Pussy." For Gunhild, Helle said, there was no real difference between desire and the gratification of desire. This explained her antipathy to Schlick or, for that matter, to any form of art; it also explained why she was such a rotten cook. But Gunhild refused to be ignored. She told Helle that she had something to show her, something important. In the kitchen. It would only take a few minutes. "Eventually I gave up," Helle said. "It was the only way to get rid of her." She followed Gunhild down the hall, taking note of the way she swung her hips from side to side, of the way the two middle buttons on the back of her blouse were missing, revealing a dirty gray sliver of chemise.

What did Helle expect to find in the kitchen? Evidence of her own domestic shortcomings—a rind of cheese on the

counter, a smear of butter on the doorknob, a sweater hanging
over the back of a chair? No, when they entered it the room
looked neat enough. It was warm, too, the windows opaque
with steam, because a kettle of water had been left boiling on
the stove. "Now that we're here," Gunhild said pleasantly,
"why don't we have a cup of tea?" She settled herself at the
table and began wagging her foot up and down, buffing her
nails on the hem of her dress. "Well?" she said. It took
several minutes before Helle realized that Gunhild wanted her
to make the tea. "Things are different now," Gunhild said.
"And the sooner you understand that, the better." She suggested that some shortbread might be nice. Wasn't there a
tin of shortbread on the top shelf of the cupboard, between
the sugar and the salt—the tin with a picture of men wearing
kilts on its lid? "The water's already boiling," Gunhild said.
"All you have to do is pour it in the pot. That shouldn't be
so hard, now, should it?"

No matter how much of her memory got erased by old age
and sickness, Helle told me, she would never forget that
moment: the room darkening as the rain, its roar more like
fire than water, began to consume the house; Gunhild's boxlike
foot wagging; the smooth and impartial wood of the cupboard
door into which some long-dead Freda had carved her name.
"I opened the cupboard door and out they flew," she said—
hundreds of small, white moths, their papery wings beating
all around her face as they made their way up toward the
ceiling, or out toward the far reaches of the kitchen. They
seemed to release a fine trail of something like flour wherever
they landed and, as small as they were, Helle was left with
the queer impression of having seen, in the instant when they
first rushed out at her, their eyes: unexpectedly large and
gray, avid with anticipation of finding a newer, more interest-

ing world than the one which they'd known inside the cupboard. Or possibly what she took for eyes may have been the markings on their wings. Who knows? A moth settled on the stove, sizzled briefly, and turned to chaff. A moth settled on the tea in Gunhild's cup, fluttered its wings wildly, and drowned.

"Poor thing," Gunhild said, plucking the dead moth from her cup. "I'd prefer some of that shortbread," she added, pointing.

Of course Helle should've known that Gunhild's plan would not be limited to the leveling of a single plague, just as she should've known that where a cupboard is full of moths there must also be a place of origin, a hatchery. But what she could never figure out was how the moths got inside the tin to begin with and how, once in, they got out. The lid was snug, hard to pry off. Still, Helle managed and was met with the loathsome sight of moths in every possible stage of development. Clusters of bead-shaped eggs were lodged among the flocculent remains of what must have, at one time, been shortbread. If you looked closely you could see that that flocculence was due to a more general distribution throughout the tin of a dense, wooly secretion, cocoons with dark pupae throbbing and pulsing inside of them, getting ready to be reborn. Worms were everywhere. They clung together in churning, tentacular groups, or they crept forth, individually, like animate grains of rice, and you couldn't tell which end was which or in what part of their bodies the mind, if you could call it that, was hidden. There were also several actual moths in the tin, sluggishly creeping across the crumbs, as if they hadn't yet figured out how to fly.

Gunhild meanwhile continued to sit at the table; when Helle looked back at her the image had acquired an unnatural precision, a strange detachment, not unlike the images you see through binoculars. The shortbread, Helle remembered, had arrived in the house shortly after her mother's death, an offering from Old Clara. These gifts from sympathetic neighbors—the haunches of venison, the pickled herring, the loaves of bread, the fish balls, and the basins of stewed fruit—comprised what her father had referred to with mounting irritation as the "funeral meats." Though Helle had tried to avoid thinking of what happens to a human body after it dies, she became hysterical; the next thing she knew she was sitting in the middle of the kitchen floor with the contents of the upturned tin strewn all around her, and Gunhild was slapping her face.

"Well, this is a fine mess!" Gunhild said. Once moths got into a kitchen, she explained, it was almost impossible to get rid of them; she'd seen it happen to her aunt in Skagen, so she knew. They got into the flour, the dried beans; they even devoured an entire jarful of imported almonds, which her aunt had been saving to make her famous *julekage*. "Are you going to just sit there like an idiot," Gunhild asked, "or are you going to help clean this up?" When Helle told her that it wasn't her fault, Gunhild took hold of the skin of her cheek and pinched it, hard. "Wake up," she said. "The days of Princess Helle are over." Then she stuck her left hand in front of Helle's face so that she could see the ring, a thin gold band set with a single, clear stone. "Do you know what this is?" Gunhild asked. "A diamond. It's a diamond engagement ring. And do you know where I got it?"

The rain had stopped; there was only the isolated *drip drip drip* of water beading up and falling from the roof, from the branches of the trees. The sun was coming out, too, shining on the wet windows. Of course Helle knew where Gunhild had gotten the ring, just as she knew how her father had been duped. He'd been taken in by that peculiar quality—the shirred, yellowish smell Gunhild gave off, which Helle, despite her innocence in such matters, knew had to do with sex—to which men remain uniformly susceptible. Even an ascetic's head can be turned: this is why they make such a point of their asceticism, carrying it around like a shield. But men can afford to be susceptible. When they succumb, they have nothing to lose except, momentarily, their dignity. And afterwards, what they get is a wife.

II

OF COURSE I KNOW the composition of *Det omflak-kende Møl* involved more than Helle's discovery of moths in a shortbread tin; that juxtaposed against her obvious fascination with disintegration and mutability was her passion for the immutable Inger, a fairy-tale battle between darkness and light, death and life, the Queen of the Night and Sarastro. For isn't it true that in the world of fairy tales what is strange is also reliable; that the roses growing above a mother's grave might suddenly begin to jabber, but their advice, however disconcerting, is always calculated to restore order? In 1909 Helle had not yet concluded that this order might prove hostile rather than helpful—though it was important for me to remember that even after she had, she continued to find inspiration in such tales. For example, her childhood copy of *L'Oiseau bleu*, beautifully illustrated and well thumbed, was among the few books she brought with her from Denmark in 1944. She gave this book to the twins on the occasion of their ninth birthday, having first drawn a line through the original inscription—*"til min strikse og elskede Helle, 6de August 1908"* ("for my strict and sweet Helle")—and replaced it with her own: "For Florence and Ruby, the one not so strict, the other so sweet, as they want me to believe."

Nor did I ever discover who had written that first inscription. By 1908 Ida was dead, and the books Anders bought his daughter tended toward the informative: *A Boy's Guide to the Minerals, How to Build a Bark Canoe, Svendsen's History of the Danish People.* As for Inger, she seems too interested in getting presents herself, and too self-involved to engage in anything resembling character analysis. "There are a lot of things about me you'll never know," Helle said when I asked. "Are you jealous? Frances is jealous!" Then she got down on her hands and knees to play one of those endless games of slapjack with the twins, a cone-shaped party hat perched on her head. Maybe I *was* jealous—though on behalf of Francie Thorn who was never admired except for her vaguely debauched good looks, for the gap between her two front teeth, which, as one of her English teachers had told her, had been the tip-off to the Wife of Bath's easy virtue.

But what I was talking about was *L'Oiseau bleu,* among whose copious marginalia I found not only an expected gloss for translation, but also notes hinting at some larger purpose. Why else would *"Møl—Anden Akt?"* ("Moth—Second Act?") be written in the margin next to Cat's first long speech, the facing illustration completely obliterated by a note, the gist of which is that it would be a great accomplishment (*"en stor dåd!"*) to have a bag of sugar sing an aria? During Helle's adolescence this tendency to appropriate material was still raw and unformed. Indeed, her first attempts at appropriation were more like outright theft; later it was only in describing her own life, as in the Steen Steensen Blicher episode, that she resorted to such tactics. "I guess I'm like one of those birds,"

Helle admitted, "who's always finding an unfamiliar egg in its nest left there by a cuckoo. Who wouldn't hatch it—or else crack it open and make an omelette?"

I suppose *Det omflakkende Møl* could be written off as juvenilia. But even though its plot is hopelessly convoluted and its music derivative, it isn't without its share of moments foreshadowing future musical brilliance, dark hints of Helle's evolving sensibility. Besides, who was I to judge? Gap-toothed Francie, who at the age of twelve spent whatever time she wasn't glued to *True Confessions* either grilling the laundress for details about her love life or plotting ways to win Tom Lupone's heart. At the age of twelve could I have imagined, as Helle did, a curse capable of transforming a love-starved young girl into a cold-blooded and inconsequential creature, for whom the object of her desire would feel nothing but revulsion and pity? It never occurred to me that the more ardently I desired Tom Lupone, his insolent and long-limbed body, the more I would find myself changed into the very thing which would make it impossible to get what I wanted. Twelve? I didn't even know that at thirty. Nor could I have invented a character such as the Nisse, whose moony face Helle caused to pop up randomly throughout Act One, now from behind a wood stove, now from the other side of a window, now from under Princess Falena's chair, now from within a tub of potatoes—his face, in fact, like a potato, the features sprouting from it shapelessly, strangely, as if from a multitude of eyes. The Nisse tells us that he can go anywhere, be anything, passing through "walls like water, walls like air, frail as silk, dense as despair." He wears a colorless, cushion-shaped hat, alternately flaccid or tumescent, depending upon his proximity to the princess. And it is the

Nisse who puffs up his podgy, misshappen cheeks, causing a wind to blow open the cupboard door, revealing a silver tin on the bottom shelf.

This is the container which should never be opened, that element common to myth and fairy tale, the test impossible to pass. This is the backseat of Tom Lupone's father's Chrysler. Naturally Princess Falena can't resist. She picks up the tin. She shakes it, and sings a charming, brief duet with herself (Yes I will, No you won't, Yes she will, No we won't, etc.). The first act ends as the princess opens the lid, out fly the moths, and into a mouth still wide open with the final "Ye-es" (fortissimo, fermata—an unfeasible combination, since, by nature, the louder the sound, the more rapidly the human voice will decay) flies the tiny, winged agent of her destiny.

At the beginning of Act Two we're still in the farmhouse kitchen, although now our perspective has shifted: what we see when the curtain opens is the cupboard shelf, and the principals are Moth, Sugar, Salt, Tin, and Cat. Interestingly, Helle's use here of this "zoom" technique not only anticipates the overall design of her 1953 opera, *Fuglespil*, but also the sophisticated cinematic effects which influenced that later work. "A woman ahead of her time," in the words of Peter Sellars, whose recent revival of *Det omflakkende Møl* set the first two acts in the sauce kitchen of Lutèce. "A woman who, at the very start of this century, understood the dark turn toward greed we'd take at its end." Moth is the Princess Falena, a white mask dominated by two immense gray eyes covering her face. It is nighttime, and she is singing an aria to her new companions—a jarring composition, mean-tempered both musically and emotionally, in which she describes the consequences of her metamorphosis. "I might have known love," Moth sings, "without love's bite, wingless I might have flown. As the hand seeks the glove, the moth seeks the Worm, whose skin she once called home." Sugar, Salt, and Tin listen sympathetically; Cat, formerly the Nisse, crouches off to stage right, sharpening her nails, licking her chops.

Or at least that was the composer's original intention. But original intentions are rarely realized; according to Helle, the Muse's secret name was Disappointment, and the sooner an artist learned that fact, the better. In the first public performance (June 3, 1911) of *Det omflakkende Møl*, Sugar, played by Bodie Nissen, became restless and began fiddling with the hem of the bran sack in which she was costumed, unraveling lengths of hemp which she dropped down Salt's back, causing Salt (Hans Fog, Inger's future husband) to collapse, insofar as it was possible for him to collapse in his boxlike suit, on top of Tin (Torben Toksvig). Helle herself was singing the part of Moth, and despite the fact that she had perfect pitch, her voice was, by her own admission, "froglike," and all of the arias were overlong.

Of course an opera as produced could never live up to the composer's expectations; how could it do so when Helle herself couldn't manage to suggest even remotely the magnificence of her original dream? Didn't the very act of pinning the dream down, of assigning it form, serve to ruin it? Helle used to show me the notices sent by her agent that described "innovative" stagings of her operas such as the one Sellars was to mount, productions for which she had nothing but scorn. The great tidal wave which is the culminating image of *The Harrowing of Lahloo* was for some reason transposed by the Deutsche Oper into the wing of an enormous angel; the part of Fortune, in the Houston Grand Opera's production of *Fortune's Lap*, was "sung" by a tape deck. Nor was it so very long ago that a woman at Glyndebourne expressed interest in staging *The Girl Who Trod on a Loaf* in Greenham Common, with the bog represented by a nuclear waste dump. "Even God was disappointed," Helle said. "He made a world full of pleasant and colorful toys, and the next thing he knew they were stabbing him in the back. Two little girls in a beech grove, at least one of them plotting His demise."

If I recall correctly, this conversation occurred not long after the peculiar tea party at the Blackburns', during the period Helle came to refer to as our "courtship." Chances are we were walking somewhere—out toward the quarries?— either alone or with the twins and William in tow. Helle loved to walk, her daily routine having been built around a walk at nine in the morning and another at four in the afternoon. Before she met me these were solitary excursions up a steep trail leading off Quarry Road and onto West Hill. She would tread lightly through snow or mud or brambles, gratified by the continuing flexibility of her body; then, at the crest of the hill, she would pause among the apple trees to smoke a Lucky before heading back down the hill to her desk. After we met, however, she would walk by herself in the mornings and with me in the afternoons. Sometimes we'd make a circuit of the town, or hike out the Branch Road, or wander along Route 71 as far as the railroad bridge. But no matter where we went, three things remained constant: we smoked, we stopped to identify birds, we talked. Which is no doubt why my memory of the walks themselves is a little vague. Helle's descriptions of her past always had the uncanny effect of obliterating the present, as if all she had to do was open her mouth and say "In Jutland," and a persistent northern wind would instantly spring forth, sweeping the blacktop clean of fast-food containers and compact cars and young men on ten-speeds, turning high-voltage towers into lighthouses, fields dotted with new corn into sand dunes, Pocket Lake into the sea.

In any event, I'm pretty sure it was on one of these walks that Helle first told me about the beech grove at Krageslund, the place she used to retreat to when she was trying to solve a difficult problem of composition. Danish beech groves! Really, she said, we had nothing like them in America, which explained the undisciplined quality of the American imagination, our preference for the unruly growth of an idea at the expense of sustained reflection. American forests were large and filled with deadfall, whereas the only sign of intemperance in a Danish beech grove was high overhead, in the contorted, twisting corkscrews of the upper branches. Below, all you could see were those evenly spaced trunks, their gray-green bark as smooth and unlined as the skin of young girls, their trunks like the pillars of an airy hall whose floor was blanketed with hundreds of the little white star-shaped flowers called anemones.

Helle would lean back against the smooth gray-green trunk of the largest of the trees, her skinny legs crossed Indian-style, and Inger would generally be lying on her stomach in front of her, her elbows firmly planted in the thick anemone-studded grass, her small chin cupped in the palms of her hands. Helle waiting for inspiration to strike, Inger off on a cloud—the usual relationship between artist and muse. *Chak chak chak* went the magpies, busily feeding their young in Ida's nesting boxes. *Chak chak chak.* Some days must have been overcast, but what Helle remembered was the enclosing tent of the tree's shadow, her body and Inger's speckled with wavering disks of sunlight. They ate fruit from Ida's untended gardens, the juice of the currants staining their teeth; occasionally Inger would bring damp rounds of cheese, each marked with a pattern of tiny squares by the gauzy cloth in which it was wrapped.

It might be a sentence she'd come upon the night before in a reference work—for example, "The antennae in the moth are feathery and unknobbed"—and that, together with the sight of Inger's juice-stained lips, would cause a sound to stir within Helle, a thread of melody sensed rather than heard, a thrilling and plaintive juxtaposition of the beautiful and the rapacious. C-sharp minor, or maybe something in the Dorian mode? Possibly a major key, but with the intimation of an impossibly high final note, yearned for yet never met? Sam, Helle claimed, would see in this situation evidence for the Platonic ideal, but men were fascists by nature. Wasn't that, when you got right down to it, the real source of the conflict between Sarastro and the Queen of the Night? All you had to do was listen to their music: Sarastro's rigid and self-contained measures, the Queen's heartbreaking coloratura runs.

As Helle described it, she was struggling to catch hold of the tail of just such an elusive thread of melody, when all of a sudden the magpies took off in their lavish, iridescent cloaks, their former casual chatter replaced by noisy "alarm notes." Bounding toward her from the edge of the grove she saw Viggi Brahe's dog—uglier than usual because it had been swimming, and its coat was flecked with mud and grit and frog spawn. First she saw the dog; it took a few moments before she noticed its owner. Who knew how long he'd been standing there on the edge of the grove, his bony face shadowed by the brim of a straw hat, his bony arms sticking out of the rolled-up sleeves of his smocked shirt?

For several years now, Viggi Brahe confessed, he'd been

spying on Helle. Like many men of a solitary and romantic disposition, he'd allowed himself to nurse along a delusion until it had acquired the weight of truth: if he couldn't have the mother, perhaps he could at least have the daughter. Certainly Helle resembled Ida, although where Ida had been pliant and melancholy, Helle was stiff and ambitious. If she was going to avoid her mother's fate, Viggi Brahe cautioned, it would require more than an unusual talent for playing the piano. He knew Helle had talent, having followed her progress on Clara's out-of-tune piano, having eavesdropped through the open morning-room windows. But what she needed, he said, was a patron.

Thus commenced the first of what Helle referred to as her "*mariages faux*," relationships with men characterized by the same warring objectives that drove the plot of *Zauberflöte*, relationships such as those she was later to form with Oswald Bingger and Rasmus Rundgren. Men were always attracted to Helle, despite her obvious dislike of them. Sam claimed to find her as tantalizing as she was repugnant, an exotic bird that sang like an angel before it ate the tip of your finger, whereas in the case of Viggi Brahe the trade-off was less ambiguous: in exchange for his patronage, he wanted to get credit for the art he was himself incapable of making. Poor Viggi Brahe. It would appear that he'd inherited Tycho Brahe's ambition without the correlative genius. Like Ruby's set of nesting dolls, Helle said—a doll within a doll within a doll. The features of the first doll, the biggest one, were always painted with precision and care; by the time you got to the smallest, all you had was a nubbin of wood. Of course Viggi Brahe was more handsome than his illustrious ancestor, and he didn't have a metal nose, for which he should have been thankful. Not to mention the fact that if it weren't for

Viggi Brahe, Helle's first opera would have had its premiere in Ove Nissen's hay barn, not the great hall at Sandhed, and the singers would've been accompanied by the plangent cooing of doves and swallows, not Sandhed's magnificent pipe organ.

As it turned out, you couldn't really hear the singers anyway: the hall was enormous, the blocks of stone comprising its walls so huge they seemed to have been set in place by giants. Similarly, what passed for windows—narrow vertical slits—were positioned up near the ceiling, itself two stories high, so only giants could have looked out through them. And the spiders! They, too, were gigantic, like fists, their webs filling the gaps between the stones, obscuring the family motto—IT IS GOOD TO HEAR THE WOLF HOWLING BE-NEATH THE ASH TREE—carved into the fireplace lintel, wrapping around and around the figures of the Apostles in the four neo-Gothic wall niches. In all, a room made by and for giants—a room designed to drain any semblance of strength or depth from the voices of children, which came out sounding no louder than the muffled buzzing of trapped flies.

Chairs were set up in rows facing the wall containing the fireplace, the opening of which had been covered by a painted drop cloth. In this way the audience would have their backs to the organ and wouldn't be distracted by the sight of its twenty-one pipes and two keyboards, its rosewood fittings carved with Alpine flora and fauna, its delicate rosewood bench, on which sat Viggi Brahe, turned out for the occasion in a frock coat of fawn silk and a pair of dove-colored breeches, his long, thin hair tied at the nape of his neck with a black ribbon. He wasn't too bad as an organist, Helle said, despite the annoying flourishes of wrist and elbow; he knew how to "work his mixtures and mutation stops," and he "didn't overdo it with the crescendo pedal and the vox angelica."

The performance resembled a bad dream in that everyone Helle knew was there: the mountainlike body of Fru Pedersen, its little outcropping of bald scalp looming over the small furry head of her husband, Junker; Old Clara wrapped round and round with scarves and draperies, like a colorful mummy coming undone; tall, hideous Constable Fog and his unusually pretty wife; Helle's schoolmates, some in the audience, others on stage; the pork butcher, the undertaker, the preacher, the whole Nissen family. Her father and Gunhild sat side by side in the front row on their delicate gilt-painted chairs, Gunhild's face as blank as a worn-out coin, indicative of neither origin nor value.

And meanwhile there was Inger, singing the part of Prince Carissimo in her pure sweet soprano, sweat beading on her upper lip and across her wide cheekbones, the bodice of her white satin jacket straining at its seams as she reached for the higher notes. Inger's breasts were well developed—unlike Helle's, who would only have been embarrassed by them—and she carried herself with a stately grace. Even Torben Toksvig appeared to be in awe of her. "Why do you hide, Bright Sisters, North Star, the woods are dark, the journey far," Inger sang (an eerily ascending segment in the Dorian mode echoed, in contrary motion, by the voice of Moth, as all the while Cat repeats a single note, B-flat, "It's time to go"). Helle's intention for the second-act finale was to imply a form of struggle in which the voice of Cat, speaking seductively on behalf of fate, would remain locked in one place even as it urged flight, while the resistant voices of Moth and the prince would never stop moving. The trio expands into a quartet, into a quintet, a sextet. "The juniper boughs are creaking," the company sings (ensemble), "Listen to what they say" (Moth, solo), "The moon through the clouds is peeking, to guide us on our way" (ensemble), "O banquet! Sweet banquet! Under the light of the moon!" (Cat, solo, addressing the audience, pausing to sharpen her claws on a tree trunk).

By the beginning of the third act, the threads of the plot had become hopelessly snarled and Helle's audience was becoming restive. Karen Holst and Elizabeth Albæk were passing notes; Fru Nissen's thickly braided head kept lolling forward as if it were about to land in her big soft lap; the undertaker was picking lint from his pants; Gunhild was knitting a striped sock. During a scene change, Helle overheard Inger whispering with Hans Fog. Can you believe it, Inger was saying, a cat going to so much trouble just for one little moth? Cats usually only toyed with moths; they didn't like to eat them. Even Viggi Brahe kept sneaking glances up toward the windows, where large clouds rolled past in a bright blue sky. Outdoors it was warm; birds were singing. The pork butcher's spindly white-haired sons were drawing pictures with their fingers in the dust on the floor. In fact, Helle told me, only her father appeared to be completely absorbed by the spectacle before him. He sat stiff as a poker in his chair, his hands clenched into fists in his lap, unable to take his eyes off the stage.

For my own part, paging through the score as I listened again and again to the Angel recording of *Det omflakkende Møl*, I knew that no matter how impatient I might get, without understanding its ending, I would never be able to meet the terms of my legacy. To undo a curse, to retrieve her human shape and hence the love of her betrothed, a princess must journey to the world's end. Once she arrives there—with the aid of her traveling companions, each of whom proves to have a talent crucial to her salvation—she crawls back inside the body of the Lindworm, her own hideous place of origin, and thus triumphs over death. A characteristically perverse triumph, however, since it isn't until the top of the princess's head is no longer visible that the prince finally arrives. "Foul serpent, hell-root, world-shoot, die!" he sings, drawing his sword and plunging it through the Lindworm's heart, never realizing that he has plunged it through the princess's heart as well. We hear her voice, its muffled and sad line of melody—"ahhhhhh"—twining around the discordant wail of the dying worm. And then there spills from the wound a stream of black, undulant creatures, the worm's grotesque offspring, followed by a fluttering cloud of moths, white and pink and gold. One of them lands on the palm of the prince's outstretched hand, and he bends to kiss it. One of them lands on the ground in front of Cat, who winks at the audience before swallowing it whole.

Hatchings and involutions, resurrections and returns—"My end is my beginning," according to that famous motet of Machaut's which Helle sometimes whistled as she cooked. Or, in the words of *Fuglespil*'s Easter duet, "Which came first, the chicken or the egg?" I made a list: the figurehead's overlapping stages of metamorphosis in *Lahloo*; the reiterated "quivering ring" motif in *Waves*; the uncanny "Xerox finale" of *Fortune's Lap*; the house of mirrors in *Delia*; the horrifying conclusion of *Fuglespil*. In this respect the lesson seemed clear enough: the heroine's ultimate fate in *The Girl Who Trod on a Loaf* must somehow reflect who she was when she first accepted the bread and put on the shoes.

And yet why did I keep returning to that second-act finale, as if everything I needed to understand might somehow be contained in its music? Perhaps it was because the music itself never failed to break my heart, that listening to it I could see so clearly those birch saplings sticking up out of milk pails, the moon-speckled ribbon of water Helle had envisioned, an approaching storm. I could see her tense face, her gray eyes squinting through her mask, and—as the music gradually brightened, breaking apart into arpeggios, into sprays of brightly hopeful notes—I could feel myself longing, just as I knew she had, for the actual onslaught of magical, imagined rain. I would listen to that music and, little by little, come to realize how implicit in every fragile human hope is the seed of its transformation into grief—the Lindworm, its triangular head draped across the lip of the well at the world's end, the rest of its long white body piling, coil upon coil, within the mica-flecked, brackish water, the very tip of its tail (or is it a second head?) dangling down through the roof of hell. Maybe it was the sound of my own grief Helle was forcing me to hear, that grief she'd known how to describe even before she brought it into being. The tip of the Lindworm's tail. Pale, white. Phallic, of course, the Nisse in its final, most deadly aspect—although I suspected that wasn't all there was to it. In fact I found myself wondering whether what I was see-ing was Inger's shoeless foot, breaking through the roof of the bog.

III

SUMMER ENDED. The twins returned to school, to the fourth-grade classroom of a Mr. Ayres, whose bald head Ruby said—no doubt under Helle's influence—shone like a Magic 8 Ball, despite Flo's claim that the only image of the future you could read there was one in which miserable children endlessly recited the names of state capitals. Boise, said Flo. Pierre, Augusta, Septembra. Meanwhile, heavy winds blew in out of the west, blowing the red and yellow maple leaves from the trees, causing the responsible citizens of Canaan to rake them into piles along the curbs in front of their houses and then set them on fire, filling the air with black flecks, with that blade-sharp smell decaying matter releases as it turns to char, the smell our ancestors hoped might ward off the coming darkness. You could feel the dark's approach since the seasons, unlike so many other things in life, are sequential. Fall arrives and you know that soon enough the kitchen will be cold when you get up in the morning, frost branching across the windows. Then, after a while, the sun will rise and the frost's pinions will melt, feather by feather, clear drops of water forming at their edges.

I never bothered to burn the leaves in my yard, mostly oval leaves with toothed edges that drifted down from three tall, shaky poplar trees. Meanwhile, a single cramped and furious apple tree continued every summer to put forth approximately ten cramped, wormy apples, the kind of bad fruit that attracts ants and wasps. Why burn the leaves, I thought—what good would it do? Why shave your legs or wash a dish? But for some reason the twins got it into their heads that year to rake the leaves into an enormous barrow at the front door, a shifting pile through which we had to tunnel in order to leave or enter the house; for a few days, a layer of brownish-gray flakes covered our floors, clung to our hair and clothes. Then, one afternoon, I came back from the diner to find the barrow replaced by two harvest figures, propped in webbed aluminum lawn chairs on either side of the door.

Harvest figures are made by stuffing leaves into cast-off clothing. Sometimes a pumpkin or a Hubbard squash serves as the head, sometimes a leaf-stuffed nylon stocking. A phenomenon of northern New England or upstate New York, these figures are generally seated on porches or hanged in effigy from trees, their presence a kind of economic indicator. In the town of Canaan, for example, you would never expect to find harvest figures along Broadway or on Rose Hill. Nor would you expect to find them dressed like the figures guarding my door. The man wore a black velvet singlet and short, puffed black satin pants, scarlet hose and black, thigh-high boots; a scarlet cape hung over his shoulders, and a scarlet, black-feathered cap was set at a rakish angle on his grinning pumpkin head. The woman was wearing a violet silk gown bisected from neck to hem by a row of small midnight-blue bows; on her feet, a pair of midnight-blue slippers embroidered with silver flowers; and on her scowling pumpkin head was fixed a hat of lighter blue, a backward-drooping protuberance resembling a cocoon, from which depended a flower-embroidered veil. Elegant and vaguely sinister, these two sat at my door, staring at the road, as if at any minute they'd get up and begin inching toward town.

This was typical of the way things happened that fall: just when I'd managed to fool myself into thinking that nothing had changed, I'd open the refrigerator and be confronted by the sight of a whole smoked salmon on a Royal Copenhagen serving platter, garnished with sprigs of dill and spring onions, wedged between an unlidded plastic carton of welfare milk and a carelessly ripped-open package of welfare cheese slices, the top slice already verging on brown. Or the record on my turntable—presumably Dion and the Belmonts—would instead be Elisabeth Schwarzkopf singing Donna Elvira's opening aria from *Don Giovanni*, the basic message being that when she finds the man who betrayed her trust, she'll rip his heart out. Of course I didn't know this the first time I heard the record, nor did I realize that the female harvest figure was wearing the costume of some former, probably long-dead Donna Elvira. Helle, it turned out, had a steamer trunk packed full of such costumes—she eventually confessed to me that the night we'd met she was dressed as Violetta. The twins had made the figures, but Helle had come up with the idea. Donna Elvira and Don Giovanni, an old married couple taking the air, right before the wife slits open her husband's chest. Imagine her disappointment when all she finds inside is dead leaves! What it also took me a while to realize was the significance of Helle's choice of costumes and her choice of records.

But that fall I was too preoccupied to catch the drift of her meaning. The truth is, it seemed to take all of my concentration just to keep each day divided into a series of discrete compartments, to make sure that the obviously hostile

elements in my life wouldn't get a chance to commingle.
What if they compared notes or, worse yet, formed their own
alliances behind my back? The twins, Helle, Sam—even
good-tempered Kosta Pappadiamantis, my boss at the diner?
I knew I was courting disaster, but even at the time I believed
that all courtship came to naught.

On the morning of the party I woke the twins at six, as
usual, and got them ready for school. Flo was a light sleeper
whom you could rouse merely by staring at her broad, grave
face or by reaching out your hand to retrieve a strand of
brown hair caught in her mouth during the night. Her sheets
were always tumbled and damp; she had no affection for the
stuffed animals she'd taken to bed with her, having selected
them haphazardly and then kicking them onto the floor. The
twin who had nightmares, who walked in her sleep, she was
relieved to get up in the morning. Whereas frail, dreamy-
looking Ruby claimed never to dream. I'd have to shake her
hard before even one yellow-green eye would open; until she
was twelve, she remained faithful to one doll, the lumpish
Marybell. Thus Ruby slept in the top bunk, Flo in the bottom—even though Flo claimed this arrangement was unfair,
even though I knew she was right, and that by insisting on it
I was contributing to her sense that there was something
undesirable, maybe even dangerous, about being large and
restless.

My twins! How often I've thought that anyone looking for
an argument against astrology need look no further: born in
the same place, obviously, within minutes of each other, yet
my twins couldn't be more different. Although I also couldn't
overlook the conversation I once had with a woman at the
diner—a thick middle-aged woman, the eccentric tweed-
dressed wife of an auto parts dealer, and a confessed believer

in astrology—who attributed this difference to the fact that Flo and Ruby were Librans, a delicately balanced set of scales. Each twin could assemble her own set of characteristics in an individual pan, and there wouldn't be any problem unless one set turned out to weigh more than the other.

So I watched them standing together at the bottom of our driveway, waiting for the school bus, Flo like a miniature sailor in her favorite flannel-lined jeans and navy-blue sweater, Ruby in one of the fanciful and ever-changing outfits she'd pull together at the last minute—on this occasion my India-print shirt, hanging down below her knees, cinched at the waist with a silver-studded, red-leather dog collar. Lily's collar in fact—for Lily was the dog we had back then, a gentle creature with the masked face of a wolf, with the two little dots of white fur called "angel eyes" on her brow, which are supposed to protect a house from evil. When the bus pulled up, Lily was lying beside me on the stoop, where I sat drinking coffee in my nightgown, both of us flanked by the crepitating Don and his angry girlfriend. An embarrassing spectacle, as Flo complained later, adding that I could at least wear a bathrobe. Bill Beck said he could see my tits. Then the red stop sign sprang out from the side of the bus, the red lights flashed, the driver tilted his head to follow the twins' progress down the aisle in the rearview mirror, gave me a brief wave once he saw they were seated, and the next thing I knew they were gone.

It was going to be a beautiful day, I thought; to the east, thousands of rose-colored pieces of sky were held together by a complicated fretwork of branches, and the air was oddly mild, almost like spring. A beautiful day for a birthday party, even though I was stone broke, even though Lily was panting heavily and there was a smear of what looked like blood on her muzzle, as if she might once again have gotten into Lyle Judkins's chicken coop, and I might once again end up being asked to pay for what she'd eaten. Her ribcage heaved up and down, and her eyes, under their closed lids, jerked back and forth, the eyes of a hungry dog looking for chickens. Was that a pinfeather clinging to her serrated black gum? Seven hours in the diner, I thought, an hour at the supermarket, back home in time to meet the bus. The party was to begin at four. William was the only guest, although he'd be accompanied by his great aunt Helle. Of course there was no question of seeing Sam. The phone rang and rang but, in case it was Judkins, I didn't answer it.

It was his land that surrounded my house; his cornfield on the other side of the road, where a week earlier he'd driven back and forth in a huge yellow machine, roughly chopping off the cornstalks, hauling them away to the dark blue silo whose domed top I could just see against the horizon, beyond the rows upon rows of shin-high sticks, their tips angled into points, like headhunters' weapons. A black pickup drove by, its headlights still on, and suddenly the whole field stirred, the comprehensive violet-gray color of predawn breaking apart as hundreds of white birds, those landlocked gulls you see wheeling over town dumps, rose into the slowly brightening sky. They flew up all at once to the same height, hung there momentarily in an undulant, squealing cloud, then dropped back to the ground, no longer in unison but intermittently, *plop plop plop*, like fat white raindrops.

The meadow to my right, sloping down toward the cedar woods, belonged to Judkins, as did the little stream which had its source somewhere in those woods, looping around behind my house until it emerged to the left as a wide and lively creek, bordered on both banks with black willows and cattails—a soggy area I called a bog until Helle corrected me. Sometimes Judkins grazed his cows in the meadow, and once he drove a backhoe into the woods in an apparent attempt to reroute the stream and reclaim the land for pasture. How many acres did the man need? Judkins, I assumed, was in his late fifties, and still handsome in a ruddy, raw-boned way; whenever he had to talk to me he traded on those looks, his banter sly and flirtatious with an ugly undercurrent of utter contempt, as if I were such an easy target that seducing me wouldn't be worth his time.

Oh, I'd never liked Lyle Judkins, but on that particular morning I nursed my dislike until it grew into hate. I imagined him standing there, smug, by the phone in the kitchen his poor wife kept sparkling and polished for him, his one hand jingling coins in the pocket of his overalls, the other dialing, as his wife loaded his breakfast dishes into the dishwasher. And it seemed to me that if you were to put one of those coins in your mouth, all you'd be able to extract from it would be the dull and bitter flavor of avarice. Once upon a time, I thought, you could walk out in the morning unhampered by a pointless urge to define land in terms of territory, to make every inch of the world familiar. Blackberries and sweet corn, hazelnuts and wild asparagus, a bird flying up out of a thicket, an arrow's quick release . . .

Eventually my hatred assumed the contours of a plan, which my hours at the diner—shuttling among strangers, removing their half-eaten meatball grinders, their soup bowls viscid with chowder, their moist cigarette butts, their parsimonious tips—did nothing to dissipate. By the time the man in the plaid suit yelled "Over here, doll," and then explained that his fork had a bent tine, I was more than ready. Of course, looking back, it's easy enough to see how hypocritical my plan was at its heart—I was reviling the very tendency to division that was my own guiding principle—but at the moment all I saw was a world divided into squares, a criminal insistence on territory.

By two o'clock, when I left work, it was almost hot out, the sun shining in a deep blue sky, the only cloud in sight rising from the exhaust fans above the roof of the silver, toaster-shaped diner. I'd changed from my waitress uniform into a blue-flowered dress; it had been years since I'd done this kind of thing, but I remembered how important it was to divert the attention of the checkout clerk. Would the tall red-haired boy with the drooping lower lip be on duty? The old man with either an accent or a speech impediment, who always sported a carnation in his buttonhole? That was the first thing I made sure of inside the supermarket, that at least one of the clerks was a man. Otherwise, prettiness becomes a liability, and even fingers as nimble and fleet as a magician's will do you no good.

There were only a few other customers, all of them women, many with toddlers strapped to their carts, mid-afternoon not being a prime shopping time at most supermarkets. Casually I wheeled my cart down the front aisle and into the section on the far right where the baked goods, resolutely unfragrant in their plastic bags and waxy boxes, sat on metal shelves in the bright fluorescent light. Loaves and loaves of bread, white and whole wheat and oatmeal and cinnamon raisin; coffee cakes drizzled with calligraphic icing; sugar-powdered dough-nuts with little red wounds in their sides; crullers like elabo-rately turned and varnished wood ... but where were the cakes for special occasions, the big three-layered birthday cakes? I finally tracked them down, on the top shelf of a detached central counter. Over my shoulder I had slung a large straw basket of the sort women brought along to Pocket Lake, only my basket didn't contain sandwiches, paperback romance novels, suntan lotion, car keys. My basket was empty, and my tongue felt small and rough in my mouth, like a cat's.

I've shoplifted all sorts of things. Once I even plucked a blue parakeet out of a crowded cage at Woolworth's and carried it, chirping and nipping, its claws digging into the palm of my hand, right past the cashier. Why did I do this? To see if it could be done, I guess. Or maybe just to watch the bird fly into the overcast sky above the dull gray sidewalks and parking meters, to watch it turn to a little blue dot and disappear like a released balloon. I didn't want a pet and never had liked parakeets. But these cakes were bigger than I'd thought. And although my basket was flexible, positioning the cake so it wouldn't get damaged wasn't going to be easy. Of course I could pay for the cake and steal everything else. I knew I had to pay for at least one item, in order not to look suspicious. But it was the cake I wanted to steal, not the ice cream or hats or candles or paper plates. I wanted to steal that cake on behalf of the twins; I wanted to steal it as an affront to Lyle Judkins and everything that he stood for—his backhoe, his chickens, his silo, his pocket full of jingling coins, his egg-yolk-encrusted plate being hosed down by his dishwasher, his exhausted wife, his slyly smiling mouth. A chocolate cake, the twins' favorite, with red roses on the vanilla frosting, and a message piped on in green to match the stems and leaves. I hesitated for several minutes, staring at the box, lifting it up and putting it back down, lifting it up and putting it back down, testing its size and bulk—struggling not to keep looking into the nearest of the convex mirrors with which the ceiling was studded, as if into one of the manifold eyes of an omniscient god.

And then, just as it happens at the opera, a miracle! Next door to the supermarket, in front of the bottle redemption center, a man in a gold Eldorado with Missouri plates—the gourmand in the plaid suit, as it turned out—was trying to angle his car into a parking space several sizes too small, and rammed backwards into a telephone pole that also served as support for a major power line. For ten minutes the supermarket was plunged into semidarkness. The music stopped and the cash registers wouldn't work; the only thing you could hear was the squeaking wheels of the shopping carts and, if you were near the fish counter, the faint tapping of lobster claws on glass. Shoppers peered deeply into bins of peaches, looking for that blush which signifies ripeness; they squinted, trying to make out the expiration dates on yogurt containers.

Exactly like in an opera: at any moment tongues of flame can lick out from the firmament; at any moment we can trick ourselves into thinking justice is being done. I lowered the cake into my basket, taking time to adjust it carefully, wedging it in place with a pair of quilted oven mitts. By the time the power came back on I was standing in the ten-items-or-less line, and the tall red-haired boy was ringing up my purchases. "Looks like someone's having a birthday," he remarked, sliding the strawberry ice cream into a clear plastic bag, then putting it into a larger bag of brown paper along with the pink party hats. When I told him he'd make a good detective, he ducked his soft pale chin down into his soft pale neck and blushed.

THE PARTY BEGAN at four o'clock, as planned. Helle arrived looking like a lit candle in a long gown of form-fitting white jersey (*Lohengrin?*), a garnet choker around her neck, elaborate garnet earrings dangling from her earlobes, the usual knob of hair at her neck contained in a dark red, lattice-weave snood, a surprising red day pack strapped to her back. Because the last traces of my own anger had evaporated the minute I saw the livid face of the man in the plaid suit watching as a tow truck bore away his golden car, I didn't know what to make of her mood. Maybe bad moods got passed around, I thought, like recipes and head colds. But even as she came marching up the driveway holding William's hand, stopping to kick irritably at a mullein plant, dislodging from its flannelly leaves a little cloud of dust, you could tell something was bothering Helle. There was a moment, after William had run in ahead of her and she stood regarding the harvest figures, when her expression brightened. But the frown returned as soon as she came through the door, shrugging off the day pack and saying *"Til lykke med fødselsdagen"* so it sounded less like "Happy birthday" than a curse.

"For you," she told Flo, removing a flat square package from the day pack; "For you," to Ruby, another flat square package; "For both of you," a larger package, book-shaped, which she dumped irritably on top of the piano. Then she handed me a bottle of red wine, told me to open it immediately, laughed bitterly, and asked if I didn't think it was stupid the way people worried about whether or not a bottle of wine could breathe. William's presents, she added, were still in the pack; he could get them out himself.

An inauspicious start, although Ruby didn't seem to notice that anything was amiss. She linked her arm through William's and drew him toward the kitchen, showing him how she'd set a party hat in the middle of each of five pink paper plates. Flo, on the other hand, remained standing in the middle of the living room, her attention apparently fixed on her beaded, fur-trimmed moccasins, the left one dented at intervals with Lily's toothprints and the toe chewed off entirely. From time to time she would sneak fast little glances at Helle, who had arranged herself, still frowning, on the edge of one of the sofa cushions.

When I asked Helle if something was the matter, she laughed again and lit a cigarette. "Don't mind me," she said, exhaling. "Just pretend I'm not here." Which of course wasn't possible. Her smoke, for example, followed me into the kitchen, hanging around me as I uncorked the wine—a Château Something-or-Other, undoubtedly very expensive—and then, after I'd sent Ruby and William out of the room so I could put the candles in the cake, gradually ascending to the ceiling, where it hovered, weary yet judgmental. Eighteen candles, two intersecting circles of nine candles each, according to our custom. "The cake, the cake, the cake," Ruby was chanting. Meanwhile, a huge block of late-afternoon sunlight had been inserted through the window over the sink, making everything in the room so bright that even after the candles were lit, you couldn't see their flames. In this yellow and substantial light to detect movement was impossible: one minute the chairs around the table were empty, the next minute they weren't; the plates had hats sitting on them, then the hats were sitting on people's heads.

"This is very good cake," said William, drawing his fork dreamily through his lips. Did he resemble Sam? He had the same hazel eyes, with a little more brown in them, but his hair was as fine and blond as Maren's, and although the expression on his face when he looked at Ruby showed traces of an expression with which I was familiar, William's adoration was clearly more forthright than his father's, less calculating. "It's good if you like dog biscuits," Helle said. "It's good if you like cardboard," echoed cynical Flo. The cake *was* stale, its crumb depressingly dry, its icing dauntingly hard, its flavor nonexistent. An abstract idea of a cake, a cake elevated to the realm of pure thought, a cake eidolon—the logical result of a plan that presumed to turn the theft of a birthday cake into a symbolic act. "Did you ever eat a dog biscuit?" William asked, genuinely interested, his left elbow planted on the table, the palm of his left hand serving as a lever to tilt his head slightly to the right.

"When I was in the Foreign Legion," Helle replied. "Years ago. It was that or the commander's arm." But she was staring across the table at me, her former irritability having turned to despair. "Where did you get this?" she asked, and when I told her, leaning forward to describe the circumstances in a whisper, her despair turned to outrage. "Why didn't you tell me?" she hissed. "I could have made a cake. I could have made you a really good cake." Appetite, she went on to explain, was nothing more than a prelude to putrefaction, unless it was an appetite for the beautiful. Oh, I was a criminal, all right, but my crime had nothing to do with theft! "My mouth is a temple," Helle said. "A temple," she repeated, and yet even I must have noticed how life had a way of dishing up the stale or the overcooked, the tasteless or the pulpy, when what you were hoping for was the sublime. "Hand me that wine," she ordered. "And would it be expecting too much to ask for a wineglass?"

Meanwhile, the twins were opening their presents: from William they both received three pairs of cable-stitched, worsted knee-socks in basic colors (a practical, condescending gift clearly chosen by Maren, I thought, with its implicit suggestion of neediness), and from Helle the aforementioned copy of *L'Oiseau bleu*, as well as matching flat tin boxes, each

with a picture of the Swiss Alps on its lid and, inside, a row
of colored pencils sharpened to perfect points. Fifty of them,
Helle explained, because it was important for the twins to
understand that there were more colors in the world than red
and yellow and navy blue—the practical colors of Maren's
wretched knee-socks—or than chocolate and vanilla and
strawberry, she added, sighing. Ruby shouted with pleasure
and began drawing on her napkin, as Flo simultaneously closed
her tin and her eyes. "Aren't we going to play any games?"
William asked. "Well, sure," Flo told him, her eyes still firmly
shut. "Isn't this a party?" She reached into her jeans pocket
and drew forth a deck of cards. "Slapjack," she said, shuffling
and making a bridge of the cards, expertly, like a gambler.
But what about pin-the-tail-on-the-donkey? Musical chairs?
Once, at Mary Weisner's, everyone had to whistle "Yankee
Doodle" after eating a saltine. At Susan Turcotte's they had
to bounce up and down on balloons with their butts until the
balloons popped. William said there were always treasure
hunts at his own parties; Tante Helle made up rhyming clues
which were great, even if they were hard to figure out. "So?"
said Flo, continuing to shuffle. She asked William if he remembered the rules—hitting cards, digging-for-secrets cards,
luck cards, love cards?

"You bring the glasses," Helle said, grabbing the wine
bottle by its neck. "I don't want any nine-year-olds digging
around for my secrets," she elaborated, pushing back her
chair and wandering into the living room. "When rain is
falling from the sky, I swallow the wet and spit out the dry.
I don't see what's so hard about that."

It was less bright in the living room, because the single
window faced north, out across Judkins's cornfield, at the far
edge of which a small red tractor was moving from east to

west, and above it a sliver of deepening blue sky. Lyle himself, I figured, heading home to his exhausted wife, coins jingling in his overalls pockets. Lily was curled up, gently snoring and twitching, in a large armchair to the right of the door—Lily's chair, we called it—its maroon fabric covered with a thin mat of gray fur. How drowsy I felt, and how relieved to sink down into the corner of the sofa! For isn't it a fact of nature that any sleeping creature emits into the air around it a thick residue of sleep? You can hardly keep your eyes open; the wings of your nostrils flare, as mine were doing, with suppressed yawns. Helle switched on the record player and then settled back into the sofa, facing me from the opposite corner, her knees hugged to her chest, her unusually big-knuckled fingers linked to hold her knees in place, her bracelet of silver birds, beak to claw, beak to claw, sliding from her wrist to the crook of her white-sleeved arm.

"The Act One finale," she said. "The Don is trying to seduce Zerlina—'Viva la libertà!' Did you hear that? As if Zerlina's liberty has anything to do with what he has in mind! But the violins aren't fooled. Listen to them, Frances. Feet racing up flight after flight of stairs. Du-du-du, du-du-du. Du-du-du, du-du-du. Can you hear it? Up, up, up they go, heading towards the bedroom. Also towards the last note of Zerlina's scream, which generally goes unvoiced—although Reri Grist sings it, if I'm not mistaken. Not Maeve Merrow, though. Never Maeve Merrow, which was a lucky thing for me." Helle leaned across the central cushion, where a large hole spilled forth yellowish crumbs of foam rubber, to grab my hand. "Can you hear it?" she repeated, and I was suddenly alarmed to see her face so close to mine: the small, gleaming surfaces of her teeth; the garnets, like tiny blood clots forming at the filigreed base of each wildly swaying, teardrop-shaped earring; the spokes of her gray irises spinning around and around her enlarged pupils; the skin pulled so tightly, so impossibly thinly, over her bones that it was as if I were looking at her skull. "Let's get drunk, Frances," she said. "Let's get ourselves really drunk. *'Fin ch'han dal vino calda la testa,'* as the Don would say." She reached down to the floor, picked up the wine bottle, and filled the two glasses—jelly glasses, I'm sorry to admit, decorated with pictures of Stone Age cartoon characters—to the brim. Then, handing me one, she said "*Skål!*" and swallowed the contents of hers in three quick gulps.

I took a sip to be polite, explaining that if she wanted to get drunk, that was fine, but I had to stay sober. It would soon be dark, too dark to walk all the way back to Quarry Road, and I didn't want to end up driving my car into a ditch. "Well, if that's all that's worrying you," Helle said, "we've got our ride worked out. Mr. Blackburn, Mr. Samuel Jenkins Blackburn, Sam to his friends and enemies alike, Sambo to his wife in her rare moments of playfulness, Professor Blackburn to his students, the devil to me, will be arriving at your house in exactly—" here Helle paused to consult my watch, a task which required that she once again grab my hand, yanking me toward her on the sofa—"in exactly forty-five minutes, as per his instructions. Drink up, Frances. The night is young."

Needless to say, I was anything but reassured. Sam coming to my house? Was he crazy? My dismay must have been obvious, for Helle held up one big-knuckled hand, palm out. "Sam's idea," she said, "not mine. He actually insisted. So let's give blame where blame is due." But I could already feel it: the walls gradually disintegrating into whirling particles, into air, into nothing, as if I were suddenly sitting on a hummock in the middle of the Great Bog at Horns, and it was just as Helle had described it to me—a flat, endless landscape of spore-shooting mosses and dwarf shrubs like fists and tongs, of insect-eating plants, of treacherous holes and fissures leading straight to hell. Nor was it as if I'd been transported there; rather, that the bog was where I'd been all along, though because my too-literal attention had been focused on those illusory, now-vanished walls, I hadn't noticed. "Calm down," Helle said. "It's not the end of the world." She gave me a strange little smile, slightly rueful, tender. "At least not for you," she said. "Not for you, Frances Thorn," she said, reaching out, this time gently, to stroke my cheek. Of course she was trying to tell me something; in her characteristically elliptical fashion she was hinting at some crucial piece of information, only I was too distracted to hear anything except for the faint soughing of peat. "Drink your wine," she said. "It's almost as old as I am, and it goes down a lot easier." Which I proceeded to do. In fact I ended up drinking two jelly glasses full of wine, one right after another, becoming drunk and, in the process, strangely garrulous.

If she really wanted to know, I said, the problem started when I was a girl in Philadelphia and I wanted to buy a square inch of Texas by sending in a cereal box top. You could do that, I reassured the skeptical-looking Helle. Hadn't she lived in America long enough to know that such things happened every day? Except my mother wasn't the kind of woman who thought children should act like children. For instance, I wasn't allowed to read comic books, only *Highlights for Children*; comic books would frighten me, my mother said, but that was because she never took a close look at that horrible wooden family called the Timbertoes, whose sinister adventures were one of the magazine's regular features. I wasn't allowed to eat Oreos, only Lorna Doones, which would still rot my teeth, but not as fast. Besides, what did I want with a square inch of Texas when I lived in a twenty-room Tudor mansion on three acres of prime real estate in one of the most exclusive neighborhoods in the city? Honestly.

She would never have understood if I'd told her that the appeal of the square inch—which I pictured as the first tiny chip in an enormous and slowly emerging mosaic, a ranch complete with cowboys and horses and a bald cook named Curly—was that it would belong to me; it never occurred to my mother that as far as a child is concerned, a house and everything in it belongs to the parents. Whereas my parents' myth held that what was theirs was also mine, which was just another way of saying that they owned my soul. Not surprisingly, as an adolescent I rebelled, although I told Helle she didn't have to worry, I wasn't planning to go into the details. The forms taken by this sort of rebellion are essentially the same, and consequently boring: the stifled soul longs for release, the methods it chooses alternately harsh and romantic, governed by warring urges to kill or to moodily expire.

In the present context, however, it seemed to me one aspect of my own predictable rebellion was worth mentioning, and that was my restless attraction to bus terminals. I started with the terminal at Broad and Chestnut in Philadelphia, although in time I expanded my reach to embrace most major American cities, and later, Europe as well, including Copenhagen, Aarhus, Odense—and once, even a tiny, moss-roofed terminal in the north Jutland village of Hvidsten, where I ate a bacon omelette with a man who sharpened knives for a living. "*Feed*-stain," Helle corrected. "*Feed*-stain." "Huh-vid-sten," I reiterated, indicating that accurate pronunciation was the farthest thing from my mind, and that I didn't want to be interrupted.

Especially not now, not when I was finally getting to the point. For what those bus terminals had in common, what drew me to them, wasn't the whiff of urine, the opportunity they offered to rub elbows with criminals and lunatics, but the storage lockers.

Silver, mysterious lockers! Walls filled with them, banks and banks and banks of storage lockers! Generally they came in three different sizes: small ones, which could hold a single suitcase and possibly a shopping bag; the medium-sized lockers, two suitcases, maybe one suitcase and a garment bag, maybe up to six shopping bags; and those big enough to accommodate a bass viol or a dead body or a pony—all three, if you were clever at packing. The first thing I'd do upon entering a bus terminal would be to locate the storage lockers, which was easy enough. The difficult part came when I had to make a choice. A medium-sized box in the middle of the middle row? A small box, top row, near the men's room, with a heart scratched into its silver door? Or should I make my choice based on a box's number? (Nineteen if that happened to be my age at the time, seven when I was reading Ouspensky.) Or shut my eyes and pick at random?

Although I never deposited any luggage. It used to be, when I went anywhere with my parents, we always had more suitcases than we could carry—matching things, with locks and monograms, good leather, lined with satin. But in the rebellious days of my adolescence all I owned was the accumulating square footage of cool mysterious space inside those storage lockers. Once I'd pocketed the key, I'd leave the terminal and walk around until I found the right place. This could be a bridge over a river, or a storm drain, or a litter basket, or a mail slot. I'd find the right place and drop the key; then I'd walk away. After a while I thought that I must own a space as big as the state of Texas, only what I owned was exotic and unexplored, separate and distinct, and it would forever remain that way because, unlike a real landscape, its parts would never be forced to come together into a single, boring geographic whole.

"Like the Gold Room," said Helle, "in Germany." She was leaning back against the sofa's arm, her skinny legs stretched out across all three cushions, her stockinged feet resting in my lap. When had she put them there? And her shoes—when had she taken them off? Furthermore, how long had Ruby been sitting there in the middle of the floor, wearing the discarded shoes—a pair of black ballet slippers—on her hands, making them walk up an invisible staircase in the shadowy air, as William and Flo stood whispering in the shadowy corner near the piano? If we didn't turn on the lights, maybe Sam would think no one was home. "They'd make new keys, you know," Flo said. "Other people would put things in the lockers. They weren't *yours*," she added fiercely. On the tape Zerlina was singing, softly, sweetly, to Masetto, "*Vedrai carino, se sei buonino, che bel rimedio ti voglio dar*"— "If you're very good, my darling, you'll see the pretty remedy I've got for you."

"The Gold Room," Helle repeated. "Remember that, Frances. One of these days it'll come in handy to remember that." Then Lily jumped from the maroon chair, her wolfish lips opening in an O, releasing that oddly conversational sound with which she greeted company. A car in the driveway, its engine running. Two short taps on the horn. He wasn't even coming in, I thought, and for a moment—the time it took Helle and William to gather their things together—I actually felt betrayed. As in a way I suppose I had been.

IV

B ETRAYAL AND PERFIDY; cowardice and censure—I
find, even now, that I'm as eager to leave Horns behind
as Helle was, as eager to place myself at a table in one
of those seedy cafés she frequented as a student, beneath
which, in basement shops, the tattooists practiced their art on
the edge of the Copenhagen harbor, where the shrouds of the
large sailboats chafed against each other, making the same
sound which is produced by bowing a violin *sul ponticello*, nasal
and glassy, and where the air smelled like fish. When, over a
glass of akvavit, a sailor would ask Helle what her name was,
she would say it was Henning, in order to differentiate herself
from the tense, duplicitous creature who was responsible for
her mother's death, who supposedly compounded one crime
with the intention of committing another. I'd like to leave
Horns behind now, but I can't. You might just as well try to
tell the story of "The Girl Who Trod on a Loaf" and omit
the fact that its protagonist enjoyed pulling the wings from
insects in order to watch their pathetic, frustrated struggle to
fly. You can choose a life of crime, or you can compose operas.
According to Helle, at least, those were the alternatives. And
sometimes the boundary between them got confused.

Did she really try to poison Gunhild? Somehow that seems

unlikely, more like wishful thinking, a predictably operatic touch. Besides, Niels never mentioned such an attempt in his letters, and given his obvious feeling of repulsion for Helle, if she'd actually tried to poison his mother—especially since it was his own birth which Helle insisted had tipped the balance—he would've been more than eager to fill me in on the details. A way of providing herself with a dramatic exit, that's my interpretation of this story: instead of allowing that at the age of seventeen she boarded a train for the conservatory in Copenhagen, Helle found it useful to announce that her father had banished his criminal daughter from her childhood home forever.

Of course it is possible that eventually Anders got fed up and threw her out. There he was, trying to make a life for his young wife and new baby, and there was Helle, busy composing a song cycle entitled *Den onde Stedmoder*. "The two horns of the moon never met in me. They met in her," Helle wrote, "in June." She liked the way her anger chimed melodiously against the edges of the rhyme, and the irony that her use of the melodious Neapolitan sixth (from C to E-flat to A-flat) granted the lyric. "Moon" and "June"—could she get away with "spoon" as well? No, what Helle was after was irony, not cheap sarcasm. She considered those things a doctor used when delivering a baby. But "forceps" sounded too technical, and besides, it didn't scan properly. A knife? A *silver* knife? But she wanted the violence to feel like a secret: "With a silver spade," Helle wrote, "my father scooped the baby out." She could imagine the singer's voice, a rich contralto scooping into the shimmering chromatic curtain of notes, revealing behind them a tangle of wet, red bedsheets. Hegel's definition of tragedy always appealed to Helle: given two impossible alternatives, there was no solution. The horns of the dilemma were of equal size and substance. Synthesis was out of the question. You had to make a choice and then be prepared to live with it.

The baby's skin was white as snow, and covered all over with a pelt of russet fur. Niels, they named him, after Gunhild's father, although privately Helle referred to him as Foxy. Her half-brother, father of Maren—it was almost impossible for Helle to reconcile that fussy, balding man from whom each Christmas she received a mimeographed letter describing the success of his dry-cleaning business in Frederikshavn, or his vacation trips to the south of France, with that small, pileous creature. At first she hated Niels; or at least she hated the way Anders sat enraptured as Gunhild drew a large white breast out of her negligée, its surface marbled with blue veins like a cheese, then nudged the baby's mouth toward the nipple. "Isn't he something?" Anders would comment. "Look at him go!"

For a while Niels slept in a fancy wicker bassinet at the foot of the huge oak bed in which he'd been conceived—an act Helle tried her hardest not to imagine. Gunhild was a fierce and protective mother, rarely letting him out of her sight. But late in the afternoon when she'd fallen asleep, poured like a boneless thing across the mattress, Helle would sneak into the room and watch the baby. She was fascinated that a separate life had been consigned to such a miniature container, and a separate soul formed within the larger container of her stepmother's body. Her hatred turned to admiration: how dauntless and brave the baby must've been to have held his own even when it was Gunhild's blood that set him leaping like a tiny fish!

Normally the lanugo, the soft fur that covers the bodies of some infants, falls out by the time they're four months old.

But Niels kept his well into his tenth month. "Don't let them fool you," Helle would whisper into his ear, which was shaped like a dried apricot, and tufted at the rim, so when she got close the hairs tickled her lips. She explained to Niels that his real mother was not the slatternly woman who eroded his sense of dignity by trying to engage him in endless games of peekaboo. No, his real mother was a fox, and when he got big enough, Helle would take him to the den. The fox thought she'd hidden it, but Helle had found it in a copse of swamp willow. Sometimes fingers would sprout from the tiny potatoes of his fists, and the baby would smile. Helle knew he was smiling, even though Gunhild said it was only gas that made his lips curve upward. Once Helle was so overwhelmed with love that she reached down and gathered him up. But then he began to howl, whereupon Gunhild awakened, outraged, and baby talk erupted from her lips, words as frightening and ill-formed as eggs from the vent of an undernourished hen.

However, as Niels grew, so did Helle's sense of isolation: Gunhild was clearly doing her best to protect him from his half-sister's pernicious influence. According to Helle, Gunhild's ideal was the pastor of the Lutheran church in Frederikshavn, whose understanding of the word "elect" held that one prepared one's place at God's right hand by exercising privilege here on earth. Though Anders never really took the hint, neither did he object to his new wife's attempts at transforming the formerly vast, breezy rooms of Krageslund into boudoirs and parlors, at decking the leaded-glass windows with yards of drapery—a sight as obscene to Helle as that of the beribboned key basket Gunhild had taken to carrying over her wrist, a custom she'd read about in a ladies' magazine and which was meant to symbolize that she was now, without question, the mistress of the house. Before the advent of the basket, all of the keys to Krageslund's many doors and wall cupboards had been tossed together into the top drawer of Ida's dresser; nothing had been locked, not even the examining room cabinet where Anders kept his most dangerous medicines, nor the strongbox containing the pair of pearl-handled dueling pistols he'd inherited from his father, as well as the gold coins which had constituted Ida's dowry. But once Gunhild assumed control, everything was locked up tight; even the drapes were tightly woven, letting in almost no sun, because she couldn't stand the nearness of the bog, especially at night, when gases rose from the peat, assuming the shapes of the tortured dead, many-fingered and greedy for attention. By now, Helle told me, the household had taken on the form of a great spiral nebula: looked at from the side, she and her father weren't visible, hidden behind the gigantic central cluster of matter and upheaval that was Gunhild and the baby. From above, however, they could be dimly perceived, guttering, in the process of gravitational collapse.

What could Helle do? By the time Niels was four he would cry out whenever he came upon anything fleet or sudden, anything wild or inexplicable, such as the newt which appeared one day, its body like a drop of liquid trapped in a net of sphagnum, sunning itself on the doorstep. "Don't worry, it won't bite," Helle told him, and Niels gave her the same worried, fretful look he'd given the newt. Nor did Helle make any real effort to court his favor, choosing to spend whatever time wasn't taken up with schoolwork or chores at the piano. She was still struggling to complete *Den onde Stedmoder*, a project more difficult than she'd originally imagined: she still had three songs to go, and the mere act of tuning and retuning the piano took hours. Far from being an ally, Helle thought, her half-brother had turned out to be a traitor, although this unfortunate metamorphosis was clearly his mother's doing.

Thus she conceived of her plan, which she put into effect approximately two months before her anticipated departure for Copenhagen, on an appropriately wind-tossed and stormy night, when anvil-shaped thunderheads trailed skirts of rain across her mother's roses, sending forks of lightning down around the house, setting fire to the garden shed. Well after midnight, Helle sneaked into the room where her father and Gunhild were lying, their heads thrown back on their separate pillows, their mouths open, snoring. She carefully lifted the key basket off the bedpost where it was hooked, placing her hand onto the keys to prevent them from signaling their sleeping mistress. According to Helle, the allegiance of inanimate objects was always unreliable; and there could be no denying Gunhild's admiration for the keys, for their capacity to discriminate and exclude. But nothing went wrong. She speculated that perhaps her mother's boot had assumed a role in this exchange. Or perhaps the keys were responding to a deeper form of kinship, for the truth is that Helle felt like a key herself, cool and smooth, her destiny implicit in that notched part of herself which remained invisible under her long white nightgown.

At last, like a character in an opera, she negotiated the stairs, holding a candle aloft to light her way. Most of the keys in the basket were fairly large, designed to open the doors of rooms. Of the three smaller keys, she somehow managed to select the one that opened the examining-room cabinet on her first try, releasing a smell of spilled rubbing alcohol and damp varnish. The good doctor, Helle thought, wasn't always as careful as he should have been when replacing his supplies. She reached into the cabinet, her shadow climbing the wall behind her, folding at its immense waist to bend out across the ceiling, observant, protective. Maybe her father wouldn't even notice that the dark brown bottle was missing. Inside was a grayish-white powder, harmless looking, though Helle had seen what it could do to rats. Then she opened the strongbox and removed five coins. Finally, for good measure, she took one of the dueling pistols.

According to the pharmacopeia, one gram of arsenic will produce severe vomiting and diarrhea in its victim within three to four hours, followed by death from circulatory collapse. But Helle assumed that such an occurrence would be bound to raise her father's suspicions: her idea was to break the dosage into smaller portions, administering it a pinch at a time, right up until the day she left home. This would, she knew, be easy enough to do. Gunhild expected to be waited on hand and foot; the poison was tasteless and odorless, so a few grains stirred into her morning coffee would pass unnoticed.

At first, Helle said, Gunhild complained of feelings of numbness in her limbs—pins and needles, she called them. The weather continued to be warm, but Gunhild was always cold. Her voice grew husky; she developed a cough. "It's your fault," she said to Helle one morning as she sat shivering at the table, and briefly Helle panicked, until she realized that the offense she was being blamed for was leaving the windows open overnight. Anders, for his part, counseled frequent naps, beef tea. Indeed, during that first week he seemed unconcerned. Gunhild, as everyone knew, was as strong as an ox. It was only when her hair began to fall out, when she claimed to be too weak to lift Niels into his bed, that Anders grew alarmed. Of course, Helle told me, what she'd really been hoping for all along was that her father would figure out what she was doing. What she wanted, she explained, then as now, was nothing less than recognition.

Still, it wasn't until the characteristic white ridges began to form on Gunhild's fingernails, the telltale Aldrich-Mees lines, that Anders actually *knew*. As Helle put it, fascination and horror are hard to differentiate, magnifying the eyes and mouth while the rest of the face remains about the same. They were sitting at the kitchen table eating supper; Anders was holding Gunhild's left hand, the one with the ring, as through the open windows came the sound of crickets chirping, the unbearably sweet smell of decaying rose petals. Summer was almost over. "Helle," Anders said, "come with me."

He led her into his examining room, where without saying a word he weighed her and checked her height, as he had done so many times before, making notations on a piece of paper. He pricked her finger, and put the slide on which he'd smeared the blood under his microscope, then asked her to take a look. "The round yellow shapes are the erythrocytes," he said. "The others are leukocytes." He was checking, he explained, to see whether Helle was human. Evidently she passed this test, because Anders next drew forth a chart printed with a series of drawings of rudimentary yet undeniably human forms. Helle's stage of physical development, he said, was consistent with that of a normal ten-year-old boy, then asked if she found this piece of information pleasing. When she didn't reply, he repeated the word "boy," and she found herself remembering how the Nissens' barn cat would choke up a dense wad of fur and bones, the indigestible parts of the mouse. Helle was to pack her bags that night and be out of the house the next day, Anders said. As far as he was concerned, he no longer had a daughter.

When Helle told him he'd never had one, he laughed. Ida, he said, always claimed that she was different, but he wondered if she'd had any idea of just how different Helle was. Because whatever else you might say about Ida, she had been kind. She never turned down a single soul who came to the door looking for help. Did Helle know that when Ida once found an old gypsy woman rummaging through the kitchen cupboards, she'd given her a purse full of money and a basket full of clothes? Did Helle know that? Or how he'd felt the day he came upon the gypsy's little dancing monkey tethered to a beech tree on the Six Bridges Road, and the monkey had been wearing his dead wife's pink satin bedjacket? Oh, Ida'd made mistakes, but *her* passions had been fueled merely by a foolish need to repeat history. When Ida set out across the bog to meet Viggi Brahe, she actually believed she was elaborating on motifs established hundreds of years earlier by the Lapp princess for whom Krageslund had originally been built. "I miss your mother," Anders said. "You probably won't believe me when I say this, but I do. I just thank heaven that she isn't alive today to see what became of you."

But he was wrong, Helle told me—Ida would have been proud. Unkind Ida, who one day had shown her that a note struck on the piano just once suggested nothing more than itself. A single note, Ida explained, was like an act of nature that took you completely by surprise, such as the meteorite which landed one night in the Nissens' cow pasture, or the small brown bird which had flung itself against the windowpane while Helle was practicing her arpeggios. The finger of a mindless god moved, then came down suddenly. You could call it an accident, for there was no doubt that the single note shot through your heart like a stray bullet from a hunter's gun, although it didn't really have anything to do with pain.

Pain had to exist in time: the note had to be struck more than once. And if you did so—struck the same note over and over—what happened was that the note wanted to resolve itself in its own dominant. D, D, D, D, D, Ida played with her little finger. Did Helle hear it? You could hardly restrain your thumb from falling onto the G. The fifth degree, the bass tone, the root of the dominant triad. Couldn't she hear it?

In this way Helle came to realize that when her father remarked on Ida's need to repeat history, what he really meant was that she wanted to be more powerful than he was. Thus the weak could strike at the root of the strong. They could learn to exist in history; they could learn how to inflict pain.

Part Three

THE HARROWING OF LAHLOO

I

So it happened that on September 4, 1914, Helle
Ten Brix arrived in Copenhagen. Copenhagen, city of
towers! How clearly I can see her standing there on the
Bernstorffsgade, a skinny creature with dark circles under her
wildly staring eyes, an expression of dark determination on
her small white face. Stiff, motionless—is she paralyzed with
fear? No, the reason she doesn't move is because she's watching, spellbound, as one by one the towers of Copenhagen
emerge around her, phantasmagoric, rising from an otherwise
featureless landscape. Lavish structures, intricately shifting,
no two alike, they rise into a deep blue sky: clocks rotating
their brilliant golden arms, spires swelling into golden onions,
the intertwining tails of bronze dragons, Jesus balanced on a
tiny green ball. Rosenborg Castle, the Church of the Holy
Ghost; the famous Round Tower, as gigantic and impenetrable
as the eyes of the third dog in Hans Andersen's story "The
Tinder Box." You never know, of course. Even a place as flat
as Copenhagen can be host to magic. Even a woman as self-
contained as a hazelnut can crack open and out can pour
towering chords, arpeggios, a tinkling of bells, shooting stars.
In the Tivoli Gardens, Helle told me, there was a tower made

to look like a Chinese pagoda, and at night it was completely outlined in lights.

Such happiness to look up instead of down, to have your eyes constantly drawn toward the sky! Helle felt as if she were in a forest of exquisite trees crafted from stone and slate and precious metals, a purely human design that would last forever. The lindens and beeches of Horns, though beautiful, were subject to rot and ruin, whereas nothing could touch the obdurate trees of this city. Obviously a different set of rules prevailed here, rules governing immortality, and she was now under their jurisdiction. She thought this, even though when she'd arrived in Copenhagen she was on shaky ground, being essentially impecunious—Ida's five gold coins had turned out to be worth less than she'd hoped, just enough to pay the train fare and settle her first-term account at the conservatory. But on the night of September 4, as she sat in the Tivoli Gardens drinking a beer, Helle was still giddy from looking upward all day long. Living among towers can tempt you into complacency; no matter how reduced your circumstances, they can seem of small consequence in comparison with the vast reaches of the heavens, blue by day, starry and black by night. God will provide, is what you will find yourself thinking, even if you are, as Helle was, a nonbeliever.

She was sitting at a small square table watching a commedia dell'arte routine in which two masked actors, the chalk-faced, moony Pierrot and the stick-carrying Harlequin, fought for the favors of budlike Columbine. Harlequin, in particular, was very good, capable of bending over completely backwards, his black cat mask staring upside-down from between his legs at the audience, transforming his smile, quick as a wink, into a frown. From time to time Harlequin's crony, Brighella, would appear, licking his lips and rubbing his palms together avariciously. For the right sum, he would see to it that Pierrot was put out of commission forever. Thus—despite the intoxicating effects of the beer and the unseasonably warm night air and the exhilarating towers—Helle was made to remember how all human affairs, including the most subtle affairs of the heart, are subject to the laws of economics. Off to the left a band was playing "A Bird in a Gilded Cage," one of Gunhild's favorite tunes. Helle could hear people singing along on the chorus: "She's only a bird in a gilded cage, a beautiful sight to see. You may think she's happy and free from care; she's not, though she seems to be . . ."

But who, in fact, would have suspected that Helle was anything other than what she appeared to be, just another happy, carefree beer drinker, a small young man of bohemian disposition, probably a student? She was wearing a man's white shirt and black trousers, a black silk vest and a blue silk cravat, a dove-gray fedora, underneath which her still-long hair was carefully braided and tightly pinned to her scalp. "Like George Sand," Viggi Brahe had said when she'd tried on the outfit for his benefit. It was the least she could do, since he'd given it to her, as well as a slightly mildewed Gladstone bag in which he'd packed another shirt, butter yellow; an emerald-green cravat; a pair of beige twill trousers. Otherwise, in the three years since the production of *Det omflakkende Møl*, Helle had done her best to avoid Viggi Brahe, whose former interest in patronage had been replaced by an interest in horticulture, specifically poppies, to support a rumored opium addiction. "You look more like Ida every day," he'd said, though his mind was obviously clouded by the drug.

Helle ordered another beer. It was going on eleven o'clock, late enough so another half hour wouldn't make much difference; if need be, she thought, she could find somewhere to sleep in the gardens, curling up on a soft, shadowy patch of grass within an elder thicket, the way the foxes did back home. The brass band was playing a waltz—Prince Orlofsky's ball in *Fledermaus*, just before the fateful striking of the clock— and couples were swooping, batlike, in front of the bandstand, their bodies welling up out of the darkness, brightly visible, then submerging as they waltzed in and out of the small pools of light cast by hundreds of faintly swaying Japanese lanterns. The beer tasted delicious. Nor did Helle bother to wipe away the foam mustache, figuring it added to her disguise. Nightjars were flying overhead—birds that roosted by day on the city's towers—and she could hear their eerie nocturnal cries, which could be easily confused with the sounds of mole crickets, if you didn't know better.

Meanwhile, tobacco smoke drifted in her direction from a neighboring table where two sailors, apparently no older than she was, rested their elbows among a great many empty beer mugs, their dark blue caps set at jaunty angles, their eyes pink and restless. How good it smelled, that smoke! All of a sudden what Helle wanted more than anything in the world was one of those exotic black cylinders tipped in gold. But how should she address them? And though her voice, even then, was husky and deep for a girl, she hadn't tried it out yet on strangers. If they guessed she was an impostor, would they rob and rape her? She must have been staring at them, because suddenly one of the sailors leaned over and asked her what was so goddamn fascinating. Never seen a sailor before? Then they both laughed, regarding her with the kind of good humor the bully accords his victim before pounding him into the ground.

Only Marius Finsen and Kai Borge—Dancer and Kayo—

weren't bullies, but two merchant sailors who decided, for some reason Helle never fully understood, to take her under their wing. Perhaps they'd perceived themselves to be a duet which couldn't achieve true musical brilliance except by expanding into a trio—beauty and brawn requiring brains to lend tension to a melody that would otherwise remain merely charming. Whatever the reason, in time Helle came to think of them as the lively, untamed brothers she'd always wanted, although it was Dancer with whom she would develop the more complex, potentially sinister relationship. Not another *mariage faux*, but a second category, which later quite possibly included Sam.

While it was Kayo—big, apparently dull-witted Kayo, destined to die two years later in the Battle of Jutland—who immediately saw through Helle's disguise as they made their way drunkenly down the Østergade that night, Kayo who took Helle's hand and pulled her to a stop while Dancer continued toward the harbor. "You're a girl, aren't you?" he asked, and when Helle admitted that she was, he nodded his overlarge, hairy head, like a buffalo's, and grinned. He had two sisters, Kayo explained; and women walked differently because of the way they were built. Then he blushed. Luckily for Helle, even though the boardinghouse where he and Dancer were staying was small, there was an empty room, a closet really—she could sleep there, at least for the night, until she found something better. Obviously she hadn't realized, had she, how dangerous the Copenhagen harbor was after dark, teeming with criminals and madmen. No place for a girl, even a tough little thing like herself.

As it turned out, the boardinghouse to which Kayo led her was located in the harbor's disreputable heart, right on that narrow channel called the Nyhavn: number 22, one door down from the house where Hans Andersen lived when he was writing his first fairy tales, two doors down from number 18, where he died. The house was white-painted stucco, four stories tall, but it wasn't until the following morning that Helle could see its façade clearly, as well as the still life—a conch shell, an ivy trained into the shape of a heart, a china polar bear standing on its hind legs, a wooden crucifix, a tinted engraving showing a cottage clinging, limpetlike, to the side of an alp—which the landlady, the notorious Daisy Huj og Hast, had arranged in the first-story window.

Such still lifes were in evidence throughout the city; they were, according to Helle, the Danish equivalent of the lawn art you saw in Canaan's less fortunate neighborhoods, those arrangements of silver balls and gnomes and whirling ducks and frozen squirrels. If you sneaked up on these still lifes at night, Helle claimed, you could hear the objects chattering away: "Now the drowned sailors do their dance before the throne of the Sea Witch; they hope she'll send their souls to heaven, but she wants them for her own," the conch shell would be saying, only to be interrupted by the polar bear, its voice surprisingly soft, childish: "I have eaten three men, and so I can tell you that a human heart is harder to swallow than the heart of the oldest, toughest walrus." "Have you seen them, have you seen them," the engraving would ask, "the goatherd's family under the thick blankets of an avalanche, all of them dreaming the same dream? They think they're standing on a mountaintop, surveying the whole frozen world," to which the ivy would reply, "Sweethearts, sweethearts! Watch them kissing in the parlor!" Meanwhile, the tiny Christ mounted on the crucifix said nothing.

The author of this still life was, however, fast asleep when Helle made her original appearance on that well-scrubbed doorstep with her new companions. They had to be careful not to knock over the dark blue bicycle leaning against the wall in the entryway. Dancer said that even though "the old girl" was over fifty, twice a year she rode her bicycle from Copenhagen to Odense, well over one hundred kilometers, in order to visit her brother and his wife. If Daisy liked you, Dancer said, then there wasn't a thing to worry about. Handsome, with tightly curled chestnut hair and wide-set, slanting eyes, Dancer had the fixed smile of a young man who knew he was physically attractive and who was, consequently, suspicious of any display of affection. He came from Kunø, in the Faroe Islands, where he'd spent most of his life on boats, so that even when he walked on dry land it was with a rhythmic, faintly syncopated sway—with the dip and glide characteristic of such exotic dances as the tango, hence his nickname. Kunø, Dancer explained, was composed entirely of mountains, and his village had been built in the one place where there was a slight break in the chain. Until he came to Copenhagen Dancer had never eaten anything but fish—the famous Faroese *klipfisk*, or salt cod, which the king of Spain himself considered a great delicacy. He hadn't known what a vegetable was until Daisy served him a plateful of spring asparagus.

Initially Helle felt nervous around Dancer—everyone did, she said, with the exception of Daisy, who clearly adored him. Even later, when their friendship became more intimate, Helle remained slightly tense in his presence. That first night, it was with something approaching fear that she watched Dancer take the stairs two at a time, lightly, on the balls of his feet, marveling that anyone could move so fast and still manage to convey an impression of languor, of sexual appetite recently appeased yet once again stirring. Did he have a woman hidden away in his room? Certainly he didn't show any sign of drunkenness, even though Kayo displayed several and he'd had much less to drink. When he got to the first landing, Dancer looked back, briefly, over his shoulder. "Shhh," he said, making a pillow of his hands on which he pretended to rest his head, and then pointing toward the door to Daisy's apartment. "A light sleeper," Kayo explained. "Light?" hissed Dancer. "She doesn't sleep at all. She's like goddamn Fafnir."

The closet was on the top floor of the house, on the harbor side, the odd slope of its exterior wall determined by the mansard roof. A room into which you could fit yourself and nothing more, Helle thought, after Kayo had tugged the door open for her, releasing the damp, clabbered smell of old clothes and dust. A room like a husk, a shell. Through the unblinking eye of a single round window a moonbeam, quivering and waterlogged, illuminated a narrow metal bedstead, hemmed in on either side by rows of shelves piled with canning jars and boxes.

It was smaller than he'd remembered, Kayo said. Would Helle be all right? And then, probably because exhaustion had given her face a pinched and frightened look, he paused to reassure her that he wasn't planning to try anything, if that was what had her worried. For, as Kayo went on to explain, he'd grown up on a mangel beet farm in north Zealand, where, unlike Dancer's, his knowledge of boats and women had been limited to taking his sisters for rides in a leaky rowboat on a weed-choked pond. From the time he was a little boy, all he'd wanted to do was become a sailor and escape the crushing life of the farmer, stuck like his father on one small piece of dirt for the rest of his life. Women were safe with him, Kayo promised. Helle reminded him of his favorite sister, Maja, the youngest; she, too, was a deep one. "Sweet dreams," he said, backing away into the shadows, disappearing into his own room on the other side of the hall. It didn't seem to make any difference that the bed was hard as a rock, that the pillow was moist and sour, that the duvet's stitching had come undone so the down rested in a single heavy lump on top of her feet—Helle fell asleep almost immediately. The last thing she recalled hearing was the sound of Kayo's voice, that high-pitched and lilting voice you sometimes run across in very large men; Kayo was saying his prayers.

In the morning he introduced her to Daisy, who was sitting in her dining room, drinking coffee and talking to Dancer. Daisy Huj og Hast had been married at the age of sixteen to a sailor, a nice boy whom she'd hardly gotten to know before he was drowned in a freak accident off the Swedish coast. She had been at one time a great beauty: you knew this not only because she told you so but because she conducted herself like a woman accustomed to receiving the admiration of others. Her alliance with Dancer, Helle said, was based upon this obvious similarity between them—whatever is beautiful in this world is always under assault. The world wants to discover the hidden flaw, and if one isn't readily apparent, then the world will strive to create it. Dancer's solution was to hold himself aloof, whereas Daisy's was to strike a series of preemptive blows, constantly reminding the world in advance of her shortcomings, each of which she managed to present as an asset. "I don't know why it is, but I've always hated the weak," she would announce ruefully the minute Oluf Froulund, the middle-aged man with a limp who lived in the room to the right of Helle's closet, had left the table.

Daisy's hair was pure white, almost transparent, and she wore it coiled into a thick knot at the top of her head. Her skin, too, had a transparent quality, through which you could see the perfection of the underlying structure, the wide blades of her cheekbones, the delicate sockets out of which her pale blue eyes regarded you with an unsettling combination of irony and sincerity. "Good morning, Henning," she said, sitting there with her back erect, gracefully buttering a slice of *fuldkorn*, that grainiest of the Danish breads, before taking a bite; Daisy still had all of her teeth, a miracle in those days. The house, she explained, was already filled with more lodgers than she could handle. Still, there was probably room for one more. "My friends accuse me of being too soft-hearted," Daisy confessed, turning to Dancer, sighing and tossing her head, providing a clear image of what she must have looked like as a tender, flirtatious girl. She guessed such soft-heartedness came of never having had any children of her own.

The dining room was like a cave, warm and windowless, heated by a ceiling-high stove—a larger, tiled version of the stove in Helle's trailer—its tiles the same forest green as the wainscoting, above whose panels you could barely make out the pale pink of the walls, concealed beneath a shadowy array of paintings and photographs, antique pipes, clocks, omelette pans, butter molds, and what appeared to be door latches. Every available surface—the plate rail, the immense seaman's chest, the gargantuan oak sideboard—was covered with china figurines: shepherdesses and chimney sweeps, lords and ladies, geese and ganders, rams and ewes, all arranged in pairs. Thus the room constituted a sort of secular altar to the idea of heterosexual coupling, and Helle felt more fraudulent than ever.

"Well, Henning," Daisy said, once each of the sailors had kissed her goodbye and let in a little pie-shaped slice of sunlight on his way out the door, "Kayo tells me you're a musician." She held up a porcelain pot painted with lilies-of-the-valley, a cut-glass dish. Some coffee? Some of her own homemade currant preserves? Ah, it had been too many years since she'd heard the sound of piano music in the house! Poor Lennart had been the one who played, and he'd drowned in 1884, the same year Christiansborg Palace burned to the ground. The sad history of the Danes, Daisy said, a sad history of loss and deception: Hother's unsavory dealings with the innocent forest maidens; the tragic marriage of Caroline Mathilde to a king she'd never seen; the rotten Swedes. Meanwhile, Helle leaned back in her chair, crossing her legs at the ankles, as she'd noticed men did. When she said that the coffee was very good, Daisy shrugged. Any woman who's used to stirring up the male libido can easily tell when it isn't there; if nothing else, she can recognize its absence by her own mounting sense of boredom. Daisy yawned and began brushing bread crumbs into a small pile, then stood and adjusted her corset, something she would never have done had Dancer still been sitting at the table. It was horrible, wasn't it, Daisy complained, the way the bones dug into you? Of course Henning wouldn't know.

So HELLE FOUND a home and, with it, a way of earning her keep. During the years she lived at number 22 Nyhavn—from 1914 to 1923, when Daisy sold the house and moved to Mariager—Helle managed to assemble a small band of piano students, mostly unwilling girls who arrived late in the afternoon to display on the yellowed keyboard of Daisy's upright the results of their halfhearted practice. As a matter of fact, only one of her students showed any talent, a big-eared and solemn little boy named Palle. For a while after his family left Denmark he stayed in touch, writing Helle letters from Lübeck, in northern Germany, where his father had gone to work in a shipyard. Two world wars, the first of which was about to begin, bracketed Helle's years in Copenhagen: the face of Europe—and with it the lives of millions of people— was about to change forever.

Although Denmark remained neutral in the Great War, that position is never passive. It was Sam who explained this to me some time during the middle period of our affair, provoked no doubt by my own apparent passivity. Evidently, the famous neutrality of the Swiss was initially accomplished by their invention in the Middle Ages of the pike, a long-handled spear with a hook on the end, the perfect weapon with which to dismount and disembowel armored horsemen. Once you had the perfect weapon, you became immune to attack. Or, as Hobbes put it, equality in nature was based on the premise that all members of a given system possess in equal measure the ability to kill. You might say, Sam explained bitterly, that the so-called success of the nuclear family was predicated on such a philosophy, just as you might recognize hints of it in the notion that world peace might be secured by causing the instruments of death to lurk expectantly in holes underground. Of course Sam didn't mean to suggest that the men who ran the world ever read Hobbes. But ideas, like germs, were always loose in the wind. Even a moron could catch the flu.

And neutrality didn't mean that the Danes weren't affected by the upheaval around them. Oswald Bingger, for example— the teacher at the conservatory who, for good or ill, asserted the greatest influence over Helle—was continually subjected to paranoid wartime speculation only because he was born in

Schleswig-Holstein, that wedge of land at the base of the Jutland peninsula over which Denmark and Germany had fought for years, tugging it this way and that like the two mothers in the Bible. According to Hr. Bingger, Lord Palmerston, the unsuccessful champion of the Danish cause in 1864, had claimed that only three men ever understood the history of Schleswig-Holstein: Prince Albert, who was dead; a professor, who went insane; and Palmerston himself, who'd eventually forgotten everything he'd ever known on the subject.

Indeed, Hr. Bingger said, the history of Schleswig-Holstein was not unlike the plot of an opera. He disliked opera, and during the four years he worked with Helle he tried in his own dismissive fashion to win her over to his point of view. Who could remember all the details of such complicated stories? Who in their right mind would want to? People jumping in and out of closets, stabbing each other, yodeling? The only reason anyone bothered to listen to the things, Bingger insisted, was because of the occasional beauty of the music. In the same way you might understand the history of Schleswig-Holstein. The melodic structure was contrapuntal: Germany's melody aggressive and highly emotional, Denmark's passive and rational. What people responded to was the endless struggle of two melodies toward resolution. Bingger encouraged Helle to study Bach's organ chorales, to recognize the way in which the architecture of the whole was made to supersede the beauty of the individual detail. You could choose to swim, forever, in the primeval soup, or you could ally yourself with the forces of reason. At any rate, that Bingger's motives ever came into question, that he was taken for a subversive element or spy, was merely a sign of the times. So what if, as one of Helle's fellow students took pleasure in pointing out, Bingger used the same curling device as that used by the Kaiser to make his mustaches turn up in points? So what if Bach was the Kaiser's favorite composer?

When Helle looked back at that period in her life, it was clear that the twin influences against which she railed— represented in more or less equal measure by Oswald Bingger and Daisy Huj og Hast—were manifestations of a single deity, and that deity's name was Compromise. Of course to all outward appearances no two people could have been more dissimilar: where Daisy was luminous and graceful, Bingger was puffy and awkward; she moved seamlessly, like water, and he in jerks, like spoiled milk falling in clots from a jar. Nor could anyone accuse Daisy Huj og Hast, at least superficially, of having allied herself with the forces of reason. For most of the major decisions (whether to take a given suitor seriously, for instance), she would rely on cards, tea leaves, dice, the stars—it didn't appear to matter which method of divination Daisy chose, so long as the result conformed to her desires. Which it always did, since Daisy understood better than anyone the power implicit in the act of interpretation. "I am to accept Hr. Lok's gifts but not his kisses," she would say, pointing meaningfully at a brown smear of leaves in the bottom of her teacup. No, Daisy's similarity to Bingger resided, instead, in her attitude toward her own womanhood, an attitude based on the assumption that her ability to get what she wanted increased in direct proportion to her ability to appear soft and malleable. Gunhild, likewise, had tried to trade on those qualities, but she lacked Daisy's subtlety, her strength of intellect, her vision. Helle would never have dreamed of trying to poison Daisy, whose pale blue eyes never blinked; she knew everything.

Thus Helle was daily forced to sharpen her new persona

against two whetstones, each of which seemed to have been designed for the sole purpose of wearing her away to a thinness verging on invisibility. Once the metal is suitably thin, it becomes pliant; you can transform a knife into a bracelet, a threat into an adornment. Besides, both Daisy and Bingger had the advantage of knowing that she was an impostor. Daisy never came right out and accused her of being a woman; instead, whenever a suitor came to call, she made sure that Helle was present to witness the force beauty exerts over all other forms of ambition. "Henning," she would demand imperiously, "come into my room. I can't decide which necklace to wear with this dress." Then, leaning into the mirror, she would begin perfecting the canvas of her face, providing a prototype from which Helle might derive a working replica. Daisy knew, Helle said, that Henning's mother had died when he was very young, and what she felt for him, if she felt anything at all, was pity. Thus in the household hierarchy Henning came to occupy a place just above that occupied by Oluf Froulund, the lowest of the low. Or perhaps Henning was at the bottom: at least Oluf Froulund understood how to capitalize on his deformity.

Bingger, on the other hand, understood Helle's imposture in musical rather than sexual terms. Had the subject of gender ever come up, most likely he would have encouraged Helle to ignore sex altogether, as he claimed to have done. Music, Bingger used to say, was the only suitable companion for a true musician. Bad enough to fall in love if you were a performer; but for a composer—how could the music of the spheres ever begin to penetrate the wall of babble and demands that was another human being? The one time Bingger invited Helle to his house for coffee and cake, she was surprised to discover that he had not only a parrot—a large red and green creature which talked incessantly—but also a wife, as colorless as the bird was bright. And while Frau Bingger hardly said a word, it was obvious that her silence constituted a demand of unappeasable proportions. When Helle told her that the cake was delicious, she sighed. From a bakery, Hr. Bingger snarled—the cake came from a bakery.

Initially Helle concluded that Daisy was the kinder of the two, that in keeping her suspicions to herself she was motivated by a desire to protect, whereas Bingger—who chose a public forum for her humiliation, her infamous first encounter with solfeggio, in which she was forced to stand in front of her peers and sight-sing—was motivated by a desire to destroy. Only later would she realize that Daisy's apparent kindness was nothing more than a means of exerting control, and that Bingger was genuinely benevolent. He knew that Helle was talented, and he knew how useless such talent could be when left to its own devices. Bingger's pedagogy might have been old-fashioned, but he meant well. Solfeggio, the nightmare which confronts every conservatory-trained student! No matter whether you're a student of voice or, as I was, a pianist who can't carry a tune to save your life, you have to prove that you can read the music and assign to it the correct syllables of solmization (do, re, mi, etc.). For this exercise Bingger relied, in keeping with tradition, on the 1786 text *Solfèges d'Italie*; when it was Helle's turn he had her sight-sing a piece by Caffaro, a piece which happened to be in the key of G.

A love of analysis, an ability to subject a piece of music to the most elaborate and painstaking analytic procedures, characterizes the successful student of music theory. You have to like to count, to assign abstract symbols to equally abstract quantities, to know the circumstances under which one set of symbols takes precedence over another. In a large and sunny, brown-paneled room, where large squares of sunlight were draped like drop cloths over the four rows of wooden chairs in which nineteen other music theory students sat breathlessly hoping for disaster, Helle sight-sang the Caffaro and waited for Bingger's response. It wasn't what she expected. How, he asked, could this Ten Brix have stated in his application letter that he had already written an opera and a cycle of songs, yet not be able to complete an exercise even his five-year-old niece could manage, and she, God help her, as musical as a donkey? Or words to that effect. What Helle had failed to take into account was that in traditional solfeggio, whatever the tonic, it is sung as "do." Instead of singing "so" for G, Helle should have sung "do." A simple enough mistake, you might say; certainly no cause for despair. But the damage had been done. Students tend to regard any sign of grandiosity in their peers as license to ridicule. Thus Helle Ten Brix became Henning the Hayseed, a farm boy from the north with the hubris to claim mastery at composition.

There was never any doubt in Helle's mind that her early training had been inadequate. Old Clara hadn't known the first thing about theory; and Ida, who did, had remained mute on the subject. Indeed, it was as if teaching her daughter what she needed to know would have required a greater effort than Ida was interested in expending on anyone besides herself. When you're raised by essentially selfish parents, you learn to turn loneliness into a virtue, just as when you're set adrift from your peers, you learn to cultivate the mystique of solitary genius. To enhance the effect, Helle took to dressing like a sailor, using Dancer for her model: a trim cap, its narrow

visor set at an angle over the right eye; a sweater of dark
wool; a red-and-white-striped scarf, both ends free to fly in
the breeze; black woolen leggings tucked into knee-high boots.
While the other students tended to gather after hours at one
of several respectable cafés in the center of town, Helle
frequented bars near the docks, places where the front doors
never remained closed long enough to keep out the smell of
pitch and fish, where cold winds blew in off the Øresund, and
where, on any given night, you might find yourself sitting at
a table with an Indonesian sailor who picked his teeth with a
knife and tried to sell you opium.

In those days, the soul of the Danish seaman had not yet
become an object of missionary zeal. As in any population
which derives its character from contention with an unreason-
ing force of nature, the souls of the men with whom Helle
spent her time were rampant and heathen, making it an easy
task for the Lutherans, when they finally moved in, to supplant
one set of superstitions with another. The method of discourse
in both cases was anecdotal: the sailors spun yarns; the mis-
sionaries read stories from the Bible. The lesson, ultimately,
was the same. A sailor lost his hand and, with it, his gold
signet ring to a shark. Years later he saw that very ring on
the hand of another sailor, who claimed to have found it
lodged in the baleen of a right whale killed off the Newfoundland coast. The two sailors fought for ownership of the ring,
and in the course of the fight the second sailor stabbed the
first through the heart. Afterwards, whenever that second
sailor shipped out, the voyage was marked by ill luck and bad
weather. Eventually his shipmates cast him off onto an island,
where he perished. The morality here was primitive, and hence
suitable, as Bingger would've quickly pointed out, to opera:
what triumphed was an inscrutable natural order. Among

sailors, the Lutherans always won more souls with stories in which Jehovah figured prominently than with bewildering parables from the New Testament.

Under cover of darkness, in those noisy, smoke-filled bars, Helle's metamorphosis into Henning was so complete that, by the time she finally entered her room and inserted her body between the salty, damp sheets, she felt as if all that was left of Helle was a single black thread of disintegrative matter, not unlike the vein you have to remove from a shrimp before you can eat it. Oh, what was left of Helle may have been vibrant with potential, but it obviously required nothing less than the broad hand of inspiration, or, failing that, the small hand of another human being, to stroke the genius in it to life! Sometimes she cried herself to sleep. Some nights she couldn't sleep at all, lying there listening to the whistling noise Oluf Froulund's breath made as it caught on the hairs in his nose holes next door. Daisy's clocks would strike the hours, but because she forgot to synchronize their action it seemed like nothing so definite as three o'clock, for instance, actually existed. Sometimes Helle could hear the loud rattling sound of Dancer or Kayo urinating into a chamber pot. She would get up and light a candle; she would try to work.

By now Helle no longer relied on a piano to compose her music. Even before she'd left Krageslund, on those long, dreamy afternoons under the beech trees, she'd discovered she could hear the sounds that emerged from the note-clogged field of her mind, at first like seepage, and then in a torrent, more clearly without one. A piano had a way of imposing its own set of tonal relationships, its own peculiarly black-and-white personality, on whatever came out of it; to have relied on a piano would have made impossible the composition of *Den onde Stedmoder* or *Sange til Inger*. During the days, when she was parading her alienation up and down the conservatory's dark brown hallways, her mind stuck in reflection on Fux's *Gradus ad Parnassum*, that loneliness remained a pose. Only late at night, in her closet bedroom, did it become a reality. A full orchestra worked itself into a frenzy, the strings soughing melodramatically, duplicating in their continuous ascents and descents of minor scales the tidal action of the sea, a little tame finger of which pointed past her window toward the heart of the city. Moonlight on the swells: a harp executing rapid glissandos in the higher octaves; kettledrums, *coperti*, their heads swathed in cloth like mummies. Helle took this down as if it were actual music, when it was nothing more than the sound of her own desperation, just one more late-night sound in Daisy's house.

When she finally got up the nerve to show her notation to Bingger, he dismissed it as *keck*, meaning audacious. Henning should limit himself to simple exercises; maybe in a month or so he'd be ready to experiment with that form of counterpoint found in the fugue. The universe could be contained in a single drop of water, so why try to describe an entire ocean? Helle could tell, however, that Bingger had decided to accord her the respect he saved for only his most serious students. He gave her a key to a private practice room, which she reached by climbing six sets of stairs, each set narrower and darker than the one before it, a room about the same size as the one at Daisy's. Similarly, the practice room had one small window and the same unpainted, grayish plaster walls. Instead of a bed, however, Helle's room at the conservatory was equipped with an upright piano, and when she stood at the window she could see a family of storks nesting on a nearby slate rooftop, instead of a forest of masts rising from the harbor. Also, she could lock the door. "*Dux et comes*," Bingger would yell at her, whenever he saw her headed for the stair-case, notebook in hand—leader and follower. Of course what he was encouraging Helle to remember was not only the tonal relationship between the parts of a fugue but the rules governing their relationship as well.

II

B UT ISN'T THIS always the problem: you never really
know, do you, who or what has the upper hand. And
even when you think you've managed to slip free of
the world's persistent grip, choosing instead to make worlds
of your own, the next thing you know the very creatures
you've given life to are standing up on their own hind legs,
waving their little fists in your face. God had this problem,
Helle said, which was why he no longer existed. The hierarchy
at the conservatory might seem clear enough, but that clarity
was an illusion. Better instead to take a ship for your model.
At least on board a ship the situation tended to change
according to circumstance. You'd begin by granting the captain absolute power, but the minute the weather threw you off
course and the food threatened to run out, it was the cook's
favor you had to court. Displays of friendship among the crew
would be limited to telling stories, rolling dice, endless games
of snip-snap-snorem. Hadn't sailors been known to kill for a
single cupful of wormy beans, boiled down to a glutinous
pottage?

This mood of watchful ambivalence, of sly caution, seems
to have been especially strong in Helle during what Kerman
refers to as her "Copenhagen period"—when she chose an

opium clipper as the setting for her first fully realized opera, when she came up with one of her greatest inventions: the singing figurehead, Lahloo. Supposedly mentioned in an eighteenth-century manuscript—which Helle claimed had caught her eye because it provided yet one more example of the essentially intractable nature of all artifacts, and which I was never able to locate, due no doubt to the fact that it was pure fabrication—this figurehead had been commissioned by Captain Harry Tuck, and was intended to represent his dead fiancée, the Lady Isabel, who turned out to be more animate and seductive in effigy than she'd ever been in life. Her delicate, lobeless ears were folded close to her head, just as an animal folds in its ears before it snarls or bites. Similarly, the grain of the wood wouldn't permit her hair to remain bound, so instead it fell in great swooping waves from her frighteningly high temples, back and down around her naked shoulders. The dress just wouldn't stay in place, and Harry was enchanted. The woman of his dreams! For, when you got right down to it, had he ever really loved the essentially boring Isabel?

At first the figurehead was nothing more than a single high note during the Act One finale of *Don Giovanni*—the very note which Helle told me about on the afternoon of Ruby and Flo's ninth birthday party. She originally heard it one night in the winter of 1915, as she was walking home from the Royal Theater, where she'd attended a production of that opera memorable not only for the presence in it of Feodor Chaliapin, who was on a police blacklist in his native Russia, but also because the role of Zerlina was sung by the as yet unheard-of Maeve Merrow. In the Royal Theater's production the scream was left unvoiced. The onstage orchestra, having abandoned the sweet melodic line of the minuet, began its rapid ascent in a series of inversions on the G-major triad, as the Don attempted to complete his seduction. Helle could hear it coming, that high sound of pure outrage, and then the key shifted ominously; the expected note was replaced by an A-flat—"*Gente, aiuto, aiuto, gente!*" All hell broke loose; lightning flashed; Zerlina escaped into the less exciting arms of her new husband, Masetto.

Oh, she was charming, Maeve Merrow, as antic and bright-eyed as anyone could hope for in a soubrette, although her voice was already too unbridled and histrionic, more that of the dramatic soprano she was to become. And though the Don's final descent into hell was handled with customary bravado by Chaliapin, Helle remained unmoved. She didn't realize it at the time, but she was instead getting ready to hear the first chord of *The Harrowing of Lahloo*.

How happy Helle was! All around her men and women were assuming their winter coats of dark fur and light fur; the lobby was filled with the combined smells of camphor and rosewater and tobacco and then, suddenly, someone opened the huge front doors and those limited human smells were vanquished by the smell of snow. For it had been snowing the whole time they'd been inside the theater: another drama had been preparing itself behind their backs, and this time they had no choice but to participate, to wander out into that blue theatrical light where every small gesture—a jeweled wrist lifted in farewell, a pocket watch consulted, a swift embrace, even a sneeze—was suggestive, operatic. Cabs arrived and departed, and in their headlamps each falling snowflake revealed its capacity to contain all the colors of the spectrum, to dazzle briefly before it hit the ground. A man drew a piece of paper from his pocket, looked at it, and sighed; a woman flung a snowball at her escort's head. Was this comedy or tragedy? Mozart understood the difficulty of making such distinctions, which is why the critics continue to disagree in their interpretation of the Don's damnation.

Helle was at once happy and edgy. If she were to go home, Daisy would be sitting in the parlor with her latest suitor, and she'd be forced to play the piano, to drink a cup of Dutch cocoa, to listen to more talk about Admiral Jellicoe's courage in the face of Admiral Scheer's audacity (despite the fact that history tells us the former had the appearance of a "frightened tapir"), as, all the while, a pair of porcelain spaniels regarded her with sorrowful approbation. Most of the theatergoers had disappeared by now, into cabs or one of the brightly lit cafés that ringed Kongens Nytorv. The air was mild and soft, as it sometimes is after a heavy, rapid snowfall, and she could understand the impulse said to overtake arctic explorers, to curl up in a snowdrift, your final dream lodged forever within the frozen folds of the brain. Eventually a door on the west wall of the theater swung open and out came Chaliapin, his huge body encased in an ankle-length coat of caracul; behind him was the smaller figure of Maeve Merrow, her auburn hair briefly visible before she drew up the hood of her black velvet cloak. "*Là ci darem la mano*," sang Chaliapin, but when Maeve Merrow pulled back, laughing, Helle could see the expression on her face in the snow-flecked cone of yellow light cast by a gas lamp, and it was anything but flirtatious. Later she heard from Dancer that the two of them had shown up well after midnight at one of the taverns near the docks, and that while Chaliapin had proceeded to consume a bottle of akvavit, the young woman had snuck away in the company of a sailor from the Argentine.

Helle began to walk north on the Gothersgade, more or less in the direction of the Round Tower. On all sides she was surrounded by the subtly altered shapes of trees and statues and hedges and ironwork fences; because she hadn't watched the snow as it fell, it seemed that these alterations were the result of a widespread internal disturbance, as if each object in the city had at last chosen to extrude the white, thick element of its inherent composition. When she got to the Krystalgade, she turned west. She could barely recognize the two bronze cherubim who customarily sat on their dark pedestal in front of St. Petri's Church. Here and there, on the crowns of their heads or on the crests of their wings, the familiar greenish metal showed through. Otherwise, the features by which she'd come to know them—the one with a slim cocked knee and an expression of friendly cunning, the other with the hedonist's plump belly and an expression of awakening appetite—had vanished. And then, turning the corner toward Vestergade, she bumped up against the trunk of a small elder tree, jarring loose the lintel of snow that rested across its clipped upper branches.

The snow fell through the strange blue air in a shower of glittering star-shaped flakes. Helle blinked, and for a moment the whole world sprang into unnatural focus; as it did, she felt a finger idly running along the keys of her spine and she saw a wooden mouth in the bark of the elder tree crack open, releasing a single note. This didn't surprise her. After all, hadn't it been at the foot of an elder tree where the student Anselmus first heard the voices of his three little green snakes? And hadn't it been with tisanes made from elder flowers that Ida used to coax her to sleep? So what if Inger insisted that babies laid in cradles made of elderwood would be pinched black and blue by demons? The elder tree's mouth closed, but the note hung in the air for an instant, and then a column of notes arranged themselves under it, creating a chord consisting of six fourths: the mystic chord invented by Scriabin, that old anchorite who was said to have repudiated the pleasures of the flesh only to die from a pimple. As much as Helle hated to admit it, she realized that Hr. Bingger was right. Trying to compose a piece of music that would somehow duplicate the vastness and complexity of the sea was a mistake. For while the sea was not without form, its form was too large to comprehend, which accounted for the pervasive and obstructive sentimentality of all of her attempts. You found yourself wondering whether the sea regretted its tendency to reduce all living things to flotsam, whether the terrible, heartless sea wasn't capable, finally, of compassion.

IT WOULD TAKE Helle five years to complete *The Harrowing of Lahloo*. She was forced to work on it at night— not unlike her method for *The Girl Who Trod on a Loaf*— because she couldn't risk working during the day without alerting Bingger's suspicions. During the day, she was perceived to be an obedient drudge, drawing forth from her piano endless permutations of counterpoint. Kerman distinguishes between the architectural form of the fugue and the dramatic form of the sonata; he claims it's the latter which informs Mozart's inspired use of ensemble singing in such operas as *Don Giovanni* or *Le nozze di Figaro*. "I knew those scores by heart," Helle told me, "every grace note, every rest, every anacrusis. And I knew that everything I needed to know was right there in the music." Mozart's music, she said, contained all the information necessary to understanding how Donna Elvira's actions are erotically motivated, and how the tendency to put one's faith in Eros can be confused with a capacity to forgive. At the beginning of the second act, when Donna

Elvira allows herself to be seduced by Leporello masquerading as the Don, it's not because she can't tell the difference between the Don and his cloak, but that she can't distinguish between her own nobility of character and her lust; and this is disclosed not in what she says but in the great music of the ensuing trio.

So Helle realized that the music she needed to create for her decadent sea captain and her singing figurehead—the eponymous Harrow and Lahloo, respectively—had to be similarly complex, or the opera would be nothing more than an extended exercise in counterpoint, something like the boring fugue in A minor which she was engaged, by day, in composing. You had to believe in God to compose such music, which asserted the existence of a basic pattern in the universe. By night—oh, that was different! By night Helle entertained the devil.

In her practice room the only actual, living company she had was a rat. First the black dot of the rat's nose would appear, sticking out of a hole in the baseboard. The stiffly whiskered nose would twitch from left to right on the seemingly boneless hinge of the muzzle; then the whole head would emerge. The eyes were small and pinkish, not without intelligence. You can train a rat, as Helle discovered, to take a piece of cheese right out of your hand. You can tame any basically opportunistic creature, so long as you maintain some advantage, so long as you yourself cannot be seen as food. This was Daisy's strategy with the suitors. And in the opening trio of *The Harrowing of Lahloo*, it was the strategy which defined Captain Harry Tuck's relationship to his body servant, a young Chinese boy whom he nicknamed Rattail because of the long, black queue which grew out of the back of the boy's otherwise bald head; it was also the strategy which defined, in that opening trio, Lahloo's relationship to Harry.

Helle's plan was that in production the stage itself would be built out to suggest the prow of a ship sailing directly toward the audience, and that, for the duration of the opera, the body of the soprano singing the part of Lahloo would be strapped to that structure, duplicating the placement of a figurehead. Singing from such a position would be difficult, but Helle figured that if the angle of the prow was sufficiently oblique, the singer's diaphragm would remain unobstructed. A diva desires, above all, the undivided attention of her audience. She desires prominence. Thus, even before the curtain was to come up at the start of the first act, even while the orchestra was busy exploring the several keys implicit in the mystic chord, with which the overture begins, Lahloo would be visible. Indeed, she would be audible as well, since Helle decided to include her voice as part of the overture, an endlessly repeating series of melismatic, or wordless, triads, in each case taking for the tonic one of the six notes of the opening chord. The effect of this was eerie, liquid, restless; each time you thought that you understood the size and shape of your surroundings, a small hole opened and you found yourself swimming through it.

A bog, like an opera, is a self-contained environment. A bog is not, contrary to popular opinion, similar to a great sponge, drawing in quantities of water which it then lets seep out into the landscape around it during periods of dryness or drought. There is nothing generous about a bog, nothing receptive; the mosses which grow in bogs reproduce grudgingly, sometimes not putting forth so much as a single spore in hundreds of years. Only the surface mat is alive, and underneath the living heads of the plants you will find a tangle of dead, translucent matter. In the same way an opera constitutes a world sufficient unto itself. Generally, all of the component parts of that world have been assembled within the first act. New characters might appear later, new plot twists, but the fundamental laws, by which you will understand the opera's outcome, never change. You are not left wondering at the end what will happen next. Nothing will happen next. The dead are thus accorded a form of immortality, the immortality of stasis. The Don may tumble into the fires of hell, but his spirit persists. "Ahhh!" he howls, and this time, we know, the consummate escape artist will discover no new walls to jump over, no new doors to slip through. All that he has succeeded in eluding is the watchful eye of the audience. If you want something to last forever, throw it into a bog, put it into an opera.

Conversely, if you want something to assert its capacity for change—if you want to remind something of its mortality—put it out to sea. Life on a ship, particularly on an opium clipper sailing the coast of China, was, Helle knew, subject to daily reversal, beginning with the weather. A pale, cloudless sky, an absence of wind, and you found yourself caught in the doldrums. The surface of the sea would be perfectly smooth, stretched taut over the encircling rim of the horizon; powerless to move, you would become easy prey for the pirates in their lorchas. Or the barometer might suddenly drop, the wind begin screaming, and before you could shorten the sails they might blow apart into hundreds of small pieces, which, only minutes later, would fly through the air above Swatow, or Hainan, where they'd be taken for a flight of birds. If a typhoon didn't threaten to capsize your ship, then a war junk might. The importation of opium into China had been decreed

illegal, as the mandarins understood all too well the dangerous
influence of the drug. Thus you usually delivered your cargo
under cover of night; but still, if the moon was up, you might
see anything: a man with a foot-long fingernail testing the
quality of a dark cake of Patna opium, or a man with no
fingers at all lifting a fallen globe of yellowish Benares with
his toes. A chest might break open, releasing a spill of silver
Mexican dollars. This was the accepted method of payment,
but sometimes the exchange was more exotic: golden and
impassive figures of deities would change hands; a bolt of
silk would suddenly unreel and fall shimmering into the sea.
Meanwhile, if you paid close attention, you could hear the
constant lapping of small waves against your ship.

It was that sound, so brainless and persistent, which Helle
was trying to capture in the overture. At first she thought it
might be achieved through the strings' simultaneous use of
two different bowing techniques: *ondulé*, an obsolete form of
tremolo, in which several notes are taken in the same bow;
and *spiccato*, in which the bow is caused to bounce slightly
from the string. But in either case the results were too jumpy,
too fragmented. The sea didn't waste its time with simple
rearrangement of your existing parts. The sea took from
you—sometimes pieces, sometimes everything. Which was
why, Dancer once explained to Helle, sailors on long voyages
carved into walrus tusks geometric patterns, flowers and trees,
ships under full sail. Carving scrimshaw, Dancer said, had
nothing to do with boredom; what the act really implied was
ownership.

My guess is that this conversation occurred not long after
Helle's mysterious experience at the foot of the elder tree. In
any event it was still the winter of 1915, around three in the
morning (*ulvetimen* again), when Dancer stumbled into the

dark parlor, where he found Helle sitting alone in the dark on Daisy's favorite sofa. "Misery loves company," he said, pulling off his boots and collapsing backwards onto the green brocade cushions, as they'd all been instructed not to. He was in a bad mood, and shook his head fiercely when Helle asked him what the problem was, squinting shut his eyelids edged with pale golden lashes. He didn't want to talk about the bitch, he said. He'd rather talk about something else. Henning, for example. What the hell was Henning doing up so late?

Even though he kept his eyes closed, Helle could tell Dancer was listening carefully to every word she said. Meanwhile, as she proceeded to describe her failed attempts at composition, she found herself memorizing the way he held his head back and to one side, disdainful and slightly suspicious, even in repose. Harry Tuck, she thought. Those curls like the sprung workings of a pocket watch! That primitive slit of a mouth! The more Dancer became an object of her imagination, the less capable he seemed of independent action, so Helle was startled when he actually began to speak. He began by making the previously mentioned point about scrimshaw and ownership, after which he held his arm out in front of Helle's face, revealing first a blue-black plume of dragon's breath on the palm of his hand, then pulling back his sweater sleeve little by little to reveal the dragon's wide-open green jaws and bulging red eyes on his wrist, the red wings tautly spread on umbrellalike spokes across his forearm, the thick green length of tail disappearing under his now-bunched sleeve. Didn't anybody realize, he asked, that this was why he'd turned his own body into an artifact? He didn't want any bitch getting ideas, least of all Aegir's wife, Ran, who with her nine daughters (She Who Glitters; the Translucent One Who Mirrors the Heavens; She Who Pitches or Dips; She

Whose Hair Is Red in the Evening Sun; She Who Is Coal Black; the Bloody-Haired One; etc.) had jurisdiction over the lives of seafaring men such as himself. What Helle needed, he said, was a tattoo. Of course he didn't call her "Helle," although when he finally opened his eyes it was obvious to her that Dancer knew he was looking at a woman. On the breast, he said, smiling. Maybe on the ass.

The same old story, Helle complained. No matter how hard you tried to keep your sexuality hidden, you were always susceptible to exposure and, consequently, punishment or ridicule. The early Christian saints, the ones who devoted their lives to chastity, found this out the hard way. There was St. Paul the Hermit, who so annoyed the Emperor Decius with his claims of asceticism that the emperor caused him to be tied down while a harlot caressed his naked body. When the saint felt his penis stiffening, he is said to have bit off his own tongue, having no other weapon at his disposal, and spit it at the harlot's face. Generally, Helle pointed out, these stories were about men. Rather than be tempted themselves by the pleasures of the flesh, women were supposed to play the temptress. Or the Virgin: in the case of Pope Leo, who cut off his hand after a female supplicant kissed him there and consequently aroused him, it was the Virgin who caused a new hand to grow in its place. No one would dream of trying to tempt the Virgin. What would you use? Certainly not the caresses of a harlot. If you want to get the better of the Virgin, you have to marry her; you have to assert the male forces of reason over the female tyranny of chaos.

Which, according to Helle, was why our culture would permit a man to change himself into a woman and not the other way around. This had nothing to do with physiology, although the fact that it's easier to take something away from a body than to add something to it undoubtedly simplified the task. Whatever you started out as, Helle claimed, determined your essential nature. Men didn't want to have to entertain the possibility of spending the night in a hunting cabin with someone who was, in the deepest reaches of his soul, a woman. Whereas a woman who had at one time been a man—at least you might be able to reason with her. The worst abuse Odin could heap upon Loki was to remind him that in the dawn of time he'd lived eight winters underground as a milkmaid.

But Helle wasn't thinking of Loki, or of the Virgin, or of twice-blessed Pope Leo on that dark winter night in Daisy's parlor when she found herself being kissed by Dancer. His mouth was surprisingly soft; his touch, where his hands cupped her shoulders, surprisingly gentle. He kissed her once and then fell back again into his corner of the sofa, regarding her with wary admiration. It made sense, he said, her disguise. If he were a woman, he'd probably have done the same thing. But Helle was crazy to think she could get away with it; her skin was too smooth, for one thing. The fire was dying down, and the stove's tile walls ticked as they contracted. The walls of the stove ticked; Daisy's clocks ticked; the room was getting smaller, colder, inching toward morning. When Helle told him that his own skin was smooth, he frowned. He knew a girl on Kunø, he said, a little girl, slim like her, and smart. In school this girl always finished her work before everyone else. When she grew up, she told them, she was going to be famous; she'd discover the cure for typhoid, diphtheria, or maybe she'd be a trapeze artist. Everyone used to laugh at her. Dancer reached over to the three-tiered end table, picked up a pair of embroidery scissors made to resemble a stork, and began to snip at the air. "A tattoo will help," he said, "but it won't be enough."

Dancer. If I shift my own position slightly I can almost feel it, that thin layer of heat surrounding his body. Oh, he was an attractive man, of that I have no doubt. And like so many attractive men, he seems to have created a vague molecular disturbance in the air around him, whereas these days I seem to be encased in a suit of bark, to be capable of disturbing nothing. Do I want him to kiss Helle again? Do I want him to kiss me? Certainly a human body is never sufficient unto itself. These days my own tongue sits in my mouth, good for nothing but forming words or opinions about the taste of food. What did Helle feel during the brief moment when Dancer's tongue made its way into her mouth? She claimed to have been interested in the sensation of an alien tongue touching her molars, but maybe she was just embarrassed to admit that she'd found the experience even remotely pleasant. "I'm going to be famous," she told Dancer, imagining how, if you were a figurehead, the salty spray of the waves would wash continually over your face, altering your composition. Helle leaned forward so that her head rested against Dancer's shoulder; she wondered whether under the wool of his sweater the huge barbed tip of the dragon's tail dangled over into the basin of his clavicle.

Over, against, under, into: the mystery was so frequently prepositional. Dancer pulled off her cap and began to remove the hairpins, one at a time, tossing them down onto the hooked rug at their feet. "Who would have guessed," he said, running his fingers through her hair, carefully working out the tangles. He seemed to be surprised at how much of it there was; Helle could feel his fingertips against her scalp, stroking, stroking. She held her breath. Only as it happened Dancer wasn't interested in seduction. He told Helle that the girl on Kunø had died giving birth to her third child, and that as far as he was concerned she was better off dead. Then he lifted a single long lock of hair and, with the stork's beak, sliced it off, almost at the roots. What has four arms, four legs, two heads, and no brains? he asked. Hold still, he said. And so Helle did, sitting absolutely still as Dancer proceeded to cut away the rest of her hair; he cut it very short, like a convict's. Once he was finished, he threw down the scissors—moonlight shone in the metal—and within its nest of hair the stork's beak was wide open. The next day they went to the tattooist.

III

I F A STORY has a beginning and a middle and an end, at what point do we say, Here, right here—this was the beginning of the end? And do we intend this to sound ominous, as of course it does, or merely to state a fact? If I were to say that the precise moment when Helle Ten Brix got the eye tattooed on her neck was the beginning of the end, it seems to me that *this* might be taken for a statement of fact; whereas to say that the moment when she claimed to have watched me with that eye—to have stared impossibly through the taut layer of paper-white skin molecules covering the nape of her neck, through the layer of silver-black moon-glow molecules simmering above my yard, through the leafless apple-tree molecules, the unclean-picture-window molecules, the furnace-heat molecules, the millions of dust molecules, and into my dark living room, where Sam and I stood kissing each other—would be more ominous. But whose end? Mine? Helle's? Sam's? The end of everything?

Sam said he had to run inside for a minute to get William's baseball cap. Or at least that's what Helle told me. William and the twins were dragging Lily on an improvised rope leash up and down the road in front of the house; I was frozen like the statue of poor vain Inger, halfway between the sofa and the door. "Frannie?" Sam said. "I didn't . . ." As long as the door remained open, what I saw was a black man-shaped hole in a bluish, moonlit rectangle, a hole into which I was careful not to fall as I made my way past it to shut the door. For he seemed to have forgotten that in the north, in the autumn, the nights are cold, and that a woman who works as a waitress in a diner can't afford to let so much as the smallest whiff of precious heated air escape her house. Once I'd closed the door, however, he was forced to turn around to face me, so that now the round lenses of his glasses, their pinkish plastic frames, caught the moonlight coming in through the picture window, making it look as if he had enormous pink-rimmed, opaque eyes; his large teeth, likewise catching the moonlight when he opened his mouth again to speak, gleamed disturbingly. "Is that a new dress?" he asked, and when I didn't answer he stuck out a hand, which landed on the dress's flowered shoulder, causing me to jump. I didn't have any idea, did I, he said, how happy I made him. But he didn't look happy; he looked severe and judgmental. "What are you doing here?" I finally asked. Helle and William were waiting outside. "Hey, Frannie," he said. "Hey."

I don't intend to describe the kiss. You might say I've already done so, having given it to Helle and Dancer, although their kiss was chaste and tentative by comparison, and although my own ambivalence certainly wasn't due to any basic hostility toward men. The truth is, my feelings for Sam were breath-stoppingly, heart-achingly strong, even if chiefly physical, at least during the early stages of our affair. He would come into the diner and I would see his wrist as it lifted the ginger ale glass to his lips—the light brown hairs and the scattering of freckles on the upper, invulnerable side of his wrist; the forking blue vein and the bracelet of creases on its soft underside—and I would have to hold onto the back of the booth to catch my breath. The bubbles would rise to the top of his glass in long, segmented chains, then burst invisibly under his nose, and he'd sneeze. When we were making love he would sometimes stop and reach out blindly for his glasses, which he always removed beforehand; he'd put them on and stare intently for several seconds off to the left or the right of me at whatever happened to be there—a framed reproduction of Monet's waterlilies on a motel room wall; a fly walking across the dusty dashboard of his car; a styrofoam coffee cup blowing across a field of flattened, brown grass toward a far-off set of goalposts—and then he'd look back at me, partly relieved, partly resigned. Only much later, when we were lying next to each other in those separate humming spheres that our bodies become after sex, would he say that he loved me. His voice was funny, not unlike an adolescent boy's, cracking at the ends of his sentences. The smell of his skin was faintly peppery. One of his knee joints clicked when he bent it.

Meanwhile, Helle's conduct in my presence underwent a subtle change. Nothing so obvious as the face jerked away as if slapped, the sarcastic remark—expressions of wounded dignity you might expect from a disappointed suitor. Mainly she seemed to be keeping a close eye on me (irony fully intended). Several weeks elapsed in this fashion: Helle regarding me sharply with her dark gray eyes as I tried to get out of the wind in the glass-paneled drugstore entry to light my cigarette, bending over and cupping my hand around the match, poised between a gigantic cobalt-blue apothecary jar filled with vitamin pills and a naked beige dummy wearing a truss; Helle sneaking quick glances at me as I stood on the railroad bridge, paging through the Peterson's *Guide* she'd handed me so I could have the pleasure of identifying for

myself the black-masked bird we'd both just witnessed impaling a lizard; Helle studying me through her binoculars as I
walked away from her up my driveway. Otherwise she kept
up her end of any conversation, sounding for the most part
like her usual cheerful and imperious self.

It wasn't until the day before Thanksgiving that I found
out what was bothering her. Kosta had let me leave work early,
and as we were walking past the quarries—Helle now fixing
me with a cool and speculative stare, going on and on about
how men just had to keep tunneling around under the world's
surface, didn't they, taking good things out, putting bad things
in—I was trying to figure out what I'd make for tomorrow's
dinner. I was also troubled by the fact that my mother's annual
letter had been surprisingly short this year, uncharacteristically disjointed and emotional, as if there might be some genuine problem at home. None of the expected references to
"your father," for example. Was he dead? It was like my
mother, I thought, to suppress such a piece of information,
and then hold it against me that I never went to the funeral.

A gray day, the clouds mixed together, moving rapidly in
one gray seething mass, and across the quarry's unnaturally
yellow-green water the whole gray sky appeared to be sailing
past the outstretched fingerbones of five birch trees, as if the
world's rotation were suddenly made visible. In a similar
quarry, I told Helle, not far from where I grew up, a girl with
whom I went to Sunday school drowned. A mean girl named
Bettina Archer, who cut tiny breasts and penises from felt
and then stuck them to the felt-board Bible figures, blaming
me. An immoral person generally suffers for *his* immoral
behavior, Helle pointed out, taking her binoculars from the
pocket of her army surplus parka and squinting through them
at a top-heavy bird roosting in one of the birches. A kingfisher,

she said—want to look? It was windy and cold; from the narrow strip of dead grass growing around the base of the dented guardrail the wind jarred loose a stinging cloud of grit and sand left behind by last winter's road crews. No! I said, to which Helle replied that there was no need to get angry; it wasn't as if kingfishers weren't a dime a dozen.

Although she was obviously being perverse, for soon enough it became perfectly clear that she knew what I was talking about. "Do you need an example, Frances?" she asked. "Suppose there's a man who thinks he's getting away with something. Maybe he's married to a placid, unimaginative woman, to a woman who's so interested in living her own peaceful life that she never notices what's going on around her. 'Judgment is mine, sayeth the Lord,' except you know as well as I do that even if there is a God, after the lesson of the flood fell on deaf ears He more or less gave up on the idea that men could learn anything from a deity. So this man thinks he's safe, thinks he isn't being watched, but what he doesn't realize is that the minute God turned His back on us, something else took over. Something that had been there all along, biding its time. You can see a kingfisher any day of the week. A dime a dozen, as I said. But this, I promise you, *this* is worth looking at."

Then—as we stood there in the dead grass at the side of the road, cars whizzing by, grit and sand blowing into our faces, the wind wrinkling the quarry's yellow-green surface into a regular pattern of ridged whorls like a giant thumbprint—Helle turned her back to me, extending her elbows so she could cup the knob of dark hair at the nape of her neck in both hands, lifting it to reveal, for the first time, her tattoo. I remembered a beach hat my mother used to wear, a white sailor-type cap with grommets set into it, the two back ones of which I thought she was referring to when she warned me that she had eyes in the back of her head.

"Like it?" Helle asked, and when I didn't say anything she released the knob of hair and turned around again, her mouth set in a tight, fierce little smile. She was eighteen, she said. She'd had it done not long after her birthday, and though she'd had it now for almost half a century, very few people knew it was there: Dancer, of course, because he'd encouraged her to get it; Kayo's spookish sister Maja; probably Inger Fog, née Nissen; the traitor Maeve Merrow; now me. Oh, and the tattooist. Otherwise she kept it covered, either with her hair or with some kind of high collar, the occasional scarf. Hadn't I ever wondered why she always kept her neck covered? Granted, lots of old women tried to hide their poor old creased, pathetic necks, like tupelo trunks growing out of the dismal swamps of their bodies, but she, Helle, didn't need to do such a thing. For wasn't her neck as smooth and unlined as a young girl's?

She went on to explain how every morning as she brushed her hair it made her happy just to think of it, that single tattooed eye staring out from the nape of her smooth, unlined neck. At first glance you might mistake it for a Masonic symbol. Only the Masonic eye which regards us from the glowing, disconnected tip of a pyramid on the backside of the dollar bill is frank and direct in its gaze: an eye you'd expect to find in the face of a man who has a firm handshake, an outward-looking eye, reflective in the literal sense of a mirror, within which you confront your own image. A *male* eye. Whereas the eye on the nape of Helle's neck, she confided, was nothing less than an aperture into a world defined by an increasingly smaller series of apertures; it was a female eye, one that invited entry without offering any possibility of discovery.

The tattooist, whom she'd been instructed to call Mandrill, was an artist of the form. Helle never found out his real name, perhaps because, as Dancer had suggested, most men who lived their lives in close contact with the sea understood the protective power of artifice. All she knew was that Mandrill had chosen his name in honor of the monkeys that swung through the forests of his native Nigeria, illuminating with their bright faces and buttocks the shadowy green places into which the sun never penetrated—she knew this because Mandrill's face had been tattooed to emphasize the accuracy of the name. Thus a red band had been made to extend from Mandrill's chin to the bridge of his nose; a network of blue and purple lines radiated out across his cheeks; black ovals encircled his golden eyes; thousands of tiny yellow dots covered his perfectly bald skull, snaking down across his temples and around his ears to replicate a mane. Nor, as Mandrill suggested, patting the seat of his pants, did the resemblance end there. He was a tall, thin man who had to stoop in order not to bump his head against the rafters of his shop. Indeed, what the shop reminded Helle of more than anything else was the root cellar at Krageslund; it was located on a side street off the Nyhavn, below street level down a crumbling set of steps, at the bottom of which stood two trash cans filled with stained gauze, wads of surgical cotton, and ambiguous brown bottles. Even Dancer, who was relatively short, was forced to bend over as he went through the front door.

A little snow had been falling, on and off, but the flakes were too large to stick; as they entered the shop Helle could feel them melting on her lips, mixing there with the familiar dockside taste of brine. The winter of 1915 was unusually cold; the Limfjord froze solid, and there were rumors of wolves in Göteborg. In Horns, Inger had written, the snow was so deep that you couldn't see through the first-floor windows of the stores and houses; the children had created an intricate series of snow tunnels through which they traveled, silent and invisible, materializing suddenly where you least expected them. There had been an influenza epidemic; many people had died, including Torben Toksvig. But inside Mandrill's shop it was warm, even hot; like a hot black stone dropped into a pond, the stove in the center of the room sent forth ripples of overheated air, causing the needles lying out on an adjacent table to appear undulant, wavery, longer than they actually were.

The walls of the shop were covered with charts of sample designs, numbered and arranged according to category. There were the predictable nautical motifs (ships in full sail, anchors resting on their three points, fish, spears, flags, mermaids, constellations); the amorous (hearts, twined hands, naked women, embellished initials); and the religious (crosses, admonitory passages from Scripture, pietistic symbols, chalices, and lambs). There were primitive geometric configurations, repeating concentric circles, tiny checkerboards, relentless cross-hatchings, straight lines and wavy ones, diamonds and stars. An entire wall was devoted to trompe l'oeil designs, many of which were calculated to excite a sexual response and which were, according to Dancer, enjoying great popularity in the local bordellos. A whore could have her breasts tattooed to resemble sunflowers, petals radiating out from the nipples, the stems trailing languidly down the torso, disappearing into the grass of the pubic hair; she could wear a tattooed chemise of the finest Chantilly lace, with a tattooed hand disappearing up under the tattooed lace hem of her tattooed knickers.

A small man such as yourself, Mandrill told Helle, could get his whole body covered for the same price it would cost a big man to do a single arm. The tree of life, perhaps? Its roots extending along the toes, its branches spreading out across the shoulders, a snake twined around the torso, an apple in the palm of the right hand?

No, Helle said; she wanted something small enough to fit on the nape of her neck. Something she could display when she wanted to but that she herself wouldn't be able to see— a quality as apparently discrete from herself and yet hard to overlook as, for instance, Daisy's shoulderblades, those small wings she customarily kept folded in place beneath a white dimity blouse. "Ah," Mandrill said, his golden eyes narrowing. And did the young man realize that the nape of the neck was one of the most vulnerable parts of the human body? If you wanted to kill someone, all you had to do was stick a sharp object into that part of the neck where the tip of the spine meets the base of the skull, where the medulla oblongata nestles unprotected by bone. Hadn't everyone heard about the milliner who was said to have murdered her wealthiest customer with a hatpin? One small slip of the needle and you could end up paralyzed forever. This had never happened to Mandrill, but he knew of a young sailor from Liverpool who'd wanted the image of his sweetheart's lips to press an eternal kiss into the soft skin just below his hairline. Now that same sailor, no longer young, could be seen any day of the week sitting propped up in a chair outside the Norwegian Gate, selling worthless spectacles, their lenses made of window glass.

Some tattooists trace the design onto the skin, a practice

for which Mandrill had nothing but scorn: you might begin with an overarching concept, but for the specific details you had to rely on the skin's hidden messages. In this way the human soul could be given visible form. You had to coax the details out; you had to learn how to overlook the body's attempts at trickery. The people of the Punjab, Helle said, believed that at death the soul, the little man or woman inside the mortal frame, would go to heaven imprinted with the same patterns which adorned the body in life. Naturally such a process was painful. The design could be applied by a variety of methods: pricking, incising, burning, and, more rarely, incrustation, in which precious stones or pearls would be set into the skin, a method favored mainly by the very rich, such as Indian maharajahs. Mandrill recommended pricking, since incision was too painful, and since burning had connected to it the stigma of slavery—a burned-in design was, after all, nothing more than a brand. Generally he used needles, sometimes one at a time, sometimes several, stuck into the head of a cork.

The eye on Helle's neck, to all outward appearances, was an ordinary eye, an ellipse about two and a half inches long and an inch wide at the minor axis, the outer canthus narrowing into a point, the inner canthus a small, rounded extension separated from the eyeball by a delicate line to indicate the presence of the tear gland; long, outward-curving lashes thickly fringed the crescent-shaped upper lid, while the lower lashes were shorter, more finely distributed, and the lid itself slightly less pronounced. On closer inspection, however, you could see that instead of an iris Mandrill had drawn a woman's face, the same small, severe face over and over—Helle's face, in fact—viewed from slightly different angles, the faces subtly overlapping, indicative of motion or changing phase; and that the pupil, the point of intersection of all of those overlapping eyes, had been made to contain another, smaller eye. You could hardly make it out, Helle said, but if you held a magnifying glass up to that second eye you would see that its iris was in fact an oceanscape, where an impossibly tiny clipper ship sailed under an even more impossibly tiny moon. In the creation of any work of art, Mandrill explained, there was a moment when the senses no longer proved useful and faith took over, in this case that moment having occurred when he came to the place where those multiple eye sockets intersected, the very place where his needle could have slipped through the skin and killed her.

Which was why he'd left that place blank. He didn't know how it had happened, he confessed, but somewhere along the line he'd lost control of the tattoo. He and Helle were alone in the shop, celebrating the completion of the project with a bottle of Indonesian rum. Ten sessions in all, stretching out over almost three months. I couldn't begin to imagine how painful it had been, Helle said; excruciatingly painful—bloodstained bandages, infections, fevers, needles pricking through tender scar tissue. According to Mandrill, it was probably during the seventh session that he'd first realized the tattoo was staring at him, and that its stare wasn't the one he'd drawn. No, this was the stare of a completely unfamiliar intelligence—lay off the rum, Mandrill, he thought, get some sleep. During the eighth session the eye seemed to throw a quick glance in the direction of the door; during the ninth session it actually winked at him. How many fingers, how many fingers? he asked Helle, wildly holding his hand up behind her neck. Nothing like this had ever happened before, and he was frightened.

"I hadn't figured out how it worked yet," Helle said, flatly, "so I couldn't tell him." A sharp, cold rain was beginning to fall, threatening to turn at any minute to sleet or snow. With the exception of the quarry water, which remained an eerie yellow-green, and the headlights of the passing cars, most of which were now lit, everything in the world around us was a deep, spiritless shade of gray. "We should be getting back," I said, adding that it must be close to suppertime, and while Maren had been kind enough to agree to watch the twins for the afternoon, I didn't want to presume on her good nature. "I bet you don't," Helle replied. She raised the hood of her parka, shoved her hands down into its pockets, and started walking in the direction of town. "Go on," she said when she was several paces ahead of me. "Give it a try. You're dying to, I can tell. Besides, you might as well see what you're up against."

So she stood there, a small damp woman on the shoulder of a wet gray road suddenly filled with rush-hour traffic, waiting for me to demonstrate once more that she could get me to believe anything. "Forget it," I said. Maybe she was the kind of person who bought those stories in the *National Enquirer*—the cowboy in Utah who'd carved the Nativity scene, complete with angels and sheep and tiny coffers containing gold, frankincense, and myrrh, onto a poker chip; the grandmother in Maine who'd embroidered the entire text of the United States Constitution onto a shoelace—but I wasn't. The tattoo was a nice piece of work, and I'd admit that Mandrill must have been an unusually talented craftsman. I said as much, loudly, trying to get her to turn around, even though she'd once again started walking, quicker than ever, back toward town. "Haven't you ever wondered," she called brightly over her shoulder, "why he does that thing with his glasses?"

Eventually, hard little pellets, part snow and part ice, began to fall from a sky you could no longer see; Helle and I walked along in an uncompanionable silence, maintaining a distance between us of about one car length. Indeed, neither one of us said a single word until we were both standing together in the weak light cast by an overhead bulb on the Blackburns' front porch, protected from the wind and the sleet, if not from each other. "Who?" I asked. "Who does *what* thing?"

Helle laughed. "Can't you do any better than that, Frances?" And when I told her spies got shot, she laughed even harder. "Shot?" she said. "Well, that's not so bad. Do you know what they do to adulterers? Cut off their cocks."

IV

ALTHOUGH THE TRUTH IS, Helle's anger didn't have anything to do with an offended morality. What made her angry, at least in part, was the fact that I would permit Sam a form of intimacy she would never be allowed; that, to be blunt, I'd let him fuck me, whereas all Helle enjoyed was the occasional sisterly kiss on the cheek. Nor do I mean to imply that she was merely jealous. She might well have been, but ultimately both this and her morality would prove beside the point. Clearly some deeper sense of outrage was at the heart of Helle's anger, some sense of a primary flaw in the universe.

Just as it probably goes without saying that Maren's plight left her unmoved, that as far as Helle was concerned, all you needed to know about Maren could be summed up in her habit of putting on gloves before working in the garden, or her peculiar tendency to eat whatever was on her plate item by item—every single pea, for example, before moving on to the lamb chop, the boiled new potatoes, the mint jelly, as if in defiance of the digestive system's inevitable squalor. In short, a nature too tritely divided to be worth plumbing for its hidden depths. Life made Maren nervous, so she found boring ways to regulate it. Indeed, the only daring thing she ever did was to marry a man she'd known only for a month, whom she met one day when she went to put flowers on her grandmother's grave (which happened to be in the same Copenhagen cemetery as Søren Kierkegaard's). She'd already deposited the flowers, and was hurrying back to her grandfather's apartment in the nearby suburb of Nørrebro, when she encountered a bespectacled and serious-looking youth paging through a guidebook, straddling his rented bicycle in such a way as to block the path. Did she know, he asked, where Kierkegaard was buried? But because the Danish word for "cemetery" is *kirkegård*, and because Sam's pronunciation left a lot to be desired, Maren's response was to cock her head to one side, scowl, and inform him that he was *in* the cemetery, a response he found charming.

If Maren had any brains, Helle claimed, she would have realized that any man making a pilgrimage to Kierkegaard's grave should be avoided like the plague. What did Kierkegaard know about women? In the *Diary*, he actually suggests that the best thing a man might do for a woman after seducing her would be to emulate Neptune and turn her into a man. Oh, you might see signs of a latent ethic in Kierkegaard's youthful decision to break off his engagement with Regine Olsen, whereas all he was doing, really, was honoring a system that allows men to singlemindedly pursue their dreams. Throw in your lot with a man, Helle contended, and forget about dreaming your own dreams. Although, to be fair, if the only image your dreams offer up, over and over again, is that of happiness with a man, then what's the profit in resisting? Sam took Maren to hear American jazz in a bar near the university; as she sat listening to a black man play the trumpet, chills of Kierkegaardian dread ran up and down her spine. She shivered, and Sam put his arm around her, mistaking dread for passion. Later, after he'd walked her back to the apartment and she'd asked him in, he was surprised to find himself seated at a parlor table, playing chess with an old, bearded man. An erudite old Dane smoking a long, curved Meerschaum pipe, stuffing its head-shaped bowl full of tobacco; a slim, blond girl pouring a dark rain of imported beans into a huge iron coffee mill; a sweet-smelling summer breeze faintly disturbing the organdy curtains at the four tall front windows—it was all too much for Sam, who'd grown up in a blue-collar Connecticut town, and whose own grandfather had been given to telling jokes revolving around the twin themes of flatulence and excrement. Not unlike Mozart, Helle said, in his notorious letters to his cousin, except that Sam's grandfather never composed an opera. If I wanted to understand Sam—which she assumed I did, for otherwise there was no reason to have sex with him, was there?—then I should remember that his character had been shaped negatively, that he'd set out *not* to be whatever he'd found most humiliating about his family. That's what we have in common, I replied, and Helle snorted. Only he turned out to be a philosophy professor and you turned out to be a waitress, she said. Think about it, Frances.

Helle customarily carried with her a breast-pocket-sized white notepad in which she'd jot down whatever useful ideas came to her, "like fish swimming into a weir," in the course of an average day. But during the early stages of our acquaintance, I remember that she also carried with her a second notepad, this one bright red, with IDIOTIC THINGS SAID BY MEN written in black Magic Marker on its cover. Unfortunately that notepad never made its way into the waxed carton, although much of the material it contained shows up in *The Girl Who Trod on a Loaf*, specifically in the infamous Act One quartet, "A man says," sung by the Bog Queen and her three daughters. Plato's thoughts on gender and reproduction, for example, those passages Helle paraphrased for me the first time we had tea together, had first been consigned to the red notepad and later transposed into libretti, along with numerous quotations from the Bible ("There are three things that are never satisfied, yea, a fourth thing which says not, it is enough; that is, the mouth of the womb"; or "And I find more bitter than death the woman, whose heart is snares and nets, and her hands are as bands"); Dryden's "Women are not comprised in our Laws of friendship; they are *Ferae Naturae*"; Greene's "Uppon a banke, bordring by, grew women's weedes, Fenell I meane for flatterers, fit generally for that sexe"; an unnamed Chinaman's "The smaller the woman's foot, the more wondrous become the folds of the vagina"; Cicero's "When a woman thinks alone she thinks evil"; St. Bernard's "Their face is a hissing wind, and their voice the hissing of serpents"; Terence's "Women are intellectually like children" . . .

Possibly worst of all, though, was Havelock Ellis's claim that as far as music is concerned, "there is certainly no art in which women have shown themselves more helpless." Helpless indeed! What he really meant, according to Helle, was that if women were suddenly to begin spending their time dreaming whole worlds into existence—such effort as is required by the creation of a symphony or an opera—then no one would be left to make sure that men's floors got polished, no one left to make sure that the old skin and hairs which regularly sloughed off men's bodies got swept up and thrown away. If women were to begin composing operas, who would feed the living and cosset the dead?

You could be sure, Helle said, that in the Copenhagen cemetery where Sam and Maren met, it was a woman who'd been hired to keep the gravel walkways raked, keeping all the rake marks perfectly symmetrical; it was a woman who followed Sam and Maren around, erasing their footprints as they looked for the place where what was left of Kierkegaard's body was undergoing similar erasure under its closely mowed square of grass. Meanwhile, all around them, a confederacy of dark-clothed women would have been spreading out within the maze of boxwood cubicles, each busy at a separate task: one clipping away the green shoots which marred the otherwise level planes of the hedge surrounding her father's grave; another setting bulbs, evenly spaced, around a stone angel. From time to time a man might appear, usually advanced in years, pausing to remove his hat before remonstrating with his departed wife or mother. How could she go away and leave him all alone? Come back, you could hear him whisper. Indifferent, the sun would continue shining on the carefully weeded beds of lilies and forget-me-nots: noon, Helle said, was the perfect time to visit a Danish cemetery, for who would want such a felicitous arrangement to be disturbed by the presence of shadows? Although even as you tried to avoid seeing them, the shadows were leaking out all around you, their dark seepage visible at the root of each tree, each flame-red tulip, each polished stone. The women would set down their little bunches of posies, and it was Death they were honoring, shadowy Death, without whom there could be no order, without whom the story of your life would rattle on and on, as inconclusive and irritating as those stories told, late into the night, by drunks or pedants.

Oh, there's no doubt about the fact that in those days I took all of what Helle told me with a grain of salt. I had to, as I think I've implied, in order to assert my right to an autonomous existence, to hold her vision of the world and, by extension, of me, at bay. She was such an *extreme* woman; so dramatic, so perverse! Thus it seemed to me that if she knew about Sam's practice of putting his glasses back on during lovemaking, her knowledge must have had an empirical rather than supernatural basis: maybe he did the same thing with Maren; possibly he'd even told Helle about it himself. Certainly he'd been more than generous in providing her with details about his marriage—things he never shared with me, our agreement being that our lives when we weren't together were our own business. I was wary, and because of that I didn't pick up on any of the subtle hints Helle threw my way, such as her frequent references to mortality; her increasingly hostile remarks about men in general and Sam in particular; her strange fascination with the twins' trailer. Why, you might ask, was she so infuriated by the space program, by the idea that disembodied eyes were circling the planet, keeping watch, and that even after we blew ourselves to bits those eyes would continue their lonely circling, would continue keeping watch over the empty space where a planet once had been?

Then one snowy winter morning not long after Christmas, I was standing somewhere near the dimly lit heart of the ground floor of Shank & Bidwell's hardware store—an establishment apparently infinite in its proliferation of dark narrow aisles forking between dark tiers of shelves, dark yawning bins, dark stairways leading to mysterious upper rooms where there were rumored to be even darker aisles, more towering shelves and deeper bins and, in the very back corner, a metal ladder disappearing into a trapdoor in the ceiling. As I stood there rummaging through a box of elbow-shaped plumbing fixtures, I smelled a peppery smell, heard the click of a kneebone, looked to my left, and there was Sam. "Where the hell have you been?" he asked, only his tone was tender, and his features, although shadowy and hard to see, had the faintly thickened, faintly softened look that signifies desire. "The holidays," I said. "You know." He bent forward and kissed me, quickly, on my neck—a little nip, really, the kind of quick kiss exchanged in the act of lovemaking that arouses you immediately no matter where you are, because implicit in it is the suggestion you've already been aroused. Of course he knew this. "Frannie," he said. "Jesus." Shadowy, so shadowy we might have been alone in a dark, infinite forest—until Mr. Shank approached wearing his usual pale blue smock, freshly washed and ironed by Mr. Bidwell, with whom he lived in a little fairy-tale cottage at the foot of Rose Hill. "Frances, Sam, nice to see," said Mr. Shank, pointedly rearranging the elbow-shaped fixtures, as if their essential order in the box had been disturbed. He was a short round man with a very long flat face, and a long flat upper lip: a two-dimensional head stuck into the neckhole of a three-dimensional body. "Help you find or just?"

No thank you, I was about to reply, when Sam said, "The Coleman mantles. The last time I needed one, if I remember correctly, they were on the second floor, near the back wall."

Mr. Shank nodded and sighed. "Light them things and nothing but ash, no wonder, folks. Too fragile. Camping season they'd be but you're right, bottom shelf in a fishing creel, the ornamental rabbits. Show if you want." When Sam said that wouldn't be necessary, Mr. Shank looked relieved. "Doing inventory, Mr. Bidwell always loses count halfway through you name it."

There was no light at all in the stairway, no railing, and with the steps' risers of differing heights you couldn't even count on a sense of pattern to help you climb them. I managed the first five steps by keeping my eye on the word COUGARS embroidered in white script on Sam's back; at the sixth, my boot trod down on something that popped moistly beneath it, COUGARS dissolved into thin dark air, and I could hear Sam's feet shuffling cautiously around above my head, floor joists moaning, a sifting fall of what sounded like sand onto the step I'd left behind seconds earlier. "The goddamn light switch," Sam said. "It's okay, there's a window, once your eyes adjust." A dark hand reached down, tentative, the shadowy fingers waggling, one of them encircled by a shadowy golden band, and pulled me up. "Get a load of this," he said. "No wonder, folks," he said, and then, as I paused blinking at the head of the stairs, he walked away, vanishing behind a teetering mountain of bagged peat moss toward the back wall. "Ornamental rabbits," he said.

The second floor seemed larger than the first, the walls exposed and creosoted wood so that it smelled like a smokehouse, brown and dark and bacony; yet it was freezing cold, whereas the heat on the first, I understood by its absence, had been stifling. And while on the first floor the aisles were at least recognizable, on the second floor nothing even vaguely resembled a path, and even if it had you wouldn't have been able to see it, since the window to which Sam referred was small, coated with a thick layer of frost on the inside, and crisscrossed with fly-studded spiderwebs. I made my way past a set of shelves where a flock of feathered shuttlecocks had come to rest around the oblate feet of a row of coal scuttles. Maybe the order was alphabetical? Seven or eight aluminum storm windows leaned up against a huge crate filled with black galoshes. Here and there something winked at me from out of the gloom—a chrome-plated faucet, a glass hurricane lamp, a tangle of brass light pulls—but for the most part the second floor appeared to have become the repository for large, ambiguous pieces of machinery, dull dark objects with wheelworks, levers, immense oak handles, black bolts oozing oil, blades and teeth of pocked iron, dusty convex disks covering arcane instrument panels.

"Frannie—here," Sam called, and at last I found him, holding the creel and leaning back against a broad wooden countertop, every available inch of which was taken up with slightly larger-than-life-sized plastic rabbits, some white, some pale brown, all of them crouched as if getting ready to hop. "Give me a hand, will you," he asked, and I thought, You were wrong, Helle, *this* is what happens to adulterers. Adulterers have to make their bed among plastic rabbits in the frigid expanse of a dark brown smokehouse, while below them they hear the constant chirring of an adding machine, its occasional *ding* as their cold bodies lock together, as their wide-open eyes discover, in the wide-open eyes of the other, the wild, futureless expression of their own lust. We kept on most of our clothes; I never even removed my red ski cap, nor Sam his glasses. "Frannie," he said, "I've missed you." This was afterwards, when we were still lying there side by side on the wooden countertop, our breath pouring in plumes from our mouths, our hearts beating fast, rabbit fast, *ding ding ding*. I repeated what I'd said before: the holidays, the twins home from school, a busy time no matter how you looked at it.

"But not too busy for the old witch," Sam said, swinging his legs over the edge of the counter and standing up. He zipped his chinos, then watched, interested, as I zipped my jeans. "Although I guess I ought to thank you."

I didn't have any idea what he was talking about. The last time I'd seen Helle was at the school Christmas concert. Let it snow, let it snow, let it snow, as I reminded him. Mrs. Sprague's punch and cookies.

Sam dipped his chin toward his neck, regarding me intently,

suspiciously, from over the pinkish rim tops of his glasses. "Helle moved out four days ago. Moving in with you, she said. A suitcase, a tape deck, a brown paper grocery bag full of notebooks and tapes—granted she's small, but not so small that you wouldn't notice. It's been my experience," he added, "that for a small woman she takes up an enormous amount of room."

"What do you mean," I asked, "with *me?*" I hadn't seen her. I felt angry, alarmed. *With me?* "Maybe we should call the police." I was just sliding off the counter when all of a sudden it caught my eye, a little circular smear of yellow light leaping sporadically from window to ceiling, from ceiling to ax handle, from ax handle to watering can, from watering can to rabbit, from rabbit to Sam's guilt-stricken face.

"You folks find?" asked Mr. Bidwell, dressed exactly like Mr. Shank in a crisply ironed pale blue smock, although in the case of Mr. Bidwell it was his body which was long and flat, and his head which was short and round. "The light must've but lucky for us batteries."

"No problem," Sam said, holding aloft a little cellophane-wrapped package of lantern mantles, white silky things like doll socks. "Right where they were supposed to be."

Mr. Bidwell bowed his head and raised the flashlight in an odd gesture of resignation. "Wiring left a lot to someday if both ain't dead."

Sam put his lips to my ear. "Do you think when they're together," he whispered, "they make complete sentences?"

THE TWINS, as I found out soon enough, had been aware of Helle's plans for almost a month. She'd sworn them to secrecy and promised them a fabulous reward if they didn't break the pact. Nor had any specific event—an especially heated fight with Sam, for instance—precipitated her decision. According to Helle, one fine day as she was walking past the open laundry-room door on her way to the kitchen, she heard the washer rhythmically chanting, apparently as a result of an imbalanced load, "Move out of the house, move out of the house, move out of the house . . ."

Initially, however, she merely put on her army surplus coat and went for a walk, her usual route up West Hill, although not at one of her usual times. It was in fact two in the afternoon, a bright winter sun shining in a cobalt blue sky. The snow had a delicate crust on it, and with every step she heard a familiar sound, the same sound you hear when you apply the butter too roughly to a piece of toast. Such a thin layer of snow, not yet deep enough to cover the red, thorny suckers the blackberry bushes had sent up last summer in the middle of the path—they made Helle angry, so that she stamped them down under the caramel-colored rubber bottoms of her boots, dislodging the small drops of melted snow which hung suspended from the tip of each thorn. By the time she got to the crest of the hill she was breathing heavily and she felt dizzy, as if there were a hole in the top of her head into which the surprisingly hot winter sun was pouring its confusing yellow liquid. She leaned back against the trunk of one of the leafless apple trees and closed her eyes.

Then it began, a sensation she knew from childhood: Donkey Man, she used to call it, because the first time it started with a dream in which a tiny man sat blowing a tiny brass horn as he sat on the back of a donkey; under the donkey's hooves was a pile of bones. An auditory disturbance, Donkey Man—the whiskery sound of the apple tree's naked branches and twigs rubbing against each other, the sound of her pulse, the sound of the world revolving in its socket—all these sounds mixed together until they became a faint piping of voices, wordless, accusatory, and mean. Over the years Helle had come to understand that what she was hearing was the sound of biological inevitability; the fact that it involved a man with a horn merely served to reinforce her belief that most Christian iconography—as, for example, the Last Judgment—had its sources in the human body.

The human body, she thought. Feh. Dr. Kinglake was a nice enough man, dauntingly healthy himself, and reasonable rather than fatuous in his concern. But what could Dr. Kinglake tell her that she didn't already know? Helle opened her eyes and looked around. Briefly, she was surprised to find herself where she was, at the crest of the hill, surrounded by trees. She reached into her pocket for a cigarette, then remembered that in a moment of misguided resolution she'd thrown the pack away. Was it possible, she wondered, that these trees were older than she was? And if they were, then how could it be that every summer they continued to put forth fruit, hard little green balls, sour and wormy, but fruit nonetheless? Whereas her latest opera was less a blossoming than an evulsion, and what was being wrenched out of her was like what came out of the front lawn the time Sam pulled loose the elm stump. Chickadees and finches were flickering in and out of the branches all around her, their bright small bodies landing and taking off; thrushes were rustling among the thick growth of dead bedstraw and blackberry bushes. The world was certainly a very lively place! Okay, she thought, have it your way. And then she began to feel as she had, when she was seven years old, standing with her mother at the doorway to the bog; all at once Helle Ten Brix realized that she was strangely exhilarated. Instead of returning to the house she decided to follow the footpath that led off to the right, winding steeply down among the trees of a complicated, dense woods until it met the Branch Road.

This was a chilly spot, this intersection, for the Branch Road cut through a narrow valley between two steep ridges thick with pines, and even on the hottest summer day the dirt surface of the road remained dark and moist. The sun might be shining, but its heat was absorbed by millions of pine needles high up on the ridges, so only cold scraps and rags of light fell into the valley. Nobody who had any choice in the matter lived on the Branch Road; poor people like me lived there, the houses becoming increasingly decrepit and small the further you got from town.

By the time Helle came out onto the road, it was about four o'clock. She hesitated for a second or two: Maren seemed to be an easygoing woman, but it drove her crazy when people were late for supper. That was what happened to you when you decided to believe in comfort; you became despotic. If you discovered an ant walking across your kitchen countertop, you imagined your house being devoured by termites. Not like Buggy Moore, Helle thought, whose house she could now see a short distance down the Branch Road, the larger pieces of litter in the yard around it—the rusting sap buckets and sets of bedsprings, the dismantled pump, the front end of an aquamarine Chevy—positioned on the white sheet of snow like objects on display in a museum. When she got closer, Helle could see Buggy Moore himself, sitting on the porch smoking a cigarette, a sight which caused to surge through her the addicted smoker's wild desire for that first inhalation, that first intake of smoke, that reminder of how there's at least one way in life of getting down to the bottom of things.

A cigarette, she thought, reaching into her pocket, which was, of course, empty.

"Evenin'," Buggy said, taking a long drag, forming his lips into a neat O; he filled the cold blue air around his head with smoke rings and then tossed the still-lit cigarette into the snow at his feet, where it glowed bright orange for a moment before going out. Rumor had it that Buggy Moore had at one time been a great ladies' man, that he was the one responsible for burning down Cecil LePan's house after he found out that Cecil had been "sniffing around" the door of the town beauty, Aggie Bent. But now Aggie Bent was dead—as was Cecil LePan—and Buggy Moore was sitting on his porch in a black-and-red-plaid hunting jacket, buttoned wrong, so that one side of the collar was lower than the other, revealing a wedge of shirt, the fabric faintly luminous.

Helle asked him if he could spare a cigarette, and he moved over a little on the porch, patting the splintering gray boards with a speckled, rachitic hand. Through one of the two front windows she could see a table, its chrome legs and rim fuzzy with rust, a big, shapeless white cat pooling out on it around a roast pan, batting with its paw at whatever was inside. Buggy told Helle that when he was a boy, girls didn't smoke. No offense, but that's the way it was. He held out a crumpled pack, and although Helle was dismayed to see that it was blue-green, signifying menthol, she took a cigarette anyway. "Allow me," Buggy said, striking a match. Maybe Helle would like a little something to wash it down with? His face was sprightly and full of suggestion, reminding her of how the habits of youth, left to languish during the dispassionate, busy middle years of a person's life, tended to reappear in old age. Buggy Moore, she realized, was flirting with her. No thank you, she said, she'd already presumed on his hospitality; it was getting late and she still had to walk back to town. Across the road, where a little stream trickled down among mossy rocks and frozen ferns, the rocks were no longer sparkling, the snow was no longer white, and obviously this was because the sun's light was no longer poking through the now-black needles of the pines growing along the ridge at their backs.

Buggy Moore asked if she knew the way, then yawned and looked around; the coming of darkness, for him, meant bedtime and, with luck, the chance in his dreams to kiss Aggie Bent on the porch swing of her mother's house, screened from the street by a wall of morning-glory vines. It was like the song, Buggy said—you could take the high road, you could take the low road. The important thing was not to get lost, although people always did. Mostly women. Well, women and cats. He held out his hand and Helle could feel his fingers—the metacarpals smooth and distinct within their sheath of dry old skin—closing around her own dry old fingers. "Don't be a stranger," Buggy called after her, as she started walking off down the Branch Road. "Fat chance," Helle replied. But she said it softly, the words blowing out softly ahead of her into the cold cold night, in the direction of the cold cold town.

What time was it? Helle hated watches, and although she admired the way the moon and the sun paraded across the sky, she never bothered to figure out how their movement might help her orient herself in space and time. Tonight, an almost full moon gave off a thin, sharp light: the trees' shadows fell onto the snowy road like troughs, and Helle found herself stumbling a little, compensating for dips where there were none—it was like climbing an unfamiliar set of stairs in the dark, thinking there was one last step and coming down hard on your foot, having the wind knocked out of you. The wind, she thought. The wind. She envied Buggy Moore the dark snowy pocket of his yard, the severity of his junk, the dispassionate gaze of his shapeless white cat. Even a little money, she was thinking, is a dangerous luxury. You get yourself a little money, and with it you buy curtains for your windows. The wind coming through them loses its force; it becomes aesthetically pleasing. How beautiful, you think, and then you start making up metaphors. A breeze draining through the meshes of the fabric like whey through cheesecloth. A breath like a hand stroking a loved one's face.

Our greatest illusion, Helle thought. As if we ever live anywhere but under a bog. As if there's any reason to think that breathing should be easy. She began to walk faster. The Branch Road, which had been proceeding in a more or less straight line between the two ridges, suddenly curved to the right, to make room on the left for a wide moonlit meadow, at the near end of which, Helle realized, although she'd never approached it from this direction, was the twins' trailer. Of course this is where she'd been headed all along. Far away, at the other end of the meadow, shone the boxy yellow lights of my house; even farther away, the tiny round white lights of the first stars. She knocked first, to be polite, although the trailer was clearly empty. Then she pushed open the door and went in.

Moonlight poured through the louvered windows, moonlight and moon shadow unrolling like a bolt of banded fabric across the narrow drain board, draping into the sink. The moon-striped floor appeared to have been recently swept by the small red-handled broom propped up in the corner; on the folding table Flo's yellow plastic tea service was set for two, and when Helle opened the moon-striped cupboard doors she found a cellophane package of Oreos and a jar of apple juice. At first she had trouble seeing, but once her eyes adjusted she discovered a box of candle ends on the counter, beside a box of kitchen matches. She lit a candle and dripped some wax into a clam shell that obviously was used for this purpose; then, when the candle was firmly stuck in position, she poured herself a teacupful of apple juice, took four Oreos from the cellophane package, and sat down on one of the beach chairs to eat. The truth is, Helle was extremely hungry. As she told me later, she'd never tasted anything so delicious as that juice and those cookies.

After she'd finished eating, Helle reached into her pocket and took out her white notebook. For the first time in a long while she felt a song—a small, inconclusive burr at first, then rigidly spoked like an asterisk, its spokes extending outward at varying rates of speed—jumping around in the place between her ears. "The bog is a tannery," she wrote, "the Bog Queen alone can turn flesh into leather, can alone give the bones to her three starveling daughters; so her wrath was unloosed when down through the water came two human shoes with human feet in them. Such beautiful shoes!"

Helle put down her pencil. This was a previously unsuspected aspect of the Bog Queen's character, but it didn't get at the source of her mounting excitement. She shut her eyes and saw once again the Great Bog at Horns, a soup plate piled full of spongy matter under a starry sky, and somewhere in the middle of it a smaller version of herself, standing there watching as her new pair of shoes began sinking into the reddish-black bog water. What time was it, and what was she doing there all alone? Where was the loaf of bread? Even though the water was cold, the night air was mild, thickening with insects, and the peat was imperceptibly sinking and rising, sinking and rising, as if under the touch of a wide, consoling palm. Meanwhile, the smaller version of herself was gasping—how slyly the bog wicked the air out of you, so you felt you'd do anything for just one deep breath, though if you succumbed you would carry the bog inside your body wherever you went, and you would grow the way the mosses did, alive at the top, dead at the bottom. "Air on top, sponge below," Helle wrote. "A stage divided horizontally?" But what she really wanted to convey was the sense of an absolute boundary being violated. One minute you could see the black and boundless sky pricked with stars, and breathe the sweet night air—for the air above a bog is unbelievably sweet, since the decay occurs so far below its surface—and the next minute your eyes and nose and mouth would be plugged shut. *That* was what excited Helle. An opera conducted in a place apparently without air, indeed without space of any kind. And what, exactly, did she mean by such a thing?

She looked up from the notepad and there was a girl, her hair coiled around her head in thick yellow braids, a stalwart figure in a long red dress and dark green boots, seated in the beach chair on the opposite side of the table. "Where did you come from?" Helle asked. "Here and there," said the girl, as if naming actual places. This wasn't a ghost, Helle knew. This was a figment of her imagination, conjured by the notion of the story Inger, plucked from the great blue beyond. The real Inger, lacking the necessary restless fixation on the future, would never have turned into a ghost. "What are you doing here?" Helle asked, and Inger cocked her head to one side. "A cookie would be nice," she said, and Helle thought tenderly, Just like you—always hungry. "A cookie would be pointless," Helle said, and when she took a breath she could feel her sorrow, like something heavy making its own hole and then sinking into it. "But the shoes are a ruse," Helle wrote. She could hardly see the words on the page; the candle had melted down into a white puddle in the clam shell, on top of which the flame ferried about, trembling. "She binds your neck with a sphagnum noose; she steals your breath." Helle looked up, and across the table Inger was frowning. "You've gotten so old," Inger said. "How could it have happened that you'd get so old?" "Because *I* never died," Helle said. Then she put her head in her arms and wept.

By the time she looked up Inger was gone, and Ruby and Flo were standing at the door, Ruby regarding her nervously, Flo with interest. They'd noticed a strange, winking light coming from the windows of the trailer, Flo explained, as they stood together in the bathroom brushing their teeth. Does your mother know you're here? Helle asked, sniffing, and Flo said I didn't, I was already asleep. Fireflies, Ruby had suggested; maybe the whole trailer was full of fireflies. But Flo had pointed out that it was winter. Probably a burglar, Flo hinted; if they hurried they could surprise him in the act. A girl who at least in her waking hours knew no fear, my Flo; a girl whose routine disappointments had left her prematurely resigned to whatever life might offer up, thus providing Ruby with an illusion of constant shelter. They'd put on their matching pink parkas and blue snowmobile boots, but there was enough snow in the meadow that when they got to the trailer, the legs of Flo's pajamas and the hem of Ruby's nightgown were sopping.

"This is *our* house," Flo said, informatively. Helle sniffed again, and dabbed at her eyes with her sleeve. "I apologize," she said. "The door was open." Only it wasn't really their house, Ruby corrected. She called Flo's attention to the open package of Oreos and the jar of apple juice. Maybe Helle was just hungry; after all, Ruby observed, she was awfully skinny—whereupon, to the girls' astonishment, Helle rolled back her sleeve and made a small, egglike muscle. "I'm fit," she said, "not skinny. As I said, the door was open. Certainly I'll be happy to replace whatever I ate, although, to be perfectly frank, the cookies were stale and the juice was beginning to turn." She went on to remind them that she was an old woman, in case they hadn't noticed. Of course the young rarely took notice of the old, unless they happened to be extremely lonely. Under such circumstances a young person might overlook the decrepitude, and turn an old person into the object of adoration. The whiskery kisses, the frightening aroma of the underclothes—all those things, Helle said, could be overlooked, if you were lonely enough. Ruby tugged at the sleeve of Flo's parka. "I want to go home," she whispered, but Flo just stood there. "Who said anything about being lonely?" she asked. Twins were never lonely. Ah, Helle replied, she'd forgotten. Twins. No doubt Castor and Pollux, those famous twins, would have had something to say on that score if their father hadn't changed them into stars, rendering them effectively speechless. "But we don't have a father," Ruby said. "Only a mother and a dog."

Like many childless people, Helle found children mildly intimidating; for this reason it didn't immediately occur to her that the twins, truculent Flo in particular, might be waiting for her to take control of the situation. Nor was it as if she hadn't already decided what it was that she wanted, only that, because she was dealing with children, she wasn't sure how to get it. "Girls," she eventually said, "I'm embarrassed to have to admit that I need your help." A rapid exchange of bright, flickering glances, during which Helle looked longingly toward the far end of the trailer and the dark, windowless corner where she'd noticed a small maple bed, invitingly made up with clean white sheets and a thick pile of blankets under a red-and-white patchwork quilt. It was late, Helle continued, and a long way back to town. Would the twins mind very much if she were to spend the night? Needless to say she didn't confess that her more comprehensive plan included moving out of the Blackburns' house and into their trailer. Back and forth the glances flew—finches in apple trees, thrushes in bedstraw. "All right," Flo said at last. She was the one who spoke, although as usual there was no way of knowing which twin, if any, had influenced the decision.

Outside it was snowing again, the wind was blowing, and the moon had disappeared. Lying on his stomach in front of the television, William was watching Boris Karloff in *The Mummy*, even though it was long past his bedtime. Go back, he told the mummy, go back, because he knew that if it didn't, people would take off the wrappings and nothing would be left of it but dust. In the kitchen, Maren was staring at the telephone, trying to decide if she should use it. A raccoon came out of the weeds at the turn onto the Branch Road, its eyes like two pricks in the dark, making Sam slam on his brakes. "Damn you," he said, and he meant Helle. He couldn't see the spikehorn walking through the meadow, nibbling at frozen clover; he couldn't see it because the lights were on in my house and Sam was thinking about me. In the top bunk Ruby was wondering whether things were going to be different now; in the bottom bunk Flo was dreaming about a new pet, a tiny black kitten that she was coaxing to drink milk out of a sky-blue saucer.

V

BECAUSE, of course, anything can happen in a dream. A fierce old woman can be turned into a soft and trusting creature; she can be made to act in ways which betray her true nature. In a dream the dead can come back to life, and make you do things you'd never have done when they were still alive. They can make you let them touch you, make you open your body to them. They can make you doubt your own true nature, leave you lying there on your bed sick with spent desire for something you never thought you wanted in the first place. How many times did Helle show up in my dreams, her skin like a sheet of water, thin and clear, an insufficient disguise for the glassy stalk of her will? Watery hands, watery mouth, turning suddenly, unexpectedly, to soft, pliant flesh. I could never resist her, whereas when I dreamed about Sam there was always an impediment to passion, a missing body part, an entire body disintegrating into vapor, thin air. Helle, I'm sure, would have seen this as yet another piece of proof that there was nothing substantial about sex, that it was yet another of the waking dreams we are afflicted with, and given its foundation in the physical world, a particularly insidious one. "There is no greed," she told me, "worse than the body's." The body, so greedy for transport, simultaneously longed to remain intact, a greedy bag of skin, forever and ever. Music, Helle said, alone of all the arts, could not only replicate but also remedy this condition. This was due to the fact that music—unlike a book, a painting, or a piece of sculpture (which she called "puppet droppings")—didn't exist as matter, nor did it require the presence of a material body to register its existence.

As for the obvious objections to this scheme—the role played by the ears, for instance, or by the musicians and their instruments, not to mention the overwhelming materiality of an opera house, its sets, costumes, and lights—wasn't that, when you got right down to it, exactly Helle's point? Body and spirit, she said. Naturally the senses played a part. They were like doorways to the mind, to its boglike furrows and folds, grayish, unfurnished. So you might provide the onstage image of a single ghostly jib sail, the moon's light filtered through it. Three singers. The doors open and there is the stage, magically reduced in size, magically lodged in the bog-like landscape of your mind. Stuck, really. It isn't until the music begins that you recognize the existence of another doorway; it's the music which calls that doorway into being, the music which enters through it, the music which suggests a way out. Unlike sex, Helle said.

Thus I came to understand the guiding principle behind *The Harrowing of Lahloo*, its musical structure all entrances and exits, just like Helle's face when she would talk about her struggles composing it, the face of a younger woman, as seductive and baffling as the three strange riddles of its open-ing trio: difficult and complex, "the fragmented voice of a dying civilization," to quote Peter Sellars. I admit that the first time I listened to that trio my own response was anything but universal, infused instead with a sense that the message it conveyed might prove crucial to my own future happiness, if only I were able to understand it. A veiled message, a veiled set; masts and sails, flickering moonlight: the vertical masts of Lahloo's unearthly triads appear and disappear within Harry Tuck's saillike sweeps of melody, within the flickering moonlight of Rattail's patter. Three voices, three riddles: What cuts but draws no blood? What has no hair but tickles going through the hole? What rooted first in earth and then in water?

It took me a while, but eventually it dawned on me that in each case the answer to the character's riddle was his or her own name, and that the reason why I'd taken so long was because the music itself defied the possibility of simple resolution. "A newborn babe," Harry Tuck suggests, in response to Rattail's query; "The soul of man," to Lahloo's. An unadorned tune in C minor—forthright enough, and yet when phrases of it intersect with Lahloo's D-minor triads, a disturbing dissonance is created, a subtle indictment of Harry Tuck's romanticism. What has no hair but tickles going through the hole? The tail of a rat, I thought: *Rattail*. Besides, hadn't Helle told me never to trust a tenor? I seem to remember the snow-covered sidewalk in front of the Blackburns' house, the wrenched and wavering sound of Sam's voice as he sang to himself while shoveling a path. "Duke Duke Duke"—*scrape scrape scrape*—"Nothing can stop me now. . . ." The shovel tearing ragged chinks in the sun-bright wall of snow, his pinkish face, his nose coated with a white paste to prevent burning—he was doing a lousy job. Dancer had been a tenor, Helle said; likewise the famous Antonio Giuglini, whose hobbies included flying kites and making fireworks and who died, mad, at the age of thirty-eight. If you were going to throw in your lot with a man, better to choose a baritone or a bass. At least with a bass you knew what you were getting yourself in for. Who ever said sex was mysterious? Those tenors! So melodramatic, so sentimental! Unlike Buggy Moore, for instance, whose attitude toward life, like Rattail's, was uniformly salacious, anecdotal, phallic. "I knew a man who loved a dame," Rattail sings, "a darling in a flowered gown. Each time he put it in she came; she got so wet he thought he'd drown."

But why bother choosing between the lesser of two evils, when there was a third, more fitting choice open to you? Why devote even a minute of your precious life to a man whose skin was the only sensitive thing about him? Look at him! That hat! Those mittens! Helle liked to do this, during the month or so immediately following her move to the trailer, to plan our walks so that they included a brief detour down Quarry Road. It was as if she wanted to remind both of us of what she'd left behind, an impulse echoed in her sudden need to re-examine that earlier period in her life when she'd likewise "snipped the thread." Lahloo, she told me, Lahloo was the key. All I had to do was concentrate on Lahloo's response to the riddles—"The spirit's egress, the flying fish, the worm in the flesh"—and, at the same time, listen to the way the triads were beginning a gradual shift from minor to major, culminating at last in the C-major triad. Arpeggiated, repeated twice, the first time ending on middle C, the second time an octave higher, eerily triumphant: "A drowning man." Do, mi, so, do. Could I hear it? The music coming to rest in that simplest and most familiar of chords? And didn't I want to extract from it the promise of a warm parlor, the smell of bread baking in a nearby oven? Didn't I want to imagine myself sitting in the Blackburns' parlor, Sam watching me as I knitted him yet one more ridiculous hat? Oh, there would be no stopping me, once I got started! The embrace of a loving husband, the comfort of the nuptial chamber, the expected intimacies, the lie of Home—wasn't that, after all, what the music tricked me into believing I wanted?

Although unless you hadn't escaped from home at least once, Helle explained, the ironic message of the C-major triad would possibly leave you cold. That was why she'd decided to elaborate on the lie, to position Skyboots, the ship's mascot, high in the sails, where he can give eloquent and invisible voice to it. Because he remains invisible throughout the course of the opera, Helle compensated him with some of her sweetest music; his first aria in particular—"Dancing Sister"—became extremely popular in the spring of 1925, following the Royal Danish Opera company's first production of *Lahloo*. In those days you could walk down almost any street in Copenhagen and expect to hear that sweetly artless melody coming through an open window: a woman humming it as she watered her Holland bulbs, a chef whistling it as he sprinkled chopped dill across a slice of salt-cured salmon. More recently Paul Simon revived "Dancing Sister," turning it into a tango—you can imagine the twins' surprise when I told them it was Helle's song. As she originally conceived it, it was supposed to be sung a cappella by a young boy whose voice hadn't yet changed: after the opening trio's complicated layering, "Dancing Sister" was calculated to drop like a silver coin into the porcelain cup of your ear. The boy confuses the skysail with his sister's white dress, billowing outward as she dances to a music box in her bedroom; he confuses the Pleiades with the string of pearls around her neck. And then the string breaks, the pearls fall, becoming the Ladrone Islands—home of pirates—their volcanic peaks shining up ahead in the moonlight. "Dancing sister, I'm your consort, you're my compass, I'm your star," the boy sings. "Touch your face and I'm there with you, wind and water from afar. Little sister, dance forever, dance me through the China Seas; the pirate's knife tucked in your sash for you to do with as you please. Dance forever, you're the treasure, you're the one who went away, golden rings are on your fingers, I'm the one who chose to stay."

SPRING ARRIVED—Helle's second spring in Copenhagen—and with it a persistent light rain, day after day. The gutters filled with rivers of gray water on which she could see floating the boat-shaped leaves of the lindens; the King's Guards shivered as they stood in their tall bearskin hats, pegging down all four corners of the Amalienborg Plaza, pretending not to notice when Helle came to a sudden halt by the central statue of a dead king on his horse, her face rigid with purpose, making a wish. The guards pretended not to notice, as if their scrutiny might make the wish turn sour. Unlike me, Francie Thorn, whose curse it is to notice everything—the rain running down Helle's cheeks, the glistening drops of rain beading in her eyelashes, the way she cheated, plucking the eyelash out instead of letting it fall naturally, wiping it off on her coat sleeve because it was too wet to blow away. A little shiver, a little sigh. You can do that, I know— you can pay too much attention to what's going on inside another person. And while you're thus engaged, a magpie can come and steal the watch from your pocket. The world might end; a magpie can sneak up and steal your darling's heart.

As for the exact nature of that wish, who knows? Certainly the libretto to *Lahloo* contains its share of sexual innuendo (the opening trio's riddles, for instance), so that if you wanted to, you could see the entire opera as the workings of a suppressed libido. Helle, of course, would scoff at such a suggestion. Blackmail from the Vienna Woods, she'd call it. Hadn't she told me that during her four years at the conservatory she resisted whatever sexual longings she might have felt, that she'd kept to herself and so developed a reputation for arrogance? For the most part, she said, the other students left her to her own devices, although after word of her nocturnal habits got out she would sometimes hear scuffling sounds in the hallway; once, when she'd been banging very hard on the piano, a note came sliding through the crack at the bottom of the door. "Not Plutus but Apollo rules Parnassus," it read, a quotation from Fux.

Still, as I am well aware, no matter how hard you try to remain isolated, autonomous behavior exerts an attraction of its own. As it turned out, there were two young women in the school who desired Henning's attentions. One was a large, alarming cellist from a Norwegian town above the Arctic Circle; the second, with whom Helle eventually formed a guarded friendship, was a brash and cheerful girl from Aalborg, Linka Grubbe, whose singing voice and sweet tooth reminded her of Inger, although the resemblance ended there. Linka was another of Bingger's pets, a fact she traded on shamelessly. Success at the conservatory, she said, might be assured in one of two ways. Either you were, as Helle was, a genuine musician, or you figured out how to act like one. Linka ended up on the stage, singing roles in light opera, a profession to which her voice and temperament were perfectly suited. Once she was even miscast as Nightingale in her hometown's production of *Fuglespil*; I know this because the clipping she sent Helle from the Aalborg paper eventually made its way into the quilted glove box. "*Hvad for noget?!*"—

"What on earth?!"—Linka had written in the margin, with an arrow pointing at a photograph showing her now elderly body perched in a large tree, her formerly brash mouth wide open, wheezing out the subtle aria with which Act Two begins.

Despite Helle's claim that her childish crush on Inger ended the minute she boarded the Copenhagen train, it seems clear that it hadn't, and that the afternoons she spent in La Glace, watching Linka devour pastries, could be explained only by her resemblance to Inger. Certainly Helle wasn't interested in the gossip Linka dispensed so freely, leaning across a delicate, white-clothed table. Who cared that Hr. Ørsted (woodwinds) had been fired because he'd gotten a third-year clarinet student pregnant? Or that the old woman who mopped the floors had once been accounted a great beauty, and was Niels Gade's lover? Linka would hide her large feet in their worn-out shoes under the table, smooth her unruly, thick hair, and then gracefully lift the chocolate pot to pour. That man sitting across the room, eating a slice of *sportskage* (macaroons, profiteroles, crumbled nougat, whipped cream), might be the owner of a shipbuilding company, or prominent in the Bourse; he might even be a member of the royal family. For Linka was hoping to trap a rich husband— a fact which she confided tenderly, so as not to hurt Henning's feelings. Whereas Helle confided nothing. "But even Mozart had a mother and father," Linka said once, exasperated.

No, it seems clear to me that Helle continued to moon after Inger. This would explain the ferocity with which I imagine her whacking her boot heel against the window frame in her practice room, eventually managing to jar it loose. Hadn't she just received Inger's letter informing her of an anticipated trip to the city, asking her if she'd help choose a trousseau? "I have decided to marry Hans Fog," Inger wrote.

In the country, when it rains, the air fills with smells of vegetation and dirt. In the city, even one as dedicated to cleanliness as Copenhagen, what you smell is prodigal and human—coal fumes, soggy paper, drenched pavement, blood and fat from the butcher shops on the far side of town, hothouse flowers and carnal sweat, bilge and tar. Rain was pattering on the windowsill, making a small damp spot on the floor. The rat had vanished into his hole, either to sleep or to eat; maybe he had a family in there, she thought, a wife, little rats.

Helle stuck her head out the window and let the rain wash her face. What was Inger doing now? The Nissens all went to bed early, so Inger was probably sound asleep in the large bed she shared with her sisters, their soft arms and legs braiding together under a light-blue quilt filled with duck feathers. Everything at the Nissens' farm was well padded. The one time, years earlier, that Helle had been invited to spend the night, the sisters had complained about her skinniness and the unpleasant sharpness of her knees and elbows. "Helle sleeps by herself," Inger had told them, but they hadn't believed it. If she were to lean far enough out the window, Helle wondered, could she see the Nissens' chimney rising up on the other side of Mogens Stream? Of course if you looked back you turned into salt; you sent the person you loved best straight to hell. In certain circumstances this could be yourself. "I'm your consort," Helle sang. "You're my compass." The aria, which she had recently completed, pleased her. In the building across the way she could see into a lit room where a bald man sat in an armchair reading a book. What was so bad about sleeping alone? At least she would never have to share her bed with Hans Fog, who no doubt ground his teeth and slept with his eyelids half-open.

"If anything," Helle told me, "I'd gotten skinnier since leaving home. Skinnier and sharper." A gaunt young man with cropped hair and circles under his eyes—Helle had removed his soul in order to animate the more worthy receptacle of her opera. You could recognize the soulless by their precision of movement, she said, a precision devoid of grace, similar to the relentless ticking of a clock. Time moved along its lateral track and the soulless moved with it, which explained why she was, if nothing else, good at keeping appointments. For instance, she arrived at the dressmaker's at precisely three o'clock on a May afternoon, although there was no sign of Inger when she got there. A sloe-eyed woman with pins in her mouth and a measuring tape around her neck deposited her on a sofa, pointed briskly at a sign which forbade the smoking of pipes or cigars, and disappeared into a curtained alcove. Even though it was a warm day, the shop's windows were closed, and the air in the room was filled with the dust of cut fabric. Murmurs, the sound of pins falling into a ceramic dish—a hand reached out through the curtain, drawing it back, and out came Inger.

She'd put on weight—probably as much as Helle had lost—but otherwise her cheeks were still pink, her hair still golden and shining, her skin clear and white. Nor had she managed to achieve an air of sophistication, despite the sky-blue, tailored day suit she was wearing, hobble-skirted and lightly corseted; as Inger walked across the thickly carpeted floor, the dressmaker warned her to take smaller steps or she'd tear the seams. She twirled, towering over Helle in her new high-heeled shoes, her lofty new hairdo: a towering woman preparing to wed the towering Hans, tall and round and stolid as a tower. "But really," said the dressmaker, "your young man must leave now." It was time for Inger to try on the wedding gown, and it was bad luck for the groom to see the gown before the wedding. She affected a French accent, Helle said, but anyone could tell that the dressmaker was from Funen, "the Garden of Denmark," and that her parents were barley farmers.

Springtime, Helle thought. The linden tree outside her bedroom window at Daisy's was dying; this spring all it had put forth was a single green glove, on the hand that tapped against the panes. "Oh," Inger said, "but this isn't my young man." You could listen to the tapping all night long; you could think you were being summoned. The language of the Muse is similarly misleading. Oh, the Muse says, but I wasn't calling *you*.

VI

IT SHOULD COME as no surprise that Helle never went to Inger's wedding, or that the present she sent in her stead was deliberately impersonal, a large basket of fruit. When you finished eating the fruit, you could put your mending in the basket or take it on picnics; you could use it as a Moses basket for a newborn baby, if you happened to have one. A practical present, even if the fruit was rotten by the time it was delivered.

Besides, as it turned out, it made no difference whether Helle had planned to attend the wedding or not, for on the last day of May, 1916—probably some time during the rehearsal dinner—the British light cruiser *Galatea* opened fire on a Danish merchantman, thus starting what came to be called the Battle of Jutland, and in the ensuing confusion Kayo was killed. They never found out exactly how. Perhaps the merchantman had been, in reality, a Q-ship, an innocent-looking vessel fitted out with hidden armaments, or perhaps it had been mistaken for one. When an enemy U-boat surfaced, a "panic party"—a group of men dressed like merchant sailors, occasionally carrying with them a live parrot in a cage—would set forth from the Q-ship in a life raft, while the gun crews remained behind, preparing to strike with their rifles, their twelve-pounders, their Maxims.

According to Dancer, when Kayo had shipped out it had been for Vaasa, on the Finnish coast; he should have been in the Gulf of Bothnia, not in the North Sea. Dancer blamed Jellicoe, who continued to resist the notion of providing merchantmen with protective convoys. Everyone knew that the British commander-in-chief was a fool, a hypochondriac more interested in charting his own body's losses (of teeth, in particular, to pyorrhea) than the daily casualties of innocent lives. Meanwhile, Daisy persisted in her belief that Kayo was a hero, that he had, unbeknownst to the rest of them, taken up the cause of freedom. She hung the parlor with black baize, and propped up a small, framed photograph—Kayo on the deck of a ship, squinting into the sunlight, his cap pulled down low on his forehead—in the front window, between the polar bear and the ivy heart.

In those days, despite such technical advances as wireless telegraphy, hydraulic power systems, and long-range searchlights, naval warfare remained, essentially, a mysterious business. In the case of the Battle of Jutland, neither side had any idea that the other's main battle fleet was even *at* sea. Admiral Scheer hadn't been able to do his customary air reconnaissance, because the wind was too strong for the Zeppelins to be moved from their sheds. The weather was bad everywhere, windy and foggy and wet. Inger wrote to tell Helle that they'd been forced to hold the wedding reception inside her uncle's house. Rain on a wedding day was good luck, she insisted.

Only isn't it true that good luck is always parochial—that while Hans Fog was shoving a piece of wedding cake into his new bride's mouth, Kayo was lying dead on the ocean floor;

that while Inger was slipping into bed beside her new husband, Helle was standing alone at the edge of the harbor, cursing God? Kai Borge. How could he be dead? Born on February 7, 1897—making him almost exactly six months older than she was—in the town of Rappendam, the parish of Jorlunde, beloved son of Aksel and Hanna Borge. Kayo, whose kindness Helle had come to take for granted. But doesn't recognition always come after someone dies? Or, at least, adult recognition: when Helle was a girl, it never occurred to her to think that she'd taken Ida for granted. Death had nothing to do with time—it was a location, a place where Ida had gone. At first Helle patiently waited for her to come back, until she was eventually forced to give up, preparing for the more adult confusions about death we think of as facing reality. Of course, later I would learn that death *is* a place, and that it's inside us, waiting for each of us to come to it. It's like one of those problems in non-Euclidean geometry wherein a shape proves capable of sailing through a tiny hole in itself, its points rearranging themselves in a previously uncharted neighborhood that was there all along.

The funeral was held in the church Kayo had attended as a boy; the Borge family had its own pew, and it was here that Helle eventually found herself, wedged between Dancer and Maja Borge. This was Kayo's youngest sister, the one Helle was supposed to resemble, although obviously the resemblance Kayo had seen wasn't physical, for Maja turned out to be tall and big-boned, with the same large head and crown of thick, kinky hair as her brother. After they sang the hymn for the drowned, the pastor, gripping the edge of the pulpit as if to prevent himself from falling out of it, delivered a barely audible eulogy. "He can't trust himself," Maja told Helle, explaining that the pastor had always favored Kayo and was

infuriated when he'd decided to become a sailor. "Like everyone else," Maja said, "he always thought I was a bad influence." She pulled out a handkerchief and handed it to Helle,
though she was the one who was crying. Helle was never able
to weep in front of other people, preferring, like God, to
provide her grief with form.

The church at Rappendam was small and white, set in the
middle of its own cemetery. All around the grave markers the
yellow flowers of the spring primroses would have been opening up, their delicate stems rising from within clusters of thick
hairy leaves; further down near the roots, where the stalks of
the leaves were veined with red, water beaded, each drop
overlarge and tremulous. First there was shadow, then there
was sun, then there was shadow again: the clouds were moving
fast from west to east toward Rappendam fen, where in 1941
peat cutters found the broken pieces of several prehistoric
wagons, tossed down among the bones of cows and horses
and sheep and wild pigs. But in 1941 the world was being
torn apart by another war, and Denmark hadn't managed to
escape that one.

In 1916, however, Rappendam's claim to renown was its
two life-sized wooden figures of Christ, stored in a damp room
off the sacristy. Maja persuaded the pastor to unlock the door
after the service so Helle and Dancer could see them. Look,
Maja said, had they ever seen such beautiful carving? Designed to be drawn through the town during Holy Week, one
of the figures was lying down in a coffin; the other was
standing up to reveal its wounds. Scholars came from all over
Europe to study them, the pastor said. Originally the figures
had been painted; you could still see traces of bluish white
pigment in the grain of the standing Christ's chest, rusty
patches around the wounds' lips. Each rib bone was clearly

articulated, the ribcage gripping the torso as if it were the splayed fingers of a god bent on retrieval. Such detail! the pastor exclaimed. Kai was fascinated by the figures, he said, probably because they helped him believe in the miracle of heaven. "Liar," Maja whispered in Helle's ear; she had taken her hand and was swinging her arm back and forth, back and forth, like the tail of a cat getting ready to strike. But the pastor wasn't a liar. All the man was guilty of was sentimentality, a crime which generally provides its own punishment.

There are no hills to speak of in Denmark. Of course there are the chalk cliffs of the Isle of Møn, and Heaven Mountain in central Jutland, which rises a scant five hundred feet above Lake Julsø, suggesting that heaven might be a lot closer to earth than we like to think. But for the most part, Denmark is flat—flat as a board, as Helle would say, flat as a pancake. In Denmark it's difficult to sneak away unnoticed, so when she left the church and wandered off alone down the Helsingør Road, everyone could see her go. For a while she walked aimlessly. The sky was bright blue; the clouds that had raced past earlier were probably casting their shadows on the streets of Petrograd by now, or breaking apart to fall as snow on the Mongolian tundra. Looking back, she could see the church in its moving thicket of dark-clothed mourners. Looking ahead, to the point where a smaller road intersected with the Helsingør Road, she could see another thicket, also dark, but motionless. Otherwise there was nothing in the landscape except hops fields, the vines pale green, the buds tight and shining. At sea, Kayo had told her, you couldn't always tell whether the island looming up in front of you was really there or merely the reflected image of an island you'd already left behind. Kayo, she thought: sitting with his elbows propped on the table, inserting a spoon slowly through his open lips, surprised and pleased to find that Daisy had put raisins in the porridge. Everything in life presented itself to Kayo this way. And would he have been surprised and pleased the moment his soul jumped out of his body? Helle said his name aloud, just once, sharply, as if it might be possible to catch his soul's attention. But all that came back to her was the sound of crying.

At first Helle thought she was hearing the collective voice of grief, carried on a light wind from the churchyard, floating toward her across the hops fields. However, it soon became clear that the sound was growing in intensity the closer she got to the intersection, where a grove of trees, tall and blighted, marked the banks of a narrow stream. At her approach, hundreds of blue-black birds—rooks? jackdaws?— took to the air, beating their wings wildly in place, hovering and then preparing to land, their claws outstretched, their beaks open wide, screaming. They did this over and over again. The highest tree branches lolled from side to side beneath the weight of the birds' heavy, shapeless nests. Maybe there was no difference between the sounds of grief and panic. She sat on the bank, watching how the sunlight penetrated to the stream's sandy bottom, dotted with shining stones, dead leaves. Wing feathers fell from above, some landing in the water and drifting along in the current until they clogged in a pool of yellow foam. All around her dandelions were coming up, and the first tender shoots of that species of wild parsley the Danes call *billebo*, or beetlehouse. The new leaves were still curled in on themselves, and speckled with bird droppings—the people who idealized nature, according to Helle, hadn't looked at it very closely.

The birds' angry squalling continued unabated, and that, combined with the rippling of the stream, made it impossible to hear anything else—the footsteps, for example, of Maja Borge as she came creeping up from behind. "Uh-oh," Maja said. She put her fingers in her mouth and sucked on them as if they'd been burned. "The eye," she said, "the eye," although Helle didn't know how she could have seen it, since it was concealed as usual beneath the high white collar of her shirt. Crazy Maja. I could have warned you, Dancer told her later, explaining that it had always been Kayo's fondest wish that he and Maja would get married, if Helle could imagine such a thing. He didn't know the details, only that what had originally been taken for precocity eventually emerged as craziness, and that the family had at one point sent her away to an institution, but brought her back when she refused to eat. Maja asked Helle which she preferred, air or water, then told her that the Buddha also had a third eye, though his was in the middle of his forehead. She sat down, removed her boots, peeled off her black stockings, lifted her black skirts, and waded out into the stream. Kayo, she said, used to bring her here when she was little. The wings of her nostrils were red; otherwise she appeared placid, even light, as if, having spent her sorrow, she was now completely empty.

Laughing, holding her hand to her mouth like a naughty child, Maja asked if Helle wanted to talk to Kayo. Most people wouldn't understand, she said, but she knew from what he'd told her in his letters that Helle was different. They used to practice, she said, right here. It was a good spot on account of the birds, who kept the air stirred up so that things could move around without any trouble. And suddenly the sound of the birds got louder and louder, their feathers showering down faster and faster through the branches together with gobbets of light and excrement; Maja's eyes rolled up into their sockets until only the whites were visible, and she fell backwards into the stream, lengthwise, like a tree. As she lay there, hands folded across her chest, the current made her hair appear to stand on end; her neck was tilted in such a way that although the egglike disks of her eyes were completely submerged, her mouth was not. "No," her mouth said, and what came out of it was Kayo's voice. "You shouldn't do this anymore," the voice said. "You have to stop."

"Kayo?" Helle asked, "is that you?" The voice asked if she wanted proof. The place in the back of the linen press where Daisy hid her money? The location of the snake on Dancer's body? What about Helle's trick of pressing her finger on Oluf Froulund's upper lip to make him stop snoring? Helle should tell Maja that this was the last time. Absolutely. A soul could get caught this way—like trying to leave Tante Mette's house and always being called back through the door for one final kiss goodbye. Maja should know better. The last time, absolutely. After this there was no telling who might show up. It could be anyone. Helle asked Kayo what he meant, but it was too late. Already Maja was raising herself on her elbows, shaking drops of water from her hair, wiping her eyes. Her movements were mechanical; from time to time her head jerked to one side, she bared her teeth and growled. "Anyone," she said in the high-pitched, timid voice of Torben Toksvig. Then her shoulders began to heave, like a dog's just before it gets sick, and Helle averted her eyes.

Later Maja would describe in detail the method she and Kayo had devised to foil death, a method based on the odd musings of Chang Hsieh, a seventeenth-century Chinese mariner. By Helle's account, he claimed that every canny sea captain knew that the Atlas-Tortoise—in other words, the whole mysterious world—was no different from the ant you'd see carrying a grain of corn across your floor. There was no such thing as the unfamiliar, Chang Hsieh said, no more danger in meeting barbarian tribes than in "touching the left horn of a snail." The secret lay in discovering the specific nature of the similarity between, for example, the apparently unfamiliar island you were approaching and the familiar ant. All Maja and Kayo had done was to take Chang Hsieh's philosophy to its logical conclusion. Thus the soul, confronted with the five hundred and forty doors of Valhalla, needed only discover that element of similarity and—presto!—a door would swing open in the land of the living, the door in this case being Maja's mouth. Naturally such a system wasn't without its flaws: there were two sides to every door, and clearly Kayo had come to resent his sister calling him away from heaven's infinite supplies of sweet mead and roast pig merely to satisfy her own earthly longings. You could become greedy, always wanting more; the door would swing open and you wouldn't think of it as a conduit but as a mouth, as the widening jaws of a whale, opening to gather in an abundance of plankton, flotsam and jetsam, small fish, bigger fish.

It goes without saying that I was skeptical—who wouldn't have been? A trick, I said; the entire episode was a trick. If Kayo and his sister were so close, if he wrote to her regularly, then there was no reason to assume that he wouldn't have told her about Daisy's money, Dancer's tattoo, Oluf Froulund's nose. About Helle's eye, for that matter. Crazy people were notorious for speaking in tongues, and although I was willing to concede that Maja Borge might have been unusually attuned to the uncanny, the episode was just that, uncanny. "As Freud defined the term," I added, waiting for Helle to express her usual disdain at the mention of that name. But all she did was smile, and remind me there were two sides to every haunting. Remember that, Frances, she said. Two sides.

YET NOT ONLY Helle's view of mortality was influenced by the experience in Rappendam, which also clearly extended to the composition of *Lahloo*. "Scarcely bigger than an ant," begins Harry Tuck's menacing second-act aria, "a flaw in the lens, a mote in the eye, a sea pigeon riding a far-off swell, a tern's shadow fallen from out of the sky? Barbarian isle, barbarian boat, past Leviathan's smile, down Leviathan's throat." He is peering through his spyglass, looking out across the sea—that is, across the audience. You think you're safe, you think you know who you are. You might be going about your own business, for instance, and the next thing you know you're being spied on, being seen not as your dull, familiar self but as an exotic. A handsome man sets forth in an opium clipper, arrogant in his assumption that adventure, when it comes his way, will conform to his expectations. But does he suspect, even for a minute, that what he will find is merely one more aspect of what he thought he'd left behind? The long shadows of late afternoon climb the sails behind him— his own shadow, Rattail's, the figurehead's. What would Chang Hsieh have made of a man like me, his aria concludes, whereupon Rattail replies that there are creatures of the deep with bright green eyes, diabolic balls of light three feet wide staring up at you from out of the great white hill of a squid's head. Feathers, I saw feathers, Harry Tuck insists. Rattail laughs, and the figurehead lifts her arms to shake out her long, thick tresses; her face, its expression of cunning and triumph, is lit by the dark red light of the setting sun.

Meanwhile, little by little, the pirate lorcha approaches the ship and the diatonic scale gives way to the so-called gypsy scale. Skyboots calls out "Pirates!" and his cry is taken up by Rattail, by the figurehead; from within the orchestra pit, Nanna's voice is heard for the first time. "At last, my sweet, the tides conspire to set you in my path," she sings. She tells Harry Tuck that there is no need for his crew to draw their weapons. Weapons are powerless, she explains, against the intentions of the tides. "The new moon rides between the Asses' Ears, half-tide, full tide, or low. Her age is clear," she sings, "it tells you where to go." Rattail points out that women always lie about their age. "The rule of the current," Nanna sings; "Trickery," Rattail replies; "All the havens fill," Nanna sings; "Don't take the hook," Rattail replies. They continue in this vein, as Lahloo repeats the single phrase "At last, my sweet," over and over, the rhythm of the phrase varying in accordance with the rhythm of the drums.

Despite Rattail's warning, Harry Tuck throws down the boarding ladder, and up climbs the pirate queen, Nanna. She is a formidable sight, with a headdress of parrot feathers, and mid-thigh black boots. Otherwise she is naked, and you can see the vestiges of blue-green scales along her flanks. In the San Francisco Opera's 1975 staging, the singer actually wore no clothes; in 1925, the Copenhagen production was forced to make do with a printed leotard. "Prudes," said Maeve Merrow, the original Nanna. In the Berlin cabarets, Maeve said, you could see any part of a woman's anatomy you wanted. *Any* part.

Nanna boards the ship and stands balanced on the rail to the left of the figurehead, her one arm extended upward, gripping the jibboom. Her first aria is an extended narrative, the story of her life told in three contradictory parts. She claims to be the illegitimate daughter of a priest and a nun, set adrift in a coracle just moments after her birth, nursed by a sea cow, taught the thousand words for "fish" by a harp seal, instructed in the laws governing morality by a shark. "Call them by name before you eat them," Nanna explains. "Ripple-fin, Shadow-gill, Coral-darter, Ticktock." But no, that isn't right. The truth is, she was the best-loved daughter of a mandarin; her feet were bound from birth, and so she would become a creature of air and light, she was fed nothing but plums and the roe of the sea urchin. "I was bathing in the Yangtze, and the River God saw me," Nanna sings, "his yellow arms grabbed me and he took me for his wife." Together they had three children, three carp with dark eyes just like her own. Beautiful eyes, Nanna remarks—doesn't Harry Tuck agree? "Look close," she sings, "closer now. What do you see, midnight sky or sky of morning?" Because any fool looking closely enough will be able to see that her eyes are blue. "Do you want to know what really happened?" she asks. "A man had a wife and he didn't love her. Grabbed her and took her and called her by name. Oh, sad to say he didn't love her, sad to say, sad to say, but who's to blame?"

The aria is constructed in such a way that the melody, based on the gypsy scale, is carried by the cellos, while Nanna's voice seesaws back and forth between two notes, D and A. The melody is haunting and quite pretty, although its two augmented seconds come into inevitable conflict with Nanna's incantation. Musically, one of Helle's purposes for this opera was to create systems in which the ear struggled to maintain its relationship to the harmonious or the familiar, while at the same time acknowledging the inevitability of discord. She'd heard Alban Berg's songs performed at the conservatory, and while she had to agree with her peers that the lyrics ("Over the borders of the All, you looked meditatingly out") were ridiculous, she claimed to find his use of Schoenberg's atonal idiom intriguing. A recent feminist analysis of *Lahloo* suggests that this tension inherent in the score—"the twin influences of Mozart and Schoenberg grappling for ascendancy, the resultant sense of a basically harmonious form within which, inchoate, the content seethes"—was appropriate to Helle's growing contempt for the patriarchy. Indeed the entire opera, according to this analysis, "is a veritable feast of proto-feminist symbols. Not only are the three aspects of the goddess—creator/preserver/destroyer; Virgin/Mother/Crone; Kore/Despoena/Persephone—given glorious embodiment in the characters of Nanna, Lady Isabel, and Lahloo; but they ultimately overwhelm the male principle, as represented by Harry Tuck and Rattail, rather than the other way around. The Furrow triumphs over the Harrow, the cunt over the prick."

By the time Nanna finishes her aria, she has succeeded in attracting the attention of Harry Tuck's entire crew, who arrange themselves behind her in two straight rows to sing the "Blame Song," a traditional chorus in which the men blame each other for their own weaknesses and mistakes: My sweetheart was unfaithful because you made me sign onto this ship; I fell asleep during third watch because you gave me rum to drink; I lost the tip of my finger because you startled me while I was cutting bait; I lost my faith in God because your prayers never work; and so on. Rattail finally intervenes. But why blame yourselves? he asks. Why not blame the one who is apparently blameless—the one who invited the enemy onto the ship in the first place?

Harry Tuck banishes the crew to its quarters. A platform descends to stage left on pulleys, curtained in the rear by the foresail; we are meant to understand that this is the captain's stateroom. The mahogany headboard of a large bed is visible, the mattress piled high with embroidered cushions. The stage is almost completely dark, except for a single beam of blue moonlight which illuminates Harry Tuck and Nanna as they lounge against the cushions. Harry claps his hands once, twice, and Rattail appears, bearing a tray piled high with fruits, a bottle of wine, an opium pipe. A duet commences, a fugue of mutual seduction. They smoke the pipe, passing it back and forth, and as they do so, a second Harry and a second Nanna—the offspring of their drugged imaginations—appear stage right in a wavering green spotlight. The duet becomes a quartet; the fugue becomes more complicated, its motif reminiscent of the one we associate with Lahloo. "I kiss your lips," sings the Harry on the bed. "I blindfold your eyes," sings the dream Harry. "I kiss your throat," sings the Nanna on the bed. "I bind your wrists," sings the dream Nanna. Gradually, as the two figures on the bed become entwined, the two dream figures undergo a metamorphosis: little by little they wind each other round with lengths of green and blue silk until they are sleek and predatory sea creatures; drawn aloft on wires, they swim through the aqueous light, their jaws open wide. "Sweet dreams," sings Rattail, casting out a net, hauling them in. He licks his chops, he rubs his belly. Then he takes a knife from his belt, slits the fish open, and removes their skeletons, which he plays, with his knife handle, like xylophones. It is the servant's lot in life, Rattail sings, to dine on the dreams of his captain. Not much meat on *this* dream, Rattail points out.

If the above effect was difficult to accomplish, it was nothing compared with what followed. The finale of *Lahloo*, the engulfing from behind of the entire ship in a gigantic tidal wave, has always required unusual technical ingenuity on the part of the production designer, and provides at least some explanation for the fact that the opera has never been widely produced. Although I suspect there are other reasons for *Lahloo*'s limited popularity, reasons having to do with its apocalyptic ending, reasons which, needless to say, the demands of my legacy forced me to take into account. It seemed to me that while the average operagoer is generally willing to accept the possibility that one or more of an opera's characters will die at the end, what isn't acceptable is that everyone will die. It's difficult enough, after all, to exchange the charmed precincts of the opera house for the litter and discord of the world outside its doors; that loss should be enough, without having to submit to a vision of wholesale destruction while still inside. Or, as Helle herself once confessed to me, an adult who relies on apocalypse to end a work of art is no different from the desperate schoolchild who ends a story with "and then I got hit by a truck." A fascist impulse, Helle sneered; nor was it a coincidence that Wagner was Hitler's favorite composer. Consider *Götterdämmerung*. Of course, by the time that cumbersome edifice had gone up into flames, everyone was glad to see it go.

In any event, when Harry and Nanna awaken, Harry's wearing a long robe and slippers, Nanna a peach-colored dressing gown. The feathered headdress is nowhere to be seen. They sip coffee, nibble toast, maintain a respectable distance from each other on the bed, propped stiffly against the pillows. "Some marmalade, my dear?" sings Nanna. "A little cream?" "Did you sleep well, my dear?" sings Harry. "No troubled dreams?" It's almost as if they've been married for years; but the music, a nervous commingling of motifs, implies otherwise. In *Die Zauberflöte*, the essential antagonism between men and women finds reconciliation in the marriage of Tamino and Pamina; we're made to see how univeral harmony is dependent on such synthesis. Whereas in *Lahloo* the underlying principle is one of fundamental disharmony. Any attempt to force the issue will prove disastrous, as Rattail subsequently points out.

He gathers the crew around him on the deck and delivers himself of a final aria, a devilish piece which reiterates, in its use of the Chinese tonal system, his original theme. This time, however, he accompanies himself on the Jingling Johnny, a strange percussion instrument consisting of a long pole with several transverse crescent-shaped brass plates, the entire structure surmounted by a hatlike pavilion. Numerous little bells hang from the plates and from the pavilion; for the purposes of this aria the instrument was modified to include the two fish skeletons, likewise hung with bells. Rattail asks the crew to think of their own wives and sweethearts, skin as smooth as milk, eyes like stars, lips like cherries. He waxes lyrical, but his intention is ironic. What could be more boring, he implies, than the return to hearth and home? What could be more driftless than a ship captained by a man who has gotten what he thought he wanted? What puts wind in the sails, starch in the shirt, lead in the pencil? The lively whores of Woosung are waiting for us, Rattail reminds the crew, those whores with skin smoother than milk, eyes brighter than stars, lips redder than cherries. Of course we have to pay, he sings, of course, of course, of course. We always have to pay. His refrain is eventually taken up by the crew, who begin brandishing pistols and knives.

By now the only person attentive to the ship's progress is Skyboots. As the agitation on deck spreads to include the orchestra—the melody of Rattail's aria consigned to the woodwinds, the Jingling Johnny's noise augmented by drums and cymbals—it's at first difficult to make out the sound of his voice. "She sighs," Skyboots sings, "she wakes, her flanks stir from where she lies, lap-lap, lap-lap." Rattail and the crew, in the act of advancing on Harry Tuck and Nanna, freeze in place; the orchestra grows quiet, with the exception of a single cymbal, brushed delicately to duplicate the lapping sound of the sea. "She's the hand that strokes before it takes, the house that holds before it breaks. No thumb, no room, no nail, no floor, no skin, no wall, no print, no door. Lap-lap, lap-lap." The wave becomes visible, rising up from stage rear. Just as Skyboots concludes his song, just as the wave is about to crest, casting a blue-green shadow across everything below, you can see, cupped within it, an intricate pattern of fish and seaweed; you can hear the faint soughing of the strings, the ascending fourths of Lahloo's original chord. Little by little the strings are joined by the other instruments. The wave crests and the whole orchestra crests with it; you don't realize, until the wave starts to fall, which elements have combined to create the accompanying panel of sound. It's only when the wave falls that you can hear them—Harry Tuck, Nanna, Rattail, Skyboots—their individual motifs churning and disintegrative within a white surge of foam.

Theorists point out that most modern operas, because they are *durchkomponiert*, or continuously composed, are nothing more than finales extending all the way back to their own beginnings. Or, as the reviewer Aksel Bram suggested, *Lahloo*'s finale makes us call into question the meaning of the phrase "to bring down the curtain," since no curtain ever went up in the first place. The ship sinks beneath the water until all you can see is the prow, and on it the figure of Lahloo. She is standing; slowly she lifts her arms. "Through the dark lanes they travel now, fleet and unknown, Kuroshio current, Gulf Stream, coral and bone, Benguela, Somali, each one alone."

VII

T HE TREATY OF VERSAILLES was signed, ending the war. The nations of Europe, in an attempt to humiliate Germany, devised a system of economic sanctions: a heavy boot heel from under which the worst of its villains squirmed forth, hungry for retribution. You can put out poison, as they eventually did at the conservatory, but that will only serve to separate the gullible from the clever. Helle's rat survived. Just as one day in the spring of 1920, Daisy took Helle to a large field on the outskirts of Copenhagen where, in the company of picnicking families and amorous couples, they watched an airplane make loop-the-loops through a blue, cloudless sky. When the plane landed, a tall blond man emerged from the cockpit. The crowd cheered and the man executed a neat, formal bow, before limping away to a waiting automobile. This was Hermann Göring, biding his time.

I suppose you could say that Helle was also biding her time, although in her case there was nothing sinister about the awaited event. Night after night she'd come home from the conservatory dispirited and numb, as if all day long she'd been banging up against the walls of an expansive cage. At the dinner table, Daisy would fill her plate with beetroot salad and red cabbage, fresh sausage, slices of *fuldkorn*, but Helle would only pick at the food, eating like a captive, causing Daisy to comment that she was turning into a shadow. Dancer was either there or off at sea. Sometimes it was just Helle and Oluf Froulund, Daisy inexplicably having decided to spend more and more time with her most recent suitor, Thorkild Propp, the cement magnate.

Understand, it wasn't as if there weren't isolated incidents which emerged with something like the brightly suggestive glow of beetroot from the otherwise all-encompassing beige plate of Helle's life: the nocturnal sessions, for example, during which she composed *Lahloo*; Nellie Melba's rare appearance as Violetta—dressed in a gown so heavily encrusted with her own lavish jewels that Dr. Grenvil almost dropped her, mid-faint—at the Royal Opera; Rasmus Rundgren's 1917 production of *Le nozze di Figaro*, in which Maeve Merrow sang the part of Cherubino, and after which Dancer, no doubt inspired by the opera's final image of happy couples, made his surprising proposal of marriage.

As Helle described it, she and Dancer were returning from the performance, strolling along the harbor among the Russian refugees' makeshift shelters, a cramped city of tents and open fires that had sprung up almost overnight, when he suggested a brief detour onto the Langelinie for an unobstructed view of the ocean. The moon was full, its light shining down across the heaving gray surface of the water; Helle was going on and on about Cherubino's Act One aria. Wasn't it wonderful, she asked Dancer, how music could make you feel that way, as if you didn't know who you were or what you were doing? As if suddenly hollow avenues were branching out in your body, all of them waiting like streambeds in the spring to fill with water, but also like the water itself, a watery hand getting ready to pour into the waiting fingers of a glove? Of course it depended on your outlook whether this process indicated the presence of a soul or its absence.

At one end of the Langelinie stands a statue of Gefion, the legendary goddess responsible for the creation of Zealand, a monumental woman shown cracking her whip above the heads of the oxen who were once her sons, driving her plow through great billowing furrows. At the other end there's the statue of Andersen's Little Mermaid, a slender and sorrowful young woman of bronze, seated on a boulder lapped over by the waves, depicted just after she's sacrificed her tail in order to win a human prince's love. Sometimes, Dancer said, you couldn't be two things at once. You had to choose, he said, taking in the two statues with a single sweeping gesture. Sometimes you had to know what you were doing. Of course there was no question which of the two statues was more attractive. If Helle chose the mermaid, he said, smiling his rueful and seductive smile, he'd begin to court her in earnest. He'd wear her down until she'd agree to marry him. He explained that ever since the night when he'd kissed her and cut her hair, he'd known that his own salvation was a matter of throwing in his lot with a woman smarter than himself. Helle could do worse, he pointed out. She could end up alone, struggling to make ends meet in an ugly apartment in the Vesterbro. An endless procession of piano students, Dancer hinted. Besides, he'd be gone for months at a time, leaving her free to compose her operas. He'd respect the fact that she'd given up her life as a mermaid for him, and in exchange she could expect his complete devotion.

Was she tempted by this offer? Did it occur to her for a minute that she might want to spend the rest of her life with a man, even such a wild and handsome creature? Or had Dancer known all along that Helle would never capitulate?

But he wouldn't forsake her, would he? Helle asked, to which Dancer replied, Never. Never! As long as he was alive, Dancer promised, he'd be there to protect her. To protect her and to cut her hair—which was getting a little long, in case she hadn't noticed. Aimlessly, dreamily, they started walking, holding hands like lovers, something they could now afford to do since there was no longer any doubt about what the act of holding hands might mean. Aimlessly, dreamily, they walked, away from the moonlit ocean, away from the sorrowful mermaid and the monumental goddess, past the sad Russian refugees and the darkened windows of the customhouse, in one end of the Amalienborg Palace's central courtyard, around its moonlit dead horseman and out the other end, back toward the Bredgade and the three onion-shaped domes of the Alexander Nevsky Church—their gold plate brighter than the moon itself!—and the wall of lindens surrounding Kongens Nytorv, toward the empty, silent opera house, and then left onto the Nyhavn.

The parlor was moonlit and sad, empty and silent; everyone else was asleep, just as they'd been the first time Dancer and Helle sat side by side on Daisy's favorite green sofa. *Clip clip clip* went the stork's beak, and small black crescents of hair drifted to the floor. She would be lying, Helle admitted, if she were to say that she didn't like the feeling of Dancer's fingers moving along her scalp, or if she were to pretend that her pleasure wasn't a result of having renounced all claim to such pleasure in the first place. Helle must have realized, Dancer said, that sooner or later Henning was going to have to die—*clip clip clip*—and that Helle was going to have to kill him. Sooner or later, he said. When he was done, he gathered the clippings together, put them into an envelope, and handed it to her, explaining that she should hide it somewhere. As long as she was alive, Dancer said, her hair could be used against her. Only after a person was dead was it safe for her hair to be made, for instance, into a ring, as they had with Kayo's. Nothing can touch you then, he said. Then you're in the realm of Helle, daughter of Loki and the giantess Angerboda. And was it true that half of Helle's body was bright red, and the other half the palest white? That her doorstep was called Pitfall; her knife, Famine; her plate, Starvation; her bedcurtains, Mischance? In any event, Dancer said, that was what he'd learned in school. Of course he was talking about hell.

Meanwhile, Inger proved to be a prolific correspondent. She'd always claimed that she hated to write, but every week the postman brought Helle another long, dull letter in which Inger detailed her new life as a married woman. The advantages, she wrote, outweighed the disadvantages. It was nice to have a home of her own, even though it sometimes seemed unnervingly quiet. She and Hans had one milk cow and were talking about getting another. A man in England who was planning an expedition to the Antarctic had contacted them about buying a large quantity of down; even if the business wasn't flourishing, at least it provided them with a living. No babies yet, but she was hopeful. She was sorry to hear about Helle's friend. They could all give thanks that the war was over, although Anders insisted that peace was an illusion. The older he got, the stranger and more difficult he became. It was bad enough when he would eat only potatoes. Then he started to eat wool and poor Gunhild had to hide her knitting. Maybe, one of these days, Helle would swallow her pride and come home for a visit? If she felt uncomfortable about staying at Krageslund, Inger and Hans had a dear little guest room, with blue flowered wallpaper and a flowered rug she'd hooked herself. "A married woman, Henning!" Daisy would say, every time another letter arrived. "I'd never have suspected that *you'd* turn out to be a homewrecker."

For four years Daisy had played along with Helle's deception. Then, the day before Helle's graduation from the conservatory, when she was trying on the pair of custom-made, spruce-green, knee-high leather boots Daisy had given her in honor of the occasion, she found a small tissue-wrapped package containing a pair of French silk stockings in the right boot's toe. Well, Dancer said, he guessed the secret was out that Helle had great legs. His gift was a new black sailor's cap, to replace the old one, and within the crown he'd packed a set of ivory hair ornaments from the Sudan; no secret, he said, that she had great hair too. Only Oluf Froulund's gift was straightforward, a tooled tobacco pouch filled with tobacco, indicating he at least hadn't seen through her disguise.

Helle's final project, what she referred to as the world's most dim-witted fugue, was performed at the graduation ceremony by a graduating group of chamber musicians, the Norwegian cellist among them; moreover, Helle won two prizes and Bingger took her aside at the formal reception to tell her that her future was assured so long as she remembered the words of the master—Fux, of course: "Do not allow yourself to be seduced into proceeding too early to your own free compositions. The mountain of the muses is to be reached only by a very precipitous path." But Mozart composed *Bastien und Bastienne* when he was twelve, Helle replied. Ah, Bingger replied, Mozart. Little Wolfgang. If Bingger recalled correctly, though the opera premiered, appropriately enough, in the Vienna garden of a certain Dr. Anton Mesmer, not everyone in the audience was hypnotized.

And certainly *Lahloo*, Helle admitted, wasn't without its

flaws. The ending, for example. She never was good at endings, unless, as with *Waves*, she had another person's text to guide her. Indeed, she sometimes thought the first production of *Lahloo* got mounted only because Rasmus Rundgren, the quixotic director of the Copenhagen Royal Opera, was bored. He wanted a challenge, a project that would call attention to his own genius and not merely serve as a showcase for some overweight and avaricious diva. The postwar world in which Rundgren strove to make his mark was characterized by widespread disregard for the workings of larger forces: having recently been swallowed up in history's maw, the postwar world, spit out at least momentarily into the sunshine, was busy licking dry its various parts. The prevailing mood was one of exhaustion. Tired of pulling together for a common cause, people wanted to bury their dead and get on with their lives; like Candide, they wanted to cultivate their own gardens, to grow something more interesting than the beets and turnips which they'd become heartily sick of during the war.

Of course Rundgren had been notorious for his innovative stagings of traditional operas even before the war was over. His contemporary setting for *Dido and Aeneas* was accepted by the audience without complaint. Who cared about Purcell, anyway? But when he turned *Der Rosenkavalier*, a popular favorite, into a political fable, the audiences and the critics revolted. To equate Baron Ochs with the Kaiser was objectionable: there was nothing comical about the Kaiser. To replace the Baron's missing wig with the Kaiser's famous pointed helmet was bad enough, but to depict Mohammed— the little turbaned Negro boy who, at the opera's close, lifts aloft Sophie's handkerchief—as a winking Nazi was nothing short of a travesty. So what if Rundgren's vision proved politically astute? You went to the opera to escape history, not to be reminded of its inevitability.

Thus it was Helle's good luck that by the time *Lahloo* was completed, Rasmus Rundgren was eager to produce something for which nostalgia could not be used as a critical standard. It was also her good luck that Daisy had finally decided to marry the persistent cement magnate. Thorkild Propp came from Mariager, a storybook town in central Jutland, on the outskirts of which the enormous chimneys of the Propp Cement Works filled the sky, day and night, with blue-black clouds. A large and cheerful man whom Daisy called Thor, he was given to wearing clothes at least one size too small, under the mistaken notion that packing his hamlike thighs into tight gabardine pants somehow made him look trimmer, more dashing. Although she would never love anyone the way she'd loved that handsome sailor boy so many years ago, Daisy explained that Thor knew how to make her laugh and, obviously, was very rich. The war had spread economic hardship throughout Europe, but it had also created the need to rebuild. Pigs and cement, Daisy said. Denmark was still exporting upwards of a hundred thousand pigs to England every week. And people everywhere clamored for boatloads of Propp Cement.

Mange tak! Oluf Froulund said, clasping his arthritic, translucent fingers together over his weak chest. Thank you very much. He was furious, because Daisy had just finished telling her boarders that after the wedding—two Thursdays hence, Thursday being Thor's day, and a small, private affair, since anything more lavish, given the advanced age of the couple, would be in poor taste—they would have to find new lodgings. She'd be moving to Thor's estate in Mariager, and once she was settled in she hoped they'd all come to visit. The estate overlooked the Mariager fjord, she said, and was unusual for being composed, largely, of cement. "Of course it's a terrible eyesore," Daisy added. "But very big."

Helle's response to this news was not as desperate as Oluf Froulund's, although she confessed to sharing his sense of betrayal. Besides, wasn't everyone leaving? Dancer had just signed on for three years as chief officer of a passenger ship, figuring that he might as well capitalize on his looks before he lost them. As it turned out, Helle never saw him again. One morning he was drinking a cup of coffee at Daisy's table, and the next he was hugging her goodbye in his new uniform. As usual his wide-set eyes took in everything but her face, just as the ruminant appears to be watching everything but the precise blade of grass it's about to nip off at the roots. The minute the door closed behind him, Daisy poured what was left of his coffee into the sink. She hated change as much as Oluf, Helle said, the difference being that Daisy had learned how to camouflage or eradicate its traces. For this reason the visage she presented to Thorkild Propp, when he arrived in her parlor several hours later bearing tulips and liqueur-filled chocolates, was as fresh and unlined as a girl's.

"Henning," Daisy said, "come join us. Have a chocolate." Raising her pale eyebrows ironically, she held out a box that Helle recognized as yet another of Propp's creations, a wobbly wooden object decorated with muddy oil paintings of his namesake's attributes: Mjolnir, the hammer; the iron mitt and magical belt; yellow Z's meant to represent lightning bolts; a cart drawn by two oddly foreshortened quadrupeds who were, as he explained, billy goats. For Thorkild Propp was one of those self-made men of business whose aspiration is to make a larger impression on the world than is created by dumping onto it tons of cement; he was an autodidact, a dabbler in the arts.

Always an honor, Propp said, taking Helle's bony hand in his fat ones. What he wouldn't give to be able to write music! No doubt Henning was acquainted with the work of Carl Nielsen? So beautiful! So soul-stirring! The Danish Sibelius, as they called him. But why not call Sibelius the Finnish Nielsen? Although the problem wasn't really the Finns, was it? The real problem was the Germans and Italians, didn't Henning agree? Wasn't your average Dane, after all, every bit as sensitive, as musical as your average Kraut? Hamlet was a Dane, was he not? Ha! And did Henning perhaps have a project of his own which might redound favorably upon Denmark's reputation?

The tenor of these remarks was intended to be ingenuous, although Helle could see a glimmer of cunning in the twin gooseberries of Hr. Propp's eyes. He seemed to be taking her measure, just as any successful businessman does prior to striking a deal, for which reason she chose to keep her opinions to herself. When you want something from someone, it's important to trim and shape the truth in order to present the illusion of fair exchange. Yes, Helle said, she'd completed an opera, but she assumed it would never be produced because of the Danish preference for the works of Strauss or Wagner or Puccini. When Hr. Propp urged her to play him a sample tune, she complied with "Dancing Sister." Lovely, lovely, he pronounced after she'd finished; he sat with his one arm slung in a proprietary fashion around Daisy's shoulders, acknowledging his enthusiasm by beating with his free hand on the broad expanse of his thigh. Was the rest as good? he wanted to know. Helle chose humility, the safest avenue of response under the circumstances. She could only hope so, she said, at which Propp let out another loud "Ha!" and drew a card from his vest pocket. Henning was to present himself at the inscribed address at noon the next day. The wealth of the Medicis had been based, perhaps, on a nobler commodity than cement; but patronage was patronage, was it not?

The address in question turned out to be that of the Royal Theater. As Helle approached it from across Kongens Nytorv, she could see, partially obscured by the statue of Ludvig Holberg, a large signboard announcing the current season's offerings: *The Wild Duck*, *Coppélia*, the Vienna Symphony Orchestra, *La Bohème*. It was October of 1923. The sun was shining brightly, the sky was blue; leaves were falling from the lindens around the square, revealing the knobby, fistlike shapes of the upper branches. When you trim the top of a tree straight across, Helle thought, you substitute aggression for grace. She'd heard the rumors about Rasmus Rundgren—his bad temper, his debauched weekends in Malmö, his fascination with disease—and wondered if this could be the aggressive result of a similar dedication to artifice.

Initially, all she could see of the man was his bullet-shaped head, thinly smeared with hair as a rock is crusted with lichen. He was sitting in the middle of the front row of the balcony, gazing toward the stage with a bored impartiality not unlike that of the gilt angel who roosted, a crystal lamp depending from her gilt fingers, immediately beneath him. In rehearsal for *Coppélia*, the female lead was practicing her opening solo. "Delibes," said Rasmus Rundgren. He never stopped watching the stage, gesturing impatiently for Helle to sit down beside him. "Ballet." A pair of steel-rimmed spectacles, their lenses dirty and flecked with dandruff, moderated the effect of his small, quick eyes. "A second-rate art form." Without language, he explained, art was basically amoral. The evidence was right in front of them. When, toward the end of Act Two, Coppélius decides to steal Franz's brain in order to plant it in his doll's brainless head, it isn't so that she'll be able to articulate the difference between right and wrong but so she'll know enough not to dance into a wall or out the window. A second-rate art form, Rundgren repeated, its crimes aggravated by the abysmal quality of the music.

Then, suddenly, he stood up. Propp was late, but any man who could make money selling bags of dust was bound to be resourceful; if Propp wanted to find them, he would. In the meantime they would adjourn to Rundgren's private office. Rising to follow him, Helle was startled to discover that he was at least an inch shorter than she was. He told her not to get her hopes up, his tone conversational and pleasant. Propp had said that the work was "very pretty," and if Rundgren wanted pretty, he could stick with Puccini. But Propp only heard one song, Helle replied. By now Rundgren was ushering her down a hallway in which, among packing cases and framed set-pieces, the glittering pendants of Hakon Werle's chandelier spilled across Mimi's gray mattress, the clasp of the Burgermeister's purse peeked out of Gina Ekdal's straw basket, Musetta's new shoes stood side by side on top of Pierrot's drum. This dark hallway, filled with the disjunct elements of many worlds, mirrored perfectly Helle's frame of mind. There is nothing worse than having to try to please two people at the same time when each one of them has an opposing idea of what they want from you. This, she knew, was her only chance to win Rundgren's support; once Propp arrived, she would become as odd as those red leather shoes or that purse, as helpless as anything lacking context. The work as a whole was unconventional, she explained. The tune she played for Propp was merely intended to provide ironic contrast. Oh, unconventional, Rundgren said—God help us.

As he paged through Helle's score, occasionally humming to himself, tapping his surprisingly long, beautifully manicured fingers on the arm of his chair, she surveyed the photographs of the famous, each one framed and personally inscribed, which covered the walls of his small, untidy office. Most of them, she couldn't help noticing, were from women: Amelita Galli-Curci (*"L'uomo è mobile"*); Adelina Patti (*"Al mio tesoro, carissimo Rasmussimo, dalla tua piccina"*); Nellie Melba ("Keep the sword sheathed 'til I return"). "Care for an orange?" Rundgren asked, taking one from a lower desk drawer and peeling it deftly. He looked disturbed when Helle refused, exclaiming that a person could never eat too many oranges; then he lifted a segment to his lips with his thumb and index finger, fanning his other fingers out like the elegant tail of a bird. According to Maeve Merrow, Rundgren's vanity focused on his fingers because he subscribed to the theory that they provided visible evidence for the hidden qualities of the penis.

At two o'clock Propp showed up and apologized briefly for his lateness, though he offered no explanations or excuses. In fact his manner was so imperious that it created an alliance between Helle and Rundgren, two artists joining forces against the rude world of commerce. By this time Rundgren had paged through to the end of the score, sometimes pausing to scrutinize a single passage, sometimes flipping through whole sections without so much as a glance. Did Propp have any idea, he asked, how expensive it would be to produce this opera? Not to mention how impossible it would be to find a mezzo who'd agree to sing strapped to a pole? But Rundgren's exercise of power through indirection was a version of what

Helle had grown up with: she knew how to read the signs, the way those beautiful hands first lifted, then weighed, and at last fondled the score. What wonderful smells, the smells of greasepaint, dust, orange peel! Down the long dark hallway traveled the sound of the orchestra playing the cheerful tune of *Coppélia*'s first-act mazurka: *dah dee da-da, dah dee da.* Helle imagined the entire corps de ballet leaping extravagantly across the stage, where, if all went well, professional singers would perform *Lahloo*. Maeve Merrow, Rundgren was saying, would be wonderful for Nanna. Difficult, but worth the effort. A soprano with presence. Siv Sonnengard for Lahloo? The critics loved her voice and hated her acting—but if she didn't have to move? Roman Grabowski, of course, for Rattail, and Charles Prince, more popularly known as Bonnie Prince Charlie, for the Harrow. Maeve couldn't stand him, which would add to the opera's erotic tension.

Rundgren's invocation of these names, combined with the faraway music of the orchestra, cast a greasepaint-scented, dust-spiced, orange-perfumed spell under which Propp seemed to find it impossible to lift so much as a finger. A fly was walking across his forehead, pausing midway between the commas of his eyebrows; his mouth was hanging open, and where his pink tongue rested on his lower lip Helle could see a faint glistening of saliva; his eyes were likewise moist. *Dahh—dedada, dahh—dedada, dahh—dedada, dah*: the dancers were twirling around and around at the feet of the pretty, brainless automaton.

And outside, the sun made the spokes of the school-children's bicycles glitter as they pedaled home to their mothers. How separate Helle felt from that world. She was twenty-six years old, competent, adult, ready for anything.

Part Four
FUGLESPIL

I

No, she wasn't good at endings, but then who is? And even though Helle had clearly gone to great pains to provide me with a version of her life that was *durchkomponiert*, lacing every element of the composition with clues hinting at the finale, my first glimpse of it took me completely by surprise. This was on a fresh breezy Saturday in early May, one of those days when with each breath you feel as if you're swallowing water from an underground spring. We were sitting on Buggy Moore's porch, which ever since he'd given Helle a cigarette the winter before, had become one of our routine stops. The three of us were smoking; the twins and William were arranged at different levels along the stream on the steep hillside across the road, their small, stooping bodies and the landscape which contained them looking strangely precise and two-dimensional, the work of a painter ignorant of the laws of perspective. Flo, in a white T-shirt at the top, was sending leaves down the stream, the idea being that William, in a red T-shirt near the middle, would put a passenger stick on each leaf, and Ruby, in a white T-shirt at the bottom, would collect them. The stream was sparkling, the surface of each rock washed over by a thin gleaming sheet of water; you could smell water everywhere, the sharply mineral smell it leached from the rocks tempered by the sweeter smells it drew from newly unfolded ferns and banks of tiny, umbrella-hatted mosses.

"You're a lucky man, Buggy Moore," Helle said, going on to explain that as far as she was concerned, it was a mistake for a human being to try to live any place where there wasn't a lot of water. Water, not air, was our natural element. "Always so proud," Helle said, "humans. Always wanting to prove that we don't remember our origins." Her own feet, she boasted, were delicately webbed between the first two toes; and when I regarded her doubtfully, she pointed out that it wasn't as if she'd never offered me the opportunity to see her naked. "You've missed the boat, Frances," she said, "on more than one occasion." She sighed, exhaling, coughing lightly, and then, because Buggy Moore was also shaking his head, she complained about being surrounded by a bunch of doubting Thomases. Wrong, Buggy said. It wouldn't shock him to hear that Helle had fins and a tail. He was only thinking about what his daughter would say if she heard that he was lucky to be living around all this water. As Buggy described it, his daughter—Dolores Soames, whom I knew slightly in her role as the mean-spirited president of the PTA—thought that her father should be living at the Soldiers Home, playing bingo every night with a bunch of zombies. "Stubbornness is an admirable quality," Helle said. "Then you'd love Dolly," Buggy said, to which Helle replied that she was referring to the father, not the daughter.

Yes, stubbornness was admirable, Helle repeated, lighting another cigarette on the burned-down stump of the one she'd just finished, then suddenly tilted her white, nutlike face upward. "Hear that?" she asked. "*Zoo-zee zoo-zoo-zee?* That dreamy lisping noise in the treetops? B, A-sharp, B, B, A-sharp?" Spring warblers, she said; blackthroats mainly, although there seemed to be some high-pitched, rachety *zip zip zip titi tseees* mixed in, which indicated the presence of Blackburnians as well. Aptly named, didn't I think? That little wiry squeal, just like Sam's, at the end of each sentence? But you couldn't even begin to compare these spring birds with the steadfast, stubborn birds of winter, she said, the ones brave enough to stay no matter how cold it got. Spring birds were fickle, showing up only when the world was fair again, once the worms had again started to emerge from their tunnels of dirt onto the new grass. Spring birds flitted and preened, craving nothing more than a plenitude of worms and unceasing admiration. They woke you early, hundreds of jewel-bright nuggets weighing down the tree branches. They would never dream of eating carrion; it took a stubborn winter bird like a crow to understand that kind of desperation.

Only wasn't Helle ignoring the fact, I asked, that a bird hardly bigger than a pea would dare to fly thousands of miles, year after year? Understand, I felt compelled to take issue with her views on this subject not only because of the way in which they implied a criticism of Sam but also on behalf of my own powers of judgment. *Wasn't* there something admirable, I asked, in flying thousands of miles, from Peru to Northern New York? "I think you're missing the point, Fran," Buggy Moore said. "It's their goddamn flightiness she's objecting to." A strong gust of wind sprang up, stirring through the needles of the pines on the ridge; the hindquarters of the white cat perched on the Chevy's aquamarine hood were likewise stirring as it charted the progress through the knee-high grass of something we couldn't see.

"Precisely," Helle said. "Flightiness." She let out another little cough—*hhh hhh*—and then, just as Buggy Moore was reaching over to offer her a sip from his beer can, the cough darkened, acquiring a darkly resonant rattle as it moved from her throat to somewhere at the base of her neck, finally settling low in her chest, welling up in huge, wrenched barks, each of which left her gasping for air. When I tried to reach around and clap her on the back, an arm swung out and punched me in the chest; her face, tucked down over her knees, was getting redder and redder. "Holy shit!" Buggy said, and it alarmed me to see how frightened he looked. Well, he said, it turned out Dolly had been right for once, getting the phone installed right after Christmas, even though he didn't need one. Emergencies, she'd said. He glanced at me to make sure I shared his opinion—this was an emergency, wasn't it? Meanwhile, Helle continued coughing, the color of her face changing from crimson to purple to blue. Yes, I said, an emergency. I grabbed hold of her shoulders, as if each cough were a result of their frantic jerking, not the other way around; once again her arm swung out and punched me, feebler this time, but still a punch.

The coughing had finally stopped by the time the ambulance arrived. Helle was lying on her back on the porch, her face having returned to its former whiteness, although now it was the white of a marl pond, unwholesomely opaque, faintly green. At some point Buggy had managed to tuck a pink afghan—a gift from Dolly, he explained, embarrassed—up under the sharp tip of her chin. A little sliver of tongue emerged, licked her lips—she was preparing to speak, preparing to curse us all, I'm sure, except that the minute she'd croaked out a single husky "What . . . ?" she once again started to cough, and the shorter of the two ambulance attendants, a big tipper named Jim whom I recognized from the diner, ordered her to be quiet. He took out a hypodermic needle, squeezed several drops of colorless liquid from it into the air, pulled back the afghan, and jabbed the needle into Helle's upper arm. "This'll calm her down," he said, "for the ride." The other attendant, a blond, handsomely weathered woman I'd never seen before, asked if one of us would be able to accompany the patient, and when I gestured in confusion toward the children on the hillside, Buggy volunteered, stubbed out his cigarette, put on a faded Dodgers cap, and hopped with unexpected agility onto the little fold-down seat in the back of the ambulance.

What's happening, I thought, what's happening? It seemed inconceivable to me that a woman as tough and woody as old gingerroot should be on her way to a hospital, that a woman as resourceful and glib as a magpie should be rendered speechless, that a woman as fierce and proud as Helle Ten Brix should be forced to succumb to the trickery of her body. The attendants lifted her onto a stretcher and slid it through the ambulance's waiting doors the way you slide a loaf of bread into an oven. Her feet, shod: maybe I'd never find out if she'd been lying about her toes. I yelled to the children, then went inside the house to call Maren, who was, I reminded myself, next of kin. A pink Princess phone—to match the afghan, no doubt. It was sitting on the floor between a blue macaroni-and-cheese box and a cow-faced condensed-milk can. The cheese has landed on your macaroni, I thought, listening to the far-off burring of the Blackburns' phone inside my ear. Helle's favorite line from *Il barbiere di Siviglia*, an opera which she otherwise claimed to prefer in the Bugs Bunny version. How could no one be home? Maren never went anywhere, and Sam usually spent Saturdays grading papers. I was about to give up when I heard his voice. "Yes?" he said, abrupt, peremptory, aggravated. And then, to my distress, I burst into tears.

So I ended up riding to the hospital in the backseat of the Blackburns' car, Sam driving, his eyes fixed on the road, Maren twisted around, grilling me. Had there been any warning that something was the matter? It was a cigarette, wasn't it? Didn't I know that Larry Kinglake had ordered Helle to stop smoking months ago? Emphysema, he'd said. Had she been smoking when it happened? Or was it possible that something upset her? God knows she'd often get worked up after her walks. I thought of the twins and William sitting where we'd left them around Mary Kinglake's kitchen table, paper napkins stuck into the neck holes of their T-shirts, eating tomato soup. All this talk about smoking was making me want to smoke, although I knew my overall appearance— the strings of my windblown hair, the strings dangling from the bottoms of my cutoff jeans, my secondhand football jersey, through the front of which I knew my nipples were visibly erect, not from arousal but because the sun had set and Maren had rolled her window all the way down—was affront enough. The twins had looked so placid and content sitting there in Mary Kinglake's kitchen, the pristine kitchen of a childless couple, with its mirror-bright appliances, shining yellow Formica countertops, ruffled white café curtains trimmed with yellow rickrack, the nearby humming in the pantry of a giant, well-stocked freezer.

No, I told Maren, Helle hadn't been smoking. It just happened out of the blue. Out of the blue, I said again, liking the sound of it, snapping my fingers, and Sam laughed, glancing up at me for the first time in the rearview mirror. We were approaching the hospital, all of its windows lit, all of its inhabitants undoubtedly propped up behind the trays containing their awful dinners—if Helle was in any shape to eat, I thought, she'd be livid the minute she stuck her finger through the little round opening in the silver dog-dish-shaped warmer and lifted it off. Well, Maren said, if there was anything funny in this situation, she certainly failed to get the joke.

According to Dr. Kinglake, who met us at the intensive care nurses station, Helle's condition was stable, the severity of her coughing spell a result of what looked like chronic bronchitis, exacerbated by emphysema. He was going to recommend oxygen therapy, but clearly nothing would do any good if the patient continued to smoke. He'd already engaged in a tug of war with her over the pack of cigarettes she'd hidden under her pillow upon arrival, and a candy striper reported that Helle had tried to bribe her to buy another pack in the machine down the hall. "She *pinched* me," Dr. Kinglake said, holding out his arm to show us, within a nest of thick black hair, a small mauve bruise. How could she! exclaimed Maren, bending over for a closer look, and I felt Sam's lips land briefly, daringly, on my neck, the frames of his glasses brushing across my cheek.

During the week Helle spent in the hospital I came to visit her every day on my way to and from the diner. On Sunday, both morning and afternoon, she was still in a savage mood, which wasn't improved by the presence in her room—211, the same room she'd be assigned a year later when she was dying—of a man-sized green metal capsule on a wheeled trolley. Who could sleep, she wanted to know, in the presence of a nuclear warhead? It wasn't a warhead, of course, but an oxygen tank. NO SMOKING, warned the sign on her door, OXYGEN IN USE. On Monday morning she was staring blankly at the television weather map; on Monday afternoon she was staring blankly at the trellis of pink and yellow flowers in the wallpaper. Nice view, I offered, and she hissed at me. By Tuesday afternoon she'd discovered Marco, and I found the two of them playing cutthroat rummy for cotton swabs, aspirin tablets, and suture buttons. Ennui, Helle said, was the killer, not disease. *La noia*, echoed Marco, *sì, sì*. Besides, the *signorina* didn't look sick. As indeed she didn't, sitting there in her intricately tucked and pleated white gown (Lucia's mad scene, Covent Garden production, 1959), her hair bound into its usual shining knob at the nape of her neck, her bracelet of silver birds encircling her right wrist, her kohl-lined eyes darting this way and that, her lipsticked mouth dispensing orders, so that the effect was more that of the levée than of the sickroom. On Wednesday she received the get-well cards the twins had made using their colored pencils from Switzerland. Ruby's showed a snub-nosed unicorn grazing in lumpy clouds. "I hop you feel better son," it was inscribed. Flo's was a self-portrait, severe in its interpretation yet skillfully rendered: she drew herself standing in front of the trailer with her hands jammed down into the pockets of her overalls, her eyes cast down characteristically to the left, her feathery eyebrows slightly raised over the bridge of her nose, a speech balloon saying "I miss you" emerging from her tensely set lips. An artist, Helle said. People probably took Ruby for the artist, because she looked so dreamy, but people were fools. For while Ruby was merely dreamy, Flo was observant. Well, observant and patient, Helle amended. Disappointed and stubborn. An unusual child.

Indeed, I arrived in room 211 on Thursday afternoon to find Flo sitting in a chair beside Helle's bed, the two of them busy setting up a large, squarish, boxlike object on an adjustable table. When I asked where Ruby was, Flo whirled around, her irritable expression a perfect duplicate of Helle's. Just because they were twins, why did I have to assume they'd always be together? Ruby, for my information, was with William; she and William were helping Mrs. Blackburn make a Jell-O mold that Helle didn't even want. She's right, Helle said—have a seat. But how did Flo *get* to the hospital? I persisted. It was much too far to walk; and even though she was mechanically inclined, I found it difficult to believe that she'd figured out how to hot-wire a car. Hot-wire! crowed Helle. Hot-wire! She loved it when I used words like that. Meanwhile, Flo turned her attention back to the mysterious object, lifting a thin metal rod from a carton on the bed, a metal rod with something small and colorful attached to the end of it, and waving it around in the air like a wand. "I came in a taxi, Ma," she said. "Helle paid." Helle told me to sit down, for heaven's sake, and explained, as if to a child, that she needed Flo's observant eye. Also the theater. Between the two of them, she said, they were going to design an opera.

The object on the table was a model theater—one of the famous Priors Dukketeatre, or doll theaters, constructed and sold by an old man and his wife in their shop at 52 Købmager-gade, Copenhagen. It was, according to Helle, a perfect replica of the stage of the Danish Royal Theater, a wooden framework with grooved abutments into which you could insert heavy cardboard panels, some of them entire rectangles, such as the curtains, drops, and scrims; some of them die-cut, such as the proscenium arch, borders, and drops. A beautiful building, Helle said, the Danish Royal Theater— of course we'd have to imagine the domed ceiling's nine trompe l'oeil lunettes, a muse hovering in the center of each one, surrounded by a light blue section of sky, all of them arranged in a ring around the millions of glittering prisms of an enormous crystal chandelier; we'd have to imagine the three tiers of red velvet seats, the top tier held aloft by golden swans, their wings extended, their long necks arching outward, the middle tier by seraphim, their wings folded in against their golden flanks, the bottom tier by naked golden women. It was as if the potential for flight decreased the closer you got to the floor. But who paid any attention to the floor in a theater? Helle knew, for instance, that the floor of the Royal Theater was carpeted, but she couldn't recall the color. A theater's floor, after all, bore such evidence of common human traffic as dirt or mud or snow; the crumpled white bags which once held toffees or licorice allsorts; dropped gloves, coins, ticket stubs—evidence, no matter how transcendent the architecture rising above it, of everything you came to escape.

But the rugs in our opera house, Flo said, were red. She knew because the night Ruby played the part of the little dead child, when Flo had opened her pocketbook to put in the program, all of her money had fallen out. She remembered it: silver and copper circles on a red background, like planets in another universe. You see, Helle said, an observant girl; marvelously observant. The trash was different, too, Flo continued, warming to the praise. No gloves, no white bags. Just a lot of squashed soda cans and candy wrappers. Programs with black shoeprints on them. Cellophane. She didn't know what licorice allsorts were, but she was pretty certain there hadn't been any. Definitely no toffee.

Helle nodded her head, pleased. Although when you got right down to it, there wasn't any real difference, except a difference in degree, between the Copenhagen Royal Theater and the Canaan Opera House. Oh, ours was smaller, the audiences more casually dressed; usually a chamber group, rather than the full orchestra called for by the score, would accompany the singers; and the singers themselves would sometimes have to run out during matinee intermissions to put quarters in the parking meters. Still, weren't the colors of our theater also red and gold? And hadn't the anonymous, itinerant nineteenth-century artist who painted its fly curtain (Daphne in her moment of metamorphosis, her father rearing up to watch from out of the swollen currents of the Hunger River) been every bit as attentive to detail as his Danish counterpart? Helle picked up the cardboard panel representing the Royal Theater's fly curtain and slid it into place, turning the whole structure around so we could see it better: on the curtain, stage left, a red velvet drape was being tugged back by three cherubim to reveal a terrace, its floor a checkerboard of black and white marble, a single rosebush drooping over its ornate stone railing. Could that be the Parthenon, miniature and spectral, perched on a cloud-wreathed mountaintop in the distance?

Swans and muses, gods and angels! Everywhere you looked in an opera house, Helle said, you should be confronted by the sight of creatures whose proper element was the heavenly ether, reminding you that your purpose in being there was not routine entertainment but transport. Opera houses should be designed with the sole intention of transforming you—to transform your sense of scale, to reduce you, finally, to nothing more than a pair of eyes, a pair of ears, a wildly beating heart. Why else, she asked, pointing, would the Royal Theater have EI BLOT TIL LYST written over its proscenium arch? Not Merely for Pleasure. Rapture, maybe. She closed her eyes. Oh yes, Helle said, definitely rapture.

Earlier, when I'd left the diner, the sun had been shining; but now I noticed that it had started to rain: a heavy spring rain lowering its own wrinkled, drop-pocked scrim down the window, darkening the room, casting wavery shadows across the trellises in the wallpaper, across Helle's impermeable face, across Flo's face, softer-featured and broader yet similarly impermeable. I could hear wheels squeaking in the hallway, the rattling of dishes, a voice saying "No, *I* did her last time," and suddenly a matronly teenaged girl in a pink-and-white-striped uniform—the candy striper Helle referred to as the quisling?—tapped at the open door with her pink-enameled fingertip and entered, tray in hand, first flicking on the overhead light and then cheerfully informing us that we were going to go blind. Turn it off! shouted Helle. How many times do I have to tell you I hate fluorescent lights! A handful, the girl confided to me—this one was a handful. Mrs. Brick, she said, heading toward the bed, if I don't put on the light, how are you going to see your dinner? And if you can't see your dinner, how are you going to eat it? And if you don't eat it, how are you going to get well? An insane young woman, I thought. But Helle simply told her to leave the tray on the windowsill, and then asked her if while she was at it could she remove some of those depressing flowers. Those tall pink ones, in particular, were driving her crazy. Not the *glads?!* exclaimed the young woman.

It didn't pay to make them mad at you, Helle remarked after the girl had finally gone; they'd only take it out on you later. Make your bed one of the stops for the doctors-in-training, so you'd have to lie there while ten boy doctors poked their stethoscopes around your poor old naked chest, trying to figure out where your lungs were. Assign Marco to some other wing. That was the worst. It was on Marco's account, by the way, that she kept the dinner. He had an amazing appetite. Food and women, Helle said—like the

Don. She reached into the carton on the bed and took out one of the metal rods. Like *you*, she said accusingly to the little figure attached to the end of it. A slide, she explained, handing it to me for closer inspection; the characters and the props were all attached to slides, making it possible to move them in and out between the panels.

The figure of the Don had been lithographed in four colors on heavy-stock paper and then cut out with scissors like a paper doll. He was part of a complete *Don Giovanni* set which had originally belonged to the Baroness von Schadenheim, and which the baroness had given to Helle in token of their friendship—although that, Helle said, was another story. Evidently the tradition of the model theater came into existence in England around 1800; Robert Louis Stevenson wrote a charming essay on the subject, in which he described the pleasures of purchasing, for a mere two pennies, a set of lithographed sheets containing all of the figures and props and backdrops needed to create a whole new world.

And it was a whole new world, Helle said, which she and Flo were about to create—specifically, the bog world of *The Girl Who Trod on a Loaf*'s second act, the world Inger drops into when she takes that fateful step onto the loaf of bread. The difficulty, Helle told Flo, was to somehow indicate that even though the bog was a world without air, water and not air was the medium crucial to sustaining life; their challenge was to see to it that the audience understood this on the most visceral level. Obviously you couldn't fill the stage with sphagnum, nor could you leave it empty. I watched, fascinated, as my daughter gravely nodded her head, took a clean piece of drawing paper from the carton, and removed from her plaid schoolbag the tin of colored pencils. Helle had told her, hadn't she, that bog moss was transparent? What if there were lots of transparent curtains hanging from—not the ceiling; what was it called, the fly gallery?—narrow strips of curtain positioned at different depths across the stage? She sketched some lines on the paper, sighed, and crumpled it up. No, it would be easier to explain this way, Flo said, taking a roll of string from the carton and cutting off approximately ten two-foot lengths. See, if you stretched these strings from one side to the other, taping them in place like this, you could hang the strips of curtain from the strings like laundry. She cut several sheets of paper into strips and taped the strips at intervals to the strings. If only the paper were transparent! Then you could really get an idea of what it would look like. Of course the curtains, she said, would have the outlines of moss plants painted on them, some with just a single plant, others thickly covered.

Scrims, Helle said, clearly pleased. We could hang scrims, and manipulate the lighting to make the surfaces either transparent or opaque. Thus the bog might initially appear to be a solid mass of peat, but a section of it lit from behind would suddenly reveal itself as an open channel. A wolf, she said— a wolf! Yes, she said happily, that would work! And the painted outlines, Flo added, could be different colors, layering one on top of another to make new colors—like yellow and blue made green, as she'd learned in school. What they needed, Helle said, were some sheets of that acetate graphic designers used for overlays. That and whatever kind of paint would stick to it. But this would work! The bog would be beautiful, seductive; you'd think, looking at it, that what you wanted more than anything else was the chance to immerse yourself in it. Instead of seeing it as the instrument of Inger's damnation, you'd see it as magical, even redemptive.

Still, the problem remained of how to depict visually Inger's

passage from one world to the other. The music would help—
the Gasping Aria, for example, which Helle had been working
on at night ever since she'd been admitted to the hospital.
"Ah air! Addio! Ah ah dear me . . . oh! Ah! I go where no
breeze blows . . . Ah, sweet despair as down I go. . . ." In what
will emerge as the second act's most frequently reiterated
motif, this aria juxtaposes the achromatic, slowly descending
runs of the clarinet and cello against the rapid, brightly flickering ascent of Inger's voice, implying that rather than fighting
her new surroundings, the girl is elated by them. "Through
skeins of moss and lively water," Inger sings, "the Bog Queen
claims me as her daughter." Yes, the music would help; but
would the audience realize that the world of air and sky—the
world Inger was leaving behind—was inherently hostile? Sure
they would, Flo said, if the airy world of the first act looked
even denser than the bog world of the second. The stage for
the first act would also have to be layered with curtains, only
lots more of them, and these would be painted with round,
globelike shapes that suggested air molecules rather than
moss. Then the audience would know that no matter where
you were, you shouldn't take breathing for granted.

Thus began the final, infamous year of Helle's life, a year
filled with mysteries, not the least of which was her mysterious
artistic collaboration with a nine-year-old girl. Dr. Kinglake
allowed her to return to the trailer on two conditions: that
she stop smoking and that she permit someone to check in
on her once a day. "You doctors," Helle said. "Just because
a woman's dying you think she's turning into a baby." "Who
said anything about dying?" asked Dr. Kinglake, at which
Helle laughed one of her short, dark little laughs. So I would
find them, strange old Helle Ten Brix and strange young
Florence Thorn, sitting in beach chairs on either side of the

fold-down table—sometimes building sets, sometimes discussing an aria, sometimes just listening to *Don Giovanni* while they sipped apple juice and nibbled cookies. Occasionally Flo would invite Helle to our house for supper, and she would appear grimly at the door, grimly sniffing the air as if for traces of culinary wrongdoing. To compensate she'd invite us to the trailer, where we'd be given elaborate feasts. Potage aux herbes panachées, ragoût de veau printanier, freshly baked pain de campagne, a salad of mixed wild greens, rhubarb tart, if she was in a French mood. Zuppa primavera, bruschetta, shrimp grilled in their shells over an open fire, insalata di arancia, blackberry ice cream, if her mood was Italian. One summer night she served us an enormous *bisteeya*, a Moroccan delicacy made by wrapping alternating layers of pigeon, curdled egg, ground almonds, and cinnamon in warka leaves, a kind of pie you were supposed to eat with your hands, surrounded by tiny glass dishes filled with such colorful and exotic condiments as orange sections and grated radishes in orange-flower water; chopped tomatoes, roast peppers, and preserved lemons; a thick black eggplant jam; a compote of dark-green bitter herbs; sliced carrots and ginger—when you came to eat at Helle's trailer, you never knew what you were going to find on the table.

What you could count on was that after the dishes had been cleared away, after Helle—the expression on her face amused because she knew perfectly well that no one was going to challenge her—had smoked a forbidden cigarette, she and Flo would get out the Dukketeatre. They would set it up on the fold-down table, positioning a row of stumpy white votive candles at the foot of its stage, a row of taller white candles behind it. The house lights would go down, Flo would light the candles, Helle would remove the fly curtain. One time it lifted to reveal the paper figure of a girl, a sturdy blond girl in a butcher-blue smock, a pair of bright red shoes on her feet, her feet stuck to a large round loaf of bread not unlike the one we'd just finished eating, floating slowly down through shimmering veils of peat. The tape deck clicked on and we heard Flo singing the Gasping Aria, Helle humming the accompaniment. Another time the curtain opened on four shadowy forms—the Bog Queen and her angry daughters— slowly rising from the bog floor, singing the Replication Canon along with Inger.

Of course three parts were missing, since only Helle and Flo sang on the tape, weakening the overall effect of its eerily overlapping sequence of complaints about God's inability, having set the universe in motion, to halt its frightening proliferation of matter. The way it was supposed to be performed, Grudge would begin ("The first cell so lovely"), and as she continued ("he thought he'd make more"), Retaliation would enter ("The first cell so lovely"), followed in turn by Unnameable ("The first cell so lovely"), the Queen ("The first cell so . . ."), and finally Inger: "The first cell so lovely he thought he'd make more; one cell into two, two into four, four into sixteen, until God got bored . . . until God got bored . . . God got bored . . . God got bored . . . God got bored . . ." Meanwhile, mimicking the canon's pattern, the women's shadowy paper bodies shuttled back and forth through the veils of peat. God amasses many little things into a bigger thing—a heart perhaps, or a lung—then amasses the big things into even bigger things. Animals. People. His astonishment at the beauty of those first little cells has been replaced by idle curiosity. What will happen, God wonders, if he squashes one of these big things between his fingers? "A burst of light, a flash of heat?" the canon continues. "A feathered soul, a bit of meat? Will it put up a fight? Will it be good to eat?" Thus God's terrible appetite is born, and with it the terrible human appetite, for weren't we made in God's own image? Little by little the intertwining voices of the five women are drowned out by a series of loud, ominous chords: D-minor chords, the very chords with which the Overture to *Don Giovanni* begins. The women sing louder, millions of little notes piling up on top of each other, but they are overwhelmed by the chords. A boot appears, sticking down through the roof of the bog. Two boots. The strings sough darkly, ominously—*lalalala, lalalala*—up and down the D-minor scale. The Don falls into hell. The end of Act Two.

Flo blew out the candles. It was a moonless night in late summer; we sat there in the dark, in the hot trailer, Ruby softly snoring in my lap, a humid breeze sifting through the louvered windows, the metal walls faintly rattling, Helle stifling a cough. "And next?" she said. "Next, the fun begins." But when she flicked on the light switch the theater was gone, Flo having put it back in its box. Of course the Don would try to seduce Inger. The question was, would he succeed? Well matched, didn't I think, the Don and Inger? Such a proud, hungry man, such a proud, tasty girl? This was a new Don, by the way, not the one she'd been given by the Baroness von Schadenheim. If I looked closely, I'd see that this Don was wearing glasses. Flo's idea, Helle said; some children understood, didn't they, how hapless, how uncontrolled, were the lives of adults.

II

Y**OU WOULD HAVE** expected that the Dukketeatre, or at least some of its cutout figures and props, would have ended up in the waxed carton, but you'd be wrong. I spent two Sunday mornings carefully sorting through the papers in the glove box, removing the photographs from the chocolate box and arranging them in orderly piles, painstakingly flipping through the pages of the notebooks and the bound scores, yet all I was able to show for my work was a page torn from *Artforum*, glued to a piece of cardboard. Damian Spark's design for the final wave in *The Harrowing of Lahloo*, Flo informed me, adding that she thought she remembered Helle gluing it to the cardboard to use as a backdrop; and no, in case I was wondering, she didn't have any idea what had become of the theater itself, although she'd already looked for it everywhere in the trailer. Severe Flo, who ever since Helle's death had taken to wearing her lank brown hair in a tight little knob at the nape of her neck, who refused to believe that anyone else's grief equaled her own.

According to Helle, even though she herself was bad at endings, Damian Spark—who committed suicide on his fortieth birthday, the day after Hitler's armies invaded Denmark—obviously was not. He was a true artist, she said, a

man whose gift was to effect that confluence of poetic detail
and scientific illusion without which art is mere decoration, a
man whose set designs for *Lahloo* perfectly realized her own
deepest intentions. If only I'd been lucky enough to attend the
Guggenheim's 1958 retrospective of Spark's work, perhaps I
could understand how wrong those critics had been, misinter-
preting that final, engulfing wave as apocalyptic, whereas in
actuality it was teeming with life. For the wave, she explained,
had formed the exhibit's centerpiece, a huge expanse of fabric
billowing down from the museum's ceiling. One side of the
wave was a green so dark as to be almost black, and Spark
had painted its surface with strange, wondrous forms: eels
whose immense jaws yawned forth from tiny spermlike bodies;
clusters of umbellula nodding their milky, tentacular heads; a
thick dark fish composed of nothing more than a mouth filled
with pale threads of teeth, and a single eye on a wavering
eyestalk; bright red starfish; feathery, translucent crabs; glass
sponges; medusas and polyps; sea lilies putting forth elaborate
plumes like those with which harem girls would fan indolent
sultans. The other side of the wave was a delicate and nubile
green—the green of luna moths, of new ferns—and painted
with lacy scallopings of white foam. What the critics failed to
understand, Helle said, was that when the final wave washes
over the deck of the *Lahloo*, it is clearing away the refuse of
a greedy, decaying world, and therefore enabling new forms
of life to flourish.

New forms! Anything might happen! For example, you
might think you'd been watching the premiere performance
of an opera composed by a young man—a young man as
engulfed by his black evening cloak as the ship had been by
the wave, a thin young man sitting tensely in the third row,
just barely visible through your pearl opera glasses—but what

finally emerged from the folds of his cloak was a young woman. Because, as Helle told me, it wasn't Henning Ten Brix who emerged that night from the ship's wreckage but Helle herself, who walked out onto the stage to take a bow wearing a dress of sapphire-blue shantung cut stylishly short to reveal the silk stockings Daisy had given her six years earlier. Her hair was also stylishly short, her eyes for the first time kohl-lined, her lips for the first time bright red, a pearl choker hiding the tattoo on her neck, silver high-heeled shoes on her feet. A madwoman, Rasmus Rundgren no doubt thought as he watched her sinuous approach—the result, Helle said, of hours of practice in the hallway of her new apartment. If she were to so much as wobble on her heels, she knew the audience and the cast alike would fall upon her and tear her to shreds; people hate to be reminded of their own credulity.

Meanwhile, as Helle stood there listening to the tidal ebb and flow of the applause, a few *brava!*s bobbing up in the undercurrent of murmured surprise and discontent, the future was dropping its own sly hints at her silver-shod feet like flowers. There were Maeve Merrow's suggestive wink, the critic Aksel Bram's scowl, the appalling sight of Anders and Viggi Brahe propped against each other in the front row of the balcony like two dying trees, punky and swarming with bugs. Later she would find them waiting for her in the wings, sitting together on a wickerwork basket, the two of them huddled under a tartan-plaid lap robe, opera hats askew on their heads. They both looked old, although in Viggi Brahe's case, Helle said, the deterioration appeared to be the result of years of insalubrious behavior, while for her father the cause was obviously beyond his control. Whiskers were growing out of the wrinkles on either side of his mouth as well as within the deep folds of flesh beneath his chin; his body appeared faintly phosphorescent, and gave off the powdery, sour smell that no amount of washing would ever remove, because it's the smell that presages death.

"Look," said Viggi Brahe, "it's Helle." Anders lifted what had once been the proud shield of his face, and whereas before he'd deployed it in her presence as if he were Perseus confronting the Gorgon, now his face reflected back nothing. Did she feel sympathy? Panic or grief? Mainly, Helle said, what she wanted to do was run. "Who?" asked Anders. How odd, she thought, that his earlobes would have gotten longer, and that he should be ending his days in the company of a man he'd once scorned. "Helle," Viggi Brahe repeated. "Your daughter."

"Oh," said Anders, staring at a pile of rope in the corner. "Well, whoever you are, you've certainly succeeded in making a spectacle out of yourself." Then he looked her in the eye and smiled. When she asked if he'd liked the opera, his smile widened. "You know perfectly well I've never liked fish," he said, exposing a mouthful of stunningly white false teeth.

"Spectacle" was the key word, for as Helle explained— despite Aksel Bram's contention that the "monstrous crea- tures on Spark's wave provided a suitable visual counterpart to the score, each measure of which was, itself, a monstrosity," and despite Bram's undeniable status as Copenhagen's most powerful and influential critic—*Lahloo* became a popular suc- cess because both the opera and its composer satisfied the audience's taste for the spectacular. Following the war, Helle said, the tiresome god Progress had so infected the hearts and minds of her fellow Danes that they would embrace anything as long as it implied forward motion. And if they might not have shared Spark's understanding of her artistic vision, they obviously adored the evidence *Lahloo* provided of money and technology at work, just as they were titillated by the fact that the opera had been written by a woman masquerading as a man. *"Den mystiske pige!"* they called her— "that girl of mystery!" *"Hvem er den ægte Helle Ten Brix?"* everyone wanted to know. "Who is the real Helle Ten Brix?"

In this way Helle managed to secure her position as one of Rasmus Rundgren's protégées; between September 24, 1925, when *Lahloo* was first performed, and March 7, 1944, when she left Denmark behind forever, all of her composed work premiered under his direction on the stage of the Royal Theater. Four operas date to her Copenhagen period: *Despina Unmasked* (1928), *The Shepherdess and the Chimney Sweep* (1931), *Waves* (1935), and *The Heroine* (1943), in addition to a variety of pieces in other forms, including *Innocence*, a song cycle for alto voice based on the poetry of Sappho; numerous concerti, of which the Piano Concerto in D minor is the most frequently performed; and the *Resistance Requiem*.

Of course I studied those four operas for clues to help me with *The Girl Who Trod on a Loaf*. But with the exception of *Despina Unmasked*, they were faithful to the texts on which they'd been based, and therefore to the endings the authors provided, so I found them less helpful than, for example, *Fuglespil*—a fifth opera begun in that period, although left incomplete until 1953. *Despina Unmasked* is a one-act opera, its central character "stolen" from Mozart's *Così fan tutte*, in which Despina is lady's maid to the two sisters, Dorabella and Fiordiligi, around whose maligned fidelity that opera's plot revolves. According to Helle, however, Mozart's Despina was a glorious woman, clearly deserving of an opera of her own; an expert in the art of deception, she not only disguises herself as a doctor and a notary but also recognizes romantic love itself as a form of disguise. Thus Helle's Despina makes her first appearance as a maid, undergoes a series of unmaskings, each one revolving around a new romantic attachment, until at the opera's conclusion she reveals herself in her true form: a sleek, black creature, moist and clearly dangerous—a Fury, in fact, the Bog Queen's prototype. The music in *Despina Unmasked* is an homage to Mozart—the final aria, "So do we all," is obviously parodic—and sublime, though more often performed in concert, since the opera as a whole is considered too bleak to draw an audience. Like *Bluebeard's Castle*, said one critic, except that Bluebeard is a woman, and it's easier on the ears.

Whereas *The Shepherdess and the Chimney Sweep*, the only opera Helle composed for children, is frequently staged, despite its difficult atonality. Andersen's story provided the plot, Daisy's parlor the inspiration: a story of love between a porcelain chimney sweep and a porcelain shepherdess, the opera can be seen as an indictment of that flaw in the Danish character, the need to make things *hyggelige*, snug and homelike, which so infuriated Helle. A repressed landscape, everything flat and neat, clipped and polished. Andersen, Helle said, had been similarly infuriated, which explained his tendency to provide the objects in his stories with the gift of speech. It was as if beneath the bland, tidy surface of Denmark there seethed an angry river of language, looking for a way out; and since the mouths of Danish men and women refused to release such language, it had to escape through less guarded, inanimate orifices. A menacing view of the world, really. Even though the ending seems happy, obviously the lovers' happiness doesn't extend forever into the future. Indeed, the finale takes place when the two figures shatter, and while the pieces are very beautiful—not unlike the shimmering cloud of moths released from the Lindworm's wound at the end of *Det omflakkende Møl*—there is no hope that even the most skilled application of glue and rivets could ever rejoin them.

Based on Virginia Woolf's novel, *Waves* also interests itself in the revelatory possibilities of language, and in this case Helle created parodies of six musical styles for the six separate voices, limiting the encompassing atonality of *Sweep* to the book's italicized sections. Each of these styles is suggested by the character's initial speech: for example, Bernard's "I see a ring hanging above me; it quivers and hangs in a loop of light" suggests the impressionist style of Debussy; Susan's "I see a slab of yellow spreading away until it meets a purple stripe" suggests Bach, in particular the great organ preludes; Rhoda's "I hear a sound, cheep, chirp, cheep, chirp, going up and down" suggests Mozart's piano sonatas. As in Woolf's novel, each of the voices narrates its own version of what will emerge as a comprehensive story involving all of them; and because it's the nature of music to permit many voices to speak simultaneously, Helle was able to pile up voices in duets, trios, quartets, quintets, sextets. The opera ends, as does the novel, with Bernard's cry of "O Death!"—followed by an extended atonal passage representing the waves breaking on the shore.

Of these four operas, only the last, *The Heroine*, makes overt the correlation between events—specifically, the invasion of Denmark and the romance with Maeve Merrow—and their effect on Helle's life. The source was Isak Dinesen's short story of the same name, published in Denmark in 1942, in which a young Englishman's wartime encounter with a beautiful and fiercely proud young woman—a woman "like a lioness in a coat of arms"—completely alters his perception of reality. Finally, years later, she provides him with a corrected version of the truth, one which honors human weakness in the face of those twin deities Eros and Thanatos. The opera is faithful to the text, its musical structure driven not by character but by plot: there are no memorable arias in *The Heroine*, no hauntingly individual voices. Event presides over a relentlessly constructed network of sound; you almost have the sensation, listening to *The Heroine*, that it is nothing more than a single, endlessly complex, and essentially claustrophobic measure.

If Helle expected me to come to terms with Inger's and the Don's enmity, what possible solution might these operas suggest which the composer would find "compatible with her intentions"? In two of them—*Despina Unmasked* and *The Heroine*—the ending is dominated by a single powerful female figure, although in the former the vision is reductive, severe; in the latter, subtle and ambiguous. Whereas *Sweep* and *Waves* imply that whatever routine struggles we experience in our lives must be understood in the context of a disintegrating universe, the minute parts of which are, ultimately, indistinguishable. Eventually, of course, in *Fuglespil*, Nightingale would embody these two warring possibilities, although that war's outcome only serves to confirm the horrible strength inherent in such a dichotomy.

Was it simply a question of gender? Once, when Helle was playing me a recording of the Dinner Table Sextet from *Waves*, I asked whether she could similarly assign musical styles to all of us—to me and the twins, to Sam and Maren, to herself. Oh, she replied, maybe, but what would be the point? To do so would be to assume there was a formal integrity to what the six of us represented, and unless she was mistaken, that wasn't the case. Besides, the men in Woolf's novel and, by extension, in Helle's opera, posed no real threat

to the predominant, female voice of the sea. When the waves
fall, when death overtakes the characters, they're all the same.
But Sam? How could I think there was any way to render
someone like Sam musically? Prokofiev, if you had to—the
duck in the wolf's belly, duck and wolf and belly all wrapped
into one. Childish music, seemingly pleasant, annoyingly sentimental. As long as Sam's around, Helle said, the waves won't
fall; or if they do fall around here, she added coldly, only one
person will get it. A threat? I asked, and she shook her head.
No, Frances darling, she said; a prediction.

Meanwhile, undeterred, I continued my affair. If anything,
the minute Helle was released from the hospital, Sam and I
began seeing each other more frequently, becoming less cautious in our choice of trysting places. The new configuration
of alliances—Ruby and William at the Blackburns', Helle
and Flo in the trailer—made it occasionally possible for us
to meet at my house. *Ping pang pong*, the pebbles would hit
the window. He would have parked his car a half-mile away,
driving it up an old logging road and hiding it behind a glacial
erratic. The logging road skirted the back edge of the soggy
area Judkins had tried to reclaim as pasture, and Sam would
press his way through wild raspberry bushes and scrub poplar,
stepping over mossy, crumbling lengths of deadfall, toward
the pleasures of my bed. For my part, I suspect that the
thought of Helle's eye trained on us, watching us as we stood
staring at each other fully clothed, as we each waited for our
bodies' wheels and pulleys to create in the feverish space
between us a mechanism discrete from ourselves, a mechanism
suggesting its own course of action, acted as an erotic stimu-
lant. Sam, on the other hand, once the initial excitement of
conquest was behind him, became driven instead by need,
choosing like many men to present his need as passion. He

could hardly get enough of me. Not just sex, but *me*—what Helle probably meant by duck and wolf and belly all wrapped into one. And she was right: his need was the unappeasable kind of hunger that a man with an empty place in his soul will always feel for a woman. A woman can fool herself into thinking that empty place is being filled during intercourse; a man cannot. That's why some men devour women whole. And then how sad they become, how tender and loving toward the poor little duck quacking deep inside them.

Although it would be a lie to suggest that this condition is limited to relationships between men and women. Or to quote Cook, in *Fuglespil*, "The bad eggs aren't all men." For although Helle was reticent to talk about the time she spent with Maeve Merrow—years which corresponded to her "Copenhagen period," and culminated in catastrophe—from time to time something would so forcefully remind her of Maeve that it was as if, in order to go on doing whatever she'd been doing when the memory hit, she had to unburden herself. Thus it happened that one day as Helle and I were wandering down the section of the Branch Road beyond Buggy Moore's house, two young women came cantering past us on horseback, and Helle, who'd been eagerly anticipating an afternoon in search of wild mushrooms, sat down on a rock and refused to go any farther. A bucolic sight, she said, wasn't it? You couldn't get more bucolic if you tried. Midsummer, the woods alive with birds and insects, girls riding horses, an old mushroom hunter and her beloved accomplice poised in the cool shadows of the trees, listening to the sound of retreating hoofbeats.

Ah, Frances, she said, why couldn't you assign form to your life the way you could to an opera? It would be so much easier, although without any firm knowledge about the circumstances of an ending, of course it was impossible. At least the religious disposition had the advantage of being able to acknowledge the twin portals of birth and death, both giving onto a world of pure spirit. But if you didn't believe in God, the symmetry was less pleasing, and the potential for happiness implicit in the fact of having been born was outweighed by despair at the prospect of dying. Only the creator of such an arrangement could find its symmetry pleasing.

You could force the issue. You could try to *make* things fall into place, the way they did in an opera. For instance, you could say that the start of your life had been presided over by the flaxen-haired deity of Inger, while it was dark-haired Frances who commanded its ending. You could try to see in Inger's lack of guile, in her insistence on fairness, a useful symbol for commencement; in my dark skepticism, one more fitting for conclusion. But were you to do so, you'd be overlooking the lesson of the bog. You'd be disregarding the fact that for the artist, there was always the possibility of an alternative portal, that third door which, in fairy tales, you were never supposed to open. This was the horrible lesson of Maeve Merrow.

Horrible, yet like so many horrible things, including most attempts at going where you weren't supposed to, it caught you off guard by beginning on an auspicious note. Bucolic, even. Midsummer, horses—did I get the picture? A day in midsummer, the fields outside Copenhagen bright yellow with flowering rape, the sky that deep blue used by medieval painters to represent the vault of heaven. A hot, windless day, and Helle was sitting astride a tall, white gelding who continually lowered his head, pulling her down across the bony hump where the neck joined the body as he tried to grab mouthfuls of flowers. Meanwhile, several yards ahead, on a younger, livelier horse, rode Maeve Merrow, appropriately attired in jodhpurs and leather boots, a white shirt with a stickpin at the collar. From time to time she would look back over her shoulder, frowning, shouting, "Don't let him get away with that! Remember, you're the master." Flies were buzzing all around them, their sustained note, Helle noticed, pitched exactly one half-tone higher than that of the grasshoppers and crickets hiding in the rape flowers, a continuo above which she could hear the squeaking of the saddle leather, the jingling of the curb chains, the clopping of hooves.

Maeve Merrow had grown up on the west coast of Ireland and, if she was to be believed, had been hurtling over hedges and walls and streams on the back of one of her father's mares before she took her first step. All the Merrows, according to Maeve, were long in the torso and short in the leg, which no doubt explained why they delighted the eye only when they were on horseback. A delight to the eye, Helle said. As indeed Maeve was that midsummer afternoon, the broad planes of her face lit by the sun, her carriage perfectly erect, the fluid motion of her pelvis suggesting that, at least from the waist down, the distinction between horse and woman had been erased. What you couldn't see, watching Maeve ride, was how thoroughly the element of tyranny had informed this relationship. By fixing on the beauty of the myth, Helle said, you missed the operation of will that made myth possible.

They finally left the rape fields behind, and the whole surface of the earth began to tilt slightly upward, no longer yellow but green, dotted here and there with squat bushes, in whose branches horned caterpillars had erected sticky, filamental tents. The caterpillars chewed away the tender parts of the leaves, avoiding the veins; once satiated, they dropped down into pools of shadow on the ground, where the birds

stopped singing for a moment to pluck them up and eat them.
It seemed to Helle that they'd been riding for hours, moving
farther and farther from the precincts of the known world,
and that the molecular composition of things beyond the crest
of the hill—toward which Maeve had been leading them all
afternoon—would prove inhospitable to normal life. Or
maybe, she said, that was merely the way it appeared now,
looking back. Of course there was no tangible boundary
between the two worlds, such as Maeve claimed there was in
Ireland, where you could tell that you'd crossed over because
the dogs would all have red ears.

At the top of the hill Maeve reined in her horse. How are
you doing? she asked, though her blue-violet eyes in their
thicket of black lashes, the only glamorous feature in an
otherwise plain face, were focused not on Helle but on the
horizon. Do you think that's the Øresund? she asked, pointing
toward a thin sliver of water barely visible off to the east.
Helle said she didn't think so, and Maeve consulted her
wristwatch. Well, suppose it was, she said, and suppose she
had an appointment in Copenhagen at six; did Helle think if
she rode like hell she could make it in time? No, Helle
replied, smiling the shy smile of the newly elect, the one for
whom the old lover was about to be stood up. A hard smile
to sustain, given Maeve's refusal to cut loose from her past;
but despite Rasmus Rundgren's pointed warning—Maeve
Merrow will sleep with anything, he'd said, men, women,
animals, showers of coins—in matters of the heart you always
hope that you'll prove the exception to the rule. Besides, Helle
reminded me, this was her first real love affair, even though
she was thirty years old, the same age I'd been when we first
met on the opera house steps. An innocent, a naif! It hadn't
yet dawned on her that Maeve's governing obsession was not

with her but with the horse. Nor had she yet realized that
Maeve was not primarily a singer—that her astonishing voice
was nothing more than the outward expression of a will dedicated to adventuring forth on its own, heedless of the consequences.

Which was probably why Helle misunderstood Maeve's
request that she dismount, just as she attributed the subsequent weakness in her legs to an anticipation of passion rather
than the fact that her legs had been clamped for hours to a
saddle. A midsummer afternoon . . . love on a sunny hilltop
. . . birds eating caterpillars . . . the horses wandering away
. . . who cared? Though as it turned out, what Maeve wanted
was the chance to ride off by herself. Helle shouldn't take
offense, she said, but this snail's pace was driving her crazy.
A half hour at most, Maeve promised, regarding Helle as if
it were she, and not her dismal mount, who was cursed with
spavined hocks and a frail constitution. Thus the heedless will,
in order to thrive, requires that there should be a sedentary
observer, a fixed marker against which it can measure its own
velocity, by which it can calculate how far it has traveled.
Would this account for the religious bent we find in so many
explorers? Certainly it would explain the plight of women.

Chak chak chak chak, sang a magpie. B-flat. But Helle
wasn't ready to hear in its song the first hints of *Fuglespil*;
nor was she ready to hear in the *huphuphup* of the soldier bird
intimations of approaching war. Inger had recently had a baby,
Anders was dying, Helle was in love—her sensibilities were
attuned to the nuances of the human drama, which, after all,
has its roots in our animal nature. She sat watching her horse
chew grass, taking note of the way its lips turned from pink
to green; of the way the foam collected within the trough of
gum tissue at the base of its long yellow teeth; of the bright

green fly lodged, possibly dead, in the corner of its white, indifferent eye. By paying close attention to one thing you could avoid the sight of another—of Maeve's horse retreating down the hillside, the light glinting off its upturned shoes and its spiraling brown tail, an image of operatic, disturbing proportion.

According to Helle, everything about Maeve was operatic and disturbing. Her presence in their shared apartment, for example: Maeve wasn't sloppy, but she had a decorative impulse which led her to drape tasseled, sequined shawls and bead necklaces over the tops of mirrors, to hang the walls with reproductions of pre-Raphaelite paintings, the dreamy expressions on the faces of all those Guineveres and Galahads in sharp contrast to the solemn faces of her relatives looking out from their frames on top of the piano. Daisy had given Helle her upright, since the estate in Mariager was already equipped with a Bechstein, which, she pointed out dryly, neither she nor Propp knew how to play. For a while, until one day Helle swept the entire surface clean in a fit of irritation, a big silver loving cup—one of Maeve's many awards for prowess in the steeplechase—also sat on top of the piano, filled with sprays of desiccated wildflowers, their seed pods releasing a continual shower of fluff across the keys. Dead flora was everywhere, Maeve's favorite season being autumn. No matter if a spring breeze blew outdoors; leaves would be falling inside, where Maeve's two cats would pounce on them, as if to exercise such skills as might prove useful in catching live prey, although the apartment was overrun with mice.

In addition to the cats, Maeve—modeling herself, most likely, on the eccentric Croatian soprano Ilma di Murska, whose dinner companion was said to be a giant Newfoundland dog, and who traveled with an entourage of apes and parrots—had a tendency to introduce more exotic animals into the household, such as Siamese fighting fish, iguanas, snakes, a capuchin monkey, and in one particularly ill-advised moment, a baby wolverine. Unlike the cats, none of these pets lasted for very long, Maeve either forgetting to feed them, as in the case of the fish, or simply losing interest and giving them away. After the wolverine bit her, she fed it poison and carried it off in a suitcase to one of the taxidermists on the Nyhavn, who made it the centerpiece of his window display, its sleek head caught in the act of lunging back, snarling, over its shoulder. For a while, Helle said, no excursion was complete without a side trip to the taxidermist's shop. Look at those teeth! Maeve would exclaim, one hand pressed to the glass, the other to the place on her thigh where she'd been bitten. Then her pupils would dilate until her eyes were as black and luminous, as profoundly witless as the two glass beads set in the wolverine's eye sockets, and it was as if she couldn't get home, couldn't fall onto the bed, couldn't pull Helle down quickly enough beside her.

Those mad caresses, the humid landscape of another person's skin, the moment when your mind—still filled with thoughts but suddenly lacking the mechanism which makes thought possible—is funneled out of its place in your head to leap around like common muscle and nerve between your legs! Having held herself aloof from her body for so many years, Helle confessed that its awakening to sex left her both ecstatic and terrified. Or as Sappho wrote in the first of her poems which Helle set to music: "Virginity, virginity, when you leave me/ where do you go?/ I am gone and never come back to you./ I never return."

On the hilltop, meanwhile, Helle fell sound asleep; the sun

set; her horse vanished. The pools of shadow at the feet of the shrubs grew into towers, and then the towers grew taller and thinner until they were so tall and thin that they were no longer towers but masts, all of them pointed toward the city, the direction in which Maeve had steered her horse an hour earlier, and from which she was at last riding back. Look at you, she said in a voice dark with reprobation—you're covered with ants. Helle rolled over, looked up. Donkey Man, she thought, as the curb chain's jingling and the crickets' single held note became higher and higher pitched, the sound of the tips of the shadow masts and shrouds squealing against one another. Climb on, Maeve said impatiently, and then before Helle knew what was happening they'd taken off at a gallop, the rocklike sheath of Maeve's ribcage expanding and contracting within Helle's desperate grip; everything else, including Helle herself, seemed to have turned to wind, a furious blur without source or motive. Things flew by, or they flew by things—it was impossible to tell the difference. Midway down the hill they came upon Helle's horse, busily eating the bush in which its reins had gotten tangled. Thank God he didn't snap his cannon bone, Maeve said, reining in her horse so Helle could stumble off.

It hardly mattered if you and your lover were of the same gender; she might just as well have been a member of a different species, so impossible was it to develop anything resembling a sense of common purpose with another human being. Thus you might find yourself, at the end of a disappointing day, jealous of a fourteen-year-old stable boy. In the limited glow of a lantern Helle watched his face bending toward her sweetheart's over a cracked hoof. The boy was holding the tin out of which Maeve was scooping a black paste; he was whispering tenderly into the horse's ear as

Maeve painted the paste on. Maeve would never look at her, Helle knew, the way she looked at him. In fact, after her audacious masquerade, there was almost nothing Helle could do to hold Maeve's attention. It was cool in the stable; flecks of straw and horsehair sifted through the lantern light. The boy offered Maeve a bottle of beer, which she accepted nonchalantly; then they leaned back together against a post, their bodies touching along the length of their arms, their thighs, discussing the virtues of the various horses. He'll make a good eventer, Maeve said, pointing toward the opposite stall. Nice conformation. But the boy wasn't so sure. He thought he'd seen signs of unsoundness, and Bobby could already cover an oxer without even trying. What were they talking about? Helle stood off to one side, stroking the nose of a gray horse whose face reminded her of Dancer's. The skin was so soft, the little whiskers so delicate and vulnerable, that it took her completely by surprise when the horse grabbed her index finger in its teeth and bore down hard. The truth is, there are endless worlds, all different, radiating outward from the millions of inhabitants of this planet, and in each of these worlds it is possible, if you're not careful, to lose a part of yourself. As Maeve reminded Helle later, she was lucky to escape with nothing more than a bruised knuckle.

III

HELLE HAD OCCASION to recall this incident when she returned to Krageslund the following December, ostensibly to watch her father die. She hadn't wanted to go, but Maeve pointed out that this would justify the claim of some of her critics that seawater ran in her veins—strong-willed Maeve, who insisted on accompanying her; treacherous Maeve, whose reasons for doing so probably had more to do with curiosity than concern. Similarly, it was Maeve who talked Rundgren into lending them his car; and when they finally got to Krageslund, it was Maeve who pushed Helle through the front door. How strange to discover that the house had been decorated for Christmas! A huge fir tree filled the entry hall, its boughs weighed down with candles in molded tin holders, with Ida's blown-glass, hand-painted ornaments shaped like pine cones, trumpets, and drums. The staircase was looped with swags of balsam tied in place with red satin bows. On the oak table where Helle had been accustomed to seeing her father's black bag, his gloves, and his newspapers, a wooden crèche had been set up; far off, at the other end of the table, stood the Three Wise Men and their attendant camels. Every morning this group moved a little closer to the manger, Helle said, as if to provide her with a means of measuring the length of her stay, or to chart the progress of her father's own mysterious journey.

Helle had come prepared to detest Gunhild, and consequently found herself unsettled by both the grave expression on her stepmother's face and the gratitude with which she accepted Maeve's embrace. Every hint of her former voluptuousness was gone, and her yellow hair was mixed with gray. Anders was asleep, she explained, going on to say that for a week he'd hardly been able to sleep and that, when awake, he set her impossible tasks, the most recent of which was to exhume Ida's body. "He wants her in bed with him," Gunhild said, adversity having extracted every trace of coyness from her voice, leaving it as flat as the rest of her. The decorations, it turned out, had also been Anders's idea, based on his theory that Death might be fooled by festive camouflage. For instance, Niels was out looking for boxwood at this very minute, just as he'd spent most of yesterday looking for mistletoe. Helle figured that from where she stood, the number of steps required to reach the sickbed was probably equal to the number that would carry her to Rundgren's car. But she didn't know how to drive—nor did she ever learn, firm in her belief that most inanimate objects were possessed of antic and malicious urges—and it was clear that Maeve had no intention of leaving. Maeve told Gunhild to get some rest, to let her take over, and didn't even bat an eye when Gunhild stopped for a moment on her way up the stairs to explain where they could find the clean diapers. "He soils himself," Gunhild said, and then was gone.

They spent a week at Krageslund, during which Helle was forced to witness the gradual transformation of Maeve into the perfect version of what she herself was supposed to be. Indeed, since Anders remained confused about identity, it was only a matter of time before he became convinced that Maeve was the real daughter, Helle the interloper. Walking down the hallway, she would hear, through the open door of the examining room where her father sat propped up behind the bars of a large criblike bed, the sound of playful conversation. "What small hands you have!" she heard him say on one such occasion, getting the wolf's part wrong. "Small but hardy." Maeve was rubbing her father's feet, something Helle couldn't bring herself to do. "From milking," Maeve explained, and then went on to tell a long story involving a pair of kidskin gloves and the mayor's second wife. Since all of Maeve's stories were drawn from personal experience, Anders's tendency to laugh with her over them, as if in recollection of a shared past, was enraging. How could this be happening? Helle knew that the pleasure Maeve took in Anders's company wasn't counterfeit and, moreover, that her relationship to her own father, who'd died when she was just twenty, had been unusually close. Besides, Helle would never have wanted to trade places with her.

Envy and relief, a horrible combination. Mealtimes were particularly difficult. Niels developed a crush on Maeve, like every adolescent boy with whom she came into contact; they would sit at the kitchen table, bumping elbows and making faces. "Oatmeal's the best," Maeve announced over breakfast the morning after their arrival, "though you've got to mix it with something stringy. Do you have any celery?" Years later, Helle would try to locate hints of her half-brother's parentage in Maren's placid good looks, but they shared only a long upper lip, and Niels was, at seventeen, a blocky, unattractive youth with a slightly dished-out face, reddish hair, and freckles. Helle watched, amazed, as Maeve worked her charms: one minute she was filling her mouth with food, and the next she was opening it wide in order to demonstrate the rules for "Repulsion," a game she'd learned at boarding school. Later she would engage Gunhild in a discussion of the best way to remove bloodstains from linen. For Maeve managed to charm Gunhild as well. They walked around together, arms linked, whispering. They gave each other manicures. At night, when all the clocks struck nine, they kissed each other on the cheek like sisters before heading for bed.

Of course Maeve spent her nights with Helle. Was it true, as Helle claimed, that the attraction was primarily physical, or was this merely another one of her strange attempts to provoke my own jealousy? Why else would she encourage me to imagine the two of them lying there on her childhood bed, Maeve trying to see whether it was possible to circle Helle's waist—a waist evidently as slender and taut as Maeve's was plump—with her hands, her fingers avidly stroking and adjusting, describing points and arcs, as all the while Helle tried to push her away? For didn't I agree, Helle asked slyly, that no one, least of all a self-indulgent lover, had the right to make circles at night after a day spent creating triangles? Maeve and Niels and Helle. Maeve and Gunhild and Helle. Maeve and Anders and Helle. Even old age, Helle insisted, that great plot thickener, hadn't been able to thicken her waist, although she had to admit that it was no longer so finely articulated as it had been back then, back in the days when Maeve compared it to the pedestal of a communion chalice, to the neck of a hookah. Slowly, slowly she would lift Helle's gown. Every night a little more of the moon would be visible in the top pane of the window, just as every night invisible hands, an invisible tongue, would adjust the increasing pitch of her desire. What Maeve wanted, Helle said, was to make her moan out loud. Whereas I suspect that what Helle wanted, telling me this, was to create the ultimate triangle: Maeve and Frances and Helle.

Afterwards Maeve would put on the tortoiseshell glasses she used for reading, pull the standing lamp closer and reposition the tilt of its shade, then page through one of Gunhild's magazines. The lamp, Helle noticed, was new, and the formerly pale blue walls had been papered over with a rain of stemless dark blossoms; but otherwise the room appeared unchanged. To the right of the window, beckoning from the front seam of the wing chair's blue-and-white-striped cushion, was the same white feather she'd noticed the night she packed her bag to leave home forever; opposite the bed, the mirror over the dresser continued to add weight to your torso while removing it from your head. Her books, likewise, remained as she'd left them on the shelves: dove-gray Ovid between glove-leather Donne and water-stained Hawthorne; upside-down Stendhal next to sea-green, tilted Homer. When she opened the drawer of the bedside table she found two stemless tufts of cotton grass shuttling, rodentlike, around the bottom of it.

Meanwhile, Maeve would fill her in on the reasons behind the declining popularity of the Charleston, or the latest antics of John Christmas Møller, the Conservative party's boyish new leader. Damp in the walls, obviously not a problem at Krageslund, could be controlled by the application of verdigris. She introduced this particular piece of information the night after Inger and Hans had joined them for supper, accompanied by their infant son, Hans the Younger, his tiny head nestled like an apple within the soft folds of an eider bunting. The house Maeve had grown up in, she told Helle, had been as subject to decay as Krageslund obviously was not. Look at that floor! Perfectly flat. Where she grew up, you could put a marble down in the vestibule and it would roll from room to room. Furthermore, on its way through the parlor it was bound to pass a dead body surrounded by keening women, since that was the way it worked in a large family— people were always dropping off like flies. Would it interest Helle to know that Krageslund was nothing like what Maeve had expected? Listening to Helle, a person came away with the impression that she'd grown up in the castle of Otranto. You might think she'd grown up among monsters, whereas clearly Gunhild was a courageous woman, Niels was a fine boy, and Anders—well, Anders was a lamb. Good people, all of them.

But how could Maeve Merrow, a genuinely evil woman, recognize goodness? What I had to remember, Helle said, was that although she herself knew that her father wasn't a lamb, she also knew the extent to which her own character was defective, and that among its many defects was the need to keep her defects hidden. Maybe this would explain why if, as the saying goes, the shoe fit, Maeve wanted to make Helle wear it. Or maybe Maeve realized all along that the shoe didn't fit, and her real purpose was to make Helle cram her foot into an undersized shoe, an act which would require lopping off toes or the back of a heel—an act which would, in other words, draw blood.

Which was just another way of saying that Maeve, not unlike Inger, seemed driven by a love of justice. An ultimately misleading similarity that Helle had noticed during supper, when Maeve had supported Inger in a discussion of the government's latest regulations on farm production. It was the little farms, Inger had said, that would be hurt the most. Wasn't that right, Sugarpie? She was cradling the baby in one arm, while with the other she took a roll from the basket, set it on the tabletop, and then, by way of demonstration, pounded it flat with her fist. Inger's method, Helle had observed, was to address all of her comments to the baby, a strategy no doubt developed in response to her husband's habit of referring to her in the third person. *Moder*, Hans called her. Mother. What Mother failed to understand, he'd explained, was the larger economic picture, in which poultry and cheese were placed in the foreground in an attempt to adapt to the needs of the foreign market. Helle saw an austere seventeenth-century landscape, its distant watermill and delicate shade trees dominated by giant chickens and wheels of Havarti. How about cement? she asked, in bored recollection of Daisy, but Hans didn't have a chance to reply, because suddenly Maeve was lifting the squashed roll and waving it in his face. People like Hans made her so mad, she said. While they were talking about the foreign market, people were going hungry. Who cared if King George liked coq au vin? Why satisfy the needs of royalty at the expense of the people? Why talk about economics when there was a dream of common greatness waiting to be fulfilled?

Inger pressed a kiss to her baby's forehead; Gunhild wiped her mouth with the napkin she'd stuck into the collar of her blouse; Niels regarded Maeve with dumb admiration through the pale blue fishbowls of his eyes; Hans sighed and ate a turnip. The kitchen was disturbingly bright, and it occurred to Helle that this was the first time she'd seen it lit by electricity. The key phrase in Maeve's outburst was "common greatness"—it was one of her favorite phrases, and helped clarify the distinction between her sense of justice, which would prove soon enough to be tragically prophetic, and Inger's, which was always highly personal. But such a dream, Hans pointed out, couldn't exist in a vacuum. Wasn't such a dream, whether on behalf of the farmer or the merchant or the artist, dependent on the economic health of society as a whole? Surely Helle would agree that an extravagance such as opera could never find adequate support in times of economic hardship? How annoying, she thought, that Hans—stupid Hans, tall and round, his Adam's apple rising and falling like a turnip swallowed whole—should have hit upon an unarguable line of reasoning. Except that art wasn't a luxury, she replied, and was preparing to explain how the problem was cultural, not economic, when Anders suddenly yelled "Ida!" Gunhild got up to see what he wanted, and the baby began to howl.

According to Helle, if you made the mistake of returning to the cradle of deceit—by which she meant the house where you'd spent your childhood—you would shrink; go back once too often and you would vanish altogether. Eventually she extended this theory to include the discontented children of the middle class, runaways whose hazy pictures you would see in post offices, pinned up among the pictures of murderers and bank robbers. Those children weren't lost but had merely become so small, so transparent, that their own parents—the terrible agents of this metamorphosis—could no longer see them. You and me, Frances, she would say, we got out just in time. Look at us! Possibly she was right. At the very least her theory would account for her feeling of having been transformed, that December night, into something as flimsy as one of those sheets of tissue paper you find covering the full-color plates in an expensive book; of having become the expendable protector of all that is lavish and valuable.

It was a cold night. Helle slept fitfully, and some time around three o'clock was awakened by Maeve's snoring: *Puh puh puh puh*, a delicate, flaccid sound. Lying on her back, her lips moving as if to blow kisses or bubbles at the ceiling, how pretty Maeve looked now that she was no longer filled with zeal! Helle got out of bed and walked over to the window, drawn by that hidden system of cords and yokes which governs the soul's enigmatic motion. The moon was almost full, roosting in the branches of the linden. *Puh puh puh puh*—where had she heard that before? As she listened, the sound within the room was answered by a similar, albeit more resonant, sound from outside. *Puh puh puh puh. Poo poo poo poo.* Subject and answer, subject and answer. All at once it came to her: what she was hearing was the opening section of the love duet near the end of *Die Zauberflöte*, though in this case Papageno was her sleeping lover and Papagena a hungry owl—specifically, *Aegolius funereus*, or Tengmalm's owl, vagrant to northern Jutland, a little creature about the size of a dinner roll, with a child's large, surprised eyes and an appetite for wood mice. Of course Helle didn't know this at the time, only that an owl was flying across the bog, its blue shadow racing beneath it across the surface of the snow. The owl was headed in the direction of Sandhed, toward those provocative, moonlit chimneys.

The next day Anders, perverse as always, rallied. Unlike Lazarus, he rose without divine assistance, and then, trailing cerements, shuffled down the hall to the kitchen, where he came upon Gunhild kneading dough in the dark. It was very early, the rest of the household still asleep. He frightened her to death, Gunhild admitted later. One minute she was alone in the room, the next minute she could feel hot air on the back of her neck. Evidently Anders stood there breathing on his wife for several minutes before requesting a cup of coffee. As Gunhild explained it, even though this was the first normal request he'd made in months and should have been cause for celebration, she discovered that what she felt was more like dismay than gratitude. Indeed, she might have ended up paralyzed with guilt forever had Anders not suddenly started to beat with their sterling soup ladle, a wedding present from the Funen cousins, on the cast-iron lid of the teakettle. Wake up! Wake up! he yelled. Everybody up! His idea was that they should all go for a trek on snowshoes, several pairs of which, he happened to know, were stored in the root cellar.

It was the kind of winter day when everything in the world looked like it was about to crack into pieces, when the sky seemed to be made of the thinnest blue porcelain, and there was a fine black outline around each tree, each branch, each tiny drop of water depending from each twig. By the time Niels located the snowshoes the sun was just coming up over the rose garden, turning its dark lattice of canes pink, the thorns red; Anders, whose enthusiasm had turned to ferocity in the wake of Gunhild's objections, was once again yelling. What was everyone afraid of? That he'd drop dead? But wasn't that what they were all waiting for? A man couldn't drop dead while he was lying down, could he?

As it turned out, Gunhild need not have worried. Instead of striking out toward the white expanse of low hills to the east, or toward the white expanse of peat to the west, Anders led the group Indian-file around the house. Around and around the house they marched, their track deepening with each successive orbit. Was anyone else getting sick of this? Maeve asked, but Helle could see that her cheeks were pink and her eyes were shining, and realized that for Maeve there was very little difference between adventure and derangement. Eventually Anders brought them to a halt in front of the middle parlor window. The fruitwood table, he said, pointing, was to go to his dear wife. Also the bell jar and whatever that thing was that was under it. Niels was to get the clock. Panting Time toileth after him in vain, if they took his meaning. The rest was to go to Maeve.

So they continued their journey, pausing at other key windows, notably those looking into the examining room, the dining room, the kitchen, the morning room. A brass candlestick here, an embroidered cushion there, a pair of bookends shaped like hands, a set of knives—Anders's method of dispersal remained the same, consigning one or two objects to his wife or son while the lion's share went to Maeve. They were all aware of the diagnosis, that Anders was suffering from a form of dementia associated with senility; Gunhild reminded them of this fact, gathering them together in hurried colloquy behind a clump of elder bushes. Obviously Anders was not to be taken seriously, Gunhild said. She appeared anxious, chewing on the tip of her gray and yellow braid like a young girl. Well, of course not, Maeve replied, although she had to admit she'd taken a fancy to that cloisonné vase in the morning room.

By the time Anders finally ran out of steam, Helle was the only member of the party to whom he'd bequeathed nothing. It wasn't until much later, when they were sitting together eating potato soup in the kitchen, that he suddenly chose to acknowledge her presence. Three things for that one, he said, waving his soup-coated spoon more or less in Helle's direction. *Primo*, the piano, assuming she could afford to move it. Bringing them to *secundus*, a certain box of gold coins, about which one could only say, *non numero haec judicantur sed pondere*. Ditto *ultimus*, the remaining half of what had once been a pair of dueling pistols, with the stipulation that if she decided to use it she bear in mind that *summa petit livor*. While talking, he sat with his neck tilted downward, regarding his soup bowl like Narcissus at the pool. Why, he isn't crazy, Helle thought. He might be fooling the rest of them, but he knew that she could understand every word, for hadn't he taught her himself? Cicero: "These things are judged by weight, not number." Ovid: "Envy seeks the highest things of all."

Maeve and Helle left Krageslund the next day, and Anders died a month later. Because Helle had given in to what came to strike her as a coward's impulse, accompanying Maeve on a concert tour through the geographic confusion of Bavaria and Austria, by the time the telegram met up with them in Berchtesgaden it was already too late, the funeral was over. A beautiful service, as Gunhild hastened to reassure her in a subsequent letter. The Lutheran pastor from Frederikshavn had delivered a beautiful eulogy; there were hundreds of beautiful wreaths, even though it cost a fortune to buy flowers in January; the church was overflowing, and you could hardly hear the organ for the sound of sobbing. If it was any comfort, she added, they wouldn't be able to inter Anders until April at the earliest, after the ground thawed. She'd let Helle know when. In the meantime, she could take her word for it that her father was resting peacefully in a vault—and wasn't that the important thing, after all, resting peacefully? Evidently, Anders's tendency to express himself in dead languages had become more and more pronounced toward the end. His last words had been a paraphrase of Horace: "A ridiculous mouse will be born."

How charming were the towns and villages through which Helle and Maeve traveled, the roofs of the houses covered with snow, smoke curling from the chimneys! Children heated pennies and melted perfectly round holes in the frost on the windows, the better to watch these elegantly dressed strangers pass by. Garmisch-Partenkirchen, Bad Tölz, Munich, Berchtesgaden, Dachau, Ingolstadt, Nuremberg: history had not yet invested the names of any of these towns with symbolic meaning. In Nuremberg they bought slabs of hot gingerbread which they ate in the front hallway of Albrecht Dürer's house; in Dachau they visited a twelfth-century castle and then went ice-skating on the frozen Amper River. The last stop on Maeve's tour brought them to Berchtesgaden, where they were the guests of the Baron and Baroness von Schadenheim. Their chalet, a make-believe structure perched on the side of a mountain, reminded Helle of the engraved cottage in Daisy's window, just as the baron reminded her of Daisy's china polar bear, and the baroness of Daisy's ivy heart. It was only when you looked back, Helle said, that you could see the ghostly shape of future events spilling out of the contours of the commonplace, those dark humours wreathing the nearby Obersalzberg, the little house at its summit built with royalty money from *Mein Kampf.*

The routine, chez Schadenheim, never varied. Every evening the baron drove them in his white Mercedes to a nearby resort hotel where Maeve was being paid, as she put it, to distract a bunch of Munich businessmen from close inspection of their wives. Every day, while Maeve and the baron went skiing, Helle remained at home with the baroness, whose health was apparently as delicate and subject to sudden reversals as were the emotions that flitted beneath the surface of her heart-shaped face. One minute she was cheerful and distant, yielding and forlorn the next. A confusing woman— was it in the former mood or the latter that, on the third afternoon of their visit, she confessed her love of Wagnerian opera, and called Helle's attention to the upper ledge of a Gothic prie-dieu in the corner of the room, on which sat a model theater? Lush vegetation, vines and flowers—the second act of *Parsifal*, Helle guessed, after Klingsor has caused the tower to magically disappear, replacing it with a tropical garden, thereby paving the way for Kundry's destruction.

As if in confirmation the baroness began singing Kundry's famous second-act narrative "*Seit Ewigkeiten harre ich deiner*" —for an invalid, Helle said, she made a lot of noise. The usual snow was falling, tumbling in overlarge flakes past the window; the baroness was leaning back against the chintz sofa cushions printed with overlarge poppies, stretching out her long, silk-stockinged legs. Did she plan it that way, that her painted toe should touch Helle's knee, that her neat, small head should land precisely within the dark nucleus of a poppy? Poor Kundry, the baroness said, forever doomed to wander the earth because she'd laughed at the Savior's agony. This was, Helle realized, not only a seduction but also a thinly veiled reference to the way in which she'd met the news of her father's death. She felt set up, tricked. Was it possible that at this very moment, as their woolen hats turned white with snow, Maeve and the baron were tumbling into each other's arms? At night, in the hotel, you could tell whose job it was to distract whom; during the day it wasn't so obvious. I'm nothing like Kundry, Helle said. Kundry became a penitent and dedicated herself to a life of service: "*Dienen . . . Dienen*," remember? The baroness lifted a silver swan from the table, pressed a button on its head, and when its beak sprang open to release a tongue of fire, she lit two cigarettes. Oh, she remembered. But she also remembered that Kundry was a sorceress. She took a deep drag and then, having left behind the imprint of her red lips, handed Helle one of the cigarettes. A Turkish cigarette—it tasted wonderful. Helle thanked the baroness and retreated with it to her room, where she continued the endless unfolding of a phrase in the Dorian mode. "It is said that Leda, long ago, found an egg the color of hyacinths"—the first hint of what was to become *Fuglespil*. Her notebook, she couldn't help noticing, had been moved from the walnut table to the cushioned window seat.

According to Helle, there was a certain kind of married couple to whom any single woman will become easy prey, the element necessary to the creation of drama on a stage otherwise designed for farce. Of course the roles were familiar, since they duplicated the condition of childhood. In the beginning there were Anders and Ida; in the end there were Maren and Sam. If Helle refused to let the baroness have her way with her, did that refusal pave the way for future refusals? Or was Helle merely refining her role? Was she preparing to emerge, finally, as a heroine, or was she never anything more than a pawn? Your position remained clear so long as you stayed in your room composing music. The problem was that at some point you had to come out of your room. You had to come out and, when you did, you might find yourself pinned against the door handle of a car as it swerved around a curve on one side of which an avalanche warning had been posted, on the other side of which a vast, gaping emptiness waited to be filled. The baron's gloved hand might reach out to touch your knee, reassuringly, and it would be the same hand which, earlier, swatted your fingers after you trumped your partner's ace in a game of bridge. Bridge in the late afternoon—Helle said that if she'd neglected to mention that feature of the daily routine, it was because it was, arguably, the feature she hated the most. After the Great War, civilized people played bridge. Or more precisely, indoors they played bridge. Outdoors they played tennis. After the Great War civilized people thought they could substitute manners for morality. So it happened that by the time the monster had arisen, slavering, from its pit, it was too late; the habit had been formed. By that time, didn't everyone know that it was bad manners to interfere?

IV

Fuglespil, Act One. Juxtaposition of two themes, one played on the glass harmonica, one on clarinets and strings: Niflheim, realm of swirling ice crystals and fog; Muspelheim, realm of dancing fire. An empty space in the middle, out of which emerges—what, a big egg? Please. All right, how about Act One, soprano aria offstage, a capella? A pond ringed with cattails, the water clear and motionless, two blue-violet eggs in a nest on the bank? Suddenly the shadow of a female form swirls and dances across the tall stalks of the cattails; suddenly a crack appears in each of the eggs. A crack! Imagine the drama of that moment, the way in which the tension is enhanced by the tapping of a drumstick on the metal rim of a drum. Yolk or chick? *Tap-a-tap.* Really, Helle thought, if you can't be serious, you might as well give up. You might as well trot out the full orchestra, the full complement of gods and goddesses. You might as well dress up Zeus in his swan plumage and send him flying, his shadow swirling and dancing across the face of the pond where his lover has hidden her nest. She's on the lookout, her blue-violet eyes darting this way and that. Yet the question remained, Where did they come from in the first place: the god, the pond, the nest, the girl, the blue-violet color of her eyes?

And if there was an instant of separation of light from dark, sun from shadow, male from female, fire from ice, at what point did that separation also suggest the twin possibilities of good and evil?

Act One, two girls, twin sisters in matching white dresses, on a bright green lawn. White dresses with hems of scalloped lace; the delicate, far-off clink of a porcelain cup coming to rest in its saucer. Yes, that was better. The primary condition, after all, must appear to be one of innocence. Act One: A lawn extends, back, toward a raised terrace, the tapering fluted columns and rosette-studded rail of its stone balustrade intercepted at each corner, and on each side of the central portal, by an armless marble caryatid. It is Easter morning. The sun is just coming up, stage right, behind a huge beech tree; leaking through the tree's leaves and branches, its light casts a wavering blue net out across the lawn, across the sisters' excited faces. And does the sun make shadows, the first sister sings, shadows to trap itself before it can get away? Gold disks, gold disks! She leans over and from within a clump of white flowers extracts a yellow egg, which she then places in a basket at the foot of the tree. Luminiferous ether, the second sister sings, wave or particle, light must always bend around obstacles. She reaches behind a juniper bush, extracts another egg, this one deep scarlet, and puts it, too, in the basket.

I've always liked this duet, the way it's saved from mere prettiness by the perversity of its instrumentation: the first sister's theme, a cheerful music-box melody in A, is assigned to the cello and the clarinet, those most pensive of instruments; the second sister's theme, a pensive inversion of the first, is assigned to the essentially cheerful glass harmonica. Of course that was the point. Helle wanted to conjure up a world in which, no matter how hard you tried, you couldn't disentangle one little girl in white from the other, a world in which conventional wisdom is defied, and all of the eggs get put in the same basket. She wanted to conjure up that world, and she wanted it to look very pretty. The duet concludes with the second sister counting—twenty-one, twenty-two, twenty-three, twenty-four! There're all here, she sings, but the first sister refuses to believe her. How do you know? she asks. Why not twenty-five instead of twenty-four? Why not a hundred, a thousand, or more? Meanwhile the twins' parents appear on the terrace, the mother wearing a rose-sprigged dress, the father a white shirt, linen trousers, and a pair of striped suspenders. In recitative they discuss their daughters, Bluette and Viola. Apparently the only way a stranger can be taught to tell them apart is that while Bluette's eyes are more blue than violet, Viola's eyes are more violet than blue. The parents know that there are other, deeper differences between the two, but for the moment they find themselves unable to agree about which child is which. ("Captain and Mrs. Harry Tuck, at home," wrote Aksel Bram in his review of *Fuglespil*. "Refreshed from their recent bout with a tidal wave the happy couple try their hand at parenthood.")

The first sister, who is in fact Bluette, continues to hunt for eggs; the second, Viola, takes the basket on her lap and continues counting. As they do so the parents, arms linked, commence their own duet, its melodic line echoing that of the children. This time, however, the key modulates from A to A-sharp, and the resultant half-tone shift upward creates an uneasy, anticipatory mood. Is something about to change? How sweet the children look, sings the father; how sweet their faces, sings the mother. How radiant the dyes, sings the father; how sly the hiding places, sings the mother. It soon becomes obvious that each parent thinks it was the other who engineered the egg hunt. Then, at the moment when Bluette stands on tiptoe and lifts from a hole in the trunk of the beech tree an egg as large and dully colored as a cannonball, the key shifts back again to A. Was the interlude in A-sharp a "false" modulation? Did it hold forth promise of further shifts in key, only to insist, finally, on the permanence of the original? The full orchestra joins in, the parents sing in unison: "The virtues of concealment, the virtues of concealment, cannot be overlooked, cannot be, cannot be, cannot be overlooked."

Now we find ourselves in the kitchen, supper preparations under way. A drop cloth—its painted expanse of black and white tile surrounding one small viewless window—bisects the stage laterally, suggesting that the previous set's depth of perspective might have been illusory. Stage center stands Cook, a tall woman in white wearing a tall white chef's hat, as if a part of her has risen above the walls of its container like a soufflé. She is assisted by two white-robed scullions of uncertain gender, one seated on a stool, stage right, peeling potatoes, the other standing nearby at a large worktable, eviscerating a hen. The downstairs maid and the valet play cards at a smaller table, stage left. They are both dressed in black, the maid in a black dress with a little white apron, the valet in a black suit. Two dimensions, two colors—such is the limited canvas of servitude.

"Candle the egg before you break it," sings Cook, thus beginning a quintet in which the kitchen's occupants not only describe their activities to each other in a drawn-out parody of the bel canto style but also reveal their secret thoughts, sussurrando, directly to the audience. For instance, Cook's reference to candling the egg causes the downstairs maid to let the audience in on the fact that she's pregnant, and that while she suspects the valet might be the father, she isn't sure. It might be someone else in the house, she suggests, pointing upstairs. Then she turns back to the valet. "Three of hearts," she sings, playing a card, "go ahead and take it." The valet confesses his desire for the seated scullion, who is, at the same time, worrying about forged immigration papers; the standing scullion works out the details of a plan for blackmail involving an intercepted billet-doux from the mistress of the house to Cook. In this quintet the important information is delivered piano, the unimportant, forte, a strategy by which Helle hoped to emphasize the deterioration of the latter into mere doggerel: "Candle the egg before you break it; Three of hearts, go ahead and take it; Cunning, my dear, but I wanted the four; Look at the peel curling down to the floor! I get the liver, the cat gets the lights; One bowl for yolks and the other for whites."

All at once the cat, appearing from nowhere to pounce on the proffered treat, jostles Cook's elbow just as she is tapping the final egg open; the yolk breaks and spills into the wrong bowl. Ruined! the cook sings. They'll never form peaks now. And shall we have you instead? she wonders, grabbing the cat in one hand, a knife in the other. Shall we have custard surmounted by a mound of fur? O cruel feline! For there are no more eggs, and everyone knows that Easter supper will be incomplete without its traditional dessert of *oeufs à la neige*, served in the mistress's favorite cut-glass bowl. Her anguished recitative terminates in the famous cavatina "More has broken than you know," a very tender song, *andante molto* in B-flat. Cook is disconsolate, but the valet proposes a solution. He happens to have noticed that in the basket of eggs collected by the little girls there was a very large egg of mysterious derivation, the contents of which, when he picked it up and shook it, seemed not to have been blown out or hard-boiled. If Cook will just wait, he'll get it for her.

The minute the valet is gone, everyone remaining in the kitchen starts to dance, hoisting one another high into the air, revealing kicking legs and undergarments. In this fashion we see that the seated scullion is in fact a young man, although his immigration papers would suggest otherwise, and that the standing scullion is in fact a young woman, who is wearing under her bloodstained robe the black net stockings and black lace garter belt of a whore. The downstairs maid is clearly pregnant, her belly straining against the fabric of a voluminous pair of knickers; Cook is stark naked. More and more frenzied, the dancing continues for the duration of the valet's absence, and then, the minute he returns to the kitchen, the music stops; order is restored. In absolute silence the valet hands the egg to Cook, who regards it speculatively. In absolute silence the first act ends.

Of course, because the world in an opera is primarily composed of sound, such silence is profoundly unsettling. In an opera, sound precedes everything; it is the point of origin. Without her voice, what is Cook? Her tall white hat, her long naked legs, her fellow servants, the kitchen itself—all of these things have derived their form and life from the music. Without her voice Cook is reduced to an image painted on a drop cloth, to a painted face, its voiceless mouth open in astonishment or horror, staring at us through the kitchen window, stage rear, as the curtain lifts on the second act. We are once again outside the house, only this time we are looking back at it through a screen of leaves and branches, through the crisscrossing upper limbs of a huge tree which we see, extremely close up and from an elevated angle, as if we might be hovering in the air just beyond it, preparing to perch. Helle's intention was that the actual trunk of the tree exist as mere implication, a vast column forking at a point just beneath the stage floor, providing the crown with its two main structural elements. Some kind of an elm, perhaps? The bark furrowed and gray, spring's first little flower clusters fanning out from the tips of its twigs? Of course you wouldn't be able to pick out such details immediately, because the stage would be dark, the only point of brightness the far-off yellow square of the kitchen window. And then, little by little, a silver light from the fly galleries, meant to represent the moon, strengthens in intensity; it glints off the edges of the leaves, sharp, oval blades of thinly hammered metal. Little by little we see that there are creatures roosting in the tree. Little by little we watch the advance, from stage rear, of another creature: something large flies toward us, landing on the foremost of the two main branches.

Part man, part bird. The face and neck and torso of a young man, the head covered with a cap of brown feathers, each arm with a neat brown wing, the plumage extending down from the scapulae along the back, culminating at the coccyx in a short russet tail. Like water bubbling from an underground spring, the sound fresh and bell-like, Nightingale's characteristic song wells up from that human throat: *chook-chook-chook*, repeated several times, followed by a series of delicate notes, *piu piu piu*, at first slow and then increasingly rapid, rising to a crescendo of heartbreaking sweetness and clarity. *Chook-chook-chook; piu piu piu*—or such, Helle told me, was Dresser's transcription in his nine-volume masterpiece, *Birds of Europe*, what T. S. Eliot rendered merely as *jug*

jug and Hans Andersen as *klukke klukke klukke zizizi.* Although no one, she said sadly, could ever hope to furnish the words for an essentially wordless language.

Twelve birds are roosting in the tree at the start of the second act—thirteen when joined by Nightingale—each introducing its own musical motif, the text for which is, at least initially, a similar series of nonsense syllables. Only when these separate songs begin to intertwine—creating a "polyphony verging on cacophony," to quote Olin Downes—does meaning replace nonsense. Nightingale's *chook-chook-chook; piu piu piu* becomes, for example, *joke joke joke's on you you you;* Shrike's scratchy, halfhearted *queedle queedle; tsurp-se tsurpsee* becomes *we'll we'll see see* or, alternately, *cheat all cheat all usurpers.* Magpie immediately develops an extensive vocabulary—*chak chak chak chak, talk talk talk talk about the jewels I've seen, flashing emeralds in her hair, winking diamonds on her fingers, milky pearls everywhere*—whereas Bee-Eater, vain and dim-witted, never progresses beyond a single noisy *chirrup.* In addition to Nightingale, Shrike, Magpie, and Bee-Eater there are, in the tree, Cuckoo, Kite, Chaffinch, Rook, Yellowhammer, Wren, Snowy Owl, Sparrowhawk, and Sparrow. A dubious grouping, as Dame Marjory Huxtable-Bins pointed out in *Ibis,* the quarterly publication of the British Ornithologists' Union. "One not only feels compelled to direct Ten Brix's attention to her obvious gaffe in causing a sparrow to perch beside a sparrowhawk, but also to her less obvious misrepresentations, among them the elevated placement of the ground-dwelling wren."

Needless to say, it wasn't Helle's aim to create a realistic environment. Indeed, it seems clear to me that what she tried to do in each of her operas—even in *Fortune's Lap,* which took for its setting the recognizable precincts of a large corporation—was to create landscapes that duplicated the conditions of the human soul, fantastic landscapes that could embody the twin possibilities of captivity and escape. Maybe a sparrow would never perch beside a sparrowhawk in the real world. The important thing was that both sparrows and sparrowhawks actually existed, and that whatever separated one from the other in the real world was a very delicate thing, as illusory and randomly deployed as a drop cloth. For while the drop cloth we see hanging stage rear at the beginning of *Fuglespil*'s second act is apparently solid, its little window merely painted on, we're led to believe that it was, earlier, an actual window, providing Nightingale with a way out of the kitchen, just as, earlier still, Cook had provided him with a way out of his shell. In each of Helle's operas there's always a loophole in the most tightly knit fabric, a wolf in the music. Even the body, she said, offered points of exit, the problem being that it wasn't always easy to tell the difference between disease and imagination, between the brain's desire to shut off completely or to go somewhere else for a change.

A ND WAS THAT WHY, despite Dr. Kinglake's lectures and Maren's stern predictions, despite all the dictates of good sense, Helle continued to smoke? Was it actually possible that she saw in her disease evidence of the imagination's triumph, that the harder it became for her to breathe, the more deeply she felt she was sinking into the moss-stuffed world of her last opera? Once a week you would see parked in the weeds outside the trailer a dark green panel truck, sent by the medical supply company to replace the previous week's empty pale-green oxygen canister with a full one; once a week the driver—a thin young man whose upward-tilting, puzzled eyebrows, Helle said, might mislead you into considering him inquisitive, until you heard his loud and domineering voice—would explain not only that the oxygen was pointless if Helle didn't stop smoking, but also that she was in danger of blowing herself and the whole trailer to kingdom come. Thales was right, Frances, she would say; the first principle, the *ousia*, of all things is water. The seeds of all things, including the soul, are moist. Then, as if to contradict herself, she would start to cough what had by now become a dry, hacking cough, and we would sit there on the stoop, embarrassed and guilty, waiting for the coughing to stop, watching two ghostly white threads of smoke issuing from the clamshell ashtray. According to Helle, Thales held that there was no difference between life and death. Well, then, why don't you kill yourself? a friend asked, to which Thales, imperturbed, replied, Because there wouldn't be any difference.

Eventually she would decide to transform Thales, along with Anaximenes and Anaximander—the so-called Milesian philosophers—into the three hunters who ride across the frozen surface of the bog on snowmobiles during the first act of *The Girl Who Trod on a Loaf*, turning their trio into a discussion of the *ousia*, with Thales arguing in favor of water, Anaximenes of air, Anaximander of what he referred to as "the unlimited," by which he meant time. Typical, Sam said when I told him about the trio. It was just like Helle to reject Plato's clarity and embrace instead the pre-Socratics, primitive thinkers who devoted their lives to worrying about where the blue went when the sky changed color, or where the glow went when you extinguished a candle. It was just like Helle to be charmed by Anaximander, who claimed that every existing thing was a "usurper," believing that during the course of its existence it "committed injustice" by preventing its opposite from existing. In fact she probably thought the whole bunch of them were proto-feminists, never realizing that among the three blessings for which Thales daily thanked Fortune was the fact that he'd been born a man and not a woman. Thales, Sam said. Give me a break. I'd be doing Helle a favor, he said, if I told her how her hero, when a servant was leading him through the fields one night so he could observe the stars, tripped and landed in a ditch. How can you expect to understand the heavens, Thales, the servant is reported to have remarked, when you can't even recognize what's lying right under your feet?

Of course that summer we were all ignorant about what was lying under our feet. Or at least the adults among us managed to remain ignorant, notwithstanding the children's attempts to open our eyes. Children, after all, are always bent over in rapt study of the ground. Following a rain, for instance, they'll spend hours playing in the driveway, floating twigs down the muddy rivers pooling in the tire ruts. They'll make deals—if my stick gets to the bottom of the driveway before I can count to a hundred, then I'll have long golden curls, then my mother will stop going out on dates with Mr. Blackburn, then Helle will stop smoking, then I'll get a horse— and because the deity with whom these deals are struck tends to reveal itself through signs, children become, of necessity, unusually observant. An hour earlier the rain might have been clear, funneling like liquid glass through the cleft hearts of the lilac leaves, but now the yellowish foam bunching from the ruts' muddy lips—the yellow foamy place where the stick gets caught—serves as a herald of disaster.

Days came, days went, a procession of hot, dry summer days which, if you subscribed to Anaximander's system, was essentially telic, providing evidence for a moral order in the universe, like the rise and fall of nations, the life and death of organisms, the perpetual alternation between good and evil, success and defeat. Hot, dry summer days—the truth is, it was uncharacteristically hot and dry. Lyle Judkins planted his corn, and although the almanac would have it knee-high by the Fourth of July, what I saw poking up from the powdery gray dirt of his field, as the Elks Club fireworks opened their blue and red hands in the sky above it, was no higher than Ruby's anklebones. Everyone's crops failed, but Judkins seemed to take the drought as a personal affront. Dwarf corn, dwarf wheat, as meanwhile weeds flourished, the mullein erecting its tall, flannelly towers along the roadsides, the burdock putting forth its huge elephant-ear-like leaves, the fibrous fingers of witch-grass roots reaching out to choke the tender threads sent down by dying carrots, dying peas, dying beets in the town's dying vegetable gardens.

For the first time there was an advantage to my job: at the end of the previous summer Kosta had gotten a bargain on a used air conditioner, and although at the time I'd scoffed—that summer having been essentially cold and wet—it turned out to have been a good idea. In upstate New York, you didn't expect a diner to be air conditioned; now everyone wanted to come in. People wearing Bermuda shorts knew they could sit in the booths without worrying about their thighs sticking to the leatherette upholstery. Cool cool leatherette, cool Mediterranean azure! People could rest their arms on the cool white Formica tabletops and sip the cool drinks of summer, iced tea, iced coffee, lemonade; they could feel the sweat drying on their temples, on their upper lips. The smell of french fries cooking in fat, which is unbearable in an overheated, claustrophobic kitchen, became immensely appetizing. The place was always full of customers, all of whom ate a lot, after which they tipped generously. They smiled, they laughed, happy to remain in that cool white and azure world forever.

So I was unprepared for Patti Judkins's attack one morning in mid-July. Meek Patti Judkins, as I'd always thought of her, a woman who had been at one time a pretty girl, whom Lyle had knocked up in high school, turning her prematurely sour and prim—I found her sitting in a corner booth, one sunburned arm clutching a summer pocketbook of dark blue straw, the other extended across the table to page through the heavy metal-and-plastic pages of the miniature jukebox mounted below the window. You could see the hot bodies of the cars parked in a brightly colored row along the front of the diner, with here and there the more sober colors of the pickup trucks mixed in. Patti Judkins's pickup, for example, was black. I filled her water glass and then, to be neighborly, said it must be discouraging to have to rely for your livelihood on something so fickle as the weather. There was nothing fickle about God's will, Patti answered, still paging through the jukebox. Her neck was curved away from me, her hair pulled back into a French twist, revealing bug bites on the tender place behind the ears. I took out my pad and pencil. A cup of coffee to begin with? The specials were blueberry pancakes and western omelettes. Did she need a moment to think about it? No, Patti said, she didn't. That is, she didn't want anything, except to tell me that she wasn't a fool like Maren Blackburn. If I kept on flirting with Lyle I'd better start packing my bags right away, because she, Patti Judkins, was going to see to it that my life here was so miserable I'd have to move somewhere else. Her voice was thin, girlish, and she had the adolescent girl's habit of letting her sentences end on a rising note as if they were questions. I told her I didn't know what she was talking about. I'd never flirted with her husband, I said, resisting the impulse to tell her that the mere idea filled me with disgust. Oh, sure, Patti said, her voice getting louder, sure. That was why I always sat around on my front steps dressed like a whore, just waiting for him to drive by. Worse than a whore, she shouted, because at least a whore covered herself when she wasn't fucking a client. The four teenaged boys in the adjacent booth had stopped blowing straw wrappers at each other and were sitting in rapt silence; a family of tourists got up from the booth across the aisle, leaving their breakfasts untouched and, as Kosta told me later, unpaid for, the mother and father herding their two toddlers ahead of them out the door.

Hey, Francie, a voice called from the far end of the diner, how about some more coffee; but when I started to walk toward it, Patti slid with admirable grace across her leatherette seat and jumped to her feet, her free hand grabbing my wrist, her other hand raising the pocketbook to hit me on the shoulder. Hey, I said, hey! The pocketbook's silver hasp sprang open and a plaid wallet, a plaid glasses case, car keys, loose change, a bottle of aspirin, a pair of white cotton gloves, several lipsticks, a black plastic comb, and a brown plastic compact spilled onto the floor. Filth, Patti yelled, I was nothing but filth. Hers was the strong grip of a farm wife, of a woman who'd extricated from between their mothers' legs the stuck wet bodies of calves and lambs, the grip of a woman who could lift a fifty-pound bag of grain and tighten the bolts on a tractor—the grip, in short, of a woman who, having thrown in her lot with a man, would never relax her hold on him. She could only feel pity for my poor little girls, Patti said, having to be brought up by trash like me. What kind of an example did I think I was setting? Me and that old pervert, who probably had them in her clutches at this very minute. Did I think I was so special to be having an affair with Sam Blackburn? With Mr. Caught With His Pants Down? Wipe that smile off your face, girl! she yelled, even though I wasn't smiling.

In fact my response was twofold, and took me completely by surprise. To begin with, I found myself filled with respect for Patti Judkins, for her brave refusal to back down even after Kosta and the teenaged boys had pulled her away from me to a presumably safe place behind the counter, for the way she pretended to acquiesce and then, the moment they'd let go of her, picked up a cup filled with coffee and hurled it in the direction of my head, the coffee hanging in the air in a wide brown arc before splashing onto the floor, an extended *splat* immediately followed by the loud crash of the cup breaking in half against the metal rim of the table. Two pieces of blue-banded white ceramic landed at my feet, two parts of the same cup—just as the second part of my response, in which I found myself filled with a new longing for Sam, my former indifference giving way to a vision of permanence and constancy, seemed to me nothing more than the necessary correlative to my respect for Patti Judkins. It was as if I'd been infected by her violent sense of moral rectitude. Maybe I *did* want Sam for my very own. Was that so crazy? A father for the twins, a husband for me? A normal life, whatever that meant. Sam. Whatever that meant.

Of course, when you're one of the principals in a drama it isn't always easy to distinguish the underlying themes. "*Là ci darem la mano*," the Don sings to Zerlina in the popular first-act duet from *Don Giovanni*. Your hand, he urges, honey-mouthed, doing his best to woo her away from her unpolished yet faithful betrothed, the stalwart Masetto. Such charming music, so sweet, so romantic, although neither the Don nor Zerlina is aware of the fact that this is the same request the ghost of the murdered Commendatore will make of the Don at the opera's conclusion. *"Dammi la mano in pegno,"* the Commendatore will ask—"Give me your hand in token"— the implication being that since he's honored the Don's dinner invitation, the Don must reciprocate, only this time they'll be dining with the damned. Patti's strong grip across the countertop, Helle's weaker grip on her deathbed, Ida's pretty fingers lacing through her daughter's, drawing her along behind her into the bog—a net of symbolic imagery was dropping over me, but I was too involved to recognize it for what it was.

Kosta let me leave work early, and I immediately drove up Airport Hill past the limp wind socks and limp flags, the huge, heat-baked hangars and bright private planes; down the hill past the rows of small airless tract houses, their dust-caked lawn ornaments and their dead lawns; ending up at the high school at the bottom of the hill, where Adirondack Community College held its summer-session classes, and where I knew I would find Sam. The parking lot was nearly empty, a still gray field of asphalt bordered on one side by a still gray football field, on the other by a still gray building. Inside, it was even hotter; a bored-looking woman sat behind the front desk at a typewriter, her long blond hair stirred at intervals by the slow oscillations of a portable fan next to the wooden partition which during the school year would protect the administrators from the students. Mmmm? she said, keeping her eyes on the typewriter, her hands poised over the keys. Professor Blackburn? Room 109, at the end of the hall to the right. Hands preparing to pounce, a silent system of bells preparing to ring, a silent hive of rooms preparing to fill with the din of autumn. Was it my imagination, or had the woman, at the mention of Sam's name, briefly smirked?

In room 109 Sam was leaning against a chalkboard on which he'd written in his backward-sloping, loopy handwriting, "Aristotle versus Plato—the question of Free Will." Though class had been dismissed, a heavyset man in a seersucker suit remained—an insurance salesman, I thought, or a teamster, depending on whether he'd dressed up or dressed down for the occasion—who appeared to be older than Sam, and who was consequently unwilling to concede the position of authority. "I'll be with you in a moment, Miss Thorn," Sam said, his eyebrows lifting briefly above the pink rims of his glasses, his eyes briefly, waggishly, crossing. Why did Mr. Gruber persist in his misguided belief that Plato advocated a relationship between free will and body weight? Surely a bright man like Mr. Gruber should realize that such a theory would suggest that the destiny of a lightweight, like, for instance, Miss Thorn here, was more circumscribed than his own? But hadn't Plato said that any man—or woman, for that matter, appended Mr. Gruber, sending a conspirator's smile in my direction—who knew what good was couldn't choose anything else? He was grinning slyly, as if he'd at last set a trap from which escape was impossible. Well, Sam replied, he guessed the final verdict would rely on how convincingly Mr. Gruber had managed to argue his case in his paper, wouldn't it?

I'd heard the rising pitch of exasperation in Sam's voice, the pinched squeal of his vowels, so I knew what kind of mood to expect by the time Mr. Gruber had at last taken leave of us, backing reluctantly out the door. No one could pay a person enough, Sam said, slamming it shut behind him, to put up with a moron like that. This was the last summer! Absolutely the last! He was violently shoving papers and books into his briefcase, then all at once surprised me by stopping dead and looking sadly out into space, his expression tender and heartbroken, as if he were about to cry. Footsteps in the hall, a jingling of keys, the whiskery sound of a broom moving across linoleum, a deejay's hearty voice giving way to Dion DiMucci's, that unbearably erotic little moan with which "Ruby" begins. "Ruby, Ruby, how I wauncha, Like a ghost I'ma gonna hauncha"—the most sublime rhyme in the world, according to Helle Ten Brix. God damn it, Frannie, Sam said. You think you know what you're doing with your life, and then what? Maybe Gruber was right. Maybe our combined weights weren't enough; maybe what fate had set against us in the scales was a fat man in seersucker. Because I should correct him if he was wrong, but it wasn't Gruber, was it, who was stuck teaching philosophy to a bunch of morons? It wasn't Gruber who was going to be stuck grading a bunch of moronic papers until all hours of the morning. No, Gruber was off to ride across the green lawns of the golf course in his expensive, motorized golf cart. I didn't realize until I'd come close enough to put my arms around Sam—approaching cautiously, since you never can tell whether a person prefers to lick his wounds in private—that he was laughing. Gruber on a golf cart. The Platonic ideal. Better than the usual tired old examples, didn't I think? A number, a tree, an elephant, a bed? Speaking of which, how about it? The Hi-Ho, the Ho-Hum, whatever the hell it was called?

I hesitated, and as I did the fat man tipped the scales, sending Sam and me flying through the hot air of summer toward the chill air of fall, toward the moment when the typist's hands would land on the keys, the bells would ring, the classrooms would fill with noisy students. No, I said, not today. I was tired of sneaking into motels, of lying to the twins, of pretending not to care about the future. Couldn't we move away? Couldn't we decide to throw in our lot together, pack up the children and move away? It wasn't as if Sam still had anything invested in his marriage or his job— Maren would probably be happy to see him go. Of course William was a problem; she'd want to keep William. But we could sort all that out later. For now we could get in my car and start driving—east toward one ocean, west toward another. It was bound to be cooler the closer you got to the coast. We could camp out on beaches, cook fish over driftwood fires, sleep under the stars. I knew only a few of the constellations, Orion, the Dippers, the one shaped like a big W, and this would give me a chance to learn the rest. I'd always wanted to learn them, ever since I'd flunked out of the Girl Scouts, aged eleven, without earning a single merit badge.

The more involved I became in my monologue, the less it seemed to have to do with Sam. In fact, the image I was coming back to over and over again—Francie Thorn wading among dark wet rocks, plucking from nests of seaweed the iridescent mussels she would later coax open over a fire, revealing to her two little girls first the small secret of the meat hidden within each shell, and then the larger secret of the figures hidden in the black starry sky—didn't include Sam at all. Meanwhile, he was standing by one of the classroom's three tall windows, staring thoughtfully out at the parking lot. My car, his car, a car I didn't recognize, a powder-blue Corvair, probably the typist's. His white shirt was open at the collar, the sleeves rolled up, damp under his arms and between his shoulder blades. The heat made his hair curl, his eyebrows wild. I thought he looked handsome, but like a stranger.

Where were his hat, his pen? He tapped on the window, waved; the powder-blue car made a slow circuit of the lot, then drove away.

"What are you saying?" Sam asked. "Are you asking me to leave Maren? Is that it?" We were all alone in a building designed to accommodate hundreds of people, meaning we were more than normally alone. So many strangers in the world! There on that cool northern beach, for instance, as my twins dropped off to sleep under a powder-blue blanket, as the darkening sea thumped its dark green paws on the dark moist sand, a stranger approached, a man in a white shirt, the damp air making his gray-brown hair curl at the temples, over the ears, coating the lenses of his pink-rimmed glasses with a thin, salty film. While I watched, he removed them, regarded them curiously, wiped them on the tail of his shirt, one flap of which was hanging out like the tongue of an exhausted dog over the waistband of his chinos, folded them, and put them in his breast pocket. What was going on here? Who was it who was slipping his hands up under the skirt of my waitress uniform? Why was my head pressed against a flat hard surface that smelled like chalk? I could taste salt on the man's lips. "I didn't realize," he said. The building was so silent that every noise we made—the sound of a zipper, the sound of static electricity as the bunched skirt of my uniform came in contact with the small hairs on the backs of the man's hands—resounded with meaning. "I never thought you wanted anything more than this," the man said. But I didn't, I told him—not before. And now? And *now*? No, I said, not now either.

The truth is, whereas before I'd known what I didn't want, now I didn't know what I did. If I had, would it have made any difference? Would I be living with Sam and the twins in a shingled cottage near the ocean, filling the shelves of a neat wainscoted pantry with jar upon jar of homemade beach plum and rosehip jam? Sam in the next room, sitting at a large oak table writing scholarly articles; Flo standing behind an easel on the beach, painting; Ruby wandering through the dunes with her newest beau, Lily at their heels? Of course not. Of course not. As we say these days, get real. Get a life. Which I did, in a manner of speaking.

Before we left—steering our cars in opposite directions at the place where Airport Drive intersected with the Branch Road, a light tap on the horn by the way of acknowledging that we were once again about to be gathered into the desperate embrace of our separate lives—Sam removed an envelope from his briefcase. Did I know about this? It was a formal invitation, engraved in black on heavy cream-colored stock: "*Un Ballo in Maschera!*" it said. "A gala celebration of Helle Ten Brix's last birthday in this world! The sixth day of August, nineteen hundred and sixty-three." Costumes, the invitation explained, were required but presents discouraged, since the celebrant would have no use for them where she was going. Guests should plan to arrive at the trailer no later than nine P.M.; an unmasking at midnight would be followed by a light supper. When I shook my head, confused, Sam told me that he'd found it in the mail just that morning—one was probably waiting for me at home. The whole family was invited, even William. But didn't I think it was odd that Helle hadn't mentioned the party to me, of all people? Not really, I said. She was a tricky woman. A tricky, dying woman—a dangerous combination. In this world, at least. At the very least, Sam said. Frannie. Oh Frannie. In this world that had me in it, whom he loved.

V

This world, by which we usually mean the real world, the world which, by the time Helle had begun making her dreamy way into what would eventually emerge as *Fuglespil*, had come to resemble the nightmare world of that opera, its landscape controlled by such composite creatures as she was causing to roost in the branches of her invented elm. How seductive the aspect of a winged human body— how easy to turn such a man into a god! The power of the image, according to Helle, derived from the symbolic linking of bird and spirit, for wasn't the Egyptian pharaoh's soul carried to heaven by Horus, the hawk-headed deity, and didn't the souls of Christian saints ascend to heaven in the form of doves? What this implied was the purity of the soul, its innocence, although the association wasn't always so optimistic. In the Herakles legend, for example, the birds which rose from Lake Stymphalus represented the hideous issue of a stagnant soul; in the Book of Revelations, the whore Babylon became "the hold of every foul spirit, the cage of every unclean and hateful bird." Hitler, Goebbels, Göring, Streicher, Hess, Rosenberg, Himmler—Helle said it was as if by conjuring up those names you might actually be opening Babylon's expanded, causing the whole thing to lurch in her hand as if it were trying to get away. In fact, Helle told me, you might say that overnight Copenhagen itself had become overheated, labile. Possibly this was why the front windows had been cranked open on such a cool, cloudy day; as Helle ran to close them, a shower of leaflets blew in, scattering like petals across the floor. We will bomb the capital if we meet with resistance—such was the basic message, although the leaflets also promised protection of Danish neutrality so long as the Danes "cooperated." The fishwives were clustered together, their arms lifted, shaking their fists at the blunt-nosed planes which circled overhead; on the other side of the canal Helle could see Maeve pushing through a group of helmeted soldiers, heading toward the bridge. One of the soldiers tried to grab her as she passed, and another shook his bayonet in her face, but she ignored them both, picking up speed, her green dress blowing back between her thighs, her strong legs pumping up and down. Apparently nothing could stop her, not even the tank stationed in the middle of the bridge, not even the gun swiveling in its mount, holding her in its sights as she walked by—because the men hidden inside were thinking of firing or because she was pleasing to look at? Suddenly Maeve disappeared into a crowd of men and women on bicycles, and Helle didn't see her again until she burst into the apartment.

Swine! Maeve announced. Who did those swine think they were, anyway? She kicked off her shoes and fell back onto the sofa. In the streets people were saying it was only a matter of time before King Christian surrendered. Roll over and play dead like dogs, Maeve muttered. Did Helle want to end up with a collar around her neck? Did she want to live in a kennel? Back in Ireland, Maeve said, her mother had a wolf-hound named Rosie, and whenever there was a thunderstorm

cage, letting evil itself escape. Inhuman, you'd think, there
investing those names with inhuman power, thereby repeati
the error upon which the fascist, over and over again, buil
his house of human skulls and bones. So it happened that
the early hours of the morning of April 9, 1940, Germa
troops crossed the border into Jutland; an enormous mercha
ship sailed into the Copenhagen harbor and docked, releasin
its cargo of soldiers and tanks onto the Langelinie's stor
promenade. Within fifteen minutes the Germans had capture
the Citadel, after which they advanced to Amalienborg Palace
where following a brief skirmish they subdued the King'
Guard.

At the time, Helle was living with Maeve in a large apart
ment on the Gammel Strand, overlooking the Frederiksholm
Kanal. The apartment's front room had two large window
facing southeast, and it was the women's custom to start each
day seated by those windows, drinking coffee as the sun came
up, as the fishwives spread out their wares in the street below,
the first rays of the sun catching on the scales of the sturgeon
and mackerel and salmon, on the moist coils of the eels, or
the wind-puckered surface of the water. They didn't live in a
quiet place, and Maeve was not a quiet woman. Helle wa
used to being awakened by the screaming of gulls and the
shouts of the fishwives, by Maeve's voice raised in song a
she turned the creaking handle of the coffee grinder, preparing
her own secret blend of beans, a mixture she would reveal to
no one.

However, on that April morning Helle knew immediatel
that the sounds weren't the result of routine activity: th
apartment was empty, the kettle had boiled dry on the stov
and when she went to pick it up its tin bottom sudden

Rosie would hide under the bed, whimpering. That was what it was like to be a dog. Thus she anticipated the rhyme which was to become popular during the five years of occupation: "To feed the German appetite/ Pretty Denmark's cows and pigs/ Every day get turned to meat/ Of which you cannot take a bite/ For those with muzzles cannot eat."

It isn't my intention to recount the atrocities of a period with which everyone is already familiar, for although I don't subscribe to Helle's belief that a reliance on fact has never helped illuminate the truth, I am willing to admit my limitations as an historian. Oh, I could tell you that the Germans consumed millions of tons of Danish pork and beef between 1941 and 1945. And if I felt like doing the appropriate research, I suppose I'd know precisely how many millions of tons, as well as how many millions of dollars Danish profiteers made on the black market. I could go on to relate how many millions of kroner changed hands every day in the fashionable stores on the Strøget, how many millions of pelts went into the making of the fur coats worn by the wives of the profiteers—beautiful coats of ermine and lynx they flaunted as they guided their horse-drawn carriages up and down the roads from Skagen to Nykøbing, as millions of people died.

Millions of people, numbers too large to understand: as Helle described it, they constituted an edifice as overwhelming, as constrictive to the heart, as Speer's vast shrine to the Nazi dream in Nuremberg, its red banners bigger than houses, its 130 columns higher than clouds. The only possible response to something so huge, Helle said, is fear. If you're required to love it as well, what you have to do is turn your fear into a song that brings a tear to the eye, and then you have to sing that song with a million other frightened people, all of you carrying torches. The torches were a nice touch, for they presumed to illuminate an otherwise comprehensive darkness; and the more colossal the edifice, the more colossal its shadow.

That shadow, ultimately, was the element within which Helle had to learn to live. Even as the April sun shone on the deep green water of the canal, creating mutable constellations, as six or seven blinking stars proliferated into an entire galaxy with the passing of a cloud; even as the December sun turned the canal to a mirror of ice, and the brightly whirling hats of the skaters to meteorites and comets; even as she felt that sun heating her face, she understood that darkness and not light was the primary condition of the universe. Maeve subscribed to the resistance paper, *Frit Danmark*, where Helle read about the efforts of such brave Danes as Count Carl-Adam Moltke, who was responsible for helping Niels Bohr escape to London with information about German work on the atomic bomb. She read about the perfidy of the Danish police, "more deadly than Nazis," and the sabotage efforts of a group of Aalborg schoolboys called the Churchill Club, who set fire to railway cars carrying German troops to Norway.

Maeve, meanwhile, began keeping strange hours, leaving the apartment in the middle of the night and not showing up again until early the next morning. At first Helle suspected she was having an affair, and she admitted to having followed her once: along the moonlit canal, past the intertwining dragons' tails on the Bourse tower and to the Nyhavn, where Maeve disappeared down the shadowy steps of the very shop where Mandrill had tattooed an eye on Helle's neck twenty years earlier. But Mandrill was no longer there, and the man with whom Maeve entered into immediate and intense conversation—a tall man in a well-tailored black suit and a

gray homburg—was obviously not a tattooist. Better not ask
questions, Maeve replied, when confronted in the morning.
The suggestion was that the nature of her activities was
political, not romantic. "She had this way of squinting one
eye and widening the other," Helle said, "as if she was
concealing something and revealing it at the same time. Like
that fortune-telling ball of Ruby's, you know the one I mean?
The messages rising and sinking, rising and sinking. A hateful toy."

And then one day in January of 1943 Daisy arrived in
town, ostensibly to shop for drapery material. She and Helle
had stayed in touch, Helle spending the occasional weekend
at Asgard—which was, to Daisy's embarrassment, the name
Propp had chosen for his cement fortress—although these
visits had more or less come to a halt with the German
occupation. The coldest winter since 1871: hills of snow taller
than a man piled up along the streets; icicles hung from the
eaves, as long and sharp as the Greenland Eskimos' legendary
harpoons; ships were embedded in the frozen harbor, their
frozen rigging tinkling like glass. The insides of the apartment
windows were thick with frost, and because of the fuel shortage
you had to wear your coat indoors. My poor dear! Daisy said
when she saw Helle trying to assemble a cigarette out of dried
cabbage leaves.

Though she must have been close to seventy, Daisy was
still unusually attractive, even though Helle could see in her
face that peculiar blurring of gender common in the aged.
Daisy was now what you'd call handsome, a handsome woman
laughing as she reached into her alligator purse, her hand
shaking slightly as she drew forth an unopened pack of Gold
Flakes. American tobacco representatives, she said, had been

supplying resistance workers with real cigarettes for almost a year, and when Helle looked at her in surprise, Daisy laughed again. Had the shaking been another sign of old age, or was Daisy merely cold, unaccustomed to being in such a poorly heated building, even though she was wearing a full-length fur coat? For it never occurred to Helle until later that the imperturbable Daisy might have been nervous, despite the way she jumped at the sound of something hitting the floor in the next room. What was that? Daisy asked. Just Maeve getting up from a nap, Helle replied. Oh, Daisy said, going on to explain that the cigarettes were intended as a reward for bravery; a nice enough reward if you happened to be a smoker, which she wasn't.

"They simply don't get it, do they?" said Maeve, yawning and stretching as she entered the room, her thick reddish hair flattened on one side by the pillow, which had also pressed a red crease into her cheek. "They don't understand that bravery is its own reward," she elaborated, and then sat down heavily, pulling her coat—an expensive, hooded fur coat Helle had never seen before—tightly around her shoulders. "Hello, Daisy," she said, "nice to see you." Helle looked at the two of them, Maeve and Daisy, seated at either end of the long kitchen table, and at the time what she thought she was seeing was two women eyeing each other from opposite ends of the romantic spectrum. How could Maeve comprehend the cynicism of a woman whose experience of romance had been as its object rather than its instigator?

"These days," Daisy said, "there are no rewards." She went on to complain that her involvement with the resistance was straining her marriage. It wouldn't do, Propp had warned, to aggravate Hitler, whose annual birthday telegram to the king, more flowery than ever, had been met with a terse response. Everyone knew that the Führer was now referring to Denmark as *"diesem lächerlichen Ländchen"*—this ridiculous little country—and it was clear that his patience, if you could call it that, had finally worn thin.

Ever since the beginning of the occupation, the king's practice had been to ride out on his horse each day at eleven, his spine perfectly straight, his subjects waving Danish flags and cheering him on, his route so regular you could set your watch by it. The idea, as Helle said, was to console, not to dazzle. And then on the morning of October 19, as he was approaching the Yacht Club, his horse suddenly bolted, heading at a wild gallop toward a group of schoolchildren; when he tried to rein it in, the horse reared and threw him to the ground. "Don't touch me!" King Christian was rumored to have shouted at the SS guard who appeared, out of the blue, to lend assistance. What could be more repulsive than to watch the enemy's face lit with spurious concern, hovering over your damaged body, to feel his prodding hands? The king chose to rest his head in the lap of a middle-aged waitress, his blood seeping into her skirt until the ambulance arrived.

Now Daisy was eager to know whether either Helle or Maeve had witnessed the incident. Did they think it was true, as some people claimed, that the horse had been spooked by the sound of a train, or had someone, probably the SS guard, startled the horse with a slap on the rump? When you got right down to it, Helle answered, it didn't make any difference; the foul spirit that was on the loose everywhere had sought a form into which it might funnel itself, a form without which its influence on the course of events would go unnoticed. A train, a guard—what difference did it make? What difference!

Daisy exclaimed; how could Helle, of all people, say such a thing? Surely she knew the old adage, one of Propp's favorites: If the gold rusts, what will the iron do?

Although of course Helle didn't really believe this theory—an assertion I base not only on the evidence of *Fuglespil,* where the source of all evil is shown to be the terrible human heart, but also on what she directly said about that period in history. According to Helle, those men who wanted to rule the world and then, when they discovered they couldn't, plotted its destruction, weren't possessed by anything external to themselves. To assume they were would be to deny their complicity, and to predicate the existence of absolute evil was to succumb to the power of its symbols: the motorcade, the Hakenkreuz, the salute.

In fact, that day in the kitchen Helle was merely trying to find out whether Maeve's response to Daisy was going to be one of admiration or antagonism, and whether she herself had the power to tip the scales. She should have known better. Because for Maeve the two qualities carried equal weight, a fact which would, at the very least, explain her relationship to horses. Helle always talked that way, Maeve said, assuring Daisy that her suspicions were correct, that King Christian was an experienced rider, and that no trains had been scheduled to pass at the time of the so-called accident. As far as she was concerned, they could now count their own king among the casualties of the war, and she, Maeve, wanted to join forces with those courageous few who, like Daisy, were willing to spit in Hitler's eye. "Arrogant few, you mean," Daisy replied laconically. Anyone who'd ever been to a carnival knew how hard it was to hit a moving target. If Maeve really wanted to help, she would heed the advice of Marius

Fiil, the Hvidsten Group's leader, and take the rabbit, not the hunter, for her inspiration. For wasn't camouflage the key to survival in a country as flat as Denmark?

"I was so stupid," Helle confessed. "I actually told Daisy that Maeve would never be any good as a rabbit; that if she were a rabbit she'd wear her brown coat in the winter, her white one in the summer." A personality shaped by a love of opposition, a personality too flamboyant to hide—it was extraordinary, really, how you could live with someone and never know her true nature. Her foolish niece, for example. Although husbands and wives were notoriously blind, wasn't that the condition of marriage? Maybe you had to choose blindness, for otherwise how could you stand to spend a lifetime with another human being? "And what about you?" Daisy asked. Helle came from Jutland—surely she must be aware of the superstition still current there that rabbits changed their sex from year to year. Speaking of which, would she be interested to know that Dancer was engaged to a young woman he'd met on his last crossing? Once again Daisy reached into her purse, this time drawing forth a postcard, on one side of which was printed a photograph of a pretty redhead in a bathing suit, holding aloft a red-and-white-striped beach ball. Betty, Daisy said. Betty Barnes, a shipboard entertainer of some sort. Here, she said, turning the card over and handing it to Helle so she could see Dancer's writing, row upon row of dark slashes, as primitive and cryptic as his mouth.

Helle didn't even try to read the message. Instead she found herself picturing a man and a woman on a ship's moonlit deck, kissing, while under their feet U-boats drifted like sharks through the icy waters of the north Atlantic. I hope you'll be happy, she thought, realizing even as she did that it wasn't Dancer she was thinking of. Sleet tapped against the front windows; the lights flickered and went out. It was as if, Helle said, someone had darkened the house prior to shutting and locking the door; as if Maeve, though she still sat at the kitchen table watching one of her cats lap up the cream she'd spilled for it into a saucer, were already gone, the resistance's newest heroine, already riding north in Daisy's car. U-boats in the water, soldiers in the forests. You couldn't go anywhere where something wasn't prowling, charting your passage. For a moment all she could hear was the brittle sound of the sleet, the tiny, contained sound of the cat's tongue, *lap lap lap,* as drop by drop the cream disappeared into the tiny pink cave of its mouth.

And then suddenly the lights came back on, illuminating beads of cream on the cat's whiskers, as far away a doorbell rang. Helle darling, Maeve said, have you seen my shoes? She was bent down, searching under her end of the table; at the other end Daisy was standing, an unexpectedly savage expression on her face—in their fur coats they both looked more like animals than women, Helle said, and all at once she wondered whether instead of forming an alliance they were about to tear each other limb from limb. By the stove, Helle replied—hadn't Maeve left them there to dry out? Possibly, said Maeve, raising her head from beneath the table. Her cheeks were bright red, full of blood, her eyes shining.

Daisy reached for the third and last time into her purse. A sure way to ruin good leather, she remarked. Didn't everyone know that? But wasn't it a little late for Maeve to be worrying about shoes? She stood there holding a revolver, a dull-gray and surprisingly professional-looking weapon. Monster, Daisy said. If it weren't for this monster, Carl Bruhn wouldn't be dead. Carl Bruhn, whose parachute had failed to open, who'd tumbled out of the sky and into a field near Haslev. His body broke into a million pieces, Daisy said—a million pieces that scattered all over Denmark, a million lively, elusive pieces.

VI

A MELODRAMATIC PIECE of storytelling? Think what you will, it's clear something happened, whether on that particular January afternoon or at another less clearly defined moment during the winter of 1943, that would explain Helle's strange behavior throughout the next ten years. Was Maeve really responsible for Carl Bruhn's death? The truth is, I found that I didn't really care, that I wasn't so much interested in the accuracy of Helle's account, or, alternatively, in the quality of her invention, but rather in the touching suggestion provided by that next decade of a heart susceptible to routine human breakage. For, whatever the cause, Helle was struck mute, all desire to devise a form durable enough to withstand her formless seething having been drained from her, along with the desire to transform her memory of Maeve's being led at gunpoint down the apartment stairs—if indeed that's what actually occurred—into art. As Helle described it, a pair of men in heavy overcoats were waiting in the hallway, and at a signal from Daisy they pushed open the door, one of them binding Maeve's wrists behind her back with a length of whipcord, the other gagging her with a red silk scarf, the silk threads of its long red tassels branching like capillaries through her coat's lavish gray thickets of fur. The kind of scarf men wore to the opera, Helle told me. Daisy's choice, although she thought the irony might have been lost on Maeve.

Unlike you, Frances darling, Helle said. Nothing gets lost on you, does it? To which I replied, truculent, that at least the irony of that statement didn't. Which isn't to say I wouldn't eventually come to the conclusion that the entire story had been trumped up, that a ten-year silence might not have been motivated by such a single and typically operatic instance of betrayal. Certainly Maeve Merrow's appearance the following spring on the stage of the Paris Opéra—"a glorious Butterfly who, the orchestra's chronic tendency to swamp its singers notwithstanding, and despite her own instrument's lack of tonal center, managed to provide her interpretation of 'Un bel dì' with great emotional intensity"—would tend to bear out that fact. Besides, it seemed clear to me that no matter what passions had originally shaped their relationship, by the winter of 1943 Helle would no longer have been surprised by Maeve's routine infidelities and betrayals. "Love her?" Helle said, when asked. "Oh, I loved her all right, the way you love anything that promotes your own sense of righteousness. Also her voice—that wild, dark voice. I've always had a weakness for all of the wild, dark forces in this world which resist containment," Helle said. "As you, of all people, should know. Except Maeve wasn't just dark, she was *in* the dark. Stupid, really."

But what, if not Maeve's perfidy, could serve to explain a prolonged period of artistic inactivity in a life otherwise dedicated to understanding itself through the making of art? Briefly I entertained the idea that such an explanation might be found in Inger Nissen's death, which occurred, according to the obituary notice I came upon one day, folded inside a wine-stained paper napkin in the glove box, on December 30, 1942. Inger Fog, née Nissen, resident of Horns, the notice announced, died giving birth to her third child, a healthy baby boy. Hadn't Helle herself already told me, even if she'd never specified when, that Inger died in childbirth, that she'd been buried in a cemetery on the outskirts of Hjørring, and that her mica-flecked headstone wasn't centered within the plot but was set off to one side, leaving room for Hans to join her, just as she'd learned to leave room for him in the conjugal bed? *Hvil i fred*, it said on the stone. Rest in peace. Which, Helle muttered, she guessed poor Inger would finally have been able to do, albeit temporarily. Poor poor Inger. A dull husband, three boys, a flock of moulting ducks.

Of course, once a woman like Inger was dead she became immune to the living's expressions of sympathy or censure. This was because Inger's soul, as Helle assured me, would have gone straight to heaven; Jesus, that aspect of God encased in a human body, would have wanted Inger for his own, partial as he was to food-loving, overweight women. Whereas it was the Devil, Helle said, who went for the skinny ones. The skinnier the better. The Devil, she claimed, went for the ones who could sneak back, threading their way through the gaps in God's creation. An affront, she said, the ones like you and me. The stream was sending its dark tongue of water across my feet, Helle's feet. Bright coins of early-morning sun falling through the cedar trees, the twins just stirring in their beds, Lily furiously barking somewhere off to the west, a thrush in the ferns on the far bank. Three notes, *tuk-tuk tuk. Tuk-tuk tuk*; greenish ferns unfolding, bright coins falling, cigarette smoke. I could see her toes and they were *not* webbed. The notes of an opera waiting to be composed, she was saying. "Never" was the key. Only in order to be able to touch each other after you were dead, you had to have touched while you were still alive. Sam wouldn't be there. Believe me, Frances. You shouldn't count on Sam. She tossed away her glowing cigarette, startling the thrush into flight, and like two wings her hands were flying toward me. No! No! I said. Why couldn't it have been you, she said (echoing, although I didn't know it at the time, the words of Heloise's final aria in *The Heroine*). Back then. Back when I was still young and desirable. Damn it, Frances! And then Lily came running up, her muzzle stuck through with porcupine quills, and we spent the next hour extracting them with a pair of needle-nosed pliers.

Maybe it was a combination of elements, a disturbing confluence of the personal and the political—the fact of Inger Nissen's death, of Maeve Merrow's treachery and her subsequent move to Paris, of the war itself—that left Helle bitter and humiliated, grief stricken, assailed by fundamental, crippling doubts. Maybe it was the war alone, although hadn't Helle already proved how the wartime death of a friend might be turned to her own advantage, how the unsettled condition of war merely served to enhance her creative powers? Maybe, after all, what she could no longer tolerate was her growing sense that to make a thing was to set yourself up for the loss of it; that creation was nothing more than a prelude to mourning.

In any event, ten years went by. Helle left Denmark and commenced an aimless wandering from city to city along the eastern seaboard of the United States, where she became a brooding presence at the dinner tables of a variety of boardinghouses. The New World, she said, a ruthless, unconsoling, gigantic landscape filled with large, optimistic people—in which a small, dark creature like herself could easily disappear. In fact, she claimed, it was when she was living at one such boardinghouse, on Arch Street in Philadelphia—from 1946 until mid-1948—that she had seen me for the first time. How could you know it was me? I asked, and she sighed. "Even before I knew who you were," she said, "I recognized you. I may have made some mistakes before, but not then. As you say in English, the scales had fallen from my eyes. A disgusting image, no? Disgusting yet apt." According to Helle, once you'd decided to recognize your fate you had to be prepared to give up any hope of protecting yourself from what it might actually look like.

She was quick to explain, however, that there'd been nothing unpleasant about her first glimpse of the slim, dark-eyed girl she insisted had been me, a girl of about sixteen sitting with an older man at a table in one of those South Street restaurants where opera singers gathered after the performance, restaurants notable not so much for the quality of their food—even though you could always count on getting a decent plate of spaghetti, a half-decent dish of bisque tortoni—as for the tendency of their guests, once they had a little wine in them, to start singing. A tenor at a corner table would begin—"*Parigi, o cara*" perhaps, the heartbreaking duet from the last act of *Traviata*—and a soprano on the opposite side of the room would join in. "You were laughing, weren't you?" Helle said. "Of course it was silly, the dying Violetta shoveling ice cream into her mouth. The man with you had a little black mustache and a bow tie. He tried to get you to stop laughing, only you were laughing too hard to stop. That pretty mouth! That little tear squeezing out of the corner of your eye! That bright red dress with a boat neck and a white piqué collar. It *was* you, wasn't it?" Helle asked, and I

had to admit that I knew the place she was talking about, that
I'd been there more than once. Joe DiSanto used to take me,
I said—an opera buff whose wife hated classical music. He
worked for a caterer and I'd met him at Anna Clay's wedding
reception. As for the dress, I couldn't remember. Maybe I
had a dress like that. In those days I had hundreds of dresses,
most of them from Nan Duskin, because my mother wanted
me to attract the right class of husband. Except Frances liked
them married, said Helle. Even back then my Frances had a
weakness for married men. And what if she'd scooped me up,
quick as a wink, in my nice red dress from Nan Duskin? I'd
just like to have seen you try, I replied.

In any event, she didn't. Instead, shortly thereafter Helle
moved to New York, where she stayed for a while in a
boardinghouse on Carmine Street, her fellow boarders mainly
older women who made their living modeling nude at the Art
Students League, Cooper Union, Pratt. Crazy women, Helle
said, elderly bohemians, who showed up for meals in chenille
bathrobes or grease-stained kimonos embroidered with dragons and peonies, who seemed to apply their pancake makeup
with palette knives prior to painting their lips maroon, their
eyelids aqua, their cheeks bright pink. It was like living among
courtesans whose sense of dignity had been eroded by the
persistent absence of patrons, although at first Helle didn't
care, her own sense of dignity having been likewise destroyed.
She had a small inheritance from her father as well as the
money she'd earned from her operas. *The Shepherdess and the
Chimney Sweep*, for example, had been a tremendous popular
success in England, and there'd been some talk about City
Opera mounting a production of *Waves*. Still, from time to
time she would take a brainless job making doughnuts or

selling neckties, such jobs as might be counted on to turn the brain to mush.

Then, one April day, she was sitting in her Carmine Street room, another of those boxlike, single-windowed rooms in which she was apparently destined to spend her life, when a mouse came out of a hole in the wall and, instead of fleeing, remained poised for a moment on the threadbare carpet, regarding her with frank curiosity. The same luminous dark eyes, the same hinged muzzle, the same long flickering whiskers as its predecessor, that rat in her conservatory practice room—Helle quickly rummaged through her pocketbook for the pack of saltines she'd stowed there after buying a bowl of corn chowder at the Automat. Hungry? she'd asked the mouse, and it had blinked once, slid like a mechanical creature on wheels toward the hand which held the cracker, paused halfway across the room, blinked again, and run back into its hole. It seemed to Helle as if she were being shown a sign. A gentle spring breeze lively with the smell of lilacs, of coffee and moist pavement, flew in through her window; she could hear a woman hailing a taxi, and the percolating noise of pigeons on nearby rooftops. A tapping on her door and in walked Marie Lavallee, the woman from the room next door, distraught, to tell her that Cynthia Poole had locked herself in the bathroom and wouldn't come out. Cynthia, as they all knew, had been depressed ever since the man she'd pinned her hopes on had dumped her for someone younger. But by the time they finally managed to break down the bathroom door, Cynthia was already dead, lying in the now-pinkish water of the claw-footed bathtub with her eyes wide open, her fake marabou slippers carefully positioned, side by side, on the pink bath mat, which she'd likewise positioned carefully on the tile floor the way a person does who doesn't want to get the floor wet after she climbs, dripping, from the tub.

It was too much, Helle said. She hadn't composed a note of music since leaving Denmark, hadn't even listened to any music, aside from what she couldn't avoid hearing through boardinghouse walls or piped through the ceilings of restaurants and stores. Marie, she noticed, had a sentimental fondness for a certain French chanteuse with a childish tremor in her voice, recordings of whose songs she would play over and over, singing along, "*N'y va pas, Manuel, n'y va pas,*" until Helle was ready to scream. Piaf, I said, probably the great Edith Piaf, to which Helle coldly replied that if you'd heard one French chanteuse you'd heard them all. She hated the French, and in particular French opera, claiming that the language turned to an unctuous blur, a kind of audible drooling, when sung. In any event what she found herself thinking—Woman or mouse, am I woman or mouse?—at last acquired the force of a line of music waiting to be written. Nightingale, she remembered; she'd been working on an opera which was to have had a nightingale as its heroic central character. If her vision of the character had changed, did that mean she should abandon the project? Of course not. Nor, she warned me, should I be fooled into drawing the obvious conclusion—that the revised character of Nightingale was meant to represent Maeve Merrow—just as I shouldn't assume, along with the critics, that Nightingale was meant to represent Hitler, and that the entire opera was an allegory for the atrocities of the Third Reich.

This conversation occurred during the week preceding the catastrophic masked ball. We were sitting on either side of the fold-down table in our separate beach chairs, drinking tea, watching the twins and William paw through the contents of the steamer trunk, removing costumes and trying them on. "That looks good," Flo told William, after he'd settled a turban of red and orange silk onto his white-blond head. The only problem was, if they decided to use any of these costumes they wouldn't be able to keep their identities secret, at least from each other. Anyway, the hat was too big, William said, taking it off and frowning at it; too big and too hot. And too round, Ruby added. It made him look like Jack Pumpkin-Head in *Return to Oz*. Only it was Selim Pasha's turban from a 1930 production of *Die Entführung aus dem Serail*, Helle pointed out. A pity it didn't fit, because William was perfect for the part. She was trying to persuade me to wear the pirate queen's costume from a Munich production of *Lahloo*; her own costume, she said, had already been chosen and hidden in her closet. When I told her I didn't even know if I was planning to attend the party, she laughed. Was I going to turn out to be a coward, now, just as things were getting interesting? Cowardice, she said, was a crime like any other, except that it was essentially boring, a crime you didn't so much commit as surrender to. This at least was what she'd discovered that day in the Carmine Street boardinghouse; this was the discovery that eventually propelled her to Canaan, to the Blackburns' house, where she finally summoned the courage to complete *Fuglespil*. To Sam and Maren's house, where, in a room whose three windows let in the clear northern light, the shameless light of annunciation, she finally allowed the nightingale to perch on her finger. Took a good look. Saw what she was really confronting. Meanwhile, in an adjacent room, a husband and wife were making love. Making William here, Helle said, pointing. A man and a woman were making love while she, a more isolate and suspect deity, was making Nightingale.

NIGHTINGALE! Such a tender, charming creature, each wing beat and song note animated by that impossible set of desires peculiar to adolescence, by that yearning to remain a child and, at the same time, to leave childhood behind forever. Dark-eyed and lithe, a little slut really—"*Non so più cosa son, cosa faccio . . . Or di foco, ora sono di ghiaccio*" ("I no longer know who I am, what I'm doing, if I'm made of fire or of ice"), to quote Cherubino—Nightingale continues the *hosenrolle* tradition of *Det omflakkende Møl* and *Lahloo*. Helle imagined a soprano voice not unlike the legendary Nellie Melba's, which she'd heard on the gramophone at Clara's, a star sailing into the infinite. The perfection of Melba, combined with the passion of Malibran? A touch of Jenny Lind, whose famous trill, despite her reputation for moral rectitude, had at its heart a distinctly sexual, liquid throbbing? Jenny Lind, the Swedish Nightingale. For even though the typical diva is usually perceived to be exotic and larger than life, and even though the nightingale is a small, drab bird, comparisons between the two would seem to be inevitable, given the heavenly quality of the nightingale's voice. Isn't Hans Andersen's story "The Nightingale" truly a paean to his love for Jenny Lind? And wasn't Adelina Patti reported to have eaten, every night before retiring, a sandwich containing the tongues of twelve nightingales?

Lounging along the foremost branch of the gigantic elm, Nightingale is boyish and diffident, his left knee bent in a vee, his winged arms raised above his head, the wing feathers

fanning outward from their carpal arch. It is as if we have
caught him in the act of waking up, yawning and stretching.
"Calm, light air, light breeze, fresh," Nightingale sings.
"Strong breeze, fresh gale, whole gale, storm. Boreas, Notus,
Zephyr, Eurus; blizzard, willy-willy, bise, simoom." At this
point we are not yet aware of Nightingale's deeper longings,
merely of the beauty of his voice. He describes the winds as
an aggregation of limbs compassing the globe: the two long
pale arms of the trade winds cradling its green hills and blue
oceans; the thick, flaccid arms of the doldrums gripping its
equator; the polar winds clapped like the palms of two hands
over its icy extremities. "Petrel and chat, hawk and lark,
the winds hold us back from the outer dark, from its coinage
of stars, we can't get away, sparrow and plover, chaffinch
and jay."

The scene changes. We are now at a greater remove from
the house than before: the kitchen window is a tiny square of
yellow light, in front of which we see the elm's silhouette and
an expanse of moonlit meadow. Following the scene in the
kitchen, in fact, the entire opera is constructed so our angle
of perspective widens with each subsequent change of scene: a
refinement of the cinematic technique Helle first experimented
with in *Det omflakkende Møl*. Her purpose here was to visually
underscore the action's increasing distance from its point of
origin and, at the same time, to create increasing distance
among the individual birds, not unlike the dispersal of matter
into the universe following the big bang. For the moment,
however, the birds remain close enough together that we can
still see them all: several roost within a cluster of shrubs,
stage left, others in the grass, stage center; Nightingale and
Shrike are perched on the adjacent posts of a barbed wire
fence which crosses the apron, stage right. You must be

hungry, sings Shrike, thus beginning an extended stretch of recitative; a voice such as yours needs to be fed properly. How about something with some meat on it for a change?

Shrike's own voice, a dramatic soprano, emerges from the narrow, hooked beak of her feathered hood. Steel-gray her plumage, a black mask over the eyes, a black tail, and black wings—Shrike's human aspect is limited to her torso, naked from the clavicles to the pelvis, revealing breasts, navel, pubic hair. "A nice mouse?" she suggests. "A tasty salamander, caught just this morning?" By a tilt of the head she indicates the diversity of her offerings, a row of lifeless bodies impaled on the barbs of the fence. But Nightingale declines, reminding Shrike of his preference for bugs and worms. Besides, it isn't food which feeds his voice. "What, then?" asks Shrike. Can it be that such purity of sound has its source in the impure yearnings of the flesh? Can it be? she taunts, swiveling to face him, arching her back and spreading her legs. It was Helle's intention that Shrike's personality more closely resemble that of the typical basso buffo, shrewd and lascivious, than that of the typical dramatic soprano, declamatory and histrionic. In other words, Leporello, not Donna Anna. Let's appease our appetites together, Shrike suggests. Let's eat the food that, no matter how much of it you eat, never gets completely eaten up. But again Nightingale refuses. When you choose to have your cake and eat it too, he says, all you can think about is cake. Your voice becomes too sweet, too sugar-clogged, too crumbly. He then begins singing the first verse of the crucial "If only" aria, the other verses of which he will sing at intervals throughout the opera's third and final act. "If only," Nightingale sings, "I could fly forever, beyond this field, this grass, these trees. This fence, this post, this knot of wire—if only my wings could carry me to where the land breaks into water, to where the world breaks into air. Why am I cursed with just two wings? Why can't I have another pair? If only I could fly forever, then light and dark would meet in me, my voice would be both bloom and rot, salt and fire, root and sea."

As he sings, Nightingale moves closer and closer to Shrike, the implication being that the fulfillment of his wish might spell, likewise, the satisfaction of her desire. Fate's complex machinery is set into motion; Shrike assumes the role of go-between, conveying Nightingale's message to the rest of the birds, who respond by breaking into a noisy, dissonant chorus. And then out of the chaos arises the single voice of Magpie, the familiar *chak chak chak chak* culminating in an impassioned plea for action rather than talk. Magpie is the expert thief, and explains the secret of his success: you must first understand the difference between that which is truly valuable and that which is merely protected as if it were valuable. Once you understand this, you will have access to the victim's point of greatest vulnerability, and you can then steal whatever you want without fear of being caught.

As Act Three opens, we follow the progress of Rook and Kite, both partial to carrion, both wearing black feathered capes over breastplates of scale armor, the eyeholes of their black casques ringed with gold. They stand together within a small clearing, looking out across the audience as if toward the ocean; just behind them the base of a lighthouse, its twin beams—one white, one red—illuminate the stage at regular intervals. A copse of stunted trees, their trunks twisted and pearl gray, extends back toward the rear wall, on which hangs a drop cloth showing the barbed wire fence, the moonlit meadow, the dark limbs of the elm, the yellow light of the kitchen window, reduced to the size of a star. The music: a deep strand of sound, full orchestra; a series of five-note runs, up and down the scale, commencing simultaneously on five consecutive notes in such a way that the effect is of a seamless, undulant whole. Rook and Kite discuss their options. This place is obviously a nesting ground for terns. They can please themselves, eat their fill of eggs, or they can try to please Nightingale. Kite (*hi-hi-heea*, why why be a dupe?) favors the former alternative; Rook (*kaaw kaaw*, cost cost is too great), the latter. As they argue, they walk, so that by the time the valet appears, threading his way through the tree trunks, they are standing out of his sight on the apron, stage left.

The valet removes a letter from his pocket as the violins flutter into dreamy prominence. An assignation! But with whom—the scullion or the maid? *Fuglespil* is designed so that clouds of human drama drift, typically fugitive and ambiguous, through the landscape, obscuring or abetting Nightingale's plan. The downstairs maid approaches from the wings, stage left; the scullion from the wings, stage right. "Why not both?" sing Rook and Kite. Of course they're referring to their own dilemma, the solution to which presents itself in a mutual recollection of Magpie's advice. "Why not both?" they repeat, concluding on the high C toward which their duet has tended all along, on that sharp point of sound where the cloud snags, releasing the valet's passions in a sudden cloudburst of sixteenth notes. "My dear my dear press here press here your lips your lips your hips your hips . . ." He reaches out and, suiting the action to the words, draws the maid and the scullion into his greedy embrace, thereby creating a composite creature of multiple, flailing appendages, a parodic version of darker things to come. A brief trio commences, the music a cunning pastiche of sentimental favorites (*"Mi chiamano Mimì," "La fleur que tu m'avais jetée,"* etc.). "But what is this?" sings the valet, his hands having discovered simultaneously the scullion's gender and the maid's condition. "They call me Billy," laughs the scullion. "The flower you planted," sneers the maid. "*O terra addio*," sings the valet, backing away. On his final, sustained "*o*" the scene ends.

Thus the pattern is established: time and again Nightingale makes a request which Shrike communicates to the rest of the birds. With each change of scene we move further and further from the original elm, witnesses to an increasingly complicated series of events involving both birds and people. Eventually it becomes clear that what we are seeing, at least insofar as the birds are concerned, is representative activity. Rook and Kite might report back to Nightingale with the wings of a tern, only to find that he has already affixed to his upper spine the white wings of an egret, the purple-tipped wings of a mallard, the stippled wings of a plover—even the bright green wings of Bee-Eater, which Shrike confesses she could not resist. More wings than a seraph, boasts Nightingale. With all of these wings I can fly higher than God's throne. My voice, he sings, will be more beautiful, its range greater, its tone purer, its essential quality intensified by my depth of experience. Of course he ignores the fact that the company's number has been diminished by one: perfection requires sacrifice. Besides, Shrike points out, at the critical moment, as they were preparing to steal the wings of a mourning dove, Bee-Eater got cold feet. "It's not just her feet which are cold now," sings Wren, and this expression of remorse, however understated, causes the other birds to look around uneasily. They know that a new form of peril has been admitted into their world, and that they must either embrace it or succumb to its wanton displays of force.

The third act continues, its dramatic action revolving around Nightingale's persistent dissatisfaction. If only I did not have a single mouth, he sings; if only I did not have a single pair of eyes. Wary, the birds scramble to bring him what he wants. His beautiful head is transformed into a seething, spiny mass, beaks opening and closing, a ghastly hybrid combining the animate and inanimate, echinoderm and battle mace, the mindless sting, the malicious blow. His body is studded with eyes, dark and shining, vigilant, covetous— he can look everywhere at once, but this implied omniscience is limited by the absence of a governing intelligence. You might just as well expect a jewel-studded reliquary to distinguish between right and wrong, to be capable of sustaining a moral vision. Still, it's impossible not to notice that these accretions, however hideous, serve Nightingale's ultimate purpose. His voice is becoming more and more beatific, unearthly, issuing from his many mouths like light itself, like a radiant halo of sound, higher and higher, as if he might actually contain within himself a holy relic, St. Peter's knucklebone, a strand of St. Catherine's hair, a splinter of the true Cross. By the time he makes his final request, his voice has become so perfect that it is almost inaudible. "If only I could live forever," Nightingale sings. This is the music that precedes, out of nothing, the birth of a star, the cell's gasp at the moment of mitosis.

As Nightingale undergoes his metamorphosis, the clouds of human drama begin to thicken, to assume the towering anvil shapes of thunderheads, out of which flicker tongues of lightning. The downstairs maid and the scullion admit to a mutual attraction and decide, in a touching duet, to run away together. Meanwhile, the master of the house has received a

letter promising a piece of vital information if he shows up
for a midnight rendezvous on the beach. The author of this
letter is the second scullion, whose attempts at blackmailing
her mistress have proved fruitless. Cast-off dresses, a mangy
stole, a necklace of pearls with a broken clasp! the scullion
fumes. Now she will have her revenge; she will play both ends
against the middle. Indeed, the mistress of the house has
received a more explicit letter, the scullion not only threatening to tell her husband about the affair with the cook but also
describing her husband's infidelities. "To take the bait," sings
the outraged mistress, "is to kiss the traitor, to marry treason
is to bow to fate." This aria, with its great swooping leaps
from upper to lower registers, with its dramatic syncopation,
is in frank imitation of the style Mozart employed for Donna
Elvira's two similarly outraged arias in *Don Giovanni*. The
mistress goes on to lament her own credulity: "I missed the
point—the food on the table, the steaming joint, the loaf of
bread, didn't come from his heart but from his pocket, the
gleaming lure, the marriage bed. To eat the food is to love
the cook, to kiss the hands that removed the hook." And
where might she be now? the mistress wonders. In the kitchen,
it turns out, with the twins, baking cookies.

So the groundwork is laid for the opera's penultimate
scene: we see a shingle beach at midnight; stage rear, an
expanse of marram grass, its razor-sharp blades stained, alternately, snow white, blood red; a blue rowboat on the apron,
stage right. For the first time since the twins' duet in Act One
we hear the glass harmonica, an overlapping series of faint,
tingling glissandi. The sound of grass blades rubbing against
each other in a sea breeze, or pebbles and shells rattling
together within the trough of a wave? Perhaps the harmonica's
music reminds us of the twins. But they are nowhere near this

beach, we think. They are safe in the house with the cook, baking cookies in the kitchen. We can just make out the kitchen window, its tiny pinprick of light. Yes, the twins are safe, we think, and we're relieved, because the music, despite its delicacy and sweetness, is also ominous.

VII

How many days had it been since the last rainfall? You could feel the thick layers of hot rainless air piling on top of one another, an atmosphere in which it was impossible to do anything except remain motionless, inert, like the gold ring Sam gave me the day before Helle's party. A token of his intentions, he told me. I pictured the marble lips of a ghost statue cracking open, heard emerging from those lips a deep bass voice singing *"in pegno, in pegno."* Cotton wadding packed around a piece of metal, an object replete with significance but essentially useless—the depressive's habitual condition. In such monotonous, sedative heat your anticipation of things to come, whether a masked ball or the plighting of a troth, acquired an itchy, annoying texture; it nagged at you like a raveling label in the collar of a blouse, like road grit thrown into your face by the tires of a passing car.

Helle, however, appeared unaffected by the torpor into which the rest of the town had sunk. She was exhilarated, energetic, immersed in preparations. On the afternoon of August the fifth, four men began setting up a large canvas tent in the meadow behind the trailer. In case of rain, Helle explained. But it was never going to rain again, I said, never, forever. Helle glared at me, stifled a cough, and continued removing the pits from a huge bowl of ripe cherries. Never was a meaningless concept, didn't I think, at least if you tried to apply it to the physical world? The only thing she wanted to know was what had become of the man who was supposed to deliver the wine. She picked up a cherry, inserted it in the pitter, pressed down the handle, and out popped a pit. Her hands, I noticed, were stained dark red, but not her mouth. Amazing, I thought, Helle had managed to pit what looked like hundreds of cherries without eating a single one. Did she take Persephone for her model? Or was it more a case of honoring that crucial distinction she'd described to me not long after we met, between desire and its gratification? Here, she said, handing me a bag of oranges. They needed to be peeled, the white outer fiber pared away, the flesh sliced from between the membranes. No seeds. Did I think I could do it? Because they had to be perfect, these crescents of bright orange deployed here and there among the white slices of smoked turkey. It had taken her three days to get the turkey just right, and she didn't want the effect ruined by sloppily sectioned oranges. Of course, as it turned out, we never got to eat any of the food, only to admire the way it looked, to regard it yearningly as it sat on top of a long damask-covered table at the back of the tent: the woodlike gleam of braided loaves of bread, the salamanderlike brightness of smoked salmon, the blue-green veins of mold running through stone-like cheeses, a glistening red moistness here, a leafy darkness there, all of it ceremoniously lit by beeswax candles in three elaborate silver candelabra.

The first guests arrived a little before nine o'clock, two obviously nervous couples who climbed out of a Rambler and were led by Flo into the meadow. Even though there was still a thin smear of light left in the sky—its color that of the underside of a wave, a rising shadow preparing to fall—the Japanese lanterns strung around the meadow's periphery had already been lit. Rose and lilac, cerulean and pearl, they hung motionless from the twisted branches of the shrub willows growing along the stream bank to the north; motionless from the green-black limbs of the cedars to the west; motionless from a row of fence posts to the east. At the southern edge, just behind the trailer, a space had been left open, the doorway into the huge ceilingless room of the meadow and, thence, into the smaller, contained room of the tent. Music issued from a loudspeaker on the trailer roof—chiefly waltzes to begin with, though, as the evening progressed, as the sky darkened and a vague half-moon appeared in a thickening nest of clouds, the musical program likewise darkened: Barbarina's melancholy plaint on behalf of a lost pin, for example, interposed between the nebular folds of Chopin's Andante Spianato and his Grande Polonaise. Meanwhile, embracing every-thing—the meadow, the tent, the dancing guests, the winking lanterns, and the shining wine-filled goblets—was the heat.

You could remove your shoes, but it wouldn't do any good; the ground still exhaled the heat of midday, and the grass was so crisp and brittle that it hurt. No sooner had you taken your shoes off than you'd put them back on, stuffing back into them your heat-swollen toes, your poor blistered heels. By eleven o'clock several guests, myself included, had waded into the stream, where we stood trying to maintain our balance on the wobbly, slime-coated rocks, our equilibrium threatened by the current, by our mask-impaired vision, by the limited glow of the lanterns, by the wine. Where was our hostess? one of the many men dressed like Zorro wanted to know. Had anyone seen her? Marie Antoinette, suggested a woman husband, had been invited. Indeed, it would appear that Helle had invited the entire town, her ill-starred plan having been to take leave of us all on the grandest scale possible.

"How did you know it was me?" I asked, and Sam walked closer, pointing down to where I'd bunched the silver satin up over my thighs. The stream gave off a moist, reptilian smell, the smell in the shallow basin from which the zoo's oldest crocodile regards you sleepily, the smell of the lives we lived before we stood up on our hind legs and our sleepy hunger turned to greed. "Your knees," he said, and although the stream blotted out his familiar smell of pepper, I knew that was there as well; the thought of it, of his familiar, irreverent body hidden under his black, holy garments, made me listless and weak. "I'd recognize those knees anywhere," Sam said. "Those sharp little bones. Hear that, monkey face?" he shouted, but I told him not to bother. The monkey was Flo, I said, whereupon he took another step closer, reached out, and grabbed my hands. "Those bony knees," he said tenderly, "these bony fingers." How lovely I was, even when all he could see of me were the bony parts. But wait a sec—where was the ring, he wondered. Why wasn't I wearing the ring?

By now the other people in the stream were starting to move away, as if the combined weight of our desire were a heavy stone dropped from a great height, and they were the ever-widening band of ripples caused by its fall into the water. I could feel their movement, a subtle opening of the space around our bodies, creating a still and airless arena on the rim of which their masked faces hovered, expectant, wary, eager for entertainment. Isn't that the woman from the diner? I heard someone say, and someone else—Buggy Moore?— suggested that maybe they should mind their own business.

in a baseball uniform—a woman I thought might be]
Kinglake but whose features had been pressed into an om:
blur by a nylon stocking. The headless Marie Antoine
the blood-stained bodice. That would be just like Miss
Brix, didn't we think? Too obvious, replied another m
nun with a rubber death's-head mask completely coverir
face. He had appeared out of nowhere, pushing his way tc
us through the denser thicket of willows on the far si
the stream, then stepping into the water without botheri
lift the hem of his habit. Antoinette was Helen Spragu
man said, adding that he was convinced our hostess w:
little spider monkey he'd seen creeping through the w
back there where he'd come from. A sly, watchful little
key-woman, a sneaky little spy monkey, he said, and I
despite the way his voice was muffled by the rubber
mask, by the noise of the stream and a nearby grc
drunken revellers, that it was Sam.

"Hello, Frannie," he said. Had he been able to s
face he would have understood immediately that no
what gloomy predictions I might have made about our
at happiness in the dim and faraway future, for the m
I was perfectly happy to see him standing there beside
the stream. But he could see only the papier-mâché s
my mask, the eyeholes cut at an upward-tilting ang
outlined in black paint, the sneering lips painted bright
Turandot, Puccini's cannibal queen, the virgin priestess
flesh her three fatuous ministers claim wouldn't be g
eat. Helle had finally persuaded me to borrow the cc
claiming that if anyone could get away with wearing s
outlandish headdress and tight-fitting gown, it would
A bold move, she'd pointed out, a chance to spit i
Judkins's eye. For Patti Judkins, together with her loa

Suddenly everything seemed to be in motion: the stream kept pouring past us; the sky, when I cast a quick look up at it, had filled with enormous black clouds outlined in white by the concealed moon, and those clouds, like the stream, were racing away, leaving us behind, leaving us there, me and Sam, the two of us alone in the dark, reptilian water.

The ring was at home, I told him, safe in its box, and he made an angry, exasperated noise, expelling his breath in a raw *hnnuh* from the back of his throat. Didn't I understand that the ring was just the opening statement in what was supposed to be a conversation? He'd already told Maren, last night. Told her what? I asked, and he made a noise again, louder this time, a kind of stifled growl. Jesus, Frannie, he said, and began peeling away the mask, bit by bit, struggling against the rubber's grip on his moist hot skin, working it up carefully over his glasses, the lenses of which were so fogged up I couldn't see his eyes. Once the mask was all the way off he threw it angrily into the stream. It must be midnight, a male voice said. Twenty of, corrected a female voice, a voice wavering with nervous laughter. Teenagers, I thought. You could tell because their voices hadn't yet been dulled by resignation and its attendant sorrows.

Sam yanked his glasses from his nose and wiped them on his sleeve, his face glistening with what I first assumed was sweat. It was only after I'd moved a little nearer, my heart as tentatively anchored to its floor of bones as the rock I stepped on was to the steambed, that I realized he was crying. "That I was in love with someone else," he said. "I told her I was in love with someone else. What're *you* staring at?" he snarled, by which I knew he meant the people standing on the bank, even though his attention remained fixed on me. "Don't you have anything better to do?" he yelled. Had the music been turned up, I wondered, or was I only more aware of it, all those notes, those dark particles of sound clustering around me in the hot air? "To eat the food," a soprano voice was singing—Anna Moffo in the Met production of *Fuglespil*, I found out later—"is to love the cook . . ." Was this what it was like for Helle, every breath a terrible effort, the oxygen itself so thick and hot you couldn't draw it into your lungs no matter how hard you tried? And was that Helle I heard, down there among the black shapes of the cedars, coughing? "To kiss the hands that removed the hook . . ." As the clarinets began their wild, dark descent into a simmering pit of dissonant broken chords, the pure clear arrow of Anna Moffo's voice was flying upward, upward, like an arrow into the pearly film of clouds around the moon. "But you never asked me," I said. The mask had left Sam's hair in a flat cap on his head, and the cap was starting to separate into wet, curly locks, into separate curling blades. Brown and gray. A shingle beach, a glass harmonica; blades of marram grass stained alternately red and white by the slowly rotating beam of a lighthouse. "Ask?" Sam said. "What are you, my mother? *Ask?* I was telling her the truth, that's all."

The coughing seemed to come closer, although perhaps it too, like the music, had merely increased in pitch. The broken chords had reassembled themselves; I could hear their ominous and somehow liturgic progression, the sense of hooded figures making their steady way through vast hallways of stone. Dark and damp, measured organum, a steady beating of gradually swelling chords: step, step, step; cough, cough, cough. "Truth has nothing to do with it," a voice said, coughing, and when I looked past Sam's shoulder I could see Helle approaching out of the shadowy cave where the stream disappeared into the cedar woods, leaping lightly on the balls of her feet from rock to rock. Or to be more precise, I saw Helle dressed in Nightingale's hideous third act costume, her head encased in its helmet of beaks, flashing knifelike, scissorlike; her body tessellated with flashing, observant eyes; her brown wings extended on either side for balance; her russet tail trailing in the water. "*Chook-chook-chook, piu piu piu,*" she said. "The joke's on you."

So we might imagine them, Helle said, all of them gathered together for the last time on the beach: the two scullions and the downstairs maid, the valet, the master and the mistress, the cook. The twins as well; we shouldn't forget the twins. Flo and Ruby, over there in the bushes, a spider monkey and a little white cat—she knew they were there, even though they were trying to hide. An ascending chorale, could we hear it? The most beautiful thing she'd ever written. Heavenly music—listen! she said—the complicated mess of human affairs finally transformed into celestial music. Of course, the higher the music soared, the greater the danger. Nightingale and his army of birds were flying overhead, on the lookout as always for signs of human pride and arrogance. Sam and I were stealing the show, she complained. Midnight, time to unmask, but Sam and I had ruined everything; the guests were too distracted by the rumors of our impromptu drama in the stream to be interested in her own, which had been weeks in the planning. She lifted one winged arm—Oh my God, she's got a gun, said a man dressed like a nurse—and I realized she was holding her father's pearl-handled dueling pistol, pointing it, at least for the moment, at my chest. Thunder and lightning, she said—appropriately dramatic, didn't we think? Meanwhile, the birds were beginning to land on the beach.

Although the thunder and lightning came in fact from the

loudspeakers, drops of real rain were now falling into the stream, where Sam had turned to face Helle, his arm looped protectively around my shoulders. "It isn't loaded, is it?" he asked, and I heard a bitter, high-pitched laugh at my back. Maren, I thought, and absurdly wondered if she'd been there all along.

"Go ahead and shoot," Maren Blackburn called, "I dare you. What's stopping you?"

"Except Frances is not my quarry," Helle admonished, stately, annoyed. "I would never hurt Frances. *Summa petit livor*," she continued. "Envy always wants the best for itself, to quote my father. Well, to quote Ovid, really. A warning which I've decided to take as advice." With her free arm Helle tugged off the beak-studded helmet and, as she did so, the arm holding the pistol swung out toward the bank, causing the by now large crowd standing there to let out a short, collective gasp.

"I've got it," yelled a Zorro (Lyle Judkins, according to the police report), only he was mistaken: his hand closed over air, over rain.

"I may be old," Helle laughed, "but I'm quicker than you. Quicker and smarter." She lifted the gun, this time purposely aiming it at the crowd. "You stupid people," she said. "Don't you understand? I'm trying to protect you. You stupid, stupid people."

At this very minute, she explained, the birds were setting upon the people on the beach, tearing them apart, providing Nightingale with bits and pieces of their bodies—the valet's shiny black hair and eyebrows, one scullion's pretty lips, the other's nimble fingers, the downstairs maid's perfect breasts, the cook's long white thighs, the master's prick, the mistress's cunt, the twins' little red hearts. *Fuglespil*, she said, was a dark opera, an opera born out of her need to define, once and for all, the monstrous nature of the artist. "If only I were one of you," Helle sang, her raspy voice accompanying the sweet voice of Nightingale, which floated down to us out of the loudspeaker and across the rain-spattered meadow, "then you would never know, how terror stalks you all the time, how it's the force that shapes the rhyme, that steals your breath to set the beat, the rutting gib, the bitch in heat; my gift your grace, the lying trace of form with which I cursed you."

"You're crazy," Sam said, and Helle rotated her feathery arm in his direction, bringing the gun's muzzle into alignment with his head. The rain was starting to fall harder, splashing into the water, making the willow leaves quiver timidly up and down, up and down, the lanterns sway wildly to and fro, to and fro, extinguishing some of the candles. A hint of brewing wind, a vague yawning coolness, more like the idea of coolness than coolness itself, insinuated itself into the hot tunnel of air above the stream. "Point that thing away," Sam said, and then, when Helle ignored him, he held out his hand, friendly, entreating, like a child trying to get its ball back from a stubborn pup. "Give it to me," he said. "Come on, you know better." Just like a man, Helle laughed, couldn't make up his mind. Confusing craziness and ethics, direction and desire. Typical. By now the glass harmonica was playing, solo, the opera's concluding measures, a phrase repeated over and over, that simple and vaguely familiar line of melody, something like the last phrase of "Row, Row, Row Your Boat," only disturbingly altered, rendered sinister by repetition. Maybe Helle would listen to me, Sam whispered into my ear. I could feel his lips moving there, wet, tense; his grip tightening on the knob of my shoulder. How hard it was to hear him over the noise of the rain! For it was pouring. The downpour we'd all been waiting for. The sound of fire rather than water, as Helle had once described it to me, of fire consuming everything around it. Filled with poison, as Sam had once suggested. If she'd listen to anyone, he said, it'd be me. But I didn't move, didn't open my mouth.

"What I was planning this time," Helle said, "was to destroy Nightingale instead. A few months one way or the other, what difference would it make? *Bang!* and then it's supper, though I wouldn't be stuck having to watch you eat it. A fabulous supper, if I say so myself. Better than the stuff they supposedly serve in Asgard, unless you happen to be partial to pig flesh and drinking horns full of mead. But that was years ago, that opera. And now here's the Don, trying as usual to get his supper ahead of everyone else. His supper— a certain young lady in Introduction to Hegel, a C student, but cute. A certain Mrs. Pinsky, summer resident on the lake. Zaftig, a departure from his usual taste. Possibly a certain front-office secretary, blond, ditto a departure. Oh, I know what you're thinking—maybe it's not too late, maybe I could still shoot myself, yes? Sam's right, all you have to do is say the word. Three choices, as I see it: shoot myself, shoot the Don, shoot the whole lot of you. The last being impractical; the first, no longer pertinent."

Did she have a mysterious third ear, as uncannily attuned to random sensory data as that mysterious tattooed eye? Otherwise I couldn't figure out how she'd overhead Sam's remark. "There's a fourth choice," he said, shouting. "You could shoot nobody." He'd let go of me and was inching toward Helle, the rain pounding down all around us, a deafening roar that seemed to have its source inside my head, where the four confusing possibilities tore at each other tooth and nail in a frightening and predatory tangle. "Oh no you don't,"

Helle said. A clever ploy, trying to distract her with a philosophic dilemma—for who, after all, could ever hope to put a
bullet through nobody's heart?—but she was wise to his
tricks. Although in a way Sam was on the right track: once
you saw the Don as nobody, once you understood that nobody
was trying to satisfy his rapacious appetite here in the stream,
then it hardly mattered if you pulled the trigger. No one
had ever gotten into trouble for shooting nobody. Another
philosophic dilemma, Sam shouted. How could no one pull a
trigger? Besides, how could he be hungry if he didn't have a
body? Touché, Helle admitted. Her mistake. The sad truth
was, no one's life had ever been saved by art.

"Isn't that so, Frances?" she said, and I heard a small *click*.
An almost imperceptible noise, but enough to finally rouse
me—all at once I was aware of how my mask, a gluey and
disintegrative mass, was slipping loose, sliding down my neck
and onto my shoulders. Of course, I thought, no wonder I
can't think clearly. I scraped the rest of the mask away, let
the rain wash my face, turning it this way and that, feeling
the cold drops hit my skin, some of them running into my
mouth and eyes. The world at last sprang into focus: I could
see the little brown feather pasted to Helle's cheek, her tongue
licking forth from her furiously smiling mouth, her eyes like
two pinpricks in her papery head, through which I thought
what I was seeing was the far-off darkness of the cedars; and
then my view of her was completely blotted out by the darker
shape of Sam, his wet dark robes clinging to his back, a tender
white crescent visible at the nape of his neck. For just a second
he paused, turning to look at me, and I could recognize in his
expression the same happiness I'd felt when I first saw him
standing there beside me in the water, a happiness which
flickered dimly, and went out. Behind me Maren; to my left

the crowd-filled meadow; to my right a monkey and a cat, crouched on the stream bank. "No!" I yelled, but I confess my meaning was ambiguous. I confess, I confess, although now it's too late. "No," I said again, softer this time, and the gun went off. Once, twice, three times. All three bullets straight through Sam's heart.

Part Five

THE GIRL WHO TROD
ON A LOAF

I

AND THEN NOTHING. Nobody, no one. The stream kept pouring from its spring in the cedar woods, heading toward Pocket Lake; the rain kept falling, not so hard as before, yet steady, persistent; the music played from the loudspeaker, waltzes once again, as if to lure us all back to the meadow, where we would keep on dancing forever, the women locked safely in the firm arms of the men. Although the command was clear: Don't anybody touch anything, said a man in a Dracula costume, and we didn't, standing there separate and horrified on the stream bank as if we understood his warning to mean that we shouldn't touch each other. This was Tom Milkwood, I realized, the deputy sheriff, a heavyset man with a reddish beard skirting his chin and no mustache, like an Amish farmer. Even-tempered and diligent, a little shy—he used to flirt with me shyly in the diner, telling jokes and forgetting the punch lines. Don't anybody leave, he said now, until I get your names. We were material witnesses to a crime, he cautioned us, and should watch what we said. Only as it turned out, Helle was more than willing to admit that she was the one who'd shot the gun. She handed it over proudly, then asked with some concern whether the rain would have washed away the fingerprints. No such luck, said Tom

Milkwood, wrapping the gun in his cape. By now the oils in her fingers would have left their mark, and you had to really put some effort into it to get rid of them. But Miss Ten Brix should keep her thoughts to herself until she'd consulted a lawyer. In the meantime, he was going to read her her rights, and suggested she listen carefully. "But I can tell you what you'll find," Helle said. "You'll find my prints. I can assure you that the only prints you're going to find on that gun are mine. People will try to tell you there was a struggle, as if Mr. Blackburn and I had struggled for possession of the gun. But I can assure you he never so much as laid a finger on it."

What I remember is how quiet the world became, the stream quietly moving, the rain quietly falling, the music quietly playing. No sound, even though I know people were whispering, sobbing, screaming; even though I know that at some point there was the wailing of sirens, the abrupt and tense conversation of professional men whose job it was to take photographs, to gather evidence, to remove the body. They took him away; the stream washed away the blood. "Well, Frances," Helle said, "the wolf is there, all you have to do is climb through. Only be quick about it, because if you don't, someone else will." She had her arm linked through Tom Milkwood's as if he were about to escort her not into a squad car but onto the dance floor. "My own chances to fly," she added, indicating the condition of her wing feathers with a sly, birdlike tilt of the head, "are not so good." Wolf, I said—are you insane? Wolf, wound, Helle shrugged, why equivocate? Of course I suspected what she meant, just as I knew that the walls quietly assembling themselves around me were as impervious to escape as the walls of my own house were full of holes, bad wiring, mice. Silent walls, gray and silent walls.

In Dürer's famous engraving it's not easy to differentiate Melancholia from the wall of the unfinished tower behind her, from the bell and the hourglass hanging there, the bell silent, the hourglass running out; from the sorrowful putto perched beside her on a grindstone or the spectral hound at her feet. This is a world in which no single detail is allowed to achieve prominence, the burin's restless cross-hatchings having rendered all surfaces equally gray, equally stippled with a gray and melancholy light. Scales and compass, inkpot and tongs— Frances Thorn surrounded by those tools with which she once hoped to pry her spirit loose from its brittle human brainpan, tools that are ultimately the agents of her confinement. So you might imagine me, a dull and motionless creature caught in that gray, cross-hatched net where the accomplice is doomed to live out her days, endlessly weighing, endlessly measuring. Only there's no tool adequate to such a task, for, as I discovered, to have become an accomplice is to have lost all weight, all contour. You disappear, even though you can still see yourself in the mirror. Nothing, nobody, no one. "The lying trace of form," I thought, "with which she cursed you."

Sometimes at night I would find myself looking through the picture window, confusing the sound of small animals tunneling through the unmowed grass with a man's footsteps. Sometimes I would dream that a man was touching my body, a stranger, and one for whom I knew I would never feel anything more than weary displeasure, because no matter how hard he tried he never was able to figure out the places where I was most vulnerable to a man's touch. The summer turned cold and wet; the dwarf apples rotted in the apple trees, the dwarf cornstalks rotted at the root, snails clung to the undersides of the rotting leaves of dwarf cabbages, dwarf beets.

Meanwhile, tourists flocked to the Branch Road to get a look at the trailer, and business at the diner was brisk, although I had only Kosta's word for this. He'd had to let me go, public opinion, as he told me regretfully, being what it was. There was an inquest, a trial. Helle was guilty of manslaughter, according to the jury, their verdict based on witness testimony, most of which implied that the shooting had been an accident.

"So did the good people of Salem join ranks," wrote Wallace Bench in a *Sun Herald* editorial, "to uphold what they assumed was a moral imperative. We can only surmise that for the good people of Canaan murder would appear to be a less heinous crime than adultery. Or, failing that, that the surprising verdict in the Blackburn case was due to a triumph of sentimentality, to an overriding unwillingness to send an old, sick woman to the electric chair. Where, in our opinion, she most certainly belongs." Ah, Mr. Bench, Helle said, when I showed her the clipping. It would be a relief to think that there was at least one person in Canaan who understood what had really happened that night. The only problem was that Wallace Bench was merely trying to exact revenge for all the letters she'd sent the paper complaining about his use of the masculine pronoun to the exclusion of the feminine. *Basta, basta!* she cried, and then suddenly started wheezing, lifting her arms above her head the way she'd been taught by the public health nurse. The pillows, Frances! she wheezed. By now she was once again living in the trailer, ever since her failing health had made it necessary for her to be removed, after a month, from what she liked to refer to as "the slammer." An officer of the court was hired to keep guard, although, as he himself concluded after his first day on duty, Helle was going nowhere. He would show up late in the morning, make a cup of coffee and take it outside, where he'd

Certainly it made her furious to have to reveal to me her growing weakness, when even a simple task like removing the lid from a jar of herring would leave her gasping, bent over, her face blue and pleated with deep ugly wrinkles. "Go away, Frances," she would gasp, "get out of here." Only I wouldn't. Instead I would unscrew the lid, crank open the windows, fetch the pillows, wheel in the oxygen canister. For the truth is that my initial aversion to Helle, my horror at the thought of actually having to be in the same room with her, eventually had been replaced by a need for explanation. Or at least that's the way, over time, I came to understand my otherwise suspect behavior. I wanted Helle to explain the events of that night in such a way that I'd be left with no doubt about the nature of my complicity. I needed to hear it from her own lips: Would it have made a difference if I'd told her not to shoot? And if not, was it still on my account that she'd pulled the trigger?

That was what I wanted, but, unfortunately, Helle refused to cooperate. "You're blameless, Frances," she insisted over and over again. "Why can't you get that through your head?" I was a hopeless case, she complained. Here was a chance to escape and I was throwing it away. If only she'd realized the depth of my involvement. Was I in love with Sam? My eyes, my eyes! All she had to do, she said, was say his name and my pupils dilated. Even now. Look at yourself. Feh! Besides, hadn't the tribunal already passed judgment? And if I wasn't satisfied with the results, then wasn't that the usual price we paid once we let men decide that the tribunal was preferable to chaos? Or what men called chaos. Her face dreamy, wrinkled, and bluish-gray—not unlike the washcloth with which the public health nurse would cheerfully subject her twice a week to the indignity of a sponge bath—Helle would lie there sit in one of the beach chairs, reading mystery novels. A busman's holiday, Mr. Spot? Helle would ask him, when she saw him thus engaged.

I helped her onto the bed—the little maple bed in which, only two years earlier, Ruby had put her dolls to sleep—and propped the pillows up under her hips. A technique called postural drainage, another of the public health nurse's tricks for coaxing breath back into Helle's failing lungs. The idea was that if you elevated her hips, gravity would draw away the mucus pooling in her chest; she was supposed to remain in this position for at least half an hour, without talking. "Such a chatterbox," the nurse would say. "You need to relax, honey. Let your muscles go loose."

But what, you might ask, was I doing propping up pillows under this woman's hips? Why hadn't I taken Kosta's advice—moved away from town, started a new life for myself and the twins in some faraway city? What was I waiting for? The flickering apparition of a man whose greatest mistake it had been to confuse the unsound surface of my lust with a firmly planted stone in a darkly rushing stream? Did I think that if I waited around he would come back to me, his damp body once again whole, his heart in one piece, all impediments to our love finally erased by his immateriality? But even the faintest sudden noise made me freeze with terror: Lyle Judkins's tractor starting up; the telephone; a thermometer falling to the floor, cracking apart to release hundreds of tiny balls of mercury. No, it's more likely I was motivated by both the penitent's need to subject herself to the overt daily censure of her peers and the victim's need to subject Helle to a subtle version of that same censure, one which I alone was capable of inflicting. In other words, I wanted to atone for my own sins while punishing Helle at the same time.

on her back, the pile of pillows under her hips, and fix her dreamy gaze on the trailer ceiling.

No, it wasn't always like this, she told me. Once upon a time, before the fake elegance of the tribunal, there was genuine elegance, the elegance of chaos. Huge stars would drop through the black hood of night, slipping right through God's fingers, illuminating the place where the Furies leaked up out of the bog as ignis fatuus, taking on the form of animals and plants, men and women. As mutable and diverse as we were taught to believe the human soul was, Helle said. She would watch them, study their sly imitations of human activity. They would pretend to eat, to defecate, to speak, to copulate, to give birth, to die—acts they clearly found ridiculous by comparison with their own seething, unindividuated grace. Of course sooner or later they'd have to return to the bog; they couldn't stand our air. Although, Helle went on to explain, being lungless they weren't in any danger of developing, as she had, what was called a "marching cavity" in the lungs. "My own version of chaos," Helle explained. "One day you'll show up with your pretty dilated eyes and all that will be left of me will be one big hole." Then she sighed, her sigh turning into a gasp, her gasp into a wheeze, her wheeze into great rattling coughs, each of which was scooped up out of the very center of her, as if to begin the final process of excavation.

At first I stayed because I wanted explanations, and then I stayed because she was dying. Maybe I was still in the thrall of that choice I'd made on the opera house steps; maybe, once having assumed the role Helle claimed to have invented for me, I couldn't make my exit until she was no longer around to prescribe whatever last-minute adjustments she thought necessary. So I stayed in Canaan, living on unemployment

checks, doomed to watch the twins' daily contention with
their own assigned parts as outcasts, those roles it was my
punishment to know had been thrust on them by the wages
of adult corruption. Of the two, Ruby's suffering was the
more obvious, her friendly and sociable spirit shocked anew
by every taunt, by the variations on popular songs she was
forced to hear whenever she went out into the schoolyard—
"Minnie the Moocher" transformed into "Francie the
Smoocher," for example. She missed William, who together
with Maren had vanished from town not long after the trial,
the rumor being that they'd moved back to Denmark and
were living in Frederikshavn with Niels and his wife. Which,
in fact, turned out not to be the case. Some time in October
a birthday card arrived in the mail, addressed to both of the
twins and postmarked Boston. Signed WILLIAM BLACKBURN.
No message. "I wish I was dead," Ruby told Flo as they sat
side by side on the dust-clouded, sock-littered living room
floor, looking at the card, feeding Lily the crusts of their
sandwiches. "Everyone hates me." "No they don't," Flo replied. "They're mixed up. They act like something's wrong
with you, but that's because they're letting the grown-ups
push them around the way kids always do. But they don't hate
you. They like you. Everyone's always liked you." It was only
a matter of time, Flo reassured Ruby, and she'd be the most
popular girl in the fifth grade, just as she'd been the most
popular girl in the fourth. "Really?" Ruby asked, and Flo
nodded her head vigorously, her lips pressed into a tight,
judgmental smile. A doubtful advantage, you could tell Flo
was thinking. "I wish—" Ruby began, and Flo put her hand
over her sister's mouth. A bad idea to wish, Flo said. Look
at where it got Mr. Blackburn. Did she know I was right

there, on the other side of the partly closed kitchen door, listening? Look where it gets you, Flo added, fiercely.

For Flo, on the other hand, seemed dedicated to the development of an increasingly autonomous persona. It was almost as if her presence that night on the stream bank had released her from what would have proved in the end to be the pitiless grip of a dangerous and overpowering mentor. She reviled the Dukketeatre as "childish," the task of designing sets for another person's opera as "slavery." Art made on behalf of anyone except the artist herself, Flo said, wasn't art. One day I found the colored pencils Helle had given her in the garbage; shortly thereafter, with the money she made doing odd jobs for the Kinglakes—the only people in town, aside from Kosta, who remained sympathetic throughout the ordeal—she bought a set of oil paints. At first she concentrated on self-portraits. Hundreds of self-portraits in turpentine-diluted umber on ripped-open bags from the supermarket—she pinned them to her bedroom walls and, when she ran out of space, all over the house. Underpaintings, she explained, the traditional method of laying in the basic form before applying color, glazes, and scumblings. Shadows translucent, Flo said, lights opaque. That was the rule. She'd borrowed a book called *Materials and Techniques for the Artist* from the Canaan library, and was studying it with characteristic thoroughness. Precision, she announced, was at the heart of all creative endeavor.

In a way, it was a relief to see these rapidly accumulating aspects of Flo's grave and silent face all around me, to recognize within the severity of her gaze some hint of what I wanted from Helle, but which Helle steadfastly denied me. Indeed, so long as I remained at home I felt as if the world might actually be governed by a set of rules as precise as those governing my daughter. It was only when I stepped outside and wandered down through the meadow, past Officer Spot and into the trailer, that I'd feel the floor quaking under me, moist and bottomless, a great shifty pudding dotted here and there with the bodies of the anonymous dead, their acquisitive arms and mouths, their blank and avid eyes. Understand, I hadn't yet gotten the courage to assign names. Even now, remembering that period, I falter, retreating instead to images of routine activity: I see myself at the trailer stove, boiling chicken, making pot after pot of chicken soup.

For despite the strange eating habits Helle developed over the last few months—chiefly craving raw clams and oysters, although occasionally she would request rollmops of herring, steak tartare—the nurse left strict orders that she was to adhere to a bland diet. Her digestive system, the nurse said, was a mess, but that was a frequent symptom of the disease. Each day I'd cook her a fresh pot of nourishing soup, strain the broth through cheesecloth, cool it in the refrigerator and skim off the fat, secure in the knowledge that I might still be capable of sustaining, rather than destroying, another person's life. It wasn't until my last trip to the trailer, on a sunny morning in June almost exactly two months after Helle's death, that I found the pile of shells on the ground behind the louvered kitchen window. A kitchen midden such as any archaeologist would be excited to discover: oyster shells corrugated on the outside, pearly within; the smooth shells of cherrystones, the rough shells of littlenecks; empty jars which had once contained cocktail sauce, capers, hearts of palm—everything shining in the sunlight, winking bits of glass and pearl visible within a shining, buzzing cloud of flies. How did she do it? I wondered. How did she manage to pry open all of those hundreds of shells? Not to mention the even greater mystery of where the things had come from in the first place. Officer Spot? But when I confronted him, he merely shook his head and looked away. A stubborn old woman, Officer Spot said fondly. You had to hand it to her. They didn't make them like that anymore.

II

O F COURSE once she was dead there was nothing left to keep me from leaving. Was it in fact that same June morning, when I found that noisy, winking monument to Helle's deceit, that I finally knew it was time to go? Or was it the intrusion into my bathroom, several mornings later, of a noiseless, spectral chord, that impelled me? The opaque layers of snow and ice with which winter plated the hillsides had been replaced by spring's delicate smear of yellow-green; the school year was over, and the estate would clearly be stuck in the courts for months, if not years. It didn't take long to pack, the idea being that in addition to Lily we could each bring one essential possession, Ruby choosing Marybell; Flo, her paints. I hesitated, settling at last on the waxed carton, just as I think I'd known all along I would, even though it seemed anything but essential while I was struggling to fit it into the trunk of the car. It was almost as if I were trying to shove in Helle herself, the compressed rectangular shape of her earthly remains, a container filled with hints and lies and the dozing vapors of her ghost. Where were we going, Ruby asked, and I told her I wasn't sure. We'd drive due east, I said, thinking it would be just as I'd imagined that day last summer in the high-school classroom. Only now the lilac branches were plunging under the weight of their heavy purple flowers, each cluster sweet and humming with bees; the world looked fresh and rain-washed. I was overwhelmed with a feeling of incipience, of possibility—a mindless hunger for life made sharper, more stinging, by its undercurrent of desperation.

We drove until we got to the coast, and then—because this town at the end of the road resembled too closely the one we'd just abandoned, the same lilacs framing the doorways of trim clapboard houses, the same tulips bright with the achievement of having recently clawed their way up from deep in the ground, the same late-afternoon light that transformed everything into golden icons, inert and legendary—I turned left and headed north. The thinly hammered sheath of clear blue sky broke apart into mist, a haze of teeming gray particles, and I drove with my headlights on, the windshield wipers flapping to and fro, while the twins played cards in the backseat, Lily between them, panting, steaming up the windows. "Ferry to Canada," Flo read from a signboard planted in a clump of wind-tossed, violently waving bulrushes. "Are we going to Canada?" Why not? I wondered aloud, and suddenly it occurred to me that to cross a stretch of water, to consign ourselves to a ferryboat and leave land behind, might serve, as traveling the seemingly endless thread of highway had not, to at last sever that thread. Nor was I daunted by the presence on the boat of a group of Connecticut ornithologists, attired in oilskins and huddled along the blunt prow among coils of rope, their binoculars raised in a uniform gesture, one with which I'd become wearily familiar. "Dovekies to port!" someone shouted, and they moved together in a glistening yellow mass, the drizzle beading up and dripping off the yellow beaklike visors of their hoods. "How can they see anything?"

Ruby asked, to which Flo replied, "They can't. They make it all up. Lunatics to port!" she said loudly, and one of the ornithologists, a dark-eyed young man with long black curls, whirled around and smiled at her—smiled at my wild, tall daughter standing there with her head tilted back against the roof of our car, staring at the sky.

We eventually ended up in a town called Alma, on the Fundy coast. Kind of a funny name for a town, Ruby said— like the school nurse, Alma Snyder. Only Alma meant "boun- tiful" in Latin, Flo explained, unlike that old skinnybones who checked their heads for lice twice a year. Keep your shirt on, she told me when I regarded her with surprise, she'd read it in one of those dumb Chamber of Commerce pamphlets she'd picked up in the information booth at the border. The truth is, we ended up in Alma because that was where my money ran out, and because when I pulled over to the curb in front of the Fundy Hotel to consult the map, Ruby noticed a WAITRESS WANTED placard in its restaurant window. So it happened that once again I found myself ministering to the appetites of others, although this time my uniform was aqua rather than orange, the plates I carried were usually filled with seafood rather than sandwiches, and the people I waited on tended to be families of tourists rather than single farmers, truck drivers, teenagers. Or college teachers.

After we'd been living in Alma for almost a month, a man appeared at lunchtime and ordered tuna on rye toast with ginger ale; I heard what he said and nodded, but it wasn't until I actually saw the words taking shape on the order pad that I felt a stifled thickness in the place just behind my eyes, a thick feeling as if the backs of my eyes were being pressed on with cotton wool. "Is anything the matter?" the man asked. No, I told him, turning quickly to suggest that my attention had been caught by something, a trawler perhaps, inching across the far-off horizon, faintly visible through the salt-fogged windows facing the bay. "Sorry," he said. Actually, nothing was visible through those windows, the entire coast swaddled in a heavy fog that wouldn't burn off until mid-afternoon, revealing the steep cliffs of the Fundy headlands where they rose up out of the damp gray sand. Did I by any chance know the schedule for the tidal bore? he asked. A nondescript man in a green windbreaker, his brown hair cut unstylishly short, his ears small and pink, his eyes a watery shade of blue similar to my uniform. Little teeth, little fingers. The cashier's desk, I said—she had the schedule. But the nearest place to see the bore was at the tip of Shepody Bay, in Moncton, at least a three-hour drive. Or Truro, Nova Scotia, even farther. The man consulted his watch, which he wore on the underside of his wrist, then asked when I got off work; maybe we could see that bore together. Maybe I could dump this water over your head, I thought. The next day I wore Sam's ring to work. My husband was a sailor, I would explain. Sailing the China seas.

During that period we lived in a large, drafty apartment, four rooms and a kitchen, on top of Lucy's Bakery, about three blocks down Main Street from the hotel. Furnished, as our landlady, who happened to be Lucy herself, apologized, with things she'd found cast up on the beach after storms. She was exaggerating, although the furniture did have a worn, vaguely waterlogged look to it: chairs and sofas with puffy, shapeless cushions, their upholstery raveling at the edges as if stirred by deep, submarine currents; lamps made from buoys, ashtrays from shells; tables bleached to the bony whiteness of driftwood. Lucy Feeny was a young woman from Newfoundland with a raucous laugh, long red braids, silver

granny glasses. If the twins made an unexpectedly rapid adjust-
ment to life on the Fundy coast, this was due in large part to
the influence of Lucy, who allowed Ruby to help her in the
bakery, who posed as Aphrodite (on the beach, her bathing
suit draped with seaweed) for Flo. Just as you might say that
it was Lucy Feeny—or at least the warm, yeasty smells she
caused to float up into my bedroom from the bakery ovens
immediately below my bed—who helped me divest myself,
once and for all, of the gray hazy garments of my depression.

I was lying there, languid, depressed, flat on my back, when
the smell of baking bread suddenly came to me like a previously unexplored idea. I knew that the smell was coming
from downstairs, but somehow my experience of it was different, as if the bread were above me, drifting slowly toward me
from above. Why *wouldn't* it be a mistake, I thought, to step
on a loaf of bread? Certainly not merely because an old
Danish lesbian decided that bread was a symbol of female
oppression. Gifts and creatures, I remembered reading in the
Book of Common Prayer—gifts and creatures of bread and
wine. Probably it wasn't a good idea to step on something
another person had labored over, even if that person was
yourself. So I imagined it, a large round loaf of bread—
one of those feather-crumbed, faintly honey-flavored loaves,
Lucy's specialty—sifting slowly down through layer after layer
of peat. Creatures, the Episcopal minister had explained to
our confirmation class, referred to the yeast, mysterious gran-
ules that would swell into life if properly nourished, like the
human soul. The bedstead was narrow, made of white-painted
iron; its mattress and sheets and light green, anchor-printed
coverlet smelled of salt and mildew, of shady, damp places
conducive to the breeding of lethargy, despair, and silverfish.
Indeed, what I found when I finally roused myself from bed

to crouch on my hands and knees and slide the waxed carton out from under it, was a spill of them—a shimmering effluvium of those silver-scaled, segmental insects, primitive and wingless, their hideous tails bristling, their long feelers twitching brainlessly—draining through the closed surface flaps, over the sides of the carton and onto the floor. Not a moment too soon, I thought, for I knew that the silverfish thrives in the damp and the dark, and that it's dedicated to the destruction of books and paper. But the notebooks I was looking for, the five spiral-bound composition books containing *The Girl Who Trod on a Loaf*, were still at the bottom of the carton; and although the pages had thickened slightly in the damp salt air, Helle's notation remained perfectly legible.

There they were, right where she'd left them, Inger and the Don, the Bog Queen and her three daughters, having just concluded the so-called Heresy Sextet—that troubling piece which begins as a philosophic discussion of the nature of God's heart, a logical and even melodic interlocking of voices in the key of A major, but which breaks apart, no doubt spurred by Inger's reference to the heart as "a crystal hive," into an eerie, moaning concatenation of unintelligible syllables, a dense, blackening swarm of dissonant sound, where every attempt to elevate an individual voice, every upward-surging strand of notes, every brief flight into melody or meaning, is ultimately drawn back down into the prevailing hive of gibberish. A queer and pessimistic composition, it seemed to me, characteristically perverse in its view of the created world: God engages in endless replication of His form, the sextet suggests, but whatever diversity He appears to promote is limited by His overwhelming desire to see Himself wherever He looks, to be everything—this is the world "analogous to man's imagining," as Inger sings, and clearly we're meant to understand that she's making a crucial distinction, that the world as imagined by a woman might be completely different. I regarded the ring on my finger, my face in the salt-bleary mirror. So what, I thought. You make something, you have an obligation to it, even if you don't like it. A man and a woman end up in a bog, and then what? Once you're dead, you're dead, I thought—and that is the whole sad truth about the human heart, which eventually, no matter what kind of god you choose to see as its creator, stops beating.

At first I did nothing more than "watch" them, Inger and the Don, to see what they would do. Only they did nothing, standing there separate, discrete, as the Bog Queen's daughters twined their two statuelike bodies more and more thickly around with great looping nooses of sphagnum, just as Nanna and Harry Tuck had swaddled their own dream-bodies with yards of silk. I waited for them to begin talking, but their lips remained sealed. All they did was stand there, stage center, decorative in the mute, unsettling manner of topiary. I considered a possible dismantling and recombining of parts, the fate Helle had devised for Nightingale in *Fuglespil*: under their mossy coats the bodies would break apart, topple, the pieces creeping toward each other, coupling on the bog floor and then sprouting anew in fantastic androgynous forms. Or, conversely, when their bodies broke apart, the pieces would become indistinguishable from the moss, so that what ultimately would prevail would be the comprehensive network of the moss itself. The music would echo this condition, a kind of musical response to *horror vacui*. But then it struck me that this latter option seemed to be headed in another direction, the one implicit in *Lahloo*'s apocalyptic ending, Damian Spark's wave annihilating everything in its path; a cowardly the smell of things being baked. On a long stainless-steel counter, faintly dimpled hemispheres of pale dough rose slowly above their huge silver bowls; on a wheeled rack, speckled loaves of oatmeal bread and cross-marked rounds of Irish soda bread lay cooling in rows. "You were married, eh?" Lucy asked cautiously. No, I said. I was having an affair with a man who was married. Huh, she said, frowning. Never a good idea. Did I love him? Oh, yes, I said, realizing for the first time with absolute certainty that it was true, just as I finally comprehended that I wasn't ever going to see him again. I started to cry, and Lucy handed me a tissue and a cinnamon roll. Carrying the torch, eh? she said. Listen, Francie, time to blow it out. She made a little puffing motion with her lips. Blow it out, throw it away. Only it was harder, I said, if you didn't know until afterwards. I paused, considering. Then you could never be sure, I added. Besides, the truth was I'd killed him. Go on, said Lucy. No, really, I insisted. Well, we'd all wanted to, hadn't we now, Lucy concluded. Those married men. She smiled at me, refilled my cup; seriously now, her smile seemed to say, and I gave up, smiled halfheartedly back. Ongoing warfare, I was thinking, an irreconcilable gap which might be bridged only by lust. *The Heroine, Delia, Despina.* They could kill each other. Devour each other. Fall in love. There was another woman, I said. There was another woman, and I was no match for her.

Eventually I returned to the bread, the original loaf which, together with the shoes, had been the cause of Inger's downfall. In Andersen's story the loaf provides a sort of pedestal for the statue Inger; in Helle's opera, once it has served the purpose of speeding Inger's descent to the bog floor, it is appropriated by the Queen, who gives it and the shoes to her daughters as toys. They have no other use for such objects:

ending, as even Helle herself had admitted. What about the man's bad eyesight, the gap between the woman's two front teeth? Although maybe it was the case that those physical details which had drawn them together in the first place, those touching little differences, were the very things which when brought into close proximity would set the great tidal engine in motion.

On the other hand, perhaps I ought to regard the wave as a species of deus ex machina. How about the huge cupped blade of a peat-cutting machine suddenly appearing out of nowhere and dredging them up? And then a coda: the man and the woman restored to their former lives aboveground, the sheets of moss, even the sheets of air, replaced by emptiness. Or perhaps by furniture. They remove the dust sheets from the furniture: Darling! the man sings, I may have strayed but you're the one woman I've always adored. Darling! the woman sings, I may have stayed, but you're the one man I've never abhorred. They get married, duplicating the capitulation to complacency, the bored compromise of Nanna and Captain Harry Tuck. Such overstated irony! Inappropriate, I thought. For hadn't Helle insisted, on more than one occasion, that marriage was always a red herring?

A man and a woman. How many possible solutions were there? Of course one of them could kill the other. An inadvertent and romantic killing, as in *Det omflakkende Møl* or *Delia*, both of which also include thematic references to food and consumption. The princess in the Lindworm; Mr. Holly's heart in the aspic; in each instance the lover—the prince with his sword or Delia with her knife and fork—deals the final blow. Dying explorers, I knew, had tried to keep themselves alive by stuffing their mouths full of sphagnum, and a party of explorers could survive by eating moss containing the man's and woman's decomposing bodies. A party of *female* explorers, I thought, and for a moment I was excited, as if I were finally on the right track. Though I realized almost immediately that such an ending would not only be embarrassingly circular—the opera beginning and ending with people venturing into a boggy wilderness—but would also disgust the audience, not to mention the fact that it was at odds with whatever hidden truth I was in the process of discovering I believed. Very nice, Frances, I thought I could hear a familiar voice saying. Admirably circumlocutious.

For Helle, following an apparent period of silence extending from the day in the bathroom when I heard the chord to the day I began work on the opera, had once again become communicative. No matter how recondite its source, her voice was with me all the time, chattering on and on, humming, suggesting key signatures and instrumentation, criticizing and courting. "How about this? A single female explorer digs up the perfectly preserved body of the Don," the voice might say, "and takes him home with her. Uses him as a sex toy. Oboes and flutes—ticklish music with a sleek leathery undercurrent. Or maybe she sells him to the museum at Silkeborg, where he gets put in the same display case with the sorrowful Tollund man—two erotic and leathery dreamers side by side, routinely photographed by German tourists, one of whom, a nice-looking young man, sends a snapshot to Inger. Violins, C-sharp minor, very mournful. Write it down! Write it down! *Min skat—min stakkels skat, overrasket af natten!* [My sweetheart—my poor benighted sweetheart!]"

Or how about this, I thought: The concept of gender itself defies embodiment. Surely the various physical forms taken by the singers in *Waves* were beside the point, not unlike the mutating aspects of Despina's outward appearance, not unlike

the gray-suited executives of *Fortune's Lap*, that continuously growing horde of genderless figures, male voices and female voices raised in unison for the "Xerox finale," as if to imply that no basic difference existed between them. Viewed through this lens, the separate uses to which the Don and Inger might originally have put their bodies was unimportant; perhaps, I thought, the issue of gender ought to remain tangential, providing, as it no doubt had in Helle's life, a convenient arena in which to investigate the nature of dichotomy, the attendant impossibility of synthesis.

Although what about lust? Some days I would return to the apartment and find myself unable to remember a single thing that had happened while I was in the restaurant. Summer ended, fall came and went, the tourists emerged from their campgrounds in the highlands and headed south beneath the honking vees of geese; winter arrived with its dark gray, ice-spangled air, its furious winds born in the far-off Torngat Mountains of northern Labrador; the bay rocked up and down, up and down; a boat sank, then another; a moose wandered down Main Street and vanished in the fog beyond the fish-processing plant. The twins were attending the local school, Stella Maris Elementary. Star of the Sea. Ruby, bearing out her sister's prediction, was immediately the most popular girl in the class; while Flo, surprisingly, made friends with a boy named Elmo Weed.

"You should get out and have yourself some fun," Lucy told me late one November afternoon, when I stopped in the bakery to buy gingerbread and ended up staying for tea. "There you are, same age as I am," she said, "and you act like you're about eighty." We were sitting at a small wooden table in the bakery kitchen, a yellow room without windows, every molecule of air in it swelling, preparing to burst, with their toes are long and splay outward, the brown skin stretching thinly over the bones like silk over the ribs of an umbrella; they eat only insects, the linings of their throats oozing the same sticky substance, sprouting the same dense growth of entrapping hairs, as those of the carnivorous plants which flourish high above on the bog's surface. Indeed, we're told that food prepared by human hands is for them a deadly poison. One bite, that's all it takes. So we see Retaliation and Grudge playing with Inger's shoes as if they were dolls, dressing them in garments of moss, talking for them, arguing for them, banging them against each other in irritable combat. Whereas Unnameable cradles the loaf in her slick, reptilian arms. My baby, she sings, Sky-puff, Cloudlet, Dream-tuft. Easily the most perverse lullaby ever written.

The bread, I thought, bread made in a human kitchen by a human baker. Why, I wondered, should I assume that just because Inger and the Don had, at one time, been sucked down into the hell of the bog, they would have to stay there forever? So long as they accepted their lot as inevitable there was nothing I could do, but it seemed to me that to agree that it was inevitable was also to submit once again to the severity of Helle's vision. I imagined a duet in which they confessed to each other their impatience with the apparent solutions to their dilemma, such dismaying solutions as were suggested by all of Helle's other operas. No, I imagined them singing, we won't break apart, disappear, gobble or kill, battle or marry, merge or die. The force of their essential antagonism, I decided, the strength of those opposing wills which had damned them in the first place, might now prove useful. What if Inger and the Don were to put their two devious, clever heads together? What if Inger were once again to resort to the nasty habits of her childhood, setting traps for insects—millipedes and spiders, the appropriately named ambush bugs, assassin bugs—and then, relying on her talent for dissection, pry open their tiny bodies, concealing an even tinier piece of bread in each one? Naturally she'd have to sneak the loaf away from its fierce mother, but the Don could be counted on to work his diversionary charms. He could even sing his famous canzonetta, *"Deh vieni alla finestra,"* although the words would have to be changed, since there aren't any windows in a bog.

Thus we would watch them, the vile Bog Queen and her three vile daughters, sitting down to eat their deadly supper. A platter laden with the glinting carapaces of hundreds of dead bugs, carried in and set ceremoniously by Inger on the sphagnum-strewn pile of bones that serves as their table, while ceremoniously the Don ties bibs of sphagnum around their snaky brown necks. Perhaps an onstage orchestra might be playing the aria from *Figaro*, just as it does in *Don Giovanni* before the Commendatore's demonic arrival? *"Non più andrai"*—You will no longer flutter around, you amorous butterfly—a nice touch, I thought, since the minute the first fistfuls of insects vanish down their sticky, hairy throats, the Bog Queen and her daughters start to swell, the brown leather of their skin straining to impossible thinness, turning them into huge brown balloons floating slowly upward, making the hideously high-pitched squealing sounds balloons make when they bump against each other. Treachery! Treachery! they squeal, accompanied by the high-pitched notes of the violins, *staccato volante*, faster and faster, higher and higher. Higher and higher they float, as Inger and the Don cling to their wildly kicking, wildly failing legs. The opera ends as we watch Inger's shoe-clad feet, the Don's boot-clad feet—those feet we first saw descending slowly into the bog—now ascending rapidly out of it.

As for what they do next, I told myself, that's their own business. Although I could picture them standing there on the surface of the bog, a human man and a human woman, each one close enough to recognize the expression of shy admiration on the other's face, but not so close as to suggest that they now were linked by a common purpose. The air had finally cleared, the former dense and suffocating soup of air molecules having gradually vanished, the scrims lifting, bearing away all of those many-colored globes, all of those yellow and blue and green globes of air gradually having been dispersed, along with the four brown globes which had been, not so very long ago, the Bog Queen and her daughters. The reddish crowns of the moss glistened in the sunlight. An animal ran by. A bird sang, and neither the man nor the woman had any idea what kind of bird it was.

Meanwhile, from the bay, the hotel, the headlands, the roof of my apartment, the fog likewise began to lift. "Oh, Frances, Frances, how could you do this to me?" Who? I said. Show yourself! It was the deep heart of mid-winter; I put on my coat, walked down the stairs and out the door. There was a path that circled around behind the bakery and led down to the beach, where I could hear the voices of the gulls tearing long slits in the gray, foggy ceiling. Miles away the Bay of Fundy, its gray hide wrinkled and opaque, rose and fell, rose and fell, breathing in its sleep under a narrow strip of blue sky. Black grains of sand mixed with gray ones, pinkish ones; an overturned crab shell like a helmet filled with sand from which protruded the crab's bent white legs, feather-edged, hollow. Low tide. My father was a fisherman, I found myself remembering—one of Helle's first songs; how did it go? My father was a fisherman, my mother was a fish? Yes. One of the *Fantasi*, I thought, her earliest compositions. And then it went on: He threw her back, he mixed them up, desire and a wish. In Jutland when the tide is low I look among the stones and shells and bits of sea-green glass to find my mother's bones. How had we ever come up with the idea of fidelity? I wondered. For when had the animating spirit of a thing ever remained faithful to the form which contained it? The human voice, I thought, that most tragic of all instruments; the hopeful human voice singing, trying to hold a note forever.

III

A ND WHAT OF the key with the red plastic head? Would you believe me if I told you that one day not long ago I found myself standing in the Albany bus station, that very key shoved deep into the pocket of my red winter coat? I was on my way to the University of Rochester to pick up Ruby for Christmas break; Flo was in Munich, taking classes in restoration technique at the Pinakothek. In fact, it was a recent letter from Flo that had suggested this detour in the first place: "To the Gold Room yesterday, ring a bell? I went because of *her*," she wrote, going on to ask whether I remembered the time Helle had first mentioned the Gold Room, at that horrible birthday party when I drank too much wine and went on and on about storage lockers. The room in question, Flo told me, was filled with reliquaries, most of them, predictably, made of gold, all of them containing the shriveling or decomposed attributes of long-dead saints. A room lined with rows and rows of lavish, valuable receptacles, golden heads concealing scraps of colorless hair, golden hands concealing powdery metacarpals, golden feet concealing toe-nails, anklebones—enough body parts, Flo wrote, to construct hundreds of saints, thousands of saints. What you saw when you entered was, essentially, a room full of lockers, though it wasn't anything like a bus terminal. In the Gold Room every available locker was already taken. Taken for eternity. To pry a reliquary open, to insert a piece of yourself, would be nothing short of blasphemy. "A self-serving metaphor," Flo concluded, "as usual."

Of course I never dreamed for a minute that the key would still fit any of those lockers, or if by some miracle it did, that I'd find anything besides a stranger's luggage. Certainly not a sacred artifact, a shred of Christ's loincloth or a splinter of the true Cross. Number 73, the number obviously chosen to remind me of Helle's Opus 73, a pensive little song called "Rain on Thorn" she composed shortly after we met. So I wandered, speculative and apparently aimless, up and down the aisles of lockers, just as I used to do when I was myself a girl, although this time I didn't have the luxury of my own inspiration to guide my choice. How many years had it been since I'd last felt the hand of Helle Ten Brix pulling me this way and that? The Albany terminal was filled with students, independent young men and women wearing bright backpacks, and for the briefest instant I felt envy lifting its tusked head in the place at the base of my ribs—how lucky they were, I thought, and then realized with shame that I was as guilty of romanticizing them as the piped-in music was of romanticizing the season. Eventually, though, I found it, a medium-sized locker located at eye level in the middle of a row along the back wall. Bus to New York now loading on platform 3, I heard. May your daze beee mer-reee and bright. I removed the key from my pocket and tried it in the lock. Effortlessly it slid in; effortlessly it turned; effortlessly the door opened.

Nor do I suppose that what I saw when I looked inside should come as a surprise: the Dukketeatre, carefully positioned so that its proscenium arch was right behind the open door, facing out. EI BLOT TIL LYST. The red velvet curtains drawn aside, revealing a small cutout figure on an otherwise empty stage. Impossible, I thought. Helle had died ten years ago last April. I stood there waiting, strangely annoyed, strangely exhilarated; I suppose I was half expecting to be confronted by the sound of her voice, by the rasping, smoky sound I thought I'd heard for the last time that day in Alma. I stood there waiting, but all I could hear was Christmas music, announcements of arrivals and departures, a pair of young lovers murmuring sad goodbyes, a man yelling to his wife to remember that he took his coffee light. "Get a load of this!" said a girl, probably about seven or eight, to a small boy, probably her younger brother. They had crept up silently and now were pressing in on either side of me, the girl jumping up and down, a flurry of short, anxious little leaps, while her brother whined that he couldn't see. "Is that yours?" the girl asked, and I told her I guessed it was. What did I mean *guessed?* the girl asked. She was stocky and pragmatic, dressed in a pink parka, a large elflike ski cap, also pink, with a white pompom, pulled down low on her forehead. A blonde, I thought, even though her hair was hidden by her cap; a stocky little blonde with dry and wide-set blue eyes. Shut *up!* she said to the boy, who had started to wail. It's all right, I told him. See? I grabbed him by the waist, lifting him, startled by how thin he was, how there didn't seem to be anything intervening between his skeleton and the brown shell of his parka except for a hopelessly inadequate layer of synthetic insulation. Is it a play? he asked, and I said no, not really. That woman, I said, pointing to the cutout figure, was a famous composer, even if you couldn't tell it to look at her. It was an opera,

I said, only you couldn't hear the music. But you could tell the woman was supposed to be singing because her mouth was open.

Then why does she look so mad? asked the girl. I craned my neck to peer around the delicate wedge of the boy's head: the tiny paper Helle peered back. Mad? I said. Well, maybe. More like aggrieved. In pain. I recognized the figure as Flo's handiwork, her girlhood style of applying color thickly with colored pencils, blurring the edges with a finger, suggesting detail with a deeply incised dark line here, a smear of white there. Helle in her white nightgown. A black backdrop. If she's mad, I said, it's because she never planned to break my heart. Carefully I put the boy back down on the black and white squares of the terminal floor. If she's mad it's because she didn't want to die, I said, slamming the locker door shut and turning my attention to the girl. Listen, I said to her, you should be nicer to your little brother. Really, I said, sibylline, magnificent in my red winter coat, you should be nicer to him, or else.

A NOTE ON THE TYPE

This book was set in Cloister Old Style, a revival of
the Venetian types of Nicolas Jenson, designed by
Morris Benton for American Type Founders in 1897.

Nicolas Jenson published the famous *De Præparati-*
one Evangelica by Eusebius in 1470 using his roman
letter, and it soon became the model for all Venetian
type designs.

William Morris patterned his Golden Type on
Jenson's type, and the subsequent renewed interest
in the letter produced many types based on the Morris
model rather than on the original. Morris Benton
(1872–1948), however, chose to go to the source for
his design and bring back the Jenson type in the
typeface we today know as Cloister Old Style.

Composed by Crane Typesetting Service, West
Barnstable, Massachusetts. Printed and bound by
The Haddon Craftsmen, Scranton, Pennsylvania
Designed by Peter A. Andersen